R. Victoria Patterson is an ardent writer and a romantic enthusiast. After earning two diplomas at the Institute of Children's Literature, she decided to follow her passion and shift genres to contemporary romance from writing children's stories. Victoria is a country-woman at heart and the mother of three children. Other occupations have included dairy/cash crop farmer and hairstylist. Victoria believes that your perfect destination is just up the path, keep moving forward no matter what.

MY DEAREST – Captain Handsome Funnypants, your witty sense of charm and playfulness has brought more enjoyment to my life than you realize. From the day we first met, until now, I have experienced laughter, lust, wonder, fulfillment, frustration, love, sadness, pleasure, and delight. You have led me back to my true self. No matter what is next to come, you'll be forever in my heart.

MY SISTER – Sandra Patterson, for your engaging sense of humor, for always encouraging me to achieve my goals, and for your advice – "git'r done". You are my best friend, I love you.

R. Victoria Patterson

AMBIGUOUS AFFAIR

AUSTIN MACAULEY PUBLISHERS™
LONDON • CAMBRIDGE • NEW YORK • SHARJAH

Ordering Information:
Quantity sales: special discounts are available on quantity purchases by corporations, associations, and others. For details, contact the publisher at the address below.

Publisher's cataloguing in publishing data
Patterson, R. Victoria
Ambiguous Affair

ISBN 9781641826143 (Paperback)
ISBN 9781641826150 (Hardback)
ISBN 9781641826167 (E-Book)

The main category of the book — FICTION / Romance / General

www.austinmacauley.com/us

First Published (2019)
Austin Macauley Publishers LLC
40 Wall Street, 28th Floor
New York, NY 10005
USA

mail-usa@austinmacauley.com
+1 (646) 5125767

Leonid Afremov, world-renowned artist, for allowing me to utilize his name and stunning painting 'PASSION' as the front cover. Thank you for bringing such beauty and magic to our world with your amazing talent. Please visit his official online virtual gallery to view and/or purchase his other extraordinary pieces. Leonid Afremov on Facebook and afremov.com

Chapter 1

Friday, September 29, 2017

My stomach has been feeling sick for a week. The mere sight of food makes me ill. Tonight I prepared a tasteful chicken cacciatore for my family. As for me, getting down a few bites was a challenge. I've been filling my plate half as full as usual, and it's been particularly difficult to manage. No one has noticed my lack of appetite. I'm thankful because if they asked, I'd have to make up some lame story about what's wrong. In a twisted kind of way, I like the feeling of eating less. My stomach has been flatter. It barely bloats anymore and my jeans are beginning to feel loose. If my appetite doesn't return, I'm hopeful that the left over flab from carrying my twins will melt away. Maybe I've lost 4 pounds or so, but I haven't set foot on a scale for years. I think the last time was in February, two months after giving birth when I weighed 125lbs, the time before was the end of my third trimester at 38 weeks, when I weighed 165lbs. I remember the weight coming off fairly quickly, but after being pregnant, ten years ago, my body has never been quite the same. Recently for breakfast, I've been eating fruit and drinking water. I can't get a glass of milk to stay down. Toast and cereal seem so dry. This morning, my stomach rumbled and felt particularly poor. I wasn't sure if I was hungry or going to throw up. Inside the fridge, everything looked repulsive. I poured myself a 5oz glassful of blueberry smoothie, and forced myself to swallow it. I could still hear the rumbling, so I ate a few soda biscuits. When I was a child and not feeling well, my nanny, Mrs. Lauders, would say, "Maggy, I heard that rumbly tummy. I'll get you some soda biscuits." That usually did the trick.

After the smoothie and biscuits, I felt somewhat better, but I knew that my body needed more energy to get a good start to the day. I washed a handful of baby carrots and forced them down. *Who eats carrots for breakfast? Me.* I used to hate raw carrots, but today they were more tasty than carbs.

It's been hard to concentrate lately. All I can think about is sending Aaron a text message, to let him know I'm ready. I fear my body wouldn't allow me to follow through, so it's best I refrain.

In the shower, I imagined being all alone at home, and I sent Aaron a message to come over. *What would it be like to shower with him?* His hands would be well lathered, he'd rub them all over my body. The hot water sprinkling down would make it easy for him to slide them all over my breasts and down my back, he'd abruptly turn me away from him, bend me over, and with a firm hard jab, he'd be inside of me.

My body trembled at the thought, *then he'd see my wrinkly stomach. But then again, I'd be facing away from him.* So tempting, but nerve wrecking. *I want him so bad.* Only problem is…I am married.

I shut off the water and reached for my towel. It was hard to dry off because the bathroom had steamed up, leaving a moisture residue on my skin, I'd forgotten to turn on the fan. I made a vow 18 years ago which I intended on keeping, but the way my husband Joe was acting for the past while, was making it harder every day for me to stay with him.

I don't usually take Friday off from work, but today I took advantage because we were under booked. Really, I can take off any day I want because I'm the boss, except that'd be unfair to Lucy, my employee who works extra-long hours. I own a family-oriented hair salon/barber shop. Lucy has been working with me for the past eleven years. She began as my apprentice at age 19. While she learned how to apply her skills, we became close friends even though I'm ten years older than her. Lucy is single, and has no desire to bare children. Cutting and styling hair is her life. These days, she is like a breath of fresh air with her upbeat personality and humor. I work from 10:00am-4:00pm during the week, and the rare Saturday from 9:00am-4:30pm, on Sundays I'm closed. Lucy works 2–3 hours longer each day than me, and the occasional Wednesday alone, depending on how busy we are with clients. Before I gave birth to my twins Jody and Jonah, Lucy finished her apprenticeship, and became a licensed hairstylist, she then informed me that she would be "holding down the fort" for as long as I needed her, and not out of obligation, rather friendship and contentment. She wears a colossal smile to work each day, I am lucky to have her. Without her, I would have never been able to stay home as long with my babies after they were born.

10

My children are the single most important thing in my life. I love them to Heaven and back, and back again for infinity. I believe in spending as much time as possible with them. Caring for them, teaching them, and being close to them, is what I hold dear, for I know that one day they will become adults, and, will leave my side for a life of their own. When Jody and Jonah were babies, I brought them to the salon on every chance I could. While they napped, I did paper work, inventory, and occasionally a haircut. Before I knew it, they were tiny celebrities in our country village. To this very day, my clientele love to compare the differences and similarities between the two. They are identical of opposite sex, Jody has long, straight, brown hair. Jonah has short, curly hair. When Mrs. Lauders comes into the salon, she always says, "It's the girls that want the curly hair, but they don't get it, and it's the boys who want straight hair, but they don't get it."

The twins began school at the early age of three, and were the youngest in their class. I began working back at regular hours in December immediately after their 4th birthday. By then, the twins had eased into their new routine, and I was confident that they were in good hands. Now they are more independent, but I still enjoy doing the smaller things for them, such as making their beds and folding their socks into matching pairs for their cute little feet. Typically, I occupy my days off, catching up on errands, baking the twins' favorite cookies, and cleaning the house.

The school bus arrived at 8:30am sharp. I had the twins ready and sent them off without forgetting to give them each a kiss and hug. Joe had been up bright and early as usual. He left home at 5:30am this morning without giving me so much as a tiny peck on my cheek, or even a hug. As I began my morning routine of gathering up the laundry, thoughts of Aaron crept back into my mind, however he seemed always close to the surface, even when he was nowhere in sight. I spent the next couple hours pondering my situation, which was the constant urge to touch him. I kept telling myself, "No." It was wrong for a married woman to have sexual feelings toward a man other than her husband, but Joe has been less than desirable these days, unlike Aaron who looks hot, and has a killer personality. I remember the first time I saw him, last year at Laudersville Public School. There were forty kids or more scrambling around the hallway, and packing up their school bags, I approached Jody's locker, there was a dark-haired guy laughing and trying to high five my daughter. *Who is he?* I didn't recognize him from the salon or from town, when Jody said, "Mommy, this is my boyfriend's daddy. His name is Aaron."

I could feel my eyes lighting up, "Hello."

Aaron looked at me, his blue eyes sparkled with joy. He smiled, "Hi."

Jody grabbed her school bag and ran back to give Aaron a hug. He returned her affection. His son Landon, who I recognized from the school field trip, the year before, was also there. Landon gave his dad a hug too. That night, when I was tucking Jody into bed, she asked me if I liked Landon's dad. I didn't put much thought into it before she asked me. I said, "Yes, he seems nice."

"Do you think he's cute?" she asked.

I hesitated a moment to visualize him. He looked younger than me, and his body was somewhat muscular. "Do you think he's cute?" I said. She sat up in bed, covered her eyes with her hands, and let out a hoot, "Ewe."

After leaving her room, Aaron's good looks reappeared in my mind. *Damn, he was fine.*

The second time I met Aaron, was about 6 months after. There was a concert at the kids' school, and both Jody and Landon had sung solo parts. I went into the office to let the secretary know that I'd be giving the twins a ride home instead of them taking the bus. Aaron was standing to the side of her desk. I couldn't help but smile at him when he turned to face me, his body aura felt buoyant, which drew me to speak with him.

"Landon did a great job in there."

"Thank you," he looked amused. "You should hear him at home, he belts it out like an elephant."

That expression cracked me up, I couldn't believe he said that about his own son. I was trying to be polite in telling him, truth was, the boy just couldn't sing. I knew the teachers would sometimes pick shy kids to perform in front of others, to help them gain self-confidence, and that was clearly the case for Landon.

"Jody did an awesome job," he said.

"Thanks." It was obvious Jody had more talent than Landon, I could tell she was a little nervous that day. On the way home, I replayed my entire conversation with Aaron in my mind. I started to wonder how my hair looked, and if my jeans fit my ass alright. He wore a pair of denim jeans, a tight fitting black t-shirt, and a ball cap, his hair neatly trimmed around his ears. The outfit suited him perfectly. I didn't think much more about Aaron until, this past June when Aaron attended the end of the year school field trip to the Museum of Nature for the grade five's. I volunteered that day along with some of the other mom's, Aaron being the only father on the trip. I drove myself to the museum instead of going on the bus with all of the noisy kids. Jody and Jonah rode with me as well. At the museum, I was surprised to see Aaron waiting in his truck with Landon. He told me he prefers to drive himself because the buses drive too slow. I could tell by the lively expression in his voice that he was the type of man who liked freedom, but there is nothing wrong with that. The kids had a great time at the museum. They saw different kinds of rocks, animal displays, live insects, and they even generated their own fake volcano. I couldn't help but study Aaron in short intervals that day, I didn't want any of the other mom's to know I had the hots for him. I figured out that Aaron liked to talk to everyone, and he made people smile. His nature was playful, and he seemed confident. *Was he single?* Not that it mattered because I wasn't available. Aaron talked to me several times that day. I felt comfortable in his presence, and I noticed he laughs more than most men. I can be a chatter box at times, being a hairstylist, you have to have 'the gift of the gab' which made it easy to strike up a conversation. I think he liked talking to me because he seemed to be beside, in front, or behind me for most of the day. That's how I ended up with his cell phone number. We talked about how much Jody and Landon liked each other, and it would be cute if they could text each other.

It was time for lunch but my thoughts of Aaron were beginning to overpower my mind. I felt nauseous, but I forced myself to eat an apple, and a handful of cashews. I kept thinking, *what if he comes to my door at this very moment?* I tried to convince myself that my stomach would be settled if he did. I'd take him by the hand and lead him to my bedroom. That's where I'd rip off all of his clothes and ravish his body by rubbing him, teasing him, kissing him, and stroking his long hard manhood. He would then grasp my naked body gently and aggressively until I would beg him to do me.

He sent me a text message a couple weeks ago that said "I told Landon to hang onto Jody, because when she gets older, she might be as pretty as her mother." I texted him back and said, "You're such a flirt!" I found it flattering that a 32-year-old man thought I was attractive, I'm almost a decade older than him. Since I found out he is single, I have to ask myself, "Is he just lonely or desperate?" Then there is the other possibility: he truly does find me eye-catching. After all, I'm 5'3", with blonde hair, green eyes, I stay active, eat healthy, but most importantly, I do not have anger issues. If I was single and if he asked me on a date, I'd likely agree, unable to resist the temptation.

Tonight, for supper I was going to prepare pork chops with my homemade raspberry sauce, and herbed potatoes au gratin, but the chicken was easier. The kids enjoy both dishes equally. I've never had any problems getting them to eat fine cuisine. I think it's in their DNA. I heard that my grandmother learned to be a sous chef, and worked in Montreal at Le Bistro Noir - the most pristine restaurant for hundreds of miles. That's where she met my grandfather, and settled down to have children. After my mother and my uncles were born, she worked at a small catering company. She had a divine love for the artistry of food and before her passing, she handed down her knowledge to my mother. My mom passed away when I was five, leaving inadequate time to teach me everything that grandmother had taught her. Luckily, her cookbooks were reserved for my use, because Mrs. Lauders only stuck to the basics. My true devotion for cooking began as a teenager, shortly after Mrs. Lauders married the richest bachelor in town and moved out. I poured my sorrows of being a motherless child, into cooking for my dad. I had dreams of moving to Montreal and becoming a famous chef like grandmother, but I knew it would never transpire because I could never grasp the French language.

In high school my girlfriends used to tease me about being overzealous with hair, and not just my own. It always bothered me to see guys with hair growing on the back of their necks, I used to carry a sharp pair of scissors in my pencil case to see if I could trim them up. I had to admit my friends were right, and that's when I decided to become a hairstylist instead of a chef. I was always good at maneuvering my hands, and obsessed with improving the looks of anyone. After high school, I enrolled in trade school, and graduated top of my class.

Joe made it home on time for supper at 6:30. I really didn't know if he enjoyed my chicken, or any of my other meals because he's never given a compliment. Most times when I've asked him if he liked it, he's said, "It's alright." *Now what's that supposed to mean*? After I've spent my time preparing a nice meal, it would be uplifting to hear—"That was delicious," but no, I'd only ever heard those words directed at his mother when she was living. *I wonder if Aaron would like my cooking.*

After I tucked the twins in bed, I thought Joe would be in the mood for a roll between the sheets, after all, it's been ten days since we've had coitus. I heard Joe brushing his teeth in his bathroom. That meant he'd be heading to bed soon. In my bathroom, I quickly washed, freshened up, and brushed my teeth. I went into our room, and stood naked in front of him lying in bed. The moonlight shone in through the window illuminating our room, there wasn't a need to turn on my candle lamp. Joe had his eyes closed, I asked him if he was sleeping. He said, "Am I?" then opened his eyes and stared at my breasts, then he closed them again. I stood there for minutes, wondering if he would want me, he didn't budge. *What an ass.* Sexual frustration haunted me. I wasn't going to wait there all night. I put on my blue pjs and went to sleep.

Things didn't used to be this way between Joe and I. It wasn't until year eleven that things started to change. Joe had become more involved with his obsession to earn more money. He believed the more money he earned, the more people would be inferior to him, leaving him with power. *Are all lawyers like that?* He has been working 80 hours per week for years, which leaves no time for our kids or our sexual life, he hasn't shown any concern or cares for that matter. I've talked to him several times to try and improve things, but he always falls back into the same routine of ignoring everyone and spending his brain power on the next case that he's going to win. The first few years with Joe were extraordinary. He and I would go on walks through the hay fields at my dad's farm, we'd lay on a blanket along the tree line and make love all afternoon on the weekends. His touch used to send shivers of pleasure through my body, and his grey eyes would clutch my soul when he was on top of me, he looked completely gratified as if there were nothing more important to him than being there with me. We used to spend hours chatting about our future, our desires, and our relationship. We used to snuggle on the couch, and go out to restaurants. For our 5th wedding anniversary, Joe and I went to Le Bistro Noir in Montreal, and spent the night at Hotel de Monte Beau. It was amazing how close I felt to him, my life was almost perfect. Things change over time, but I believe I am still the same person that I was 18 years ago with the exception of my knowledge. My mind has grown and developed since then, and I understand most aspects of life now better than ever.

Our marriage has increasingly grown sour, I knew putting extra effort into our relationship was a must for things to work out.

It's grown more complicated, given my new-found feelings for Aaron, and the fact that Joe's zest for love seems to have vanished, leaving me with the bare minimum of his energy. Aaron seems to be everything I've ever needed, but he knows I'm married, which leaves me uncertain of what he expects from me.

Chapter 2

September 20, 2017

I received a text message from Aaron that said, "Umm, this is Maggy, right?" The name programed into my phone said Landon.

I typed, "Yes, that would be me".

"This is Aaron Freeman, Landon's dad. How is your week going?"

Oh, it's cutie pants. "Very well, accomplishing a lot. It's my day off."

"That's good, an ambitious woman is an attractive woman."

That was bold. "Lol, sure."

"It's my son's birthday this weekend and I'd like to have a party for him. Sorry for the short notice, but I've been working so much lately and I wasn't sure if I could get time off. He wants to invite ten of his friends including Jody and Jonah."

"That's right, Landon has the same birthday as me, Sunday right?" I remembered because last year Jody and Jonah were invited to his party but couldn't go on account of mine. We went into town to see a movie, Joe didn't make it home at all that night.

"Landon has the same birthday as you? So, you are going to be 25 then?"

"Ha ha, I'll never tell. What time is the party?"

"I haven't decided, but it's for Saturday. I'm not sure what to do with all those kids. Any ideas?"

"I usually get my kids a piñata and let them beat it to pieces."

"LMAO that's funny."

"Yes you'd be surprised how hard they can hit, even the girls." *He thinks that's funny?*

"Sometimes I plan random games for them, or get supplies for them to make a craft, and sometimes we just pick a sport to play."

"If Jody is anything like her mother, LOOK OUT piñata ha."

I had to laugh out loud at this guy, *he barely knows me.*

"Landon loves to play basketball, do you think the other kids would like to do that?"

"My kids do, and I've seen some of the others play at school."

"Ok, I know a great spot to play in the city, it's called Frank Robert Park. There's a court, and a play structure. One more thing...I'm going to be at work for a while, any chance you could get a hold of their friends and invite them for me?"

It is my day off, I suppose I could share some of my time helping him. "Sure, which friends?"

"There is the one with the curly hair, and that skinny one, and the tall one, and a couple more I think."

"LOL, you think? You can't even remember their names lol."

"Sure I do."

"Okay tell me then." *He has no idea, too funny!*

"Umm...I have an idea, how about you contact the girls and I'll get a hold of the boys?"

"I can do that but..."

"But what?" asked Aaron.

"But what time?" replied Maggy.

"What time do you think is good?"

"It's your party."

"Lol, right. Is from 11–5 long enough?"

"That should be plenty of time, if you are having cake and presents too."

"It's settled. Now you'd better get working on it. Please."

This man is absolutely dauntless. "I would get working if you'd quit all of your chattering, lol".

"Come on...why so mean?"

"I didn't hurt your feelings, did I?" *That'll teach him.*

"Remember, you work for me now, so no back talking your boss."

I work for him? "Actually Mr., I'm the boss."

"Okay Boss, get doing your job, and I'll check up on you later."

That had to be one of the strangest encounters I've had for a while. This man was bold, yet entertaining. I felt oddly uplifted after our texting conversation. It was unexpected and out of the everyday normal for me. Anyhow, I knew the twins would be excited to have plans for the weekend, *I'd better get to it.* I went ahead and sent text message invitations to the girls' mothers. I've had their numbers saved on my phone since our kids became best friends in kindergarten.

By late afternoon, I had received messages back from the girls' mom's saying it was alright for them to go to Landon's party. Brittney's mom Amanda wanted to know why I was inviting the girls for Aaron. I explained to her that he was at work and didn't have enough time to invite everyone on short notice. Amanda seemed fine with my answer, she said that Brittney could go.

After supper my phone buzzed, I saw a message from Aaron. "Hey, I'm still at work, but I wondered if you had any luck getting ahold of the girls, and I was also seeing if you need a raise yet?"

I smiled, "Yes, I need a BIG raise for doing all of your work." *That'll get him.* "All of the girls are going."

"Awesome, you're the best. Thank you so much for doing that. So...what are you doing on Saturday?"

Why does he want to know what I'm doing? "You are welcome. Yes I am the best and don't you forget it." *I won't tell him what I'll be doing.*

"I won't forget...and one more question...I asked you what you were doing on Saturday."

He's persistent. "I'll be dropping my kids off at your place for the party, then I'll be doing random errands."

"I have to ask another favor from you. I may need an extra driver, and I'll pay you for gas."

Oh crap, he wants me to go, I hope he knows that I'm married. "I'll have to find out for sure what is going on, and let you know." Strangely, the conversation was causing my nerves to act up.

"Ok thank you, and please let me know because if you don't, I'll have to get you fired."

"You can't fire me, I'm the boss, remember?"

"Good point, but if you're the boss then who am I?"

"You can be the Captain, now get back to work before you actually get fired."

"Lol, ttyl."

"Bye."

Captain? Where did that come from? I wonder why his wife or girlfriend isn't going, or is she? He talks to me as if he's my good friend. I like it. He's fun, but should I drive for him? What would I say to him when we got there? What if there is nothing to talk about? I'm being silly, I've talked several times to him in person before, and I talk to people all the time at the salon, there is always something to talk about. Maybe I can drive the girls and Jonah into the city and drop them off at the park with Aaron, then I can leave, run errands, and check out that new salon supplier in the city, then be back on time to drive the kids home at the end of the party. Hmmm...that might work. I don't want things to be awkward, especially if he thinks I'm single. I feel like a school girl crushing on a school boy. He's just a friendly guy who has asked me to drive and there is nothing more to it. Right?

The following morning my alarm rang at 6:30am. I opened my eyes and saw the light flashing on my phone. I reached for it on my nightstand, and saw a new text from Aaron that read, "Get out of bed Sunshine."

Goodness, what time did this man wake up? Sunshine? That was a surprise. I got out of bed and texted back, "I'm awake." Five minutes later, my phone buzzed.

"Finally."

I had to smile. "Good morning to you."

"So you going to drive on Saturday or not? Come on. You were to find out by now!!!"

He added a happy face emoji at the end of his sentence. *He is being funny. I won't give him a direct answer.*

"Have you found out yet how many boys can go?"

"Not yet, because some of the parents haven't gotten back to me."

"You have to find out how many kids are going first to know if you need a second driver."

"Well, my truck can hold 5 more, Silly, and with all of the girls going, and your kids, there isn't enough room."

Silly? No one has called me that for years. How do I respond to that? He is looking for an answer right now, crap. "I likely can, but just to let you know, I'll be ditching you while I go into town and do some shopping."

"Ahaha, women and their shopping, don't you want to stay and play basketball?"

What would the other moms think of me if they knew I stayed for the party?

"I can't. Just feel lucky that I can drive Mr."

"Okay Boss, I'll take what I can get. I'll keep you updated about the boys."

"Have a good day, Captain." *There I go again calling him Captain, but it just suits him.*

Again, Aaron left me feeling cheery and in good spirits.

That day was hard to concentrate on my clients. I managed to get through all haircuts, and colors with satisfaction, but if you asked me to repeat anything my clients told me, I'd be at a loss for words. I tried to place my texting conversation with Aaron out of my mind, but I just couldn't. It made me feel happy to think of him, and when I saw my reflection in the mirror while styling Mrs. McGregor's wavy hair, I looked almost excited or even glowing. Lucy asked me if I was on a sugar high. She said I seemed full of energy, truth was I did feel extra bubbly. I had Aaron pegged as someone who liked to tease people, he had impacted my feelings for the better. *Had he any idea?*

Later that evening, Aaron sent me a text message, "Hey, I just came home from work, but I forgot to order a cake, what should I get?"

Why isn't his wife or girlfriend helping him make that decision? "What kind does the birthday boy like?"

"He likes ice cream cake."

"Are you having it after playing basketball, or before?"

"I'm thinking after, what do you think?"

"Unless you have a big chunk of ice beside it, it's going to melt before the game is over."

"A smart lady."

"That I am."

"I'll think of something. Now, what's for supper?"

Hmm, he's eating late enough. "Chicken."

"I love chicken, if only I had some. Pogos or hotdogs?"

"Pogos."

"Pogos it is, day three for those." *The man has to cook for himself. Is he single or not?*

"Did you find out yet how many boys can come?"

"Yes, they are all coming, so you won't get out of driving, Missy."

Joe is always grumpy after a long day at work. Why is this guy so cheerful? Missy? "Mr. Funny Pants I see, even after a long day of work."

"Talking to people like you, keep me smiling."

"Well, I do have that effect on most people, lol". *He is so fun to tease.*

"Yes, you do."

Aaron seemed to know exactly what to say all the time, I was almost carefree when talking to him. *He must know that I'm married. He is so flirty, but I've been a flirt with him too.* This behavior was completely out of character for me. I never teased other men, but it was too easy with him. I wasn't sure what I was doing with Aaron, but I hadn't crossed any lines. I knew he wanted to plan a fun birthday party for his son, but I wasn't sure if he needed my help as much as he let on. *What is he up to?*

When I tucked the twins in bed that night, Jonah asked when we could get Landon's birthday gift. I had completely forgotten about a gift. "What do you think we should get?" I asked.

"I'm not sure what he'd like."

"Maybe Jody would know."

Jody said, "Boy stuff."

I told the twins we'd think it over, and go gift-shopping tomorrow evening.

Joe had fallen asleep in his chair while watching a documentary about volcanoes, so I decided to get ready for bed. I wasn't sure what kind of gift the twins should get for Landon. *Aaron would have ideas. Would it be terribly bold if I texted him to find out?* After pondering the situation, I decided to go ahead text Aaron, after all he was bold enough to text me.

"Hey, what is Landon asking for as a birthday gift?"

Aaron wasn't responding, *maybe he's fallen asleep already, or is taking a shower.* I wasn't tired, so I popped in a movie and crawled under the covers on my bed. I began watching *The Lucky One*, which is one of my all-time favorites. Just as the movie was getting to the part where the main character kisses the girl for the first time, my phone buzzed. I paused the movie, and saw that it was Aaron returning my text. "Hey, sorry. I had to go back out to work."

Wow, a man apologizing, that's unusual.

"Landon really likes Lego, nerf guns, and water balloons. Really, anything you choose I'm sure he'd love."

"Ok thanks, that'll help. Another long day for you?"

"Yes. I'm up at 5:30am every day. I try to work overtime to stay on top of the bills, and have some extra left to give my son a few nice things."

"You are a good dad. Kids make everything worth it."

"Yes, kids have a way of making a person want to reach their full potential."

"True. Hopefully, someday you won't have to work so hard."

"Maybe not, but in the meantime, if you hear of anyone looking for a contractor, could you please give them my number?"

"Sure."

Aaron hasn't cracked a joke at all. His serious side is alluring. He hasn't texted me for a few minutes...likely gone to bed. I pressed play, and after some time, I was about to drift off when my phone buzzed, startling me, my eyes sprang open. Again, it was Aaron. "All cleaned up. Nighty night."

Okay...weird. He's saying goodnight to me. "Night."

"You better get some shut-eye, 5:30 is going to come early for you."

Um, okay. "That's what you think, I don't get up until 6:30. Goodnight."

I pushed stop on my movie, and closed my eyes. Aaron's last words ran through my thoughts over and over until I fell asleep.

Friday morning at 7:09am, "Time to get up, Sunshine." It was Aaron buzzing my phone.

My heart flipped, I took a short breath of air. "Too late, I'm already up. Did you sleep in?"

"No, Missy, I've been up for a couple hours and I'm already at work."

"Is that so?"

"I thought I'd be easy on you and let you sleep in."

Let me sleep in? Wow, the nerve of this man. I really like the nerve of this man. "How generous of you."

"I know."

"Do you normally text unfamiliar women this time of the morning?"

"No, just the one who's going to play basketball with us tomorrow."

Ha ha, what a joke. "You are texting the wrong one then."

"Nope, I'm texting the right one. I know you'll change your mind."

"Ha ha, I won't change my mind."

"Yes, you will."

"I will not, Mr."

"It will be more fun for the kids if there are two adults playing. Ttyl."

And that was it, the full extent of our morning conversation. I couldn't believe him, he was determined to get what he wanted. *Is he always like this? I will not be giving in to him.*

After getting the twins off to school, and myself to work, the day moved forward fairly quickly due to my jovial yet wavering thoughts of seeing Aaron in less than twenty-four hours. I talked with Lucy about driving the kids into the city for the birthday party tomorrow. I don't think she suspected my anxiousness, because she would have asked me all sorts of incriminating questions, which she didn't.

That night after supper, I began to tell Joe my plans for Saturday. He wasn't the least bit interested in listening like usual, so I finished the dishes and made a quick trip to the store with the kids to get Landon a gift. By the time we arrived back home, the kids were getting sleepy. I tucked them in bed and began unpacking our random purchases. I put my purse in the closet, but not before pulling out my phone. The light was flashing. Again, a message from Aaron appeared. "How was your day, Missy?"

There he goes again, calling me Missy. I could get used to that. I texted him back saying, "Very productive." *I'll cut to the chase.* "What time do you want to leave tomorrow?"

Moments later, Aaron texted back. "After the kids are all buckled in."

"Funny Captain. Do you even know where the place is, or are you going to get us lost?"

"I'll tell you what time we leave, if you tell me your age?"

What does my age have to with this? What a crazy man. "A lady never reveals her true age."

"A lady…ahaha."

"That's right, a lady. Have you ever met one?"

"I might have once, but it's rare to find one these days."

"So what time do you want to leave, Funny Pants?"

"You're the Boss, lady."

"Good. We will leave at 10:15am. That's right, I'm the Boss."

"Sounds great, should we meet up someplace, so you can lead the way?"

"You're the one who knows the way, I will follow you."

"But you're the Boss."

"That's right, and as a Boss I'm telling you Captain, that you will lead the way, after we meet up at the bakery in town, and go from there."

"Ok Boss, and you are playing basketball too."

"Lol, no I'm not."

"Remember what I said? You want the kids to be happy, don't you?"

"I'm sure you'll be able to keep them entertained."

"I can find out your age from them, and you're playing by the way."

"They will never tell you, and I'm shopping."

"We'll see about that Missy. Goodnight, get some rest. You are going to need it."

"Lol. Yes, for all of the shopping and errands I'm going to do. Goodnight, Captain."

Playing basketball sounded appealing, I hadn't played a game in years, unless you count all of the times that I've played with Jody and Jonah for fun. I pictured Aaron and myself tossing the ball back and forth on the court, to warm up with the kids. Aaron would be clowning around, he'd pretend to toss the ball and then quickly retrieve it back, and we'd both laugh. Then, the thought of me playing with another man other than my husband, didn't seem right, and the other kids would be sure to tell their moms, and that might make me look like a tramp.

I took a quick peek upstairs in the twins' rooms, they were already asleep, I could hear Joe's loud snore echoing from our bedroom. In the bathroom I brushed my teeth, and it occurred to me that I hadn't decided what to wear to the party. I wanted to choose something sexy that would almost knock Aaron's sock's off, yet be just enough to give him a taste of my docility. Him being such a tease, I felt the urge to tempt him a little. On the other hand, I'd have to choose something respectful enough for being a mom. *If I wear jeans, my legs will be covered and he can wonder what they are like underneath, I'm not sure if he's noticed my legs before? The weather is supposed to be 24 degrees. I can wear shorts, but would that be too showy? A sundress might be pretty, but what if I do end up playing basketball, that might be awkward. I'll have to go through my closet and see what I can find.* I wanted to search through my closet then and there but I didn't on account of Joe, he couldn't bare to have any lights on because it would disrupt his sleep, leaving him extra grouchy the next day. In bed, I pictured all of my tops and blouses, the slinky ones compared to the sophisticated ones, I tried matching certain tops with bottoms in my mind, but it was no use, it'd have to wait until morning. I wasn't at all tired so, I read through my phone messages, and emails from random clients, and friends. I found myself staring at my conversations with Aaron from the past few days. *He seems so sharp and witty, but playful.* Those qualities linked together in a man, seemed foreign to me, perhaps I'd become too immune to Joe's mundane attitude that anyone else seems interesting. Aaron is flirty, I couldn't remember the last time Joe had flirted with me, I missed the times he used to. *Maybe I've been over thinking Aaron's blithe nature, certainly my mentality will be back to normal after the party.*

Morning arrived more quickly than I had anticipated. The smell of cinnamon toast was bursting into my bedroom which meant Joe would be on his way out soon, he eats the same damn thing every morning before work. *He must be going in for 8am.*

I rummaged through my closet, trying to find the perfect outfit. Dress shorts, jean shorts, short shorts, skirt, dress, etc. I made a pile of bottoms according to which things looked new, and felt comfortable. Then I searched for the appropriate top. Maybe a t-shirt, but not a blouse, or tank top. Nothing too fancy, or nothing see through. I made another pile of possibilities. I tried on my sleek blue top with my flowy grey skirt, but that said mom all over it. Burgundy dress shorts, with light pink fitted top, pretty but not sexy. Short shorts with purple V-neck t-shirt; too showy for a kids party. Surprisingly, I could still fit into those shorts and still look half decent at my age. Nothing was looking that great. I opened my dresser drawer and searched through the stack of tops that I seldom wear, and that's when I came across my black, short sleeve-fitted top that had black see through lace along the back from shoulder to shoulder. It was not too revealing, yet not too boring, it was slightly sexy. *Boom, this is the one.* My blue jean shorts would match perfectly. They were a couple inches longer than my short shorts, reached almost to mid-thigh, fit my ass comfortably, looked appropriate, and appeared to be unintentional of possible temptation, in case he did bring his wife/girlfriend. *He did say basketball would be more fun if there were "two adults" playing.*

After my toenail polish had dried, I showered and gave my legs a shave. I rubbed a sweet rose scented body lotion down my arms, mid-section, and legs. I dried and styled my hair in soft curls, put on a light dusting of make up with pale pink lipstick, and black mascara. My stomach had begun to rumble, the thought of breakfast made my stomach quiver, I had begun to feel as nervous as if I were getting ready for a first date. *This is not a date! What was I doing? I am married, and I'm trying to tempt another man, one of which I had no idea if he was single or not. I did agree to drive today and I couldn't back out now. Should I wear jeans instead?* My outfit looked borderline hot when I looked in the mirror. My breasts were perky today, and the bra I chose, made them look full and round as my top clung to them. My legs were not swollen from being on my feet all day, I could see a slight but favorable amount of muscle definition in my calves and thighs. *Shorts it is.* For shoes, I had decided on my ebony-colored leather sandals without socks, rather than my running shoes with socks. Socks shorten the appearance of the length of my calf muscle, which was not the effect I wanted to achieve.

I checked my phone for messages from the girls' moms, there was nothing except a text from Mrs. Lauders wishing me a great weekend. I text her back wishing her the same. I didn't know how a seventy-five year old woman who ran her own empire found time to keep in touch with me? After she moved out, she and I held on to our relationship, myself being motherless, and her childless. The twins were dressed, washed up, and had eaten breakfast, I hadn't been in the mood to eat, in lieu, I slowly sipped on a glass of orange juice. Just as I was brushing Jody's hair, my phone buzzed. It was Amanda saying that Brittney was running a bit late. I texted her back saying a few minutes wouldn't matter much. The twins wrote their names on Landon's card, I wrapped the birthday gift in red foil paper with a large Minecraft ribbon. Time was getting on and I hadn't heard anything from Aaron. I was still wavering my true intention for agreeing to drive. *Do I really want to help out, or do I just want to see Aaron face to face?*

A few of the girls had arrived and were playing in Jonah's room. *No message from Aaron yet. Was everything going okay with him, the boys, and were they running on time?* I couldn't wait any longer to find out, so I texted him.

"Hey, how are you and the boys for time?"

Seconds later, he texted back. "Not good here at all."

Oh no, a problem? "Is there anything I can help with?"

"I've got explosive diarrhea."

Ewe. That was not I was expecting. "Umm, well okay…" I had no idea what to say.

"LOL, I'm joking. Everything is great."

Phew. "You are too funny for your own good."

"It's going to be even funnier when I beat you playing basketball."

"Oh no, I'm shopping, remember?"

"We'll see about that Missy."

Amanda pulled into my driveway, I saw Brittney out the kitchen window, running towards the front door. The girls sounded like wild elephants charging down the stairs to greet her.

I texted Aaron back. "You ready to go or what?"

"I'm always ready," he said.

I bet you are. "Ok. I'll meet you in fifteen minutes."

"Sure thing, and don't forget your running shoes."

We'll see about that.

Chapter 3

When the kids and I reached the bakery, Aaron was already there waiting. He was standing outside of a sparkling new, four-door GMC truck, the boys bopped around inside the truck. *Hmm...No woman in sight. Of course he'd have the newest vehicle in the parking lot. How did he get here that fast? He supposedly lives further away from here than I do.* I pulled up beside him in my minivan, and lowered my window. He came directly over to me, and rest his left hand against my door. He looked so clean in his royal blue t-shirt, and plaid shorts. His face appeared babyishly smooth, and the faint scent of aqua cologne wafted toward me. His delicious fragrance allured me to take in an extra breath as he leaned inward and looked directly into my eyes and smiled. "You're late, Missy."

What nerve. "I'm right on time Mr. You must be early." I couldn't help but smile back at him.

The girls in my van all shouted at Aaron, "Hey, we're not late."

"See? The girls know we're on time." I raised my upper brow and gave him the evil eye, just for fun.

"Okay, okay. You girls win. I'm early."

"Ya, ya, ya," the girls screamed and laughed at Aaron.

"Do you girls have everything?"

"I believe we do."

"Okay then, we'd better go," said Aaron. "Think you girls, and Jonah can keep up with me?"

"Maybe it's you boys who won't be able to keep up with us?"

His eyes brightened. "Is that a challenge?"

"Do you want it to be?" I challenged him back. Last night I googled, and scribbled down the directions to the city park. I didn't want to rely on following Aaron all the way there, I like to know exactly where I'm going.

"Let's beat him there," the girls cheered.

Aaron stood back from my van, pointed his index finger towards me, and said, "We need to have a bet in place."

"What type of bet?" I said.

Aaron scratched the bottom of his chin with his thumb, squinted his eyes, and pondered a few seconds. "If I win, you have to play basketball with us."

I should have seen this one coming. "I can't, I have places I need to go."

"Are you saying that you girls are scared, and you won't be able to beat us boys?"

The girls whaled, "We can beat them."

"Come on Mom, can we?" said Jody.

"Of course we can beat them, girls. Don't be silly, but we are not racing. It is not safe."

"Did you hear that boys?" said Aaron.

The boys stuck their heads out his truck windows.

"The girls are afraid of losing a little race because "the mommy" doesn't want to play basketball."

"The mommy," now he has another name for me. He's creative.

The boys went crazy and began laughing, they teased by calling us girls chickens.

"Ha ha, no I'm not afraid of anything, and certainly not of a bunch of silly boys," I said. "We could have been half way there by now Mr."

"It's a bet then." Aaron turned and rushed into his truck with the boys.

"No, it's not," I yelled out my window.

Aaron started his truck. He looked over to me and nodded his head up and down. He revved his truck engine. "Yes it is," he called out.

"Come on Mom. Let's beat him," said Jonah.

This man is acting so juvenile. He's hot, and egoistic, damn he knows how to excite me.

"Buckle up girls. Let's go." I sped out of the parking lot, ahead of the boys. The girls waved their hands good bye toward Aaron's truck. Their giggles told me that they were eager to be in the lead. Even though I had no true intention of racing, I believed I could still beat Aaron to the basketball court, depending on which route he chose to get there. If he travels on the highway, he will get stuck in the Saturday morning rush, whereas if I take a few side roads, I can stay ahead of him and win this non-race. We both travelled along Jefferson Street. There was a slow poke driver in front of me, I decided to pass. Just as I pulled back into the line of traffic, Aaron and the boys zipped past us girls, and the next vehicle ahead of me.

"How dare they?" I was surprised Aaron was that determined to win.

"Mom, let's pass him," said Jody.

I told the kids that it wasn't safe to pass because other cars were approaching and we weren't a safe distance away. I kept watch on Aaron's truck, as he continued to speed in and out of the traffic. He was at least 8 cars ahead of us by now.

"Can't we catch up to him?" asked the girls.

"Just wait, girls. We'll catch him sooner or later." I took a quick look at the directions I made for myself, and Aaron was headed straight for the highway. *Good.* "Don't worry kids. I think we can beat him now." A couple hundred meters up the road, Aaron merged onto the highway, and was now out of sight. I continued driving past the highway, and I turned onto Pony road. There wasn't as much traffic as the highway, which made it simple for me to pass random cars safely. The road had thousands of acres of hay fields, corn, and some brush land on both sides. The girls noticed a field with at least eight ponies, some were brown and black, others were grey. Sadly, there wasn't time to stop and pet the ponies. The non-race was on, and we had to keep driving. I was about to turn onto Clark road, when my phone buzzed, I pulled off to the side to check the message.

"Don't stop, Mom," said Jody.

"I have to. It could be an emergency."

It was from Aaron, "Are you there yet?" No emergency.

Quickly I sent him a message, "Maybe we are, maybe we're not," and placed the phone down. I zoomed along Clark road, Sandy road, Neptune road, and then to Hwy 70. My phone buzzed again, I neglected to check the message. I wasn't going to lose any time on the possibility of beating Aaron. The park signs began to pop up along the roadside that read Frank Robert Park–2 kilometers. Either, Aaron and the boys were in front of us on the highway, or somewhere behind us. The traffic wasn't as thick as I had anticipated.

"Kids, keep your eyes peeled for the boys."

Where were they? We reached the exit ramp for the park and pulled up to the intersection. An arrow to the park pointed left, we waited for the stop lights to turn green.

The kids shouted, "They're right behind us."

"No way," I said. My heart began to pump a few extra beats. I looked in my rear view mirror and there was Aaron with the boys. I chuckled at the boys waving their hands out the side windows. According to my directions, the park was just a few blocks ahead. The traffic light was red, the car in the lane beside us turned right, which gave Aaron room to drive up beside us and wait for light to turn green. I had to settle the girls down. They were laughing and waving their hands at the boys through the window. I could see the boys sticking out their tongues and grinning at us girls. The light changed and we took off like a shot, leaving Aaron in our tracks, until he revved his engine and caught up to us. His truck had a lot more horsepower than my minivan. He sped past us, then was forced to stop at the second set of red lights, where we caught up to him. He had a happy smirk on his face, as if he knew something I didn't. He tried to taunt me by looking our way, pressing the gas causing the engine to roar. I knew he could easily win as soon as the light changed. The sign for the park said Frank Robert Park, next left. The light was green and the traffic moved forward, Aaron changed lanes and was right behind me. The girls were certain that we'd win this non-race. At the park entrance, I signaled and slowed to turn left. I had to wait for the vehicle ahead of me to get moving. They were taking forever. Before I realized it, Aaron and the boys zipped past us girls and into the park. They had literally beaten us. The girls shouted, "No fair." I think my worst nightmare was about to come true. Aaron would try to get me to play basketball, my insides rumbled, maybe caused from the jitters, or anxiousness, or maybe I was still hungry from not eating. When we reached the parking lot, the boys were racing around the truck, and Aaron was leaning up against his truck with his arms crossed, and a pleased expression. I carefully pulled up, and parked near the boys. Before we got out, I told the girls and Jonah to remember that it wasn't a real race, so the boys didn't actually beat us.

As soon as we got out of the van, the boys started yelling, "We won."

"It wasn't a race, so you guys didn't win," said Jody.

The boys and girls continued to taunt each other about who won. I looked at Aaron, I could almost feel his aura touching mine as he moved closer to me. My body shivered in delight.

"You lost the race," he said. "Now you'll have to play basketball."

"It wasn't a race, and I won't be playing Mr."

"Coping out of our bet, Missy?"

"There was no bet, Funny Pants."

"Okay, I'll be the one to give in. Play because you want to, and it will have nothing to do with any bet."

He sounded sincere, his voice was tender enough to make me want to stay, but I knew that it would be the wrong decision. "I can't. Do you want help getting them settled on the court before I go?"

He looked downward, and sighed, "I've got it," he smiled. "Thanks anyway."

"If you're sure?"

"I'll be fine, Missy."

On my way to SP Supplies, I replayed the morning in my mind. Aaron seemed genuinely disappointed that I didn't stay for Landon's party. If it wasn't for my disconcerted feelings, I'd have stayed in the blink of an eye, but my conscience told me to go and do my errands.

At the supply store, I was completely mesmerized by the large variety of stock, and products. My mind was overwhelmed in delight with new patterns and styles of materials. I picked up a box of new wave combs, 6 blue water resistant capes, and a new pair of clippers. On the wall hung a silver clock in the shape of a pair of scissors, I knew it'd be perfect in my salon, so I had to buy it. Thoughts of Aaron had temporarily left my attention. My stomach had begun to relax, and I was ready to have some lunch. After my stop for a quick salad, I scooted over to the mall for some new clothes. I was able to find two new tops, shoes, and a light fall jacket. The afternoon was getting on, but still too soon to pick up the kids. After I pondered the comparison of wasting time around the city, and heading to the party, I decided that it wouldn't turn me into an awful person if I did go back early.

Before I got out of my van at the park, I pulled a toothpick out of my purse and ran it between my teeth, and popped a fresh piece of mint gum in my mouth. I touched up my face with my compact powder, and fluffed my hair with my brush. A fresh appearance was important to me, and after going to all the trouble that morning, I wanted to leave a lasting impression with Aaron. *I shouldn't care what he thinks of me, but I just do.*

I remembered I hadn't checked my phone messages in hours, then I remembered the message I received on the way to the party. I took a quick peek, and sure enough, the message was from

Aaron. It said, "I'll be a gentleman and slow down, so you ladies will have a slight chance of beating us." *Ohhh, that man loves to torment me. Was the non-race actually that close, or did he drive slower on the highway on purpose?*

I texted him back from the parking lot. "Gentleman, ha ha ha. FYI I let you win the non-race on purpose. I didn't want your ego to tarnish." I waited a few minutes to see if that would spark his fire, but he did not respond. Random kids played on the play structure, others rode their bikes around the paved trail. I looked toward the basketball court, where I could see Aaron and the kids sitting at the picnic tables under the trees. When I reached them, they were all stuffing their faces with pizza. Jody popped up out of her seat to give me a hug and kiss. Aaron looked at me and smiled, "Pizza?"

The tempting smell of pepperoni wasn't going to lure me into eating in front of him. I smiled back, "No thanks."

"I thought I'd offer with my tarnished ego and be a gentleman, in case you were hungry." *He was referring to my last text message.* I wasn't sure what to say because my nerves were beginning to act up, so I ignored him. His gaze fixed on me. I walked around the tables, asking the kids if I could get them more to eat. Just in time, the magician he hired had shown up to do a few tricks. I kept my distance from Aaron, I didn't want to come off as being needy or clingy. I sat beside Jonah, the magician pulled a bird from his hat, and did card tricks with the kids. The kids clapped after each trick until the end of the show, then it was cake time. After the kids sang happy birthday, Aaron started to cut the cake, but he was having difficulty getting the pieces onto the plate without messing them up. I told him to step out of the way, and I'd take over.

"You're the boss." Tingles ran through my body, like a school girl, as his fingers almost touched mine when he handed me the knife. I cut a slice for everyone, including an extra-large one for Aaron.

"Aren't you having cake, Mommy?" asked Jody.

"Oh, I'm full, sweetheart. You go ahead." Chocolate cake always turned my white teeth brown, and there was no way I was going to use my toothpick in front of Aaron.

"Trying to make me fat?" said Aaron, his soft lips enticed me as a bite of cake slid off his fork and into his mouth.

"Maybe you can wear it off."

He began to laugh, "What kind of exercise would I do? Any ideas?"

I laughed, "Nope," I knew he was referring to sex. Thank goodness that the kids weren't paying attention to us.

"You must have some kind of idea," he teased.

I had a lot of ideas, none I'd dare speak out loud. I didn't want our conversation to get out of hand, so I focused on scrapping the icing off the cake knife. I was at a loss for words until I spotted a couple of basketballs along the fence, "See ya," I said.

"Going shopping again?"

"Maybe, or not." I ran off before he could speak. I retrieved the balls and placed them inside the bin at the side of the court. It had been a while since I dribbled a basketball, I took one and bounced it on the spot. *Amazing.* I moved around in my own little space, getting the feel of the ball. The kids chomped down their cake, and Aaron kept busy pouring them more juice, no one looked to be paying attention to me, so I dribbled the ball down the court and took a shot at the hoop. *Missed.* I tried again, *missed.* After six misses, finally the seventh, a win. I must have been more focused on getting a hoop than I realized because when I reached down to grab the ball, Aaron had snuck up and quickly snatched it before I could lay my hands on it.

"Hey, give it back," I pretended to be angry as I tried to seize the ball.

"Ah, she's a feisty one." He waved the ball around, and above his head, so I couldn't reach.

I jumped to try and get it from him, but his arms extended too high. We both laughed, as I continued to lunge for the ball. My heart rate began to increase, as I was determined to get the ball back. He lowered his arms just enough to taunt me, and that is when I slapped it out of his grasp and it bounced onto the court. I ran after it and began dribbling it towards the hoop. He ran after me, I tossed it up and it went in the hoop.

"Ha," I said.

He raised his dark brows and grinned. "Quite the talent you have."

He looked surprised, and frankly, I was too. I wasn't expecting to get it in, but since I did, it was icing on my cake.

"That's right Mr., so don't mess with me."

Aaron squinted his eyes at me. "Did you finish all of your 'shopping'?" he emphasized shopping.

"I did."

"How about playing that basketball game, after all, you do owe me one."

I paused momentarily to think. *Would that be wise of me?* "Listen, Funny Pants, I don't owe you anything, besides I don't have proper shoes on to play."

"Excuses, excuses."

I heard my name being called, "Mom, Mom?" It was Jody, and Jonah running toward me and Aaron. Landon and the other kids were following close behind. "Mom, are you playing basketball?" asked Jonah.

"Not today, sweetheart."

"Okay. Is the party almost over?" said Jonah.

"Soon."

"Okay because I'm thirsty," he said.

"I'm thirsty too," said Jody.

"Didn't you guys just have a drink?" I said.

"Yes, but the juice ran out," said Jonah.

I looked at Aaron, "Yes, it's all gone," he said.

"We can stop on the way home and get something to drink," I said. I looked at Aaron, he was tossing the ball back and forth amongst the boys.

"The presents aren't opened yet, are you doing that here?"

"Do you think we should?" said Aaron.

"I thought you were in charge," I smirked at Aaron.

He smirked back at me. "I didn't want the wind to blow away the gift paper, Missy."

There's that name again. I preferred hearing his deep, yet soft, almost seductive tone in person compaired to reading my name in a text message.

"If we are careful and collect the paper as he unwraps, it shouldn't be a problem, Silly." *I couldn't resist throwing that back at him.*

"Alright, if you say so. Let's get back to the picnic table kids."

Landon opened all his gifts which were either Lego, or nerf guns. A couple of his friends ran around shooting each other with foam bullets. The girls began to play tag. Aaron and I sat on opposite sides of the picnic table, and had our first mature conversation since our texting had begun. We talked about how well the party was going, and different events coming up at school. He asked what I did for a living, which led to questions about my hair salon. Apparently, he had heard about it, but he'd never been. I found out he works in construction, but after hours, he works side jobs. He said he liked to stay fairly close to home because he wants to be available for Landon, since his mother is not in the

35

picture anymore. I didn't press him for reasons why, but I was curious. I asked him who took care of Landon when he was at work, and he mentioned his neighbor Mrs. Finnegan, "the sweetest lady ever" keeps him before and after school every day until Aaron gets home. There was no mention of a spouse or girlfriend. He pointed to my wedding rings. *Why wouldn't he? I have a 2 carat diamond on my finger.* He asked how long I had been married for. I told him 18 years. He looked flabbergasted, then he told me that my husband was a lucky man. I felt my cheeks becoming warm, I hoped it wasn't noticeable to him. *Was he flirting? Was he being polite? Or, did he have a realization of my age and was trying to make me feel good? He must have clued in that I was around the 40 mark, but he didn't mention anything.* He asked what Joe did for a living, the only thing I said was, "Joe's a lawyer and he works long hours." I preferred if details about my marriage stayed private.

Five o'clock was approaching, the kids were still running wild, filled with fuel from the cake, and pizza. I knew they weren't thirsty anymore, earlier I saw them sipping away at a drinking fountain near the washrooms. I extensively enjoyed my chat with Aaron, I wasn't ready to leave, but I knew the parents would be expecting their kids to be home around six. I mentioned to Aaron about taking the kids home, he asked me if I was trying to get away from him due to boredom. I couldn't contain my laughter,

"Yes, I'm terribly bored and I can't wait to get away."

Aaron's facial expression beamed with vivacity, as if he knew I enjoyed talking with him. I felt a warmness inside that travelled from my neck down to my stomach. I was at ease with him, more so than I figured I'd be. The kids were having so much fun with each other, it didn't appear that they were taking note as to how long Aaron and I were chatting.

After getting the kids and myself settled in the van, Aaron came over to my window, and handed me a bunch of twenty dollar bills folded in half.

"What's this for?"

"That's for your gas and your time."

I briefly stared at the money, then tried to hand it back. "Here," I said.

"No," he said, "You keep it."

I'm not that cheap. "No, you take it back please, I had to come into the city anyway."

Aaron refused to take the money, I could tell by the twinkle in his eyes, he was amused with my persistence in trying to get him to take it back. I told him if he didn't take it, I'd let it fall to the ground and the wind would blow it away.

His lips pushed out, and his eyebrows turned into a frown, "You wouldn't do that."

His hand was resting slightly inside my window, so I reached for his hand and tried to open it. As I placed my hand on his, I felt a jolt of intense want. He held his hand tightly shut, I looked him straight in his eyes, and he relaxed his grip, allowing me to place the money inside his palm and close it. He then accepted the money, and in all sincerity said, "Thank you for all of your help."

"No problem." I didn't want the afternoon to end. I hadn't had that much fun in a long time. "And, are you going to be able to find your way home from here, Captain?"

"I don't know. But I won't follow you, you're a crazy driver."

"Ha ha, me, a crazy driver? But I'm the boss remember, and you're supposed to do what I say, and I say it's gentlemanlike to let the ladies go first."

"Yes, you're the boss," he smiled, "I'll let you wild girls go first."

On the way home, I decided to take the highway, according to my directions it was a straightforward hike back, instead of all the side roads. Aaron and the boys followed us half way back, and then he began to get crazy. Since there were two lanes, and not much traffic, he drove in the lane next to us, and the boys waved their hands at us. He took me by surprise and I began to laugh, so did the girls and Jonah. He sped up leaving the nose of his truck slightly ahead of my van. I tried to speed up to get ahead of him, but every time I did, he sped up a bit more. I could see this was entertaining for him, as it was for myself, and the kids. I slowed back, because I had to think of the safety of the children. Had I been alone, I would have given him a run for his money. However his truck's engine was bigger than my van. I'd never have won. I'd love to try one day, but I'm certain I'll never get the chance. *Would I even hear from him after this party?*

Chapter 4

Sunday morning, my phone buzzed at 8:03am. The text read, "Happy Birthday," along with two birthday cake emoji's. It was from Aaron.

He remembered. "Thanks," I responded.

"Hey, look who's finally up."

"I woke up at six, and couldn't fall back asleep."

I had woken up several times in the night due to overthinking the events from the afternoon, Aaron's text messages, our non-race, him trying to keep the basketball from me, the way the arms of his sunglasses rest over the sides of his hat instead of pressed against his head, and the attraction I felt when I touched his hand. Every time I thought about Aaron, a fire lit up inside my mind, bringing warmth to my inner core. *Was it just me, or had Aaron felt something too?*

I swear an hour had passed and he hadn't responded, but reality said it was only a few minutes. I was too anxious, so I texted him again, "I'm surprised that you're up."

"I'm working."

"Really? You aren't off Sunday's?"

"Yes, but I had to make a deal with my boss man, to get yesterday off."

"That's too bad."

"Only until noon today, weekday's I'm off at two. Then I go out for a couple hours for custom jobs, and come back for supper with my boy. When I get hired for an evening job, I don't get to bed until midnight."

"Makes a long day for you."

"Somedays are too long."

"That's what happens when you're the Captain."

"I like to please people, and yes, I AM, the Captain."

"Maybe you'd get home earlier if you weren't texting on your phone all day!"

"Screw you. Don't take that the wrong way."

I'd love to screw you. Whoa, did I just think that?

"I have a perfect answer for that, but I'm a lady, so I won't say it."

"Lady...ha ha ha. Tell me, what do ladies do on their birthdays?"

"This lady is going to her cousin's, for lunch today with her children."

"Shouldn't a 29 year old, such as yourself, be going out on the town?"

"29? Lol. I can't believe you think I'm that old."

"Really though, how old are you today?"

"I told you I'll never tell." *If he finds out I'm forty, he'll think I'm a cougar waiting to pounce.*

"Well, if you don't mind me saying, you look great...for now".

"Lol, for now?"

"Lol, someday you will tell me, but I'll say, whatever you're doing, it's working."

He thinks I look great. My heart did a somersault.

"Smart answer, Mr."

"I'm naturally smart."

"You are a natural flirt."

"Maybe."

What does he want?

"Are you actually getting anything done this morning?"

"For sure...The reason for my text is that I wanted to let you know how much I appreciate your driving yesterday, and for everything you did."

"You're welcome. I had fun."

"Me too. You're the best, Missy."

"That's right Captain, I'm the best and don't you forget it."

"Is that an order, Boss?"

"Absolutely."

"Lol. I should get back at it now. Talk to you later?"

Talk to me later? Does he mean that?

"Okay. Ttyl."

"Have a great birthday, and a nice visit with your cousin."

"Thanks."

I was not expecting any messages from Aaron today because the party was over, and he had already told me yesterday how much he appreciated my help. *Could it be that he enjoyed texting me? Or was he only being polite? He said I looked great. Did he mean it? So many questions.*

Strangely, my lack of sleep hadn't affected my energy, texting Aaron filled me with happiness, my smile reached from ear to ear. I began to sense a tingling throughout my body, a butterfly sensation inside my stomach. I hadn't experienced those feelings for quite some time, but what did it all mean? I stared at my phone, and scrolled back to the beginning of our conversation. He sent birthday cake emoji's. That was special. *Maybe he sends this kind of stuff to other people too? Or maybe he doesn't? Either way, I love it, but I can't let these feelings for Aaron get out of hand. I'll only be setting myself up for heart break. Joe is my husband, and it isn't fair to him that I'm letting another man inside my head. Our flirting back and forth needs to stop, but I don't like the idea of that and I don't understand why? The only thing I know for sure is, texting Aaron has been adding that extra bit of spark to my life, but I know I have to cut off contact with him soon, but when?*

My younger cousin Meredith, and her husband Peter live several houses down from us, on Belle Street. Meredith and I didn't get along as kids, but we matured and became closer after her mom passed away from breast cancer 20 years ago.

Meredith and Rory greeted us at the front door. Meredith with open arms, Rory with a wet nose. Meredith caressed my cheek and said, "Happy Birthday, Maggy."

The smell of beef lasagna filled my senses, I returned her affection. The twins removed their shoes and placed them on the mat. They gave Auntie Meredith a squeeze and ran off to play in the living room with Rory, the only Dalmatian in Laudersville (that I knew of). Joe went out on the back deck to talk to Peter. With Peter being a judge, it gives Joe and him a chance to compare notes about cases, even though they'd both lose their jobs if anyone found out.

Meredith's kitchen was bright and spacious. Her butcher block table held a stunning bouquet of yellow sunflowers, arranged in the crystal vase that I had given to her on her thirtieth birthday. A beautiful wine and cheese basket wrapped in cellophane sat to the right. "It's for you," she said.

"Me?"

"Yes, there's card attached. It's from Mrs. Lauders, she had it delivered earlier because she wasn't able to make it."

"How did she manage that on a Sunday?"

"She's Mrs. Lauders, that's how."

"True. Did you know she's hasn't ever forgotten my birthday?"

"She does think of you as her own daughter."

I shared a sample of the Havarti in my basket with Meredith, then made myself useful and poured pop juice (a mixture of concentrated grape punch mixed with ginger ale, and water) into all of the glasses at each place setting on the dinner table, while Meredith turned off her oven. Aunt Nancy used to make pop juice for us as a treat when we were little, and ever since her passing, Meredith has it for every occasion.

Lunch was as scrumptious as always. Meredith served tossed salad, garlic bread, baked potatoes, and sweet peas, along with her lasagna. Joe and Peter continued with their tedious conversation among themselves at the opposite end of the table, Jody and Jonah tried to sneak food under the table for Rory, while Meredith and I chatted about my dad. He couldn't make it for lunch because he wanted to go fly fishing with his friend Lou that morning, he guaranteed he'd be coming by later for some birthday cake.

After doing the dishes, Meredith wanted my opinion concerning her television room. She wanted to tear out the wall for the walk in cupboard because they never use it, and either build a wall in the center of the room to make two rooms, one being a sunroom, or build an entirely new room onto the house and put in large windows. I have always loved renovation projects, taking something and turning it into something better stimulates my mind on many levels. Obviously, the project was big enough to hire a professional. Peter isn't much of a handy man, and Meredith is Peter's judicial assistant, neither of them have the time, or skill to do it. Meredith couldn't think of anyone to consult, so I searched my phone through the online yellow pages for local companies. The only names I recognized was Williams' Construction, but they did industrial work, not residential. Then there was Abbot's Home Repairs, but I heard through the grapevine at the salon that Mr. Abbot was off work due to a broken ankle. Then it occurred to me that Aaron does construction and he did say to give anyone his number who needed work done. *That would mean Aaron would be working up the street from my house.* My stomach rolled over as I pondered the situation. *Should I mention him or not?*

"Can you think of anyone else?" asked Meredith.

Mention him, not mention him? "I might know of someone, can I let you know?"

"I'd be grateful if you would," she said.

I stood gaping toward the TV room, visualized Aaron pulling out his tape, and jotting down measurements. He would begin to remove old drywall and nails from the closet wall, causing him to get overheated enough to remove his coat. Underneath, he'd be wearing a tight t-shirt that would reveal the firmness of his biceps. As he'd use his pinch bar to loosen the studs, beads of sweat would begin to form on his forehead, under his arms, and on his chest, which would lead him to remove his damp t-shirt, exposing his bare chest, revealing his contracting and relaxing pecs as he continued to work.

"Everything alright?" asked Meredith.

I was quickly jarred back into reality. *How embarrassing, I'm twirling a strand of hair between my fingers and rubbing, and pressing it between my lips.*

"Everything is fine. I was just picturing which would be the best idea."

Meredith's eyes brightened up with stars, "I could have a skylight, and place a couch underneath, roomy enough for two."

I smiled, "I see you have a motive behind this renovation."

That's sweet. After ten years of married life with Peter, she wanted to keep the romance alive. *Joe hasn't cuddled with me for years.* I'm happy that Meredith and Peter have been able to keep their intimacy strong, however, on a deeper level, I was envious of their relationship. Throughout lunch, I noticed the two of them passing sensual looks back and forth while sitting at opposite ends of the table. Anytime I looked at Joe, he had his mouth full and was staring downward at his plate, he didn't seem the least bit interested in my whereabouts.

"Grandpa's here," called Jonah.

Meredith and I went back into the kitchen to see dad.

"Happy Birthday, sweetheart," said Dad.

He draped his sweater over the wooden arm chair, and approached me with his arms wide open. Dad's hugs were always the best because he gave more than a pat on the back. He'd tightly squeeze for three seconds, pause, and let go.

"Thanks, Dad. I'm so glad you could make it."

We all sat at the table, I blew out my 40 birthday candles. The heat from the flames were hot enough to almost singe off my nose hairs. Meredith made sure every year to bake me a chocolate-frosted birthday cake, and I do the same for her on her birthday. While eating cake, Dad talked mostly to Peter about fishing with Lou that morning, Joe expressed his interest by moving onto the sofa in the other room, and leafing through a magazine. He and Dad have never had much in common. Dad raised me on the same farm that his parents raised him, Joe was raised in the suburbs. They are men with two different outlooks on life. That's what first attracted me to Joe, he was always clean-cut and had unique ideas which made me view life in another contrast. On the farm, home life and work life were two in the same. With Joe's life, you could separate work from home, and that seemed appealing at the time.

I opened the gifts from Jody and Jonah that Auntie Meredith helped with. Jody gave me a silver bracelet, and Jonah gave me a bag of chocolate-covered almonds, and a white rock that he found at the park.

After I helped Meredith tidy up, we sat down for a cup of tea, and trip down memory lane. Soon after, the twins said they were getting bored because Rory had fallen asleep, they started nagging me to go home, but my dad insisted we stay at least until I opened his gift. I unwrapped a little purple box, inside was a heart-shaped locket, tiny white pearls adorned the lid, and the chain was white gold. I had never seen anything so exquisite. Dad said it belonged to my mother, and her mother before her, apparently he'd been saving it since my mom's passing, for a special occasion. The pearls were stunning and felt smooth to my touch. I opened the locket and there was a black and white photo of my mother placed inside. Joy and sadness tugged at my emotions. Her hair was long. I remembered it as blonde, and it appeared to have two pins holding up each side, the length was pulled over her left shoulder. Her eyes looked lively, and her smile suave. Dad said she was twenty-five when the photo had been taken. I was almost speechless until Meredith said how much resemblance I bared to Mom in that photo. I thanked Meredith for saying that, and Dad for giving me something I would treasure always. I unhooked the clasp and Dad fastened it around my neck. *Best gift ever.*

I made vegetable soup for supper that night, after stuffing ourselves at Meredith's, no one was hungry. I finished tidying the dishes and packing the twins' lunches for school tomorrow. Joe was laying on the couch in the living room. He hadn't made a peep all evening. However, he did leave a birthday card for me on the counter. It wasn't anything special, just a picture of flowers on the front, and the words 'Happy Birthday' on the inside. He didn't write my name at the top, only his name was signed at the bottom. It was easy to see that he didn't spend much time choosing the perfect card. I placed it in the center of the kitchen table with my other cards.

I thought about Meredith's renovations, and remembered that I needed to contact Aaron. I sat at the island in the kitchen, my phone in hand, but I was hesitant to text him because that would mean keeping in contact with him, and I told myself earlier that I should cut off contact with him. On the other hand, Meredith couldn't find anyone else to do the job, and Aaron was looking for extra work. *It can't hurt.* My stomach told me different by the amount of gurgling I heard. I wasn't feeling uneasy, just a little guilty with a touch of aspiration. I convinced myself to go ahead, and send Aaron the request for Meredith. I waited a few minutes, but he was not responding. *What could he be doing on a Sunday night?* I heard Joe walking upstairs, *on his way to bed no doubt.* I wanted to hear back from Aaron, but I couldn't sit there all night and wait for my phone to buzz. I slipped into my sweat pants, and began my cycling routine—thirty minutes, three times per week or whenever I felt like it. I turned on the television to keep myself entertained while I rode, I kept eyeing my phone for the flashing message notification, but after an hour, I still hadn't received anything. It was starting to get late and work would be here sooner than I wanted. *Was he at all interested in the job? Was it that he didn't want to talk to me anymore? Had he gone to bed already?*

Chapter 5

I went into work fifteen minutes early today because I wanted to hang up my new scissor clock that I purchased on the weekend. It looked befitting on my rose-colored wall in the reception area, above the guest chairs. Lucy said it looked adorable, I completely agreed. The morning was passing quickly. Mrs. Patterson was in bright and early to have her hair set on rollers, Mrs. Yang and her husband William came in for their monthly trims, Ms. Peters had a perm, and my neighbor Shelley wanted a blow dry and style for a lunch date. I wondered if she actually had a lunch date, or if she just came in to snoop around. Her complexion was pale today, she insisted she was feeling fine until after I washed her hair. When she sat up from the sink, her face turned white, she rushed to the washroom and I heard her throw up in the toilet. Shortly after, she apologized and left. *Poor girl.* I tuned on the fan, opened the windows for fresh air, and sprayed air freshener. It didn't seem to take long for the stench to clear, and it was back to business for me. Lucy did trims for a few walk-in customers. Because of Shelley, I was running ten minutes behind, then it was one client right after the other without a break, the rest of the morning. I assumed Aaron would have responded to my request by now, but I simply had no time to check my phone. At twelve-thirty, Lucy had surprised me with a fortieth birthday gift. It was a new tip jar that said, "Maggy's Old Age Fund." I had to laugh, as Lucy would be one of the few people I'd let get away with an old age joke. She also brought in chicken Caesar salad with French bread for lunch today. For dessert, she made me a giant red velvet cupcake with cream cheese icing, topped with fresh raspberries. What a treat, as we haven't enjoyed lunch together for some time due to the daily flow of customers. I didn't dare check my phone to see if Aaron had left anything, Lucy said she had rescheduled Mr. Crawford's appointment, so we could celebrate together, and I wasn't about to let my phone interrupt her good efforts.

From there on, the afternoon was steady. It was three-thirty, I had to take a washroom break. After washing my hands, I finally took time to check my phone messages. Still nothing from Aaron. *That is not like him to ignore me. Maybe he was finished talking to me.* My stomach tensed up, as I sincerely hoped that was not so, even though I knew it'd be for the best. *I suppose it hasn't been that long. Not even twenty-four hours. He's not obligated to check in with me, but you'd think he'd give me an idea if he can do the renovation or not.*

That evening, I placed my phone near the stove while cooking supper incase Aaron sent a message, but another hour had passed and still nothing. Perhaps, I focused too much into why Aaron wasn't getting back to me in a timely fashion. *Last year the internet provider took two full days to return my call for service. Aaron is a business man, maybe he handles his personal calls differently from his business calls.* This was unsettling. I didn't want to pester him, so I carried on with my evening routine while curiosity wavered.

When I tucked the twins in bed for the night, Jody told me Landon was not at school that day, and she missed playing grounders with him at recess. She was nestled up under the blankets, her head propped up on her fuzzy purple pillow. I stroked her soft hair and tucked it behind her ear. I kissed her warm cheek, and told her that he was likely fine and maybe she'd see him tomorrow. *Why was Landon not at school today? Was something wrong?* I briefly contemplated texting Aaron to see if Landon was alright, but quickly declined the idea because I didn't want to give the impression that I was sticking my nose into his business. If Landon was sick, he'd be Aaron's first priority and that could have been the reason he hadn't returned my message.

It was a warm night, I went outside in my silk nighty, and bare feet to sit on the back deck. I enjoyed a glass of Merlot from Mrs. Lauders' gift basket. The sky was dark except for the millions of stars sparkling in their natural beauty. The air was still, I could hear water circulating around in my neighbors' back yard pond. It reminded me of walking by the river near my father's farm as a teenager. I used to go there occasionally after school and during summer break, to let my mind wander and think about life, all of its mysteries, and plans for my future. I remember feeling lonely at times as I watched the rapids continuously carry a gentle flow of water over the rocks and branch off into a narrow stream, only to reach a dead end. In a dry summer, the pool of stagnant water would settle, and eventually dry up without any chance to continue the journey of meeting up with another body of water, where it would be free to expand and spread into unfamiliar places. It made me examine the possibility that there was no purpose to anything, but then I considered all of the organisms, insects, and species of nature relying on it, then it all became clear that there was a point to everything because without it everything would migrate elsewhere, leaving the area barren.

As I relaxed, I could see Joe from inside our house. The large window in his office revealed him sitting at his desk, with the desk lamp on, his full concentration seemed to be focused on reading a document. Watching Joe, and listening to the water from my neighbors' pond, made me feel the same type of loneliness I felt all those years ago. Joe was inside and I was outside alone again. Our marriage was that pool of stagnant water that had begun to mold. *If only he would lift his eyes for a few seconds, he could see me sitting out here and have the desire to join me for a chat, or a snuggle on the hammock. Will he ever give me affection and attention, as he used to?* If it wasn't for the love and affection I received each day from my children, I'd likely have turned into either a cold hearted woman or a desperate one.

Occasionally, I fantasized about taking the twins and leaving Joe for good, but then I'd think about all the time and work I've put into making our house a home, and it would have been all for nothing. *This house is the only home that the kids have ever known, they are happy here, and I don't want that to change.* Aside from the twins, there was Joe, he'd be all alone in the house with nothing. *He'd have to prepare his own meals, and do his own laundry. I suppose he could hire a maid, or get a girlfriend who enjoys the domestic life, but then there'd be another woman involved in my children's life. I'm not thrilled on that idea. I like this house and I can't fathom living anywhere else. Everyone tells me what a perfect life I live, and they are right except for the part about having a perfect husband.*

My thoughts drifted back to the birthday emoji's and text messages Aaron had sent me. *If only Joe could be more like Aaron.* Aaron seemed interested in talking with me. *Why? I'm still not sure?* I replayed the whole basketball scene from Saturday over in my mind, how flirty and playful Aaron was towards me. *Does Aaron realize how much I desire those qualities in a man?* They are the exact qualities that Joe is lacking.

The mosquitos had begun to find delight in my blood, shortly after Joe had turned off his light. *Bed time.*

I lay under my covers and kept to my own side of the bed, Joe kept to his side, exposing only his shoulders, broad with fine brown hairs scattered here and there. It's been over two weeks since he's lay a hand on me. *I have no idea how a man can go so long without penetration and release, unless he's using his hand when he showers? I don't know why he keeps away from me?* I turned to my left side and lay away from him, my arm tucked under my pillow to elevate and support my head. I rest my phone flat on the bed, close to my chest to keep it hidden, and began scrolling through my texts from Aaron. *Obsessed? No...just infatuated...a little?* Liveliness bubbled under my surface every time I read over them, my lips pressed together and formed into a smile. The text messages that we exchanged from that Thursday before the party, held a special place in my mind. He had said, "Talking to people like you keep me smiling."

I said, "Well, I do have that effect on most people, lol."

He then responded back with, "Yes, you do." I was trying to be playful in my speech, I had expected a quick-witted remark back, but instead his response was as charming as him. He's telling me I have a good effect on others, him included, and the thought of that had moved me. He knows exactly what to say to keep things interesting, and me buttered up.

"What are you doing?" I heard Joe's gravelly voice turn toward me.

My insides clenched. I pressed my 'off' button, the screen went black. "Nothing much," I said. There was no way I was going to tell him that I was in deep thought about Aaron. I reached outward to place my phone on my nightstand, then I snuggled my arms under the covers and closed my eyes. A few moments later, I felt Joe's uncalloused hand slide up my nighty, he rubbed my thigh up to my hip. *He must want it.* He had moved in closer to me pressing his warm, naked body up against my back. His hand then slid between my legs, and he stroked my genitalia, I heard him groan, as if he was gaining pleasure from the feel of my skin. *Sex with Joe was not what I had expected tonight. He had not given me any indication earlier that he was in the mood, and now I have to turn my switch to "On" for him. I hate when he does this, I mean goes for days and weeks without giving it to me and then he expects me to be ready for him as soon as he is ready.* My mind was with Aaron until the sweet sensation of pleasure had kicked in and taken over my body as he fondled me. I turned to lay on my back and splayed my legs, Joe's fingers were slipping in and out of me with ease. I reached for his erect penis, and began to stroke him up and down, but he pulled my hand away and placed it above my head, and held it there with his left. He then clambered on top of me, and with his right hand, he placed his length inside me. He had begun to breathe deeply as he moved in and out of my body. My breath had become intense as he touched upon the depth of my inner sensitivity over and over. Sweat beads had begun to form on his forehead and ran down the sides of his flushed face. I grabbed the edge of the bed with my left hand, and clutched the sheets in my fingers, he released my right hand and I felt his manhood shrinking, but he continued to move in and out of me. The pleasure was minimal. I placed my hands on his back, hoping to sense intimacy, but there was nothing. His thrusts seemed to give him pleasure. I desired more. My body had been lacking for too long. I tried looking him in the eyes, but his eyes were closed and his head was turned away from me. His speed had escalated, and his many deep breaths had turned into one, as he released himself completely inside of me. I rest my hands on his shoulders. I could feel the weight of his body resting on mine. I closed my eyes. I felt an uncomfortable chill as his sweat dampened my face, I wanted to push him off me because of it, but I refrained, not wanting to discourage him from being physical with me. After his breaths had calmed, he withdrew and rolled over onto his own side of the bed, to face the wall.

I freshened up in the washroom, and thought about our lovemaking session. Joe knew exactly where to touch me to get me aroused quickly, and he knew how to bring me to climax, but he chose not to, he seemed more absorbed in getting himself off without concern for my needs. He used to fondle with me after intercourse to make certain I would get off, anymore he doesn't put in any extra effort, which leaves me half satisfied. *Lord only knows when I'll get it from him next.* I craved physical contact, but even more than that I yearned for emotional intimacy, communication, and feeling secure while being held in loving arms. I found fulfillment in Joe years back, but he is different now. My passion for kissing is not being met anymore, and I'm not talking about a simple peck on the lips. I'm talking about the kind of kiss that warms you inside and out as soon as your lips touch. The motion is rhythmic as both of your mouths open and close in unison, taking time to feel the softness and magnetism drawing and holding you together, every tingle and sensation arouses you a step higher as your body absorbs hunger, thirst, and desire from the other, leaving you wanting and confined to indulge in your longing until all control is lost. Kissing and love making with Joe in general had a way of leaving an emptiness in my heart, however getting some was better than none. Aside from not 'making it' my insides were somewhat soothed from the physicality. As for the next time, it wouldn't be until Joe gets an urge, unless I can come up with a new way to seduce him. *Maybe that would help to get our marriage back on track.*

I was just about to drift off, when I heard the vibration of my phone, and the light began to flash. *Someone is up late.* The message read, "Hey, sorry I just got your text. I was away with my son. Left my phone at home by mistake." *Aaron.* My heart fluttered. I turned to look at Joe, to see if he was paying attention to me, but he was zonked out.

"No problem," I responded.

"I'm not waking you, am I?"

"If you had waited another ten seconds, you might have."

"I'm sorry. I can message you tomorrow."

No, I want to talk with him now. "It's alright, I'm fine."

"I just wanted to let you know that I might have some time this week to look at your friends' place."

Meredith's place, he is interested. I subconsciously reached for a piece of my hair and twirled it around and around in my fingers, then I slid them down the shaft and felt the smoothness and placed it between my lips and squeezed my lips together. *Aaron, working up the street from my house.* I visualized myself checking up on him in the evening, to see how he was doing. I could even bring him a fresh slice of pie. *Way off topic Maggy.*

"Great, I'll let Meredith know tomorrow."

"Thanks, Missy. I guess you are on the job again, Boss."

"Lol, yes I am, Captain." *I love when he calls me Missy.*

"I should let you get back to your sleep. I hear older people need extra beauty sleep."

I had to catch my burst of laughter in my throat, and contain it to ensure Joe wouldn't wake. My eyes began to water. I rubbed them dry with the back of my hand.

"What's that? You need extra sleep because you are getting old. You don't look that old to me." *Ahahaha that should make him think.*

"You are right, I am getting old and if I want to look as good as you, I'd better get some sleep too. How old did you say you were?"

There he goes again with that flattery, damn. "I didn't say, lol".

"Someday you'll tell me."

"That's unlikely."

"If I guess it, will you tell me?"

"Does it bother you not knowing?"

"Well…kind of."

Crap, he really wants to know. I suppose it won't matter much if he knows, it's not as if he has notions of running off with an older lady and hooking up, and the reality of it goes back to me being unavailable. Keeping my age a mystery won't change anything between us, unless he thinks I'm too old to flirt with, but then again, we shouldn't be flirting with each other anyway. I'll just blurt it out.

"40"

"You just turned the BIG 4 0."

"Grrrr, don't say it like that." *He thinks I'm old.*

"I'm sorry, but I have to tell you, you truly look fantastic, and my guess would have been 35, based on how long you've been married, not on your looks."

"Lol, and if you didn't know how long I've been married?"

"I definitely would have guessed 29, like I said before."

This guy is absolutely charming. "Sure. That's what you thought, Mr. Funny Pants."

"It's true."

How do I respond back? A soothing warmth grew inside my body, as always, when I thought about, or texted Aaron. I reread his last couple texts, trying to decide what to type, finally I decided to send him an emoji with blushing cheeks. Moments later, he sent me an emoji face blowing a kiss, and the words, "Nighty night. Sweet dreams. I'll let you know what day I have available to look at your cousin's house." He then sent me a moon shaped emoji.

There he goes again saying goodnight, and a kiss this time.

"Thank you. Good night, Captain." I did not send anything more because it was past midnight, and time for our conversation to end.

I wish Joe could be more like Aaron. I miss having someone to talk with who relates to what I'm saying, a best friend to play around with, and makes me feel happy like I do when I talk with Aaron. Aaron actually says goodnight, unlike Joe. What did that emoji face with the kiss mean? I just don't know why Aaron is being so nice to me, but he is beginning to get inside my head.

Chapter 6

On my lunch break, I ate left over soup, then took a five-minute stroll to the post office. The weather was gorgeous, with the sunshine and gentle breeze caressing my skin. Mrs. Johnson, the postal worker, gave me a little wave, and nodded as I walked inside. She had stood at the counter, and talked on the telephone. It looked like an important call because she jotted something down in her black book. I didn't want to bother her, so I went straight to my postal box and unlocked #76 for the salon. There wasn't much to carry back except flyers and the hydro bill, so I unlocked #123 and grabbed the mail from mine and Joe's box. There was an envelope, greeting card size, with gold writing addressed to Joseph and Magnolia Edwards. The return address read Kylie Edwards, Brockville, Ontario. It was from Joe's older sister who we haven't heard from in years. *A belated fortieth birthday card for me? I doubt she'd remember.* Time was getting on, so I tore into it on my way back to work. It was a wedding invitation, Kylie was marrying a man named Benjamin Walker, who we'd never met. The wedding date was October, 7th. *12 days from today. Would Joe go to his own sister's wedding? It's time he put the past where it belongs.* Apparently, the two of them had a falling out, some years ago, but neither of them would ever say what it was about. Kylie and I used to go out for coffee, and take shopping trips together. One day, Joe didn't want me associating with her anymore, which put an end to our relationship, he never said why. The invitation must have been a piece offering in hopes of putting the negativity aside, otherwise she wouldn't have invited us. *Hopefully, Joe will be able to accept this invitation as a positive step in the right direction.*

Back at the shop, Lucy was finishing up Ms. Smith's hair. I could hear them talking about the fabulous sale prices from this past weekend at the grocery store. She came in every Tuesday for a shampoo and roller set. She is the ideal customer because of her mild-mannered personality, and her hair is always so easy to comb out, as well, it only takes her hair 14 minutes under the dryer, which is 8 minutes less than most of the other elderly ladies. I placed the mail in the back room on the table, the bell on the front door tinkled, followed by quick footsteps.

"Anyone have time to cut my hair today?" called a raspy voice.

It was Mr. Pollock, he comes in the second Tuesday of every month without an appointment and asks the same question. I poked my head out in the salon and told him that I could do it right after Mr. Barnes who had come early, as he usually does, and was already sitting in my barber chair at my station, waiting for me. Mr. Pollock looked satisfied with my answer and began searching through the stack of magazines on the coffee table. I went over to Mr. Barnes with a fresh cape in my hand, "Hello," I said, but he didn't say 'Boo,' or anything else, I smiled at him in the mirror then draped him for a cut. Lucy stood at the cash with Ms. Smith who was paying out twenty dollars for today. Mr. Pollock had finally selected a read, and sat in the waiting chair under my new clock. The clock reminded me of the birthday party and Aaron, my stomach flipped as I pictured him trying to keep the basketball from me, and myself trying to reach for it. If it had only been he and I there that day, I could have snatched the ball away, tackled him to the ground, and tore his shirt off, we'd begin kissing, I'd rub my hands all over his chest, and down his arms, his skin would have been warm and soft to my touch, exactly what I desire. I reached for my water sprayer and began to wet Mr. Barnes' hair as the clock chimed, snapping me into reality. It read 12:30am and that was Lucy's lunchtime.

"See you ladies next week," said Ms. Smith, as she reached for her sweater.

"Thanks for coming," I said.

Lucy had her purse in hand," Be back in thirty." She left out the front door with her ponytail swinging from side to side, right behind Ms. Smith. Mr. Barnes kept silent the entire nine minutes it took for me to cut his hair, and that was fine with me, I could cut a lot faster when no one talked, however Mr. Pollock was a different story. Chatty today while I cut his hair, I knew he wanted his voice to be heard by Mrs. Lauders, who came in five minutes early for her appointment. He had a noticeable crush on her ever since he moved into town last year, and why wouldn't he? She's polite, confident, wealthy, and the best looking senior around. Ideally, she is every old boys' dream girl. As far as I saw, the only thing the two of them had in common was poker, they both played at the seniors hall every Friday night. He looked towards her, making it impossible for me to continue his cut without snipping his ear off, he told her he lost the game on purpose last Friday night to be a proper gentleman, and let her win. She smiled politely, and when he turned back, I saw her eyes roll. She tilted her head away from him, and glanced out the window.

Before I knew it, Lucy was back from her lunch break, Mr. Pollock had left, and I had washed Mrs. Lauders' hair at the sink, which was a change for us both, as I usually went to her home. She preferred to keep our visiting conversation private, as well it gave us a time out from life to enjoy each other's company. I felt my phone vibrate in my back left pocket, but my hands were covered in hair conditioner, I had to leave it be. *Could be Aaron getting back to me with a time to look at Meredith's house.* I had Mrs. Lauders settled in my barber chair, and my phone buzzed the second time, into my butt, which sent a little tingle through my body. *I hope it's Aaron.* I wanted to check in the worst way, but I knew how unprofessional that'd be. I heard the bell on the door again, it was Lucy's twenty-year-old niece Everlea, who came by to hand in her resume at my salon, and to see if she could get squeezed in for a haircut. Lucy couldn't refuse a family member even if it meant putting her behind with her appointments. Mrs. Lauders wanted a trim, and style with extra curl, as she wanted to look her best for her five o'clock business meeting. She was sharp as a whip, and still as savvy as any fifty-year-old professional. When the salon telephone rang, I let the machine answer because my fingers were now covered in snipping's of Mrs. Lauders' hair, Lucy was washing Everlea's hair, her hands full of bubbles. After the beep, I heard Carol Brice leaving a message saying that her son Mitch would be 10 minutes late for his appointment because his soccer coach insisted on a last minute practice.

After I finished Mrs. Lauders' style, I spun her chair around to face me, I held up my hand mirror to give her a clear view of the back of her head in my large mirror. I felt a sense of pride as she admired her reflection by turning her head from left to right.

"Wonderful job darling," she sounded full of delight as she pat her hands together in one solid clap.

At the cash, she told me I seemed happier than normal, she wanted to know if I had any good news to share with her. I couldn't dare mention my good mood was due to the influence of Aaron, instead I told her I must have had a leftover glow from drinking my birthday wine last night. I wished her good luck at her supper meeting, she gave me a quick hug, and said, "See you next week." She looked revitalized, and there was a light bounce in her step as she left the salon.

I had a few minutes before the arrival of my next client, and Lucy had finished Everlea's hair. The two of them were scrolling through photos on Everlea's phone, so I slipped into the back room unnoticed, to finally check my phone. I had received two messages from Amanda, Jody's friend Brittney's mother. She wanted to invite Jody over this Saturday night for a sleepover. The second message said that I could reach her on her cell. *No message from Aaron yet. What's taking him so long? He said he'd let me know as soon as he found out...maybe he's hard at work. I should be more patient.*

After my last client of the day had gone, I showed Lucy the wedding invitation, and marked the date as tentative on the calendar for me to take off work. I joked with her about being my date for the wedding instead of Joe, she was way more fun. Lucy wasn't a huge fan of weddings, but she liked to dance, unlike Joe. She said she'd go to if I needed her to. I don't know what I did to deserve a friend like her?

Just as I was getting into my van, I received a text. *Aaron.* It read, "Hey."

"Hey," I texted back. I wasn't anticipating the warmth that I felt in my chest last night, to fire up again over a simple text message, but it had.

"How's your day going?"

"Great, and yours?"

"Not bad, but the lumber I had ordered for the job I'm doing was put on back order. I was expecting it to arrive today, but since it hasn't, I'll have some free time tomorrow night to look at your friend's house."

Tomorrow night? So soon?

"Should I get ahold of Meredith for you?"

"Well, you're the boss, you tell me."

"Lol, okay, I'll text her right now, and by the way, Meredith is actually my cousin."

"Really? Is she hot?"

"Lol, she's happily married."

"That's okay, is she hot?"

"I guess she is, Funny Pants."

"Is she hotter than you?"

"What? Lol."

"Okay, never mind. I'm sure she's not as hot as you."

"Too funny, Mr."

I quickly text Meredith asking if it would be alright for Aaron to check the house out tomorrow night. She said that both her and Peter were attending a conference after work and they wouldn't be home until after 9:30, which would be too late for her. Then she practically begged me to show him the house because she wanted to get things moving as fast as possible. *Me show him?* I asked her if she was sure about that, she then assured me that she trusted I could explain everything to the T. I didn't want to disappoint her, so I told her that I'd be happy to show Aaron her place. I just had to figure out a time, and what to do with the twins. *Unless I were to bring them with me. If I left them at home it'd mean Aaron and I would be alone together, in person, inside a house, face to face with each other. Can I handle that? I'll have to for the sake of helping Meredith. The twins will likely be bored if they came, but they would ensure me keeping my hands to myself.*

I texted Aaron back to tell him the situation with Meredith, and it'd be me meeting him there.

"That's too bad, I won't get to see if she's hot," he teased.

Again, I had to laugh out loud, this man had a twisted sense of humor. "Okay, do you want me to set up another time, when she'll be able to show you herself?"

"Lol, no. I guess you'll do."

I sent him an emoji face with its tongue sticking out. "Alright then, Mr. What time do you want to meet?"

"Any time after 3:00 works, but it's whatever you say, Boss."

I like the sound of that, 'Whatever you say.' He's giving me the freedom to choose the time, and he'll show up when I say.

"I'll get back to you Captain, but for now I've got to get home to see the twins off the bus.

"I shall be waiting, Missy."

"Lol, ttyl.

For supper, I made meatballs with sweet pineapple sauce, homemade French fries, and steamed carrots. We all sat in our usual spots at the kitchen table, Joe and I at opposite ends, the twins faced each other from either side. I tried to think of a simple way to tell Joe about meeting Aaron at Meredith's place tomorrow evening without upsetting him, I knew I'd have to talk down the situation because I didn't want him to sense my excitement. Joe ate his supper, eyes fixed on the local news channel, so I decided to wait and not bring up the conversation until it was over. Jody asked me if Brittney's mom had talked to me today about the weekend sleepover. I had basically forgotten about the text she'd sent me that afternoon. I asked Jody if she wanted to go, and without hesitation, she said, "Yes," and she let out a screech of excitement. Joe's eyes darted toward Jody, and glared. I suppose she was interrupting his concentration geared toward details of a convicted murderer getting turned down for an early release trial. Jonah wanted to know if he could have a friend over since Jody would be away. I told him we'd have to wait and see what was going on first. Joe had finished his main course before the rest of us, I jumped up and brought him a piece of apple crisp on a desert plate, and placed it in front of him. There was a story on the news about school busses, I grabbed that opportunity to tell him about tomorrow night. He crinkled up his nose and asked me why Meredith couldn't meet this guy a different night? I explained to Joe that the contractor had a full schedule, and this was only possible because his other job was put on hold for the moment. He mumbled under his breath words I couldn't make out, then cleaned his last chunk of apple crisp from his plate. His raised eyebrows and wrinkled up forehead told me he wasn't impressed, as he shoveled the last forkful into his mouth and began watching the end of the news. I told him I wasn't sure what time I had to meet him, so I might not be here when he got home from work. He wiped his mouth with his napkin and he asked what I was planning to do with the kids when I was gone? His voice sounded strident, forcing me to give a quick answer, even though I hadn't made up my mind, but before I could think more about it, I told him they'd be with me. His response was zilch, and he moved into his favorite after supper chair.

He is so unpleasant to talk to anymore, and his attitude is unbearable. I'm getting tired of trying to communicate with him, his unreceptive attitude is uncalled for. I have always given him my best, without a reason to deserve the displaced treatment. How is it even possible to repair a relationship like ours?

The kids carried their plates to the sink. They seemed oblivious to the conversation between their father and me because they chatted amongst themselves about playing volleyball for gym class. They each grabbed a gingersnap out of the cookie jar and went upstairs. My appetite for supper had diminished, and desert was out of the question, thanks to Joe. Instead of sitting at the table for an extra 10 minutes to relax as I usually do, I immediately began tidying up. I figured now would not be the best time to show Joe the invitation to Kylie's wedding. *Who knows how he'd handle that? Frankly, I've heard enough of his negativity for the night.* As I loaded the dishwasher, my thoughts had switched from thinking how much of an ass Joe was, to meeting Aaron tomorrow night with the kids. *It'd be better anyway if the kids were there, they'd help me stay focused on the real reason for meeting Aaron. I know nothing can ever happen between Aaron and me, but I can't help but feel a magnetism towards him.*

I lay in bed alone. Joe was somewhere in the house, but at that point, I just didn't care of his whereabouts. As I scrolled through my texts to Aaron, I felt an inner piece as I took in every word. Aaron was becoming a part of my everyday routine. *How did this come to be? A birthday invitation, to texting, to an attraction, and now working for my cousin. Why was all of this happening?* The thoughts rolled around and around in my head, until my hand began to vibrate startling me. It was my phone, with a message from Aaron. "It's been a long day. I'm off to bed, Sunshine."

My heart skipped a beat, filled with fascination that I'd be on his mind again tonight.

"Same here, Captain. I'm in bed ready to doze off."

"Everything still on for tomorrow night?"

"Sure is, and I'm bringing the twins along."

"No problem, I'll bring Landon as well. The three can occupy each other while we are figuring things out. If that is okay with you, Boss?"

"Sounds good, I'll text you tomorrow with the time."

"Nighty night. Sweet dreams."

"Thank you, Good night."

And that was the last I heard from Aaron that night. I drifted off with the words "Sweet dreams" in my mind.

The following day, I could barely eat and I had to run to the washroom every hour, or it seemed. My nerves were getting the best of me, I knew this would be my first time seeing Aaron in person since the birthday party. I made sure to conceal my thoughts from Lucy and my clients by keeping a paramount smile on my face, while chatting up a storm with everyone. *I'm an infatuated teenager. No. I'm a grown woman who is supposed to have her emotions in check. After the party he told me I looked "hot," but what would he think after seeing me in my work clothes? I would not be wearing shorts and a fancy top, but rather a sensible pair of slacks, and a blouse, with my comfortable under armour runners. Would his opinion still be the same of me, or would he think I look like an old lady? I've got to stop thinking this way, I am who I am, and that is not going to change.* I told myself that very thing all day, but a part of me wanted Aaron to find me desirable. *He says all the right things to me, and I don't want that to end.* Aaron was adding that extra bit of happiness to my life and I didn't want to be without it.

At 3:15, my last client of the day called to reschedule her 3:30 appointment. I didn't mind because I had it in my mind to go home and change my clothes before meeting Aaron, in spite of the lecture I'd given myself. I wanted to look more appealing than just a hairdresser. The twins would be home just after 4:00 and then we'd have to go. I sent Aaron a quick text asking him if 4:15 would work. Quickly he responded back with, "Sure thing, Missy."

"Great, see you then." To the point I was, because of my urge to rush home and freshen up. I stuck my phone in my purse when it buzzed. *Aaron?*

"Aren't you forgetting something, Boss?"

"What's that?"

"Telephone number and address, Silly."

Wow, I had completely forgotten to send him Meredith's info. How embarrassing. "I'm sorry. Its (613)772-6853, 15 Belle St. House has blue siding, grey brick at the entrance, with a wooden wishing well out front. You won't miss it, if you pay attention to my description, lol."

"I'll always pay attention to you, Missy."

Damn. He knows how to hit my soft spot every time?

"Sweeter than ever, I see. Okay, see you there."

"Wanna race?"

"Lol, not this time, Mr."

"Lol."

I made it home before the kids, and rushed to get myself ready to avoid any unnecessary questions that they might have about my shower, and change of wardrobe. The outside temperature was still warm, around 23 degrees. I didn't want to overdress and risk Aaron thinking I look ridiculous, so I put on my clingy blue V-neck t-shirt, with my pale blue shorts. I looked in the mirror and noticed my clothes weren't fitting as tightly as they used to. I must have dropped a few pounds from my lack of appetite. I decided it was alright because they still displayed my figure appropriately, and looked preferable to my work clothes. As well, they were free from the hair collection, the others had accumulated throughout the day. I pulled my hair back into a high ponytail, and freshened up my make up with a light dusting of powder, and blush. By the time I had finished, the bus was letting the kids off at home. I slipped on my grey sandals, and grabbed my purse. I texted Aaron

59

to see if he'd left yet, however I knew he hadn't arrived at Meredith's because I could see the side of her house and driveway from my front porch. He responded, "Well, yes I'm already here and waiting for you."

"Lol, you are, are you?" I briskly walked along the sidewalk to Meredith's with the kids, making certain we'd get there first. When we arrived, I unlocked the house with the spare key behind the 'Welcome' sign on the front door, we let ourselves in. Rory was there to greet us with leaps, kisses, and barks. The twins wanted to know if they could take Rory outside in the backyard to play fetch. I said, "Sure," and out they went.

By 4:30, Aaron hadn't arrived yet. *Had he changed his mind about doing the renovations? Perhaps something came up, or worst scenario he didn't want to see me.* My stomach had begun to rumble, I took a drink of water from Meredith's kitchen tap to make it stop. I made up my mind to not think the worst, instead I sent him a quick text asking his whereabouts.

"Right here, Hunny."

Hunny? Just like that the doorbell rang. Without time for analyzing my nerves, or the fact he now had another nick name for me, I answered the door and let them in. Landon immediately went into the backyard to see Jody, Jonah, and Rory. Aaron stood there in the entrance, wearing a flannel shirt, blue jeans, and a navy blue Nike cap. His face appeared clean shaven, and his delicious aqua essence stimulated my senses. He looked me straight in my eyes, and said, "Hello, Sunshine."

His eyes were intoxicating when I held a three second glimpse into his. "Hello," I said. My nerves were at ease, almost joyous in his presence due to his contagious smile. I motioned for him to come inside with a sway of my hand. He stepped inside, I watched him bend down to untie the laces of his work boots. He maneuvered his fingers quickly with great control, and he placed his boots aside. Taking a quick look around Meredith's place, he said, "Great house."

Her home was filled with neutral tones of grey, white, and cranberry for accents. She had real house plants, and bricks around her propane fireplace. Her main floors were birch wood, and ceramic in the kitchen and bathrooms.

"It's beautiful." I led him around the corner towards the living room. His aura kissed mine as he kept within close proximity. A sunbeam of warmth travelled through my body as he followed.

I was comfortable explaining Meredith's ideas to Aaron about the transformation. He looked professional, tape measure in hand, pencil secured between his teeth. He moved from one end of the room to the other, serious expression on his face. He jotted down notes, and figures. *Aaron at work...a sight I could get used to.* He tucked his notes into his shirt pocket, and took a few photos of the walls with his phone. When he had finished, I asked him if he would like a coffee but before he could answer, the kids came running inside saying they needed some juice because of their desperate thirst. Aaron said he wasn't thirsty but if the kids were having juice, he'd have some too. I headed into the kitchen and got some glasses out of the cupboard, the kids tagged along waiting to be served. I asked Aaron if he'd like to sit at the table. I found a large picture of ice tea in the fridge, and began pouring it into the glasses. When finished, I looked upwards and I caught Aaron staring at me. The corners of his mouth were turned upwards. He looked pleased, as I carried two glasses to the table. On my way back to get the others, Aaron got up from his chair and helped me carry them over. *What a gentleman.* The kids guzzled down their juice like there was no tomorrow. Rory began to bark while looking out the window, which attracted Jody to do the same.

"There's a big, black cat outside," she said.

Immediately the kids ran for the door, Rory tagged along, leaving Aaron and I alone sipping our drinks. I set my glass down, and couldn't help but take a closer look at Aaron. He was still wearing his baseball cap, his shades rest over the peek, and his carpenter pencil tucked behind his right ear, sticking outwards and even with his temple. He looked young, not a laugh line present, and there wasn't a trace of dirt anywhere on him. Tucked inside the neckline of his t-shirt, he wore a silver chain that brought attention to his thick neck.

"Is there something on me?" said Aaron.

My eyes grew large, and my eyebrows raised. I took a deep breath. "Oh, I'm sorry." I could feel my cheeks getting warm as I looked away from him.

He laughed at me, "So nothing on my face then?" He rubbed his hand around his mouth to make sure.

"No, no. There's nothing wrong with your face." *I hope he didn't take that the wrong way.* "I mean...you look great." *Oops,* "I meant to say, no. There is nothing on your face. I was just thinking about how much you look like Landon." Okay, a little white lie wouldn't hurt. No way I was telling him that I was checking him out.

"You weren't checking me out, were you?" Aaron's eyes were filled with excitement and mischief.

"What?" *Holy crap!* "Checking you out? Of course not." Feeling slightly ashamed of myself, I drank half of my ice tea, and set the glass down.

Aaron began to chuckle. "Relax Missy, I'm just teasing. Besides, Mrs. Finnegan says it all of the time."

"That you look great?" Puzzled, I raised my eyebrows.

"No, silly. That Landon looks like me."

I could tell he was amused because he smiled, and turned his head back and forth while looking straight at me. He was poking fun at me. I couldn't help but laugh at myself. I cupped my hand over my mouth to gain control over my laughter. "Well, she's right."

"He's a handsome kid, don't you think?" He winked at me.

"I'll never tell," I squinted my eyes and beamed at him, trying to make him aware I knew he was trying to catch me off guard again.

His glass was almost empty, I asked him if he'd like a refill.

"No thanks, Boss."

I gathered up a couple empty glasses and took them over to the dishwasher. My back was away from Aaron, as I placed them on the rack. I turned back to go and collect the others from the table. Aaron was standing smack in front of me and holding the other glasses. "Whoa," I said almost bumping into him. His aura was inside of mine again. I could feel our chemistry building inside my chest. He set the glasses on the counter as he held his glance directly on me. We were only inches apart, and I looked him in the eye. I wanted to kiss him so badly, and place my arms around him. Slowly, I took in a breath and held it, he leaned in toward me. My body was beginning to draw closer to him. He placed his hand on my hip and my heart rate increased. I felt his breath gently caress my parted lips, when I spontaneously turned my face away from his and released my breath. I stepped back from him to prevent our lips from touching. "I'm sorry," I said.

Standing firmly in his place, he smiled at me, "Don't be." He said, "I'm not."

Feeling flattered, and wicked. I wasn't sure what to do or say. With perfect timing, Jody, Jonah, and Landon came inside with Rory, all jabbering about how Rory chased that big cat, Mel, up the tree. Instantly my focus shifted toward the kids,

"Is Mel alright?" I asked.

"Yes, Mom," said Jody. "She's up really high. Rory can't reach, but I'm scared she can get down."

Aaron went over and looked out the back door. He said, "Don't worry guys. The cat will come down eventually. Cats climb trees all the time."

"What if she never comes down, Aaron?" said Jody.

"She will."

"Ya, but if she doesn't, what will happen to her?"

Aaron squat down to talk to Jody who was now seated on the sofa. "Don't you worry a bit about that, honey. Cats are designed to climb up and down things. She probably likes it way up there."

"If she doesn't come down, will you go up and get her?" she said.

"Of course, I will. But I didn't bring my ladder this time. I'll tell you what…"

Jody paid full attention to Aaron as he spoke to her. His tone was gentle and caring with her, she grasped every word he said. He was a natural, and our 'almost kiss' was completely undetectable in his emotions. "…if the cat is still up there next time I come here, I'll go up and bring her down."

"That might be a long time," she said.

"Nope, it won't," he said, "I might have to come by tomorrow."

Tomorrow? So soon.

"You'd do that?" said Jody.

"Just for you," he said.

Jody threw her arms around Aaron's shoulders, and said, "Thank you, Aaron. You're the best."

He placed his left arm around her back and squeezed her tightly. "Or I could just put you up the tree with the cat," he said.

Her giggles allowed me to see how truly comfortable she was with Aaron. In fact, he is the only man I've seen her hug other than her grandfather, since she was about seven years old. Joe was never receptive of receiving hugs from the twins, and I believe they could sense it from him which led them to stop trying.

Jonah and Landon sat on the area rug beside a sleeping Rory, and played rock, paper, scissors. I grabbed the dish cloth and began to wipe the table clean. Landon said, "Hey, Dad? Would it be okay if Jody and Jonah came to our bonfire this weekend?"

Aaron let go of Jody, and stood to his feet. "It's fine with me, son. But you should ask Mrs. Edwards."

'Mrs. Edwards' always sounded so old, but hearing it from Aaron sounded reverential, and polite. "Mrs." flowed off his tongue with such ease, as if our intense moment hadn't happened at all. It's the first time I've ever heard him refer to me like that. Perhaps he was acknowledging the fact that I indeed was married.

"Can they please come, Mrs. Edwards?" Landon put his hands together, and begged.

"Jody is going to a sleepover, but Jonah's free."

"Can I go, Mom?" said Jonah.

I gave Aaron a quick glance, trying to see his facial expression for an indication if Jonah was welcome or not. Aaron nodded my way, implicating a yes.

"It's okay with me, as long as Aaron says it's fine."

"I'm taking this weekend off to spend some time with Landon, and do a few things around my house. It would be great if Landon had a friend over." Aaron pointed to his wrist, giving Landon the sign that it was time to go. He turned his head sideways to meet my eyes. "You can come for the bonfire too, Missy."

"Me?" I questioned him.

"Sure, why not?"

At that point, I had no idea what to say. I could feel my nerves beginning to act up again. *How I would love to sit around a fire with Aaron, roast marshmallows, and converse back and forth.* With the exception of the occasional jitters, his presence fulfilled me with inner happiness as I've never experienced with anyone else. Briefly, I fantasized of our intense encounter from only minutes ago, I then snapped back into the reality that I could not stay for the bonfire.

I rubbed Meredith's peach scented lotion evenly over my hands. "No, I can't stay. Joe might need me for something at home."

"Bring him along if you like."

"Thanks, but no. Joe isn't one for bonfires." *That would be awkward, Joe and Aaron talking together. Basically, it would be Aaron trying to talk and Joe sitting there like a statue, unenthused, and bored. I'd be in the middle trying not to laugh at whatever crazy thing Aaron spiels out, and fearing Joe getting upset with me for acting like an adolescent.*

"Joe isn't afraid of a little heat is he?" Aaron said with a smirk, his shoulders back, and chest puffed outwards.

I smirked back, knowing that the two words 'Joe', and 'heat', did not belong together in the same sentence, plus, there was truth to what Aaron had said. I could almost hear a hint of jealousy in his voice. Again, I was flattered. *How could he be jealous? Unless he'd fallen in love with me.*

Chapter 7

Thursday evening, Joe arrived home early and was in another huff. Like a child, he turned his nose up and refused to talk about what was going on. Again, I chose to not mention the invitation for Kylie's wedding, I knew him well enough to not bring up new ideas when he's in a bad mood, or his answer would be negative for sure. The twins were all excited about going to their friends' houses this coming weekend, they'd begun to write down lists of the things they wanted to take with them. Joe had been in his office for a couple of hours, and he didn't come for supper when I called him. I went to his office to see if everything was alright, he was riffling through a stack of file folders scattered all over his desk. It was obvious something had gone wrong at work. I asked him what he was doing, but he didn't answer me. He was consumed with concentration in trying to find something. I felt an overall stress wash over my body, and my insides clenched tightly. "Are you eating tonight?" I asked.

He let out a sigh of exhaustion, and shook his head, indicating that he wasn't. I asked him if he needed my help with anything, his response was, "Nope," his tone, gruff.

The sun had begun to lower in the sky, but it'd be a while before darkness would take over. I went on the front porch to get some fresh air, as I was frustrated with Joe again for leaving me in the dark. *Must everyday be miserable with him? I married him for better, for worse, and this must be the worst part. How long until the worse passes? Will it ever pass? I'm trying to be patient with him. How long until our marriage is back on track? Does he even realize that our marriage is not working? I wonder if he even loves me anymore. All these questions, and I haven't an answer for any of them.* I sat in my rocking chair, and rest my head on the back. Our street had many different houses; all varieties of sizes and colours, some had siding, others had brick, some had verandas, others had walkways and front steps. Mr. Carter adorned his yard with an array of bushes to produce different blossoms for every season, while Mrs. Morris preferred wild flowers growing every which way. The Thompson house had a love for neatly trimmed greenery, without a blossom in sight. The Bailey's loaded their property with lawn ornaments that make your head spin just from walking past. Each home had a certain individuality of its own which was a true reflection of the uniqueness and choices of each home's owner. Our home is grey stone, and the largest on our street. I prefer hanging baskets, and keeping potted plants on the front porch until frost hits in the fall. I don't like clutter, but I do enjoy looking at our four-tier bird house that sits on top of a fourteen-feet pole in the front yard. Everyone in the neighborhood has commented on how much they love our stained glass windows, in my opinion, ours is the most beautiful in the area, aside from Mrs. Lauders' mansion. People have come up to me and said, "Life in that house must be a fairytale." It's funny how things appear on the outside to others, if they knew what was really going on between Joe and I, I'm sure they'd change their minds about the fairytale.

As I looked around, I wondered how well the other married couples were getting along. Everyone always appeared to be content, with the exception of the odd scrap that you could sometimes hear, echoing through an open window. I glanced towards Meredith's house, her and Peter seemed to be the perfect couple, and completely in love with each other. They have a beautiful home, with great jobs, and they seem happy most of the time. The motion of swaying back and forth on my chair helped to relax my tension, I closed my eyes. I wasn't jealous of Meredith...well...maybe a little about being 'completely in love with each other'. I'd love to be married to a man who was truly my best friend, and lover. A man like Aaron. Even though I still don't know him that well, I can tell from his attitude, and his actions that he is a genuine person, not to mention, he is a great dad, Landon is proof of that. Several times at work, today I had relived last night's moment with Aaron. I wanted to kiss him profusely, but my conscience had made me stop. *Was it a possibility he could be falling for me?* I thought he made it obvious by trying to kiss me, I'm not sure how I'd feel today, had I let it happen? Cheating is against everything I believe in, but I can't help but feel that kissing Aaron would have felt amazing. His prolonged gaze into my eyes was unforgettable. The force of attraction was more intense than ever as he leaned inwards. *What am I supposed to do with all of these feelings I have for Aaron? I want him. I want him to wrap his arms around me just for a minute, so I can feel what he feels like. I want to express all of the warmth I feel inside for him, but I cannot.*

The sun was beginning to lower, I'd have to tuck the twins in soon. Upon opening my eyes, I saw a truck sitting in Meredith's driveway. *It was Aaron's truck. He didn't text me to set up a meeting with Meredith. He did tell Jody last night that he was planning on going back today. Why didn't he let me know? I did give him her phone number, but I assumed he'd get a hold of me first. Why did he choose to leave me out of it? I hope he wasn't upset, or hurt that I pulled away from him last night.* I watched Meredith's house, hoping to get a glimpse of Aaron, after a few minutes, I had seen nothing. *The cat would be out of the tree by now, he must be going over the plans with them.* I was beginning to feel like a stocker, and the air was getting chilly. *Time to go inside.*

I heard the twins babbling while brushing their teeth, as they always did. I took a quick peek out the sitting room window, but still no sign of Aaron, just his truck. On my way upstairs, I could hear Joe snoring, he'd gone to bed without saying goodnight to me again. *Had he resolved what was troubling him earlier? Who knows?*

After saying goodnight to Jody and Jonah, I went back downstairs to turn off the lights, and lock the doors. I was tempted to take another peek towards Meredith's driveway. Aaron's truck was gone. Knowing that his truck had been there, and gone before I had the chance to see him, left me feeling poignant.

Saturday, September, 30, 2017

By late morning, the twins had all of their things packed to take to their friends' houses. I was to drop Jody off at four o'clock, and as for Jonah I hadn't a clue. I hadn't heard a thing from Aaron, but Jonah said he talked to Landon at school yesterday, and everything was still on for the bonfire, and now he was invited for a sleepover. A confirmation from Aaron would have been nice, and I needed to know that everything was okay between us before showing up at his house. Actually, I wasn't able to show up at his place without an address. I could have googled it, but I preferred him to send me directions, so I knew the invitation was in good standing. *How was Aaron feeling about almost kissing me the other night? He said he wasn't sorry, and he seemed perfectly fine, but he's had a couple days to think things over. I hope he isn't embarrassed, or feeling regretful, or worse, thinking I'm angry with him.* I didn't want to be the one to contact Aaron first because of my uncertainty of his feelings, but Jonah was getting anxious, so I decided to bite the bullet and get to it.

"Hey there," I said.

I waited a few minutes, and he texted back, "Hey, stranger. How've you been?"

I had mixed emotions. My longing for Aaron had begun to grow almost as strong as my dissatisfaction with Joe. I didn't know how to control my feelings, nor did I know if I wanted them to stop. "Not bad," I said.

"Sorry, I haven't gotten a hold of you. I've been busy working overtime to take this weekend off."

"It's fine. You don't owe me an explanation." *He really does owe me an explanation, almost kissing me, and then not contacting me?*

"Did you want me to pick up Jonah or do you want to bring him over?"

I was relieved to hear that he hadn't forgotten about the bonfire. "I'll drive. What time should I have him there?"

"Five-thirty, okay? I can start the fire about five."

"Sure, what time should I pick him up at?"

"Tomorrow, Sunshine, if he's staying the night? Landon was to ask him."

Sunshine, he can't be upset with me if he's calling me that. Immediately, I could feel a release of tension that I'd been unknowingly carrying around. "Yes, he did."

"See you tonight then, Missy."

"Ummm Captain...exactly what is your home address?"

"1980 Willow Rd. Want directions from me, or are you going to search up a variety of different directions to find the best shortcut? LMAO"

Hmmm, witty. I knew he was referring back to the shortcut that I made at Landon's birthday party.

"Thank you, I can get my own directions, Mr. Funny Pants."

"Suit yourself, Boss."

I'm glad that our 'almost kiss' hadn't interfered with Aaron's sense of humor. I truly appreciate a good laugh these days due to lack of it with Joe. I realize now that I have been overanalyzing what Aaron may have been feeling, and why he hadn't contacted me. If he was offended, or hurt, he likely would have cancelled the bonfire. The truth was, I honestly hadn't a clue what Aaron was feeling, but I have to assume that our friendship or whatever we were would be fine. I knew it was wrong for me to care so much

69

about Aaron's feelings. That kiss could have changed everything for us, and that wouldn't be fair to Joe, or would it? He is such a bonehead sometimes that I think he deserves it, but I can't allow myself to think like that if our marriage is going to work out.

Before lunch, I had made a special point to try and talk with Joe. He ignored me, as I took a seat on the spare chair next to his desk. I smiled at him, hoping to get his attention, but he kept his eyes glued to his computer screen. I asked him if he had plans for the afternoon. He responded with a grunt. I told him about the kids going to their friends' houses for the night, and that we'd have the whole house to ourselves. Being that we were married, I hoped it would spark his arousal, because I wanted to get laid. Everything I'd been feeling for Aaron over the past few days, had gotten me revved up, and if Joe couldn't have verbal communication with me, certainly he could give me physical. Joe said nothing, I suggested that we go on a date to the movies, and go out for supper together. I was hoping if he'd take his mind off work for once, it'd be like old times. He said he couldn't go because he'd taken on a new case, and he'd have to prepare some documents for Monday. I tried to compromise with him by telling him we could stay in for supper instead of going out, I'd prepare beef wellington, and after, I'd do the dishes, and he could work until it'd be time for fun in the bedroom. Again, he turned me down. I explained to him that we really needed a few hours for ourselves to reconnect. Joe stopped typing, his face turned red, "We're not kids anymore Magnolia," he said.

What the hell did that mean? "I'm aware of that Joe, but that doesn't mean we can't spend time together."

"That's the problem with you, the more time I spend with you, the more you expect."

My nerves jumped as he slammed his fist down on his desk. "I rarely ask for us to spend time together, and that is what married people do, Joe."

"No, you expect for things to be as they were in the beginning stages of our relationship."

"Things like what?"

"You want hand holding, kissing, and snuggling. We are adults, we don't have time for nonsense." He looked back to his computer.

Nonsense? "There is nothing wrong with wanting those things."

"You're too demanding, and you're never happy with what I give you."

Anger festered. I wanted to scream. Instead, I stood my ground in my own defense. "Wow, I can't believe you just said that. I pull my own weight. Where is all of this coming from Joe?"

"A hairdresser's income would never allow us to live in this house and have all of the fancy things. It takes my job to provide these things for the family."

"Sounds like you care more about the fancy things than your family. Someday the kids will be all grown up, and they will have no memories of us doing things together because you are never home, and by then, what will we have left?"

Joe's phone buzzed. He looked at it and set it on his desk.

"What we've become is two people living in the same house, doing our own things separately. You are living your life and I'm living mine. We have no connection anymore. That is not how it's supposed to be."

"Magnolia, I have work to do. This is pointless."

Joe's phone buzzed again, and he sent a quick text.

"Pointless? So, you want to continue our relationship the way it has been, with no communication, and no intimacy?"

Joe closed his laptop, and put a few files in his brief case along with his phone. He reached for his car keys.

"Where are you going?" I said.

"Away on business. I might not be back tonight."

"What about your precious documents which you have to have ready for Monday?"

Joe didn't look at me as he headed for the door.

"So that's it? You're walking away without resolving the issue?"

"There's no issue." Joe, wearing his grey dress shoes, strided professionally out of his office.

I'm so tired. I remained seated in the chair to collect my thoughts. I placed my face in my hands and leaned forward to rest on my knees. My head began to pound, as I replayed our conversation over in my mind. What harsh words from him. *"You're too demanding? You're never happy?" Why is he saying all of these things? I was not the person he had described.* Tears formed in my eyes, and my throat began to tighten. Breathing was difficult because my lungs would only allow a few short gasps of air. I wanted to cry out as a lion in anguish over a lost cub, but I held myself together, fearing that the twins would hear. At that point, I knew our relationship was over, unless something were to drastically change inside of Joe. It was obvious he's been keeping his feelings deep inside for some time to have it all come out like that. *I do not deserve to be treated like that. I'm so tired of walking on eggshells around him, with hopes of doing things in the exact fashion that would draw him closer to me.*

I heard the twins calling me, saying they were so hungry. I got up off the chair and grabbed a handful of tissues from Joe's desk and wiped my eyes, and blew my nose. The skin around my eyes felt raw and tingly from the dampness of my tears. I took a deep breath, put a smile on my face, and proceeded to the kitchen to make lunch. Jody being extremely observant, asked me why my eyes were red. I simply told her there was something in my eyes, and I rubbed them too much. I wasn't about to taint her mind with the fear of her parents splitting up.

I had a hard time trying to eat my turkey sandwich with the twins, so I wrapped it up for later. I tried to take my mind off the fight with Joe, so I went over my rules for sleeping over night at a friend's house with the twins. Afterwards, I listened to them talking about all the fun they were going to have, I was delighted to watch their happy faces. Jody's almond-shaped eyes were glossy and bright, and filled with enthusiasm. Jonah had a permanent smile that revealed his gleaming teeth, his gleeful chuckle was contagious to anyone within earshot. One thing I knew for sure was I'd always have their love. They'd be mine until the end of time, if Joe and I ever did split, I was secure in knowing I'd never be alone.

It'd be another couple of hours until it was time to go, so I did a quick cleaning around the house while the twins played Monopoly. It's amazing how quickly you can clean a house when your adrenalin is powered by anger. I ran through the possibilities of how Joe's thoughts could have developed into such nasty words. I tried to think of anything I may have done in the past to form his beliefs into motion, but there was nothing that could have created such an impact. After drilling myself over and over I gave my brain a rest because it started to pound.

The twins packed their stuff in the van. I put on an extra sweater, and searched inside my purse for the keys, but the stupid things weren't anywhere. I turned it upside down and shook it silly, emptying every last thing out onto the console near the front door. The contents of my purse resembled an emporium of partially essential crap. I came across, a bunch of old receipts, a package of thank you cards, used and unused tissues, lip balm, and about a zillion pens, various business cards, a tea light, candy blush perfume, wet naps, tampons, loose change, change purse, wallet, gum, a spare pair of scissors with a comb, several crumpled notes from Jody that read 'I love you,' and the invitation for Kylie's wedding. At last, my keys toppled out onto a growing pile of tangled hair elastics. I placed them inside my pocket, and shoved everything else inside the drawer, except my wallet, and the invitation. The beautiful envelope enticed me to open it for a quick read. The wedding was to take place at the Presbyterian Church in Brockville, reception at the Country Club (Banquet Hall). I knew Joe wouldn't go, but I didn't really care. I'd have a better time without him, I could get caught up with Kylie, and anyone I've lost touch with. Joe would hate me if I went, but after everything he said, his opinion wasn't substantial to me. The invitation stated that everyone was to log onto Kylie and Benjamin's wedding website and RSVP, and that's exactly what I did. I searched them up on my phone, found our names on the guest registry and I checked off that two people were attending. *If Joe doesn't go, I'll bring Lucy.* Upon hearing the twins calling me, I left the invitation on top of the console, with a big, fat check mark in the 'yes' box.

Jody was as ecstatic to see Brittney, as Brittney was to see Jody. The two of them started to chatter as soon as they saw each other. I thanked Amanda for inviting Jody to stay overnight, and I gave Jody a big kiss and hug goodbye. Amanda said she'd drop her off tomorrow mid-afternoon. When I got back in the van, Jonah asked me how long it'd be until we arrived at Landon's. *Oh my goodness.* I had been so upset with Joe that I'd forgotten to look up his address. I was going to google it, but my phone was on low battery, and I didn't have my charger. I decided that it would be faster to text Aaron and ask him. *He'll have a hay day with this one.* I wasn't about to drive twenty minutes back home again to look it up.

"Hey, Mr. Wanna help me out, and give me directions to your place from the general store?"

I told Jonah to keep an eye on my phone for a message while I headed to Mason's General Store.

"Hey, Missy, are you lost?"

Jonah read Aaron's text out loud, and then he asked me why Aaron had called me Missy. I told Jonah that Aaron was the type to kid around, and that was his way of teasing me. Jonah was satisfied with that answer. I pulled into the store parking lot to text Aaron back.

"I'll explain when I get to your place. My battery is on low, can you send directions please?"

"Please? Wow! Take Queen Street out of town. Turn left on Burns road, keep going until you see a horse statue on the right, and turn there, travel half kilometer and take another right on Beach rd. Go past the bush, and turn left onto Willow road. My place is on the left. House #1980. It is two-story, white-siding with wrap around veranda."

I had an idea of where he lived but, I never had a reason to venture the side roads around there. "Thanks, Captain. See you soon."

"She's after something, first a please, and now a thank you? What is she up to?" said Aaron.

I sent him an emoji face with the tongue sticking out, and proceeded on my way.

As I drove along Willow road, I understood how it got its name. Growing adjacent with the road, there was a line of weeping willow trees which looked to be spaced within ten-feet of each other. Their swaying branches dangled over the deep ditch, but not enough to cause interference with the traffic. Opposite the trees, were country style homes; each one having a couple acres in between. I followed the house numbers to 1977, Aaron's wasn't much further. I passed a cute little red brick bungalow with a wooden mailbox that said, Esther + Ralph Finnegan. That name rang a bell, then I remembered Aaron saying his neighbor watches Landon regularly after school. Next house number was 1980, *Aaron's house.* It looked exactly as he described to me by text. I drove in his driveway, and parked beside his truck at the garage. Jonah and I got out of the van, I could see smoke coming from behind the house.

"It must be from the bonfire," I said.

The smoke smelled clean, as if he was burning softwood, possibly cedar. He had the place looking tidy, with the grass cut short and no clippings left behind. There was fresh soil spread out on the ground around the house, as if he was attempting to make flower beds along the veranda. His lot had pine trees scattered here and there. I could see a tire swing in the back yard, under a tall maple tree, an above ground pool, and little cedar shed with a blue bicycle leaning against it. Jonah and I walked toward the smoke in hopes of finding Aaron and Landon. Behind the house, I saw Aaron bringing a wheel barrow of wood to the fire pit. He was wearing a flannel shirt, and jeans. Landon was tagging along behind him, carrying a skinny log in his arms. They both seemed to spot us at the same time. Aaron's eyes were fixed on me as I neared him. I looked straight at him, blissful warmth filled my chest, which had lately become one of my favorite feelings. Then it occurred to me, I was still wearing my sweat pants which I changed into before cleaning the house. *Great, I look like crap.* Again, thanks to the fight with Joe, I hadn't thought of changing. My hair was in a side ponytail gathered at my neck, and I felt some of the loose strands falling onto my face. I quickly tucked them behind my ears, hoping Aaron wouldn't notice. Jonah yelled, "Hello."

Landon lifted his right hand and waved, he placed the stick near the fire pit, and ran to meet up with us.

"Where's your stuff?" said Landon.

"My suitcase and pillow are in the van," said Jonah while pointing at the driveway.

"Come on, we can put it in my room," said Landon.

Jonah looked up at me, "Is that alright, Mom?"

"Sure, if that's where Aaron wants it to go," I said.

"Good idea boys, then Missy here won't forget and drive off with your stuff," said Aaron, his mouth formed into a full on smile as he gazed at me, now standing an arm length away. I returned his smile.

"Make sure to take in both bags Jonah," I said.

"Ok, Mom." The boys swiftly raced toward the van, and Aaron and I were alone once again. I noticed Aaron had brown stubble over top of his lip, covering his chin, and along his jaw. It appeared as if he hadn't shaved for a couple of days, which made me feel more comfortable in my sweats.

"I see you've found the place," said Aaron.

"Yes, I must say, your directions were pretty good."

"Pretty good? That's it?"

"Well, I'm sure I would have been able to find a shortcut somewhere, had I searched directions myself."

Aaron let out a playful laugh. "Of course you would have." He gently tapped my forearm with his hand.

"And…what's the reason you insisted on my help tonight? You were lost, weren't you?" he teased, and pointed his index finger at me.

"No, I was busy and forgot to search directions, then I noticed my phone was almost dead." *Not very intelligent.*

"Laugh my ass off," he said.

We both stood there momentarily staring at each other. I took a deep breath.

"I have to throw a log on," he motioned to the simmering fire.

"Ok, I should be going anyway."

"No, you don't have to, besides you might want to wait for the boys to come back out. Jonah will wonder where you are."

He had a point, so I followed him to the fire pit, which was constructed from three layers of field stones that fit tightly together, each about the size of a grapefruit, and placed to form a circle. The tranquil flames were soothing to look at, but weren't producing much heat. Aaron stirred the fire with a long tree branch, then placed a few sticks of cedar in the middle as kindling. The fire began to crackle as the cedar fueled the flame. Aaron asked me if I wanted to sit down. There were six lawn chairs arranged around the fire, and a little wooden table to the right. Beside the table was his picnic cooler with a bag of giant marshmallows resting on top. It looked cozy enough to sit and relax, and it would have been a nice change from my trialing afternoon. I watched Aaron reach down to grab his bottle of beer that was resting on the arm of the lawn chair closest to him. He tilted his head back to take a sip, after seconds of holding it in his mouth, he swallowed causing his Adam's apple to shift up and down his neck. Tilting his head downwards, a drop of beer remained on his bottom lip. I pictured myself walking over to him and sucking it off, I would run my tongue inside his mouth and biter and malty flavors would tickle my taste buds. His tongue would twist together with mine, and I'd feel the roughness and smoothness of his mucosa. His tender looking lips would mimic mine, and we'd indulge in the pleasure of each other's caress. My day dream was interrupted as I saw him take his shirt sleeve and wipe the beer from his lip.

"It's been a long day, if I sit down I might not want to get back up. Then you'd be stuck with me all night, glued to the chair, so, no I'd better not sit," I said.

"It'd be alright with me if you stayed all night."

"You're saying that you'd like an old lady, like me, to camp out here?"

"No, just you."

Just you. Deep. My every nerve tingled as my body consumed his words. *I want him.* A seriousness washed over me as I looked him in the eye.

76

"Why are you so sweet to me?"

Aaron moved in a few steps closer to me, he rest his hands on my shoulders. His voice was calm, and composed.

"I see a beautiful woman in front of me, who deserves every sweet thing."

Beautiful? I hadn't heard that word for a long time. I paused, unsure of what to say. I looked away from him, toward the ground.

"You don't really know me that well."

He placed his fingers under my chin and elevated my face, "Missy, I've been around you, and I've talked to you enough to know what type of woman you are, and one thing for sure, if there were more women like you, the world would be a better place."

My insides were tingling, but there was nothing I could do about it. "Now, you're just being too nice."

His hands slid down my arms, and he placed his hands around mine and held them. I closed my fingers around his. "If you were mine, I'd always love and appreciate you."

I've waited years to hear those words from Joe, and I'm hearing them now, from a man who is not my husband. *Why now?*

"Why are you doing this, Aaron? I'm a lot older than you, and I'm married. I don't know what you want from me?"

"The first time I saw you, something triggered inside of me. I felt an inner piece, and happiness that I've never felt before, and now every time I see you, and all the times in between, I feel the same thing. I can't stop it, and I don't want to stop it." He stroked my fingers with his fingers, moving them in and out and rubbing the backs of my hands with his thumbs. My fingers followed his lead, and the sweet sensation of his skin stroking my skin, emitted a rush of arousing chills throughout my body. I couldn't pull away from him, the intensity was more powerful than ever. "I'm not sure where these feelings will take me, but I can't keep them a secret anymore," he said.

Wow. A hundred things came rolling into my mind at the same time. I wanted to tell him I was feeling the same as him, I wanted to throw my arms around him and give into passion, but I held back. I stopped stroking his hands, and kept them still inside his. *What do I have to offer him? I can't exactly leave my marriage for someone I barely know, and I've never cheated on Joe.* Trapped inside of my own thoughts, I couldn't speak.

"Please say something," he said.

"I can't give you what you need Aaron."

"I know you are feeling it, the same as me, tell me you are."

There was no use in hiding my feelings any longer.

"I am...feeling it...Aaron."

The words were out, and there was no going back. Aaron wrapped his brawny arms around me, and pulled me close to him. He smelled of tree bark, and musk. The warmth from him filled me up, as I put my arms around his waist. He tilted his chin down, and tipped his face to the left so his lips would meet up with mine. I tilted my chin upward, and I felt the essence of his lips nearing mine. My mouth had begun to part, ready to brush his, and I heard the porch door slam shut. Startled, I released Aaron and backed away, Aaron did the same.

"Mom?" *Jonah.* My nerves jumped at the sight of the boys clumping down the veranda stairs.

"Mom, are you coming in to see where we're sleeping?" They ran across the lawn to Aaron and I. Caught off guard, I said, "Yes, of course I will." I didn't think to ask Aaron, I was hoping the boys hadn't seen us. How terrible that would have been for Jonah to see Aaron and me almost kiss.

"Dad, are you coming too?" said Landon.

I put my arm around Jonah's shoulders, and looked at Aaron out of the corner of my eye. He turned away from Landon, and picked up his stick. "No, I have to get this fire going stronger, if we're going to cook those hotdogs." He begun to stir the fire and threw on an extra piece of wood. "You boys go ahead, and show Mrs. Edwards."

Mrs. Edwards. Jonah put his hand in mine and tugged my arm. I turned to Aaron, "I prefer Maggy." I gave him a wink before walking away.

Inside Aaron's house I expected to see man clutter, shoes and boots scattered by the entrance, dirty dishes piled up in the sink, and unsavory décor from the early 90's, but I was pleasantly surprised to see everything in order, with beautiful upgrades inside. The kitchen was open concept with a cathedral ceiling. The walls were white, and of smooth texture. It smelled like freshly painted drywall. As Jonah led me past the counter, I noticed it was made from granite and the cupboards were red cherry wood. There was an island with four bar stools, separating the kitchen from the rest of the room. The appliances were stainless steel, and appeared to not have any dirty fingerprint markings. *Strange for a man.* The floor was ceramic tiles, with an area rug under the kitchen table. The stairs to the second level were also made from red cherry wood. I held onto an iron railing as the boys and I went up.

Landon's room was covered in posters with everything from famous hockey players, to Lego, to Superman. The boys had set up a two-men pop tent in the middle of his room. They had their pillows, blankets, flashlights, and tablets inside. I could tell they were proud of themselves for setting the whole thing up because they were bragging that they did it without any help. I was proud of them, so I praised them for doing such an amazing job.

"Come on, Mom. Let's go out to the fire," said Landon.

The boys raced ahead of me and down the stairs before I even made it out of his bedroom. I saw down the hall another room which I assumed to be Aaron's bedroom, because the bathroom was across the hall from Landon's room. The door was open a crack, I wondered what his room looked like. *Was it as well kept as the rest of the house? What size of bed did he sleep in?* I took a few steps toward his room, my heart rate began to increase, I didn't want to get caught snooping around. *I'm not snooping, I'm just curious.* I tiptoed to the door, and poked my head inside the room. It smelled the same as Aaron did, the day of the birthday party; fresh shower aqua scent. He had a queen-size bed with an oak headboard, with a matching night table, and dresser with six drawers. The comforter was blue and grey checkers, and his pillows looked crisp and fluffy. The floor was hardwood, with a foot mat on the left side of the bed. Three walls were beige, and one was medium blue. Light shone in through a large window, adorned with dark grey curtains to the right of the bed. Another door was along the right side of the room, I assumed it was a closet or bathroom. As I looked around the room, I noticed there weren't any pictures on the walls. *That is typical for a man.* I eyed the bed once more, and pictured Aaron tossing me down, and climbing on top of me. I'd wrap my legs around his as he would passionately kiss my lips. I'd squeeze him and pull his bottom toward my pelvis, and I'd groan, feeling his hardness through my clothing. He'd flip me over, so I'd be on top of him, kissing his soft lips. He'd remove my sweater over top of my head, and he'd pull me inwards to unhook my bra. I'd sit up and my breasts would be exposed, so would my wrinkly stomach, but he wouldn't care. He'd eagerly lift his head off the pillow and pull me close to him, his lips would meet my nipples, and he'd aggressively caress them as I indulge in the pleasure.

Almost paralyzed from my fantasy, I heard someone come in the house downstairs. *Aaron?* How I would have loved for him to come upstairs and finish our kiss, and run his hands all over my body. I knew that was not a possibility because the boys were here, and it would be so wrong. I rushed to get downstairs in fear of getting caught.

Chapter 8

In the kitchen, I saw Aaron at the fridge, getting some ketchup. He looked hotter than ever with his shirt hanging out of his pants, *I'd love to place my fingers up that shirt and feel his back, and scrape my fingernails considerately over his skin.*

"There you are, Missy...or should I say Maggy?"

"Either one will do." I walked toward the bar stools.

"Did you get lost up there?"

"Oh...um...no." *What should I tell him? The truth would be best, but I couldn't bare to tell him I was checking things out.* "I was taking a second look through Jonah's bag to make sure he has everything for the night."

"That's what a good mommy does," he teased.

Him still being so sweet, made me feel bad for telling him a fib. *I'd better come clean.*

"Actually, I was admiring how beautiful the house is. Did you do the work yourself?"

"Thanks. Yes, I've been working my ass off the past couple years, trying to get the renovations done."

"It looks very professional."

"I've been in this business since I was fourteen. During high school, I started working for a guy who owns a wood-working business. I loved it, so I stuck with that profession after I graduated."

"That explains why you are so good at it."

"I'm good at a lot of things, Missy."

"I bet you are," I winked at him. "So am I Mr."

He paused staring at me. "What are you doing tonight?" he said in a soft tone.

Not much of anything with the kids away, and Joe, Who cares?

"I'm doing a few odd jobs at home tonight."

"Why don't you stay with the boys and me for hotdogs?"

I wanted to say yes in the worst way, every minute with Aaron was enjoyable. I loved talking and laughing with him. I wanted to learn more about him, in spite of our age difference, it was uncanny how well we communicated. *Aaron is interested in what I have to say, and he said he thinks I'm beautiful. It's been so long since another man has shown interest in me, but I haven't shown interest in anyone else before. The fact that I'm married doesn't stop Aaron from trying to get close. Why does that not bother him? I know I should stay away from him, but I've never felt a strong attraction like this before. What is happening?* It felt so good to look at Aaron, and realize I was still capable of having emotions other than emptiness. When I looked at Joe I felt as though I was suffering a slow and agonizing death. I wanted to believe our marriage could last, so I ignored my true feelings that something was missing. *It's become more clear every day that Joe is not giving me what I need. Aaron has so much to give, and he gives it naturally. The two of them are completely different people.*

"I don't know," I said.

"Come on. Let's go out and check the fire. You can decide after."

"Alright," I said.

Walking across the grass beside Aaron seemed organic, especially after our embrace earlier. I wanted to reach for his hand and hold it in my grasp, but I didn't. Upon reaching the fire pit, I stood in the exact same spot where Aaron and I had almost kissed. The boys were sitting at the fire pit, roasting their hotdogs on sticks. Nothing looked burnt yet. They had their buns ready and on their plates. Everything looked under control, so I mentioned to Jonah that I'd be leaving. Jonah begged me to stay and eat the hotdog he had just cooked. Aaron squat to the ground, pulled out two cokes and two beers from his drink cooler, and set them on the table.

"You can't say 'no' to a boy who's cooked for his mother, can you?" Jonah looked at me with his fake puppy dog eyes. He started doing that a couple years ago as a joke, after he tricked me into buying him a new video game by using them. I raised my eyebrows at Jonah, and said, "I know what you're doing."

Jonah grinned and said, "Please...Mommy."

"Mommy? You must really want me to stay," I laughed.

Aaron handed me a beer, and said, "The boy is trying. Why don't you stay?"

I took the beer from Aaron, and said, "Okay. Just for a little while."

Aaron's eyes lit up, he pointed to the chair. The fire felt toasty, as the outside temperature had begun to drop. Aaron sat in the chair next to me, the boys sat across from us. Aaron was a complete gentleman as we ate together. He poured my beer into a tall glass, warmed my bun over the fire, and made sure I had enough condiments. Normally, I'd take care of my own things, but I could tell that Aaron was getting satisfaction from taking care of everything, so I let him, including stoking the fire. I could tell he wanted me comfortable because he asked me several times if he could get me anything else. The boys put marshmallows on their sticks, and waved them around in the flames. Landon began to cackle when his caught on fire. He held it up in the air swinging it back and forth until it flew off and landed back in the fire pit. We all burst out laughing, and Aaron teased Landon about having to call in the fire truck to extinguish his marshmallow. The boys thought that was hilarious and begun acting out a crazy scene of how that would go down. After the boys settled, they cooked a few more marshmallows, and wadded them in. Jonah cooked one for me, it was crispy on the outside and gooey on the inside. I didn't want to get it all over my fingers, so I carefully ate it off the stick. I noticed Aaron sipping his beer and watching me, but I pretended not to notice, not wanting to stare back at him until I had a chance to remove any marshmallow goo that may have been stuck to my face.

Time was getting on, I reminded Jonah that I had to be leaving soon. I was surprised to hear him say, "Why? Jody is at a sleepover, and Daddy probably isn't home like always. You will be all alone if you go."

I crossed my arms, feeling embarrassed Jonah had said those things in front of Aaron. The last thing I wanted was Aaron feeling sorry for me. "I'll be fine, don't worry about me."

Aaron tried to hand me another beer. I said, "No thanks, but I will help tidy up."

"It's getting dark, you boys should go in and wash up, and get your pajamas on," said Aaron.

Jonah looked at me, and said, "Mom you will come in and say goodnight to me right?"

That would mean me going back upstairs in Aaron's house, when his bedroom is just down the hall.

"Of course she will," said Aaron.

"Sure," I said.

The boys ran off inside, I started to gather up the paper plates and napkins. Aaron told me I didn't need to lift a finger, and he'd take care of everything. I have to admit, I was feeling a bit lazy having everything done for me. I'm not used to a man doing the dirty work. Aaron asked me if I'd sit with him for a few minutes. He was being genuine, my heart was telling me to stay, so I sat back down beside him. My stomach was feeling good, and I was relaxed. I looked up at the dark sky, it appeared so wide and open with nothing blocking my view, as it did in town. Only half was lit up with stars scattered here and there, it seemed as though the rest of the stars were covered with clouds, or far enough away making them invisible to the naked eye.

"Everything okay, Missy?" said Aaron.

I looked at Aaron, "It's so beautiful here."

"Only a true country girl would notice the beauty in a half-lit sky."

"Is that so? And, do you know a lot of country girls?"

He leaned back in his chair. "Well, yes. Hundreds of them," he began to chuckle.

I knew he was teasing, I looked at him and tapped him on his left hand that was resting comfortably on the arm of his lawn chair, "Sure you do."

He placed his right hand on top of mine, and gave it a squeeze. He looked me in the eye, and said, "Where have you been all of my life?"

My insides fluttered. It was an absolute turn on, hearing those words come out of his mouth, almost déjà vu-like from a previous lifetime, if there was ever such a thing. All my life, I knew there was something missing, but I could never hit the nail on the head. I've filled my life with family, friends, and my career. I had almost everything I set out for, but every so often my internal emptiness resurfaced, and at that very moment sitting with Aaron, the hollowness had disappeared, as always, when I was with him. *Why is this happening now?* I wasn't sure how he wanted me to respond, I could only speak what felt true, "No, where have you been all of my life?"

He squeezed my hand tighter and held it inside of his. "Come here."

I held back briefly. He closed his eyes, nodded his head sideways, indicating for me to come to him, he reopened his eyes. I stood, as he held my hand. He stretched his arm out further, not letting go of me, and gently he pulled me to him. I willingly

84

complied, moved closer to him and sat across his legs, leaving my legs dangling over the arm of the chair. He put his arms around me, I placed my arms around his back as he leaned forward. Our bodies perfectly snugged together, I rest my chin sideways on his left shoulder, my cheek brushing his neck. I held my breath, as I felt my heart rate increase, my body absorbed every movement of his hands as he rubbed them slowly up and down my back. His embrace felt authentic, as if he could hold me forever. Tingles shot up my spin, and down my arms. I felt he was hugging me because he wanted to, not because I asked him to. *Lord, he feels good.* I took in some air, and rubbed my cheek on his. His stubble felt soft instead of prickly, like Joe's. He turned his face toward mine and ran his lips along my jaw line, up to my cheek, and over to my mouth. My lips brushed his lips softly, back and forth, his aura was completely synced with mine. With our lips still touching, I tilted my head to my left, and he tilted his head to his left. I felt his mouth open, as did mine. Together we opened and closed our mouths, sucking smoothly, and gently, in unison, kissing. It was the kind of kiss that completely consumes your emotions, blocking everything else out. I pulled his body tighter against mine, and I could feel his heart beat against my breast as our kiss intensified, and grew more powerful. My breaths became heavier, as did his. His hands adventured all over my body, through my clothes. He ran them up to my shoulders, down my back, his right hand moved to my ass, he gripped my buttocks and smoothed it over in a circular motion, then he continued down my thigh, he squeezed, and rubbed me as if he couldn't get enough. I placed my hands on both sides of his jaw, and slipped my tongue inside his mouth, he responded instantly with his tongue meeting mine. Our tongues moved together entangled with excitement. I felt the urge to get closer to Aaron, I released his jaw with my hands, and stood to my feet. I flipped up the arms of his lawn chair, and casually sat back down straddling his legs. I inched myself closer to him by pushing off of the ground with my toes until my pelvis was resting on his. Both of his hands cupped my buttocks, he pulled me in even closer. I wrapped my arms around him and held him. I stroked his back, and rubbed my lips along the side of his face. His skin was warm, and I gently caressed his right temple. He lifted my sweater enough to allow his hands to fit up inside to explore my bare skin. I could feel all 10 of his fingers lying flat on my back and pressing into me, massaging me all over. It felt soothing and arousing, giving me the urge to place my lips on his lips again. As our lips moved together, I felt his hands moving up and down my sides over my ribs, I leaned back bringing my hands to his chest and unbuttoning his shirt as I looked him in the eye. He remained still with his hands resting on my hips. I opened his shirt, and placed my hands on his hairless chest. I massaged his chest around and around until I reached his shoulders. I rubbed and squeezed them, feeling his firmness, and strength. I wanted his shirt completely off to feel his biceps, but I refrained. He slid his hands up my sides to my breasts, his left hand ventured under my bra and rest it over my nipple, taunting me. His right hand slide up my back and he single handedly unfastened my bra, leaving his left hand room to tease my breasts. I lifted my sweater up and over my breasts, and moved his hand down to my hip. I pressed myself against his bare chest to feel his velvety skin on mine. I sucked the middle of his neck below his ear, he tilted his head to the side for easier access. His hands slide to my thighs, he rubbed them, and tried pulling me into him. I slid up his shirt sleeves, and rubbed his forearms down to his hands, and back. He placed his fingers inside of mine, locking them together. His lips met mine again, he moaned and I could feel his manhood getting larger, as I pressed my womanhood on him and remained in a straddling position. *Lord, I want him so bad.* While we were kissing, I ran possibilities through my mind of where I could have him, maybe in the back of his truck, or in his shed, or standing up behind the tree. *I could unzip his pants and have him in this very chair, but then I'd have to free one of my legs, and that would leave me in a vulnerable position if the boys come back out.* The shed and the truck seemed too slutty, and I had to rule out behind the tree because I didn't think it would be appropriate for a first time. Having Aaron kiss and fondle my body was amazing, but I knew we had to stop. We were placing ourselves into a dangerous situation, I did not want my son to find me like that.

I pulled back from Aaron, leaving him with a look of contentment. "Aaron, we have to stop."

"I know," he said, "but my feelings for you are genuine."

"I have to be honest with you. I've never felt attracted to anyone like this before, but we can't do this."

I got up and off of him, I took his hand and helped him to his feet, his shirt hung down and remained open, revealing his six pack. He placed his arms around my shoulders, and I placed mine around his waist, my face rested on his left shoulder. He rocked me gently back and forth.

Into my ear, he whispered, "I want you."

Those words rolled off his tongue effortlessly, I didn't ever want to let him go.

"I want you too," I said, "but the timing is wrong."

"I've wanted you from the moment I saw you five years ago."

I raised my brows, lifted my head up from his shoulder, surprised. "Five? We only met three years ago."

"I remember," he said. "The first time I saw you was five years ago, you were walking out of the post office in town. It was late June, you were wearing a short sleeve, light blue dress that tied at the waist, and you carried a large package in your arms. You took my breath away. I sat in my truck parked along the street, and I watched you, this beautiful woman walk up the street and go inside a hair salon, but you didn't look my way. The second time I saw you was a few months later, I was driving past the park and I took a glance in. I saw again this beautiful woman—you, swinging on the swings with your children, I remember thinking what a wonderful mother you must be. I couldn't stop thinking about you for weeks, and before I knew it, a year had passed without seeing you. When Landon came to live with me, I registered him for school. He and I were sitting with the principle in her office, and I saw you come in the reception area to talk to the secretary. I couldn't believe I was seeing this beautiful woman again. What are the chances of that? I knew it must have been in the cards somehow for you and I to connect. The most outstanding day of all was the first time you and I actually met."

"I remember. It was in the hallway, when I was picking up the twins, and Jody introduced us."

"You remember?" he seemed surprised.

"Of course I do. And, I remember all of the times after that, like the field trip last year. I wasn't sure how much you wanted to talk to me, so I stayed reasonably close in case you wanted to, and to keep my eye on you."

"You weren't stocking me, were you?" Aaron teased.

"Just checking you out." I grinned. "You weren't stocking me, were you?" I teased back.

"No, just checking you out."

Aaron took me by the hand. "Come on," he said.

"Where are we going?"

"I'll show you the trail that Landon and I made through the trees."

"What about the boys?"

"Wait here, I'll go and check on them, and lock the door."

"I'll go too, then I can say good night to Jonah."

Aaron tossed a bucket of water on the fire to put it out. It sizzled and smoked, but he said it'd be alright after he tossed the second bucket on it. Aaron held my hand as we walked to the house, going inside he held the door open for me. I removed my shoes, and hung my sweater on the coat stand. I told Aaron we should go up to see the boys separately, so they wouldn't suspect anything.

I knocked on Landon's door and walked in. I heard music and guns shooting, neither of them spoke, I unzipped their tent, and peeked inside to find them tucked inside their sleeping bags.

They didn't look at me because they were too focused with playing games on their tablets. I told Jonah that I'd be leaving soon. Immediately he set down his tablet, sat up to give me a hug and a kiss, and said goodbye. Feeling proud that my boy wasn't ashamed to kiss me in front of his friend, I said, "I love you." I asked Landon for a hug because I didn't want him to feel left out, but he turned me down, saying,

"No thanks, I'm good," as he kept his eyes glued to his tablet.

I stepped out of their room, and looking down the hall, I noticed Aaron's bedroom door was wide open. *Was he in there, or had the boys been in there and left it open?* I listened, but the only thing I could hear was water running, then shutting off. I decided it'd be wrong for me to look inside his room again, instead I went straight downstairs. Upon reaching the bottom step, I heard footsteps upstairs, then Aaron's voice. *He must be saying goodnight to the boys.* Luckily, I didn't go into his room, because I'm not sure if I'd be able to control myself with him in the same room as a bed. I sat at the bar stool in the kitchen while I waited for Aaron to come down. My hands were feeling dirty, so I got up to wash them at the kitchen sink. As the bubbles washed down the drain, I had a chance to inspect his handiwork more closely. His back splash were one inch glass tiles, beige, grey, and white placed in an exact pattern, filling the entire space between the counter and the top cupboards all the way around. I dried my hands on the towel hanging on the stove handle, putting it back, I noticed the toe board under the bottom cupboards were wood and had a leaf design etched into it. The cupboard door handles were pewter, and had a leaf engraved into each one. He had such a talent with his hands. Everything looked gorgeous. Aaron was gorgeous. I shivered, *his skilled hands had touched my body and they felt wonderful*. I couldn't believe what Aaron and I had revealed to each other. It was obvious to me now that Aaron had been feeling the same things for me as I was for him. My mind was lost in the freedom for a moment, fantasizing that I could keep him.

"Would you like a drink?" I heard Aaron speaking, so I turned away from the counter to look at him.

"Thanks, but no."

Aaron approached me, he had changed his clothes, now wearing a long sleeve black sweater, and a clean pair of jeans. He smelled of hand soap, and his hair had been brushed. *If I hadn't been so angry with Joe before I left home, I would have changed into something nicer than these stupid track pants, but then again, if I hadn't been mad at Joe I might not have made out with Aaron...or maybe I would have?* Feeling self-conscious, I tucked my falling strands of hair behind my ears again.

"You look beautiful," he said.

"I'm sure I don't look beautiful right now."

"But, you do," he said, and placed a short quick peck on my lips.

"You're not checking me out, are you?"

"Of course I am, and I'd like to check out the rest of you too."

We stood together at the end of the counter, he stroked my back, and gently kissed my neck. I wanted to stay there forever with him, but reality kicked in, and Joe's face appeared in my mind. *It's not as if I could divorce him, and run off with Aaron, or could I? I didn't know I was capable of falling for another man, and now that I have I'm not sure how to handle it.*

"I didn't know you were into older, married ladies."

"I didn't know you were married when I first saw you, I just knew I had to have you."

"Oh really," I teased, "Is that a fact?"

Aaron kissed me again. My lips and his fit perfectly together. The kiss was smooth, and slow, and gentle enough to get me aroused all over again. It was so easy to get lost in him, but I forced myself to pull back from him.

"Aaron, I don't ever do this kind of thing."

"What kind of thing?"

"The cheating kind of thing."

"Oh, that, but it's not really cheating if you aren't in love with your spouse."

"Who says I'm not in love with my spouse?"

"No one said it, but I can tell."

"How can you tell?"

"First thing, you never talk about him, women in love talk about their spouse a lot. Second thing, women in love bring their spouses with them at one point or another. I've only seen you alone or with your kids, never with him. Third thing, women in love play with their wedding bands because they are subconsciously thinking about their spouse, and I've never seen you do that either. Fourth thing, a woman in love would have told me to screw off by now, which you haven't. Should I go on?"

"Well, aren't you a smarty pants. However, you are wrong. It is cheating, and I don't want to say that I don't love him."

"That's right, you don't want to say that you don't love him, but inside you know that you don't."

"Actually, my marriage is in a bad spot, and it has been for a while," I paused. "Honestly, I can't stand being around him right now, and please do not tell anyone I said that. You are the only person I've admitted that to."

"You've never cheated on him, feeling like you do?"

"Never."

"One question. Why me?"

I led him to the bar stools, "Good question and that I don't have the answer to." We sat side by side. "All I can say is I feel really good when I'm with you. It's as if I've known you forever. I can ask you the same question, Why me?"

"That's simple, you're hot." He laughed as I raised my eyebrows at him. "I'm drawn to you, Missy. Every text message you send me, puts a smile on my face, and I really like being with you."

"You're so sweet, Captain. You deserve to have a nice woman who can give you more than I can. Why have you not found the right one?"

He led me to sit on the sofa near the French doors in the kitchen.

"It's hard to find a good girl out there. Most want a man who has a nine to five job, and earns over a hundred and fifty grand a year. I'm a simple guy, I was taught to work hard and earn everything I have. I have a job that I enjoy doing, and I earn enough to cover everything I need. The girls I've dated would rather have more, even if it means being unhappy, and I've never been in love with any of them."

"What about Landon's mother?"

"Emily is her name. She and I had a one night stand after a party. We tried dating after finding out she was pregnant, but we couldn't make it work. Even though there was no love between us, I asked her to settle down with me for the sake of our son, but she didn't want to give up her freedom. Her mother took Landon and raised him until she passed away. After that, Emily refused to take care of him, that's why I have him now. I've always wanted Landon with me, even as a baby, but Emily's mother threatened to fight me in court to keep him herself. Rather than going through all of that, I knew it'd be better for my son to be raised by a woman with experience, and if she was willing to fight me, I knew she'd take excellent care of him. I visited him every week, and on holidays until she passed. Landon only sees his mother twice a year, but at least he has the chance to know who she is."

"Incredible. I'm sorry you had to go through all of that."

"You know, Missy, life goes on, and you just have to make the best of things. Now tell me about your man, why is he such a fool to let your head turn from him?"

Not really wanting to talk about Joe and spoil the great mood I was in, I reminded Aaron that he was supposed to take me for a walk through his trail, but he said he could smell rain coming when he closed his bedroom window earlier, and he thought we should stay inside. I told him it was getting late, and I should go home. He said that since he told me his story, it would only be fair if I told him mine.

I sat criss cross style at the end of the sofa, turned to face Aaron, who sat legs spread shoulder width apart, only his head turned to look at me, his left hand rest on my knee. I told him the short version of how Joe's personality had changed into becoming more self-involved after the twins were born, and how he has become more obsessed to be superior over everyone including his co-workers. I said Joe is barely home, and does not spend time talking, or taking time for the twins, or myself. I said he only cares about representing the best clients, to make himself look better. I told him that my feelings for Joe had become numb, and I couldn't help but think Joe has brought it all on himself. I said I hadn't felt love for Joe in a very long time, one reason being every time I've tried to get close to him, he's pushed me away. He doesn't even say goodnight anymore. I'm literally exhausted from his attitude. I'm just finished with Joe. He puts in zero effort to keep things interesting, he makes me feel that I am nothing more than a thorn in his side. After I began talking to Aaron, everything seemed to pour out and I couldn't stop. Aaron was attentive and taking everything in. I asked him if he was bored by listening to me rattle on. He said he could never be bored listening to my sweet voice. I was so touched in him saying that, I've never had a man make me feel so important. It wasn't that I craved the attention, rather just being appreciative of the words that he chooses. After I had finished filling Aaron in about my relationship, I rest my chin on my hands, my elbows on my knees, and I stopped talking. Aaron looked straight at me and said, "Missy, if you were mine, I'd never leave you alone, and I promise, I'd always say goodnight to you."

"There you go again, saying the right thing."

"Sunshine, I mean the things I say to you."

"I know you do, but Captain we have to face reality. We still don't know each other that well, and we can't just walk off into the sunset together."

"Sure we can." He poked my arm and teased me.

"It's not like we can start dating, I live with my husband, and then there's the fact that I am older than you."

"Never too old," he said.

I had to laugh. "You mean if I was seventy years old, you'd still be interested?"

"If you were seventy now and looked as good as you do, there'd be no problem."

I punched him in the shoulder. "Ya okay, Captain."

"You're not much older than me. You and the kids could move in with me, and then we can date."

"You don't mean that."

"Remember, I don't say things I don't mean. Will you consider moving in with me?"

"Wow, Aaron. That would be moving quickly. I don't know what to say?"

"I know, but I want to make sure that you are being treated properly, and the only way to do that is to take care of you myself."

"I'm a big girl, Aaron. I've been taking care of myself for a long time."

"And, you have done a wonderful job, but I want to show you how much love you deserve. Please consider it."

"There are a lot more people involved than just us, but I will remember your offer."

"I knew you couldn't resist me," he smirked.

"I'm not promising." I checked my watch. It said 10:46. "I have to go home now, it's late."

"You could spend the night."

"Aaron, honestly, I wouldn't control myself being overnight in a house with you."

"That's fine with me, I'm sure the boys won't mind."

I leaned in, and passionately kissed his lips. "I'm sorry, I have to go."

I put on my shoes and sweater. Aaron handed me his extra phone charger to keep in my van. He said my phone might be at 30% by the time I reach home. He walked outside with me. I could smell moisture on the air, as if we were standing underneath a hundred clouds, the warm wind had blown the strands of hair out from behind my ear. Aaron held me. The strength of his arms was comforting.

"I wish you could stay," he said.

"Me too." I leaned in to kiss him goodbye, and naturally, his lips responded exactly as I needed. *It would be so easy to tear his jeans open right now. I could have my way with him against my van, but no, the timing is wrong.* After getting in the van, I put my window down. "You owe me a rain check for that walk through your trail," I smiled.

"My trail is always open," he said while leaning in my window, and giving me a peck on the lips.

I turned around in his driveway, and gave him a little wave. As I drove off, I saw him standing still, like a pet watching its owner fade into the distance. His hand lifted to wave goodbye.

All the way home, I replayed our entire night in my head. I could not get over everything that happened, how much information we had shared with each other, and how much fun the boys had with Aaron and I at the bonfire. With the exception of Jody missing, it felt like we were a family, everyone sitting around talking, laughing, and enjoying each other's company. I could still feel Aaron's lips on mine, and his hands seeking my body. My breasts ached to feel Aaron's skin pressing up against them, my hands yearned to touch his firm body. Driving past the bakery, I turned on my whippers due to the light sprinkle that covered my windshield. I pictured the first time Aaron had met me there for Landon's birthday party, I was amazed how much had happened in a short time. *Aaron is such a bright light, he makes me feel as though I don't have a worry in the world. I want to know him better, and spend more time with him, but how? It's not as if we can date, or be seen together in public, and sneaking around is something I have looked down on other people for.*

By the time I had reached home, the light rain had turned into a heavy downpour, I parked the van inside our car garage. Joe's car was inside too. *Great. He's back.* I knew he was ticked for not knowing where I'd been because the house was in complete darkness inside and out. Normal people call or text their spouse to find out what time they'll be home, but not Joe, he'd rather do something he thinks will irritate me. I turned on my phone flashlight to unlock the door going inside from the garage. Just getting inside, my phone buzzed. *Aaron.* "Home yet?" I sat on the bench beside the back door, and texted him saying that I just got in, and I thanked him for the phone charger, and for a fun night. He texted me back asking me if I had my overnight bag packed yet? I burst out laughing, and texted him saying, if I was going back, I wouldn't need an overnight bag, I'd just go around naked all night. He told me he had no problem with that, and I should hurry myself back to his place. I knew that was out of the question, especially with Joe being home. *Why was he home? He said he wouldn't be back. I'm sure it's not because he's sorry for all of the nasty things he said to me.*

I tiptoed upstairs, hoping not to wake Joe, and went straight into my bathroom to get ready for bed. I removed my sweater, and I got a whiff of Aaron's cologne. I pulled my sweater up to my nose and inhaled, and exhaled, and inhaled again. He smelled delicious. I covered my face with my sweater, and sniffed it in various places to find out where the cologne smelled the strongest. The front left shoulder had the highest potency. *Wonderful.* I folded it tightly to contain the smell, and I placed it in my vanity drawer instead of the dirty clothes hamper, for a quick sniff later. My skin felt clammy, I undressed, and hopped into the shower. The water felt amazing, trickling down onto my body. I smelled smoke from the bonfire coming out of my hair as soon as the steam hit. I washed it and rinsed, and gently scrubbed my body with soap and a cloth. I remembered all of the places Aaron's hands had touched me, and I didn't want to wash off his germs, but since I shared a bed with Joe, I knew I had to.

I wanted to tease Aaron, so I sent him a text telling him I just got out of the shower. He quickly responded saying he'd be right over. I told him it wouldn't be a good idea because Joe was home. Aaron joked, and said that we could lock Joe in his room and go at it in the living room. With all truth in the matter, we probably could and Joe wouldn't have noticed. I slipped into my nighty, and quickly dried, and brushed my hair. Aaron said Jonah and Landon were finally asleep after I had asked about them. It was just past midnight, I told Aaron I was heading to bed now. He said, "Goodnight, Sunshine. Sweet dreams xoxo."

"Goodnight, Captain." I said. I wanted to send him 'xoxo' back, but to me those letters meant more than hugs and kisses. To me, they mean complete love, and as much as I feel for him, I didn't want to jump the gun.

I avoided turning on my bedroom light by using my phone flashlight, to make it across the room to bed. I gently folded back the covers, and cautiously sat on the edge with the intention of not waking Joe. I carefully lifted my legs and slid my feet under the sheets, slowly pulling them up. I could only hear Joe's shallow breathing, but he didn't budge. I was nicely tucked in when I saw my phone light blinking, knowing it would be Aaron, I smiled. He had sent me a flashing pink heart. It was beautiful. I sent him a blue heart, and a half moon. He sent me the opposite side of the moon to which I had sent him. *I don't understand how the women he has dated would want more in a man? I adore every simple thing he has done. If a man takes time to send a woman a moon, or a heart by text, it represents the extra effort he is willing to put into the relationship. Who wouldn't appreciate that? I would so love to keep this man, and move in with him as he's already suggested, but my whole life, and the twins' lives would have to change for that to be an option. I have fantastic kids. They've been doing well in our situation. I'm frightened to think if I did leave, would they be negatively affected forever? Or would they accept my decision, and continue to succeed? Why did Aaron come into my life? He seems to be everything I desire, and he's great with the kids. I don't want to give him up.*

I felt warm and fuzzy on the inside, as I studied the last few texts that we had sent each other. I turned off my phone and clutched it in my hands as they rest on my chest. I smiled, rested my eyes, and visualized Aaron and I together on the lawn chair, him pulling me in closer, as we kissed and fondled each other. I felt safe in my thoughts because Joe was turned away from me. I rolled to my left side, away from Joe, I lost grip on my phone and it crashed to the floor. I stretched my hand to the floor to feel around for it in the darkness, Joe maneuvered himself to a sitting position in bed.

"What are you doing?" he said.

I didn't feel like responding to him after the fight we had earlier, but I forced out the words, "I'm just getting my phone."

"It's 1am, where have you been all night?"

After being in my happy state of mind, I didn't want to argue, nor did I want to risk Joe finding out that I'd been with Aaron all night.

"Why, did you miss me?"

I could feel Joe's eyes glaring at me, as I set my phone on my nightstand.

"Don't you think it's kind of late for you to be getting home?"

"I'm a grown woman Joe, and bedsides, you said you weren't coming home tonight."

"I was doing business, what's your excuse?"

Tension had built inside my chest. "Jonah asked me to stay with him for a while, so I did. Is that okay with you, Joe?"

Joe laid back down, and didn't answer me. *Why did Joe think he had the right to ask me where I had been after the things he said to me earlier? I was certain that he had no idea about Aaron, but it crossed my mind that, what if he had found out somehow? How would I explain that I had been fooling around with my son's friends' father?* I waited a few moments for him to say something, but he didn't. Both of us kept silent laying on our own sides of the bed. Flashes of Aaron and I kissing stayed fresh in my mind. I knew I should be feeling guilty about everything that happened with Aaron, but I wasn't. My eyes were feeling heavy, I closed them and tried to sleep. I felt Joe moving closer to me until his body was pressed up against my back. *No way am I having it with him tonight.* He placed his right hand on my hip and began to rub it. I laid as still as I could to make him think that I was already sleeping. He tried placing his hand between my legs, but I kept them tight together, making it impossible for him. He pressed his pelvis up against my ass, and again I laid still. *Sex with Joe is out of the question. What the hell is he thinking? Does he think I forgot what he said today?* I wanted his hands off me. The thought of him touching me was repulsive. *Get away from me. Get away.* A few minutes had passed, and Joe let out a sigh of irritation and turned back to his own side of the bed. *Thank goodness.*

Chapter 9

In the morning, I was feeling well rested, even though I barely slept more than thirty minutes at a time without waking up. I kept imagining what it would have been like, had I unzipped Aaron's pants on the lawn chair, and gave it to him over and over. *I'm sure he wouldn't have stopped me, or turned me away like I'm used to with Joe.* I was glad I ignored Joe's advances last night, it would have been repugnant, knowing I had been kissing Aaron just an hour before. I was starving when I got out of bed around eight, so I didn't bother to get dressed before eating. I fried up a western sandwich for myself, and enjoyed it along with a glass of orange juice while sitting at our bar table in the breakfast room - my favorite room in the house because of the large window with six-inch stained glass squares that frame the perimeter. The sun was out and shining after the big rainfall, which aside from Aaron, might have been another reason, I felt extra cheerful. I read over a new text from Aaron. "Good Morning, Beautiful." I read it over a few times, because it made me happy. Joe's breakfast plate was in the sink, but I didn't feel his adverse presence in the house. I sent Amanda a text to see how Jody was doing, she texted back that everything was great, the girls were up and painting their fingernails.

Being Sunday morning, and not in a rush, I decided to sit criss cross on the sofa and scroll through Facebook. An hour had passed before I finished checking out everyone's posts and photos. The morning was almost over, and I was still in my nighty. I heard the front door open, and keys being tossed onto the console. I could tell it was Joe because of the loud thump his feet made when he stepped inside. Joe has said several times over the years that he doesn't like me going around the house in my nighty. He'd rather, I get up and make myself look presentable first thing in the morning. I didn't feel like getting a speech from him, or talking to him, so I headed towards the stairs. I heard Joe grumbling, and cursing in the entrance, I took a quick peek down the hall to see what he was doing. I saw him holding Kylie's wedding invitation. I wished I hadn't left it out in the open yesterday, so Joe wouldn't have seen it until I was ready to discuss it with him. I turned to go upstairs, when I heard Joe calling me, I went to him because we had already made eye contact. He tossed the invitation down on the console, and he glared at me.

"Why the hell do you have the box checked that we're attending?"

"Because we're going."

He crinkled up his nose and said, "No, we're not."

"I haven't seen your sister for years, and I've decided to go."

"Magnolia, you are not going."

"Excuse me?" I stared him directly in the face.

"You heard me, Magnolia."

The tension was growing between us, but I wasn't about to let him tell me what to do.

"I can go if I want, Joe, and besides, I already emailed her saying we are going."

Joe shook his head back and forth, threw his hands up in the air, and hoofed it down the hall, leaving me there.

My heart was beating faster, and I could feel my body temperature raising. I shouted at him,

"What is your problem with Kylie?"

Joe continued on, and didn't look back. My nerves were rattled, but I wasn't changing my mind. I was going to that wedding. I walked briskly towards the stairs, and I was jarred from the sway of the front door swinging open, bags dropping to the floor, and the tapping from rubber-toed shoes. I heard Jonah calling, "I'm back."

A sharp breath entered my lungs, as I knew I had been caught in my nighty. Turning to face the front door, about ten meters from where I stood, I saw Jonah, Landon, and Aaron all facing me. *Oh boy.*

I held my breath, "Hi boys," I said.

Aaron was standing tall, hands resting at his sides, with the biggest smile on his face. I was embarrassed, and my cheeks grew warm and rosy, as I tried straightening my hair with my fingers.

"Did we get you up, Missy?"

I was stumped for words, after the scrap with Joe, I needed to process proper wording to hide my inner frustration.

"Umm...nooo, I've been up for hours, I just haven't gotten dressed yet."

Aaron looked pleased as he scanned me from head to toe. *Thank goodness, I had my shower last night. Do I look hideous?* My unkempt hair didn't seem to have a negative effect on him, because his eyes were glossy, and they beamed when he checked me out. Seeing Aaron, had sparked enough delight in me to almost forget about Joe's anger. Jonah asked if he could quickly show Landon his room. I told him it was fine, the boys raced upstairs without removing their shoes. Aaron and I stood in the entrance. I folded my arms, not quite sure what to do with my hands. Aaron crossed his arms, and placed one hand up to his chin, and rest his chin on his thumb. He gaped at me, squinted his right eye and said, "Is this what I'll be looking forward to?" His voice sounded seductive.

I straightened my nighty down with my hands, hoping to smooth out some of the wrinkles. I smiled, then whispered, "Careful, Joe is home."

"And, what would Joe do if I bent you over right now on that console?"

I burst out laughing, and so did Aaron. "Shhh," I said.

My laugh was soon quieted by the sound of Joe's voice echoing from the hall, and his heavy footsteps approaching Aaron and I. Aaron's face became serious, but he looked me in the eye, and his smile prevailed.

"Magnolia?" called Joe, his tone was gruff. I watched Joe look upstairs and yell, "I forbid you to go to the wedding."

I didn't answer. Joe turned and looked down the hall towards the door, and his eyes were fixed on Aaron and I. He looked baffled. It was obvious he didn't know that we had company. Joe took a few steps toward us.

"Magnolia, go and put on some clothes." He spoke to me as if he was scolding a child. Aaron's face dropped when he heard the condescending tone in Joe's voice.

"Actually, I don't mind," said Aaron while holding his head high. "I understand what it's like being Sunday morning, and wanting to relax a little before taking on the day."

Joe was at a loss for words, he stood there, mouth half open with nothing coming out. Aaron had caught him off guard, and he didn't know how to handle it. Being a lawyer, he should have had a nifty response ready to fire back, but I guess without any preparation time, he was speechless. It felt good having Aaron defend me.

"Excuse me, Aaron. I'll go and tell Landon you are ready to go."

I walked past Joe without making eye contact. At the top of the stairs, I listened for words being exchanged between Aaron and Joe. Aaron's voice echoed upstairs.

"I could accompany Magnolia to the wedding if you are unavailable, sir."

Whoa, that was bold. I couldn't believe my ears. Aaron had stepped up and put Joe in his place, right in his own home. I couldn't see Joe's facial expression, but I knew it had to be raunchy. Then I heard Aaron say, "Magnolia has helped me out a few times. I don't mind returning the favor, especially when it seems to be an important event for her."

I heard a few muffles coming from Joe, but not clear enough for me to make out the actual words. The door then opened, and closed. It was nice hearing my full name roll off Aaron's tongue. *Sexy, yet mature, Magnolia.* Of course, he wouldn't have dared to refer to me as Missy, or Sunshine in front of Joe. Aaron now had a taste of Joe's predominant personality, which could have been the reason he had the urge to tear him down a notch. *Would Aaron really go to the wedding with me, or was he just saying that to provoke Joe?*

I let the boys know that it was time for Landon to go, then I grabbed my house coat from my bedroom, covering my nighty. I assumed it was Joe who walked out the door. I went back downstairs behind the boys to say goodbye. Aaron looked relaxed near the console, leaning his left shoulder against the wall, standing with his left foot crossed over his right, thumbs inside his jeans pockets. The boys booked it outside to play a quick game of tag.

"Are you okay, Missy?" said Aaron.

"I'm fine, why do you ask?" I didn't want Aaron feeling sorry for me.

"I don't like the way he spoke to you. Is he like that all of the time?"

"He's just upset with me right now."

"Over going to a wedding? That is ridiculous. You don't deserve to be talked to like that."

"I'll handle it. Don't worry." I reached out and placed my hand on Aaron's shoulder. "What did Joe say to you before he left?"

"Nothing for you to worry about, Missy." He stood up straight, took my hand in his, and slowly raised it to his lips, kissing the back of my palm.

"It would be so easy for me to have you right now against this wall," I said.

Aaron checked his wrist watch, and gently let go of my hand, "I've got to go," he said.

"I'm sorry. I shouldn't have said that."

"Don't be. There's nothing I'd love more, but I'm meeting up with a client to go over a few things."

"On a Sunday? Are you trying to get away from me?"

"Never," he said, pulling me towards him. He tilted his chin upwards, looked down his nose and into my eyes. He studied my face, then placed a quick peck on my lips. "See you later."

"That's it? Not a bigger kiss?"

"I'd prefer not to in this house."

"What's wrong with kissing in this house?"

"Nothing, just not under his roof."

"It's my roof too."

"I know, but it is also his."

"He's not here right now."

"He'll be back to be under his roof."

"My money helped pay for this roof, and the things under it, so I get half the say of what happens under this roof."

"I'd love to kiss you, and have you right now," he paused. "Just not here." His voice sounded loving and sincere.

Like Aaron, I knew it was wrong, but my lack of love for Joe, made kissing Aaron seem so right. I pulled back from Aaron. "Okay." Changing the subject, I asked, "Are you taking Landon to your meeting?"

"Yes, Mrs. Finnegan and her husband are away, so she can't watch him."

"Why don't you leave him with me? He'd have fun with Jonah, and I'm picking Jody up later, she'd like to see him."

"You're probably right, and...you are a good mommy, so I guess it'd be alright." Aaron teased.

I laughed. "This mommy has to take a quick shower, and get ready."

Aaron's eyes grew large, "Shower? Hmmm. Tempting, Sunshine."

"Want to join me?" I raised my eyebrows at him, fully knowing that he wouldn't.

"Someday, but not here," he said.

I wanted to respect Aaron's feelings, so I held back from kissing him. "See you later." I gave him a little wave.

He put his arms around me, he squeezed me, and rocked me back and forth. "I'll send in the boys," he said, then turned to leave.

That afternoon after picking up Jody, I decided to take the kids for ice cream. We sat at our usual booth at Jack's Ice Cream and Burger Shop in Laudersville. Jody had a strawberry milkshake, the boys each had two scoops of ice cream on a cone, I had my favorite, a hot fudge Sundae. I listened to the kids chatter and giggle while they devoured their treats. Jody filled me in on every small detail at Brittney's sleepover, from what they ate for supper, to all of the games they played, and every movie they watched. The boys basically talked about their Pokémon cards and which ones were most powerful. On the way out, I took a peek at the bulletin board beside the door, to see if anything was going on that afternoon. I came across a movie, Avery Brown's *Spectacular Adventure*, it was to play that evening in town. The kids had mentioned wanting to see it several times over the past few weeks, so I knew they wouldn't turn down the opportunity. I sent Aaron a quick text to let him know where we'd be. He didn't respond, so I knew he had to be occupied with his client.

The theater had gone out of business years ago, rumor had it that the old Wilkinson brothers snatched it up for a nasty price because they couldn't stand to see it abandoned. They had it renovated in hopes of keeping part of our town's history alive.

By the time we paid for our tickets, went to the washroom, bought popcorn and drinks, it was time for the previews to begin. Inside the theater was dark, and about three quarters filled with people. I didn't take time to notice who the people were, I just focused on finding enough seats for us to all sit together. I finally spotted five empty seats in a row, we had to squeeze in past a large lady who was seated beside a boy, whom I presumed to be her son. The two of them were mowing down popcorn like there was no tomorrow. Landon wanted to sit between the twins, so I sat with Jody to my right, the boy and his mom to my left. Throughout the movie, the boy and his mom fussed in their seats, and made all kinds of racket. I kept hearing packages opening and squishing, the smell of gummy bears and chocolate kept wafting over from them. The ice in the boys' drink clattered together for minutes on end until he had eventually spilled some on himself, and the floor, I was happy none had splashed on my runners. My phone buzzed half way through the movie, when I read my message, I felt the mom's glare burning into the side of my head, as if I was disturbing them, I decided they could suck it up considering how irritating they had been. The message was from Aaron wishing us a good time at the movies. I texted him back a smiley face. After ten or so minutes had passed, I heard the boy complaining about having a sore tummy, he and the mom got up and left. I wasn't the least bit upset, after all, she should have known better than to let him sit there and consume all of that junk. My kids had half a bag of popcorn left over, and shared one bag of gummies. The movie had just past the part where Avery Brown had figured out the location of the dragon's lair, and my phone buzzed. *Aaron again.* He asked me where we were seated. I wasn't sure why he was asking, I texted we were on the left side, three rows from the back. I turned to have a sip of Jody's soda, and I felt someone sit in the seat next to mine. *Please Lord, let it not be that awful boy and his mom.* I slowly turned my head using my peripheral vision, I could tell it was a man. I didn't want to turn towards him and stare him in the face, so I looked straight ahead at the movie screen. I got a waft of aqua scented cologne, instantly my senses were aroused. I looked at the man, his eyes were already fixed on me. I smiled and whispered, "What are you doing here?"

Aaron smiled, and nod his head, "Watching the end of the movie."

I was tickled that he was joining us, and thankful that the two noise makers hadn't returned. Aaron inconspicuously placed his hand on my upper thigh, and stroked it as we watched the screen. *Feels great. What if someone sees?* I carefully removed his hand, sliding it to his own seat. I saw Aaron remove his jacket. He draped it over the arm connecting our seats. Part of it covered my leg. I felt his hand slide under the coat. He pulled my hand underneath. He rest his hand on top of mine, and locked our fingers, he massaged my thumb with his thumb. I looked over at the kids. They were completely into the movie. I knew they wouldn't notice the whereabouts of my hand, so I let it be. *I've found this man who does everything I need, too bad that I can't keep him.*

My eyes squinted as the lights turned on, I quickly took my hand back, and reached for my purse. The kids were excited to see Aaron, they greeted him with high fives as soon as we made it into the main entrance of the theater. The place was packed, which was to be expected being the only theater in town. We stood in line waiting to get outside, everyone moving at a turtle's pace. I cautiously looked through the crowd to see recognizable faces, more specifically, anyone who would place Aaron and me together. I saw a few acquaintances of mine, I doubted if they saw me, I couldn't get a good look though the bobbing heads to see who was behind us, I kept moving forward with the kids and Aaron, hoping to blend in.

Outside, the sun was lowering, the mouthwatering smell of grilled ribs from Zac's Diner filled the air. Jonah asked me if we could go to the restaurant. I told him it was getting late, and we could grab something at home. Aaron quickly spoke up saying, "Come on, Mommy. It'll be fun."

Jody then started in on me about getting something to eat as well. Aaron said he hadn't had supper yet, and would love if we joined him. I took Aaron aside, and suggested that it might not be a clever idea for us to be seen together in public, it might give people the wrong idea, *or the right idea.* Aaron said there was nothing wrong with friends having a bite to eat. Landon, and Jonah both said they were hungry. I took a last scan around outside the theater to see if I knew anyone, in fear of getting caught. I saw Sandra Malone, a client of mine, with her granddaughter heading down the stairs of the theater, but I didn't think she'd notice us. Everyone seemed to be minding their own business, and getting settled in their cars. It was a risk being seen out with Aaron. Gossip spreads like wildfire in our town, and despite my uneasy gut feeling, I said yes we'd go.

Zac's Diner was located at the intersection, a short walk for us. I tugged on the door. It was heavy and made of thick glass. Aaron reached for the door to release the pressure for me. "Wimp," he teased.

"Meanie," I smirked.

The smell of barbequed ribs, and fried onions tantalized my senses, as my eyes swept over the customers eating in their booths. The place wasn't jam packed for a Sunday night, however it was already past peak supper hour. *Thank goodness I don't recognize anyone.* I pointed out a table for us in the secluded dining room, hoping to keep invisible long enough to get through the meal.

Seated at our table, a waitress with short spikey brown hair handed us menus. I noticed her beautiful pink porcelain finger nails, as she carefully filled each of our glasses with ice cold water. Her voice was peppy, she told us she'd be back to take our order.

Jody wanted a hotdog, and fries. Jonah, and Landon wanted chicken fingers. Aaron said he was starved, and he couldn't resist having Zac's famous ribs, with a baked potato. I decided to have the same because it had been over a year since I've had the pleasure of sucking the seasonings off those babies.

After our waitress, Anne, had taken our order, I sent the kids into the restroom to wash up. I kept scouring the place in paranoia, Aaron asked me to relax, I wanted to, but I had the nagging feeling of someone watching me, I couldn't figure out who. There was an old white-haired couple sitting in the dining area with us, they looked like city folks due to the lady's Channel pant suit, and designer handbag that elegantly hung off the arm of her chair. She wore a pearl necklace and earrings to match. Her dress shoes were bright red that matched her long fingernails. Her hair was shoulder-length, parted, and swept to the right. It appeared to have been straightened by a professional. The man wore a dark grey suit and tie to match the woman's purse. They looked over dressed for the diner. *Maybe they are passing through town and the smell from the ribs caught their attention.* The two of them appeared intensely involved in a quiet conversation, they weren't eating. *Were they waiting on their meal?*

I could see the reflection of the booth area in a large wall mirror close to our table. Each person seemed to blend with the others, some middle-aged guys wore t-shirts, others wore hoodies, and caps. A young lady, about twenty or so, with red curly hair sipped on a cappuccino with a group of girls of similar age. *I've never seen any of these people before.* I looked back at Aaron, who was having a sip of his water. The dim lighting made him look five years younger than he was. *Do the lights have the same effect on me?* He looked so handsome in his black and blue-checkered shirt, sleeves neatly rolled up to his elbows. The blue almost matched the color of the table cloth. His hair looked freshly washed, his face hadn't any trace of stubble, he almost always carried a permanent smile on his lips, the light in his eyes calmed me, and I realized there was nothing to worry about. I felt Aaron's foot rub against mine, under the table.

"Everything okay, Missy?"

"Yes, I think so."

"I think so too."

"Of course you do." My hands rest on the table, he stretched his over to meet mine, and held the tips of my fingers.

"Nothing to worry about," he said.

I heard Jody giggling around the corner, so I knew they were finished in the restroom, I removed my hands from Aaron's grasp and placed them on my lap. Out of the corner of my eye, I saw Jody skipping back to the table, with the boys briskly following.

The ribs were delicious, the perfect blend of spice with sweetness. I noticed Aaron had impeccable table manners, he used his fork and knife to cut his ribs into individual strips and picked one up at a time to eat, after each bite he'd take his napkin to clean his mouth, and in between each rib he'd place the bone under a napkin on a separate plate off to the side of the table, and clean his fingers. It was pleasing to watch him eat compared to Joe, who always had some type of sauce or crumbs left behind on his face much like a child, a complete turn off.

I was getting full. The serving size was too big for me. I offered the rest to Aaron, since his was all gone. He said, "Sure," and took his fork and picked the ribs off my plate. Jody teased Aaron, saying that he'd catch mommy's germs. Aaron teased back saying, if she wasn't careful, he was going to eat the rest of her hotdog too. I managed to let my guard down, enough to appreciate the wonderful time we were all having. To play it safe, I kept my hands free from Aaron, I kept my voice quiet, hoping not to draw attention to our table. I dipped my fingers in the little bowl of lemon water that the waitress had left, and dried them on the napkin. Before Aaron had finished, the kids begun to play X's and O's on the back of their paper place mats. I noticed another man had joined the old couple, his back was to us. He must have entered the dining room without me noticing. His briefcase rest on the floor to his right side. The waitress took her tray to their table, and placed a coffee in front of each of them. The uneasy feeling had returned in my stomach. I gathered up our plates, and set them at the edge of the table, hoping the waitress would see, and bring us our bill. Jonah had begun to tell jokes as we waited, the waitress was taking her own sweet time. I couldn't help but stare at the man with that couple. *His hair looks familiar.* He was going over papers of some kind with them. His hand gestures were smooth, and when the old lady was talking, he sat back in his chair, and nodded his head. *Familiar.* I kept an eye on him, he turned to the side and looked at the old man, giving me a better look. *Oh my goodness, It's Joe.*

My nerves began to quiver, I turned my head away. He was the last person whom I'd expected to see there.

"We should get going," I said.

Why would Joe be at the diner? And, who does business on a Sunday night?

"Big rush, Missy?"

I didn't respond to Aaron. I told the kids to put their sweaters on. Aaron looked puzzled, I texted him saying that Joe was in the dining room. Aaron pulled his phone out of his shirt pocket, and checked his message. He looked at me and raised his eyebrows.

"Why don't you take the kids out, I'll go to the cash."

In fear of Joe hearing my voice, I didn't want to speak, so I nodded my head. I took Jody by the hand, and calmly told the kids that we were going to wait outside. I took a quick peek at Joe, he was focused on his discussion with the old couple. *Had he seen me earlier?* As the kids and I made our way to the door, I saw the manager point her finger towards Joe's table, she told the waitress to refill coffee at the Westinmalins' table. *Westinmalin? That's a strange last name.* We made it outside, I was relieved that Joe was too involved with the Westinmalins to notice us leaving. *Thank goodness.*

My van was parked at Main Street, a few blocks away. We headed straight there, I wanted to be far out of sight incase Joe left the diner. The kids and I waited in the van for Aaron, his truck was not far from mine. Aaron was taking a long time, I hoped he hadn't run into Joe, especially after their confrontation that morning. Five minutes had passed, and still no Aaron. *There must be someone ahead of him at the cash.* Ten minutes had passed, I started to worry. I told the kids to play a DVD while we were waiting. I texted Aaron to find out if everything was alright, he didn't respond. My mind was driving me crazy, thinking of the possible scenarios of where Aaron could be, so I told the kids to lock the van door, and I'd go check on him. I cautiously strode back to the diner, and hid behind a parked car that gave me a clear view of the diner. The curly red-haired girl walked out with her girlfriends, and right behind them was Aaron. I was relieved to see him until Joe stepped out behind him. Nerves rattled my body, as I crouched in position. Joe reached forward and placed his hand on top of Aaron's shoulder, as to stop him from leaving. Aaron turned to face Joe, and removed Joe's hand from his shoulder. I saw the two of them conversing, but I didn't hear what they said. Joe pointed his finger, and moved in closer to Aaron. Aaron stood straight up, his chest puffed up. Joe looked furious, he made sharp, fast arm movements. Aaron's arms rested at his sides, his hands clenched to form a fist. A few more words were exchanged, and Joe stormed off. After Joe was out of sight, I watched as Aaron stood near the steps and looked downward, he removed his cap and stroked the top of his head twice before putting it back on. He looked almost sad, or worried. I wasn't sure what to do, so I inconspicuously headed for the van. Halfway there, I looked back at Aaron, he had his hands tucked inside his pants pockets, and started towards Main Street.

Aaron came to my window, as I put it down. He smiled as if nothing had happened between him and Joe. I asked him what took so long, he said it was nothing for me to worry about. I didn't quiz him because I didn't want the kids to become aware that something might be wrong.

At home, I had the kids each take a shower, even though it was past their bedtime. I knew they'd be tired for school the next day after their eventful weekend, but I wasn't about to send them to school dirty.

After I climbed into bed, I told myself I wouldn't think anymore tonight about what I saw at the diner, otherwise I wouldn't get much sleep. Joe hadn't returned from town, or wherever he went. I was glad he wasn't home, I was too tired to argue with him. Aaron sent me a text asking me if I was home and settled. I text him back saying I was, and thanked him for the evening. He said it was his pleasure. I wanted to ask him details about him and Joe, but then he'd know that I had seen them, and I wasn't sure how that would go off. Aaron texted me back saying, "Goodnight, Sunshine, xoxoxo."

"Goodnight, Captain."

I was almost asleep, when I heard Joe obtrusively enter our bedroom. His feet pounded on the floor as he made his way to the bed. My senses heightened, not being entirely sure if he had seen Aaron and me together at the diner or not. He breathed deeply as he sat on the edge of the bed, he clicked on his table lamp. I opened my eyes a crack to see what he was doing. He sat there, his back away from me, staring at the wall. I stayed still, so he'd think I was asleep.

"Magnolia?"

My stomach turned in circles when he spoke, I didn't want to answer him, instead I grunted with a question, my eyes remained shut.

"Magnolia, I want to talk to you." His voice was calm and quiet.

I opened my eyes, and saw he had turned on an angle to face me. "What about?"

I figured that the moment had come where I'd have to explain what was going on between Aaron and I, my jittery nerves had worked their way through my body, I hoped he couldn't hear it in my voice. Joe began talking, he said he wanted to apologize to me for the way he had been treating me for the past while. He said he's been under a lot of pressure with the last couple of cases he was working on, and he could tell that I wasn't as happy as I used to be. I was speechless, unable to grasp the idea of him apologizing, 'Sorry' was not a word in his vocabulary. *Was it true that he'd seen me with Aaron tonight? Did it agitate his sparkling ego? Maybe it was enough to make him think that he might lose his family. Did he expect me to say that I'd forgive him, and we'd pick up where we left off years ago?*

"Where is this coming from Joe?"

"I've been thinking, and I'd like things back to the way we used to be."

I was so mad at him, how dare he tell me that? "What kind of things?"

"I'd like to see my family happy again, and us spending more time together."

No way he's getting off that easily.

"You said the other day you weren't interested in doing that. What has changed?"

The muscles in Joe's jaw clenched tightly together, he appeared frustrated with me questioning him.

"Magnolia, I'm looking to the future, and I want things to be better."

I was having a hard time accepting what he was saying. I couldn't even look at him, instead I focused on the rainbow of colors in my crocheted blanket that hung over the back of my rocking chair at the end of the bed. *I don't know how we'd ever get back what we had, or even if I want it anymore?* My feelings for Joe were off, and it sickened me to think of turning them back on because of my love for Aaron. *I love Aaron.* What I felt for him didn't compare to anything I'd ever felt for anyone. I didn't want to tell Joe that I didn't love him, those words seemed too harsh, instead I told him things were fine the way they were, and nothing needed to change. *I'm not going to pretend that I want things to change between us for his benefit.* I knew Joe wouldn't be capable of change, he'd been too nasty for too long. However, if it was possible for a miracle to happen, I'd have to give up Aaron. *I can't lose him. I want him.*

Joe looked puzzled, as if he was wondering why I wasn't instantly accepting his request to make up.

"I'm tired, Joe. We can discuss this tomorrow night." I had nothing more to say to him. *He is crazy if he thinks that my affection can be gained back at the snap of his fingers.*

The buzz of my alarm clock screeched in my ears as I stretched my hand out to feel around for the off button without opening my eyes. Finally I found it, and tucked my arm back under the covers for an extra five minutes rest. My head pounded from a lack of sleep, caused from everything Joe had said before bed, to seeing Joe and Aaron outside the diner. I rubbed my eyes and massaged my head to relieve some of the stress. I heard my bedroom door open, and the twins were there holding a breakfast tray, Joe stood behind them. *What the hell was this?* Jonah placed the tray on my lap, and Jody said,

"Good morning, Mommy."

I tried to smile, as I saw toast and jam on a plate, cheese, a bowl of grapes and strawberries, coffee, and a glass of orange juice. My voice cracked, "Thanks, guys. This is so sweet."

Joe sat on the bed bedside me and lifted the tray, so I could sit up. Jody hopped up on the other side of the bed and placed a pillow behind my back for support. Jonah handed me the toast.

"What's the special occasion?" I said.

"No occasion, it's just something for my special lady," said Joe.

His special lady? The breakfast in bed deal was unnatural and foreign to me, knowing that Joe was involved. *Why was he doing this? He said last night he wanted to make things better, but this behavior is peculiar.*

"Are you going into work late?" I said.

"I've decided to work from home today."

I took a bite of toast, "Okay."

"I was thinking I could pick you up from the salon today, and we'd go out for lunch."

I tried to swallow the bite of toast but my mouth had become terribly dry after his comment, I reached for the orange juice and chugged it down with the toast. *No way.*

"I can't. Lucy and I are overbooked today. I won't have any extra time."

The conversation was making me feel nauseous, Joe looked away from me and down at the floor. *Disappointed? Why? I was certain that he wouldn't be heartbroken.*

"Thanks for breakfast, but if I don't get up, we are all going to be late." I hugged Jody, and Jonah, they squeezed back, and both placed kisses on my cheeks. Joe took the tray and said,

"See you downstairs."

I nodded, as they left my room.

Joe and I waved bye to the twins as the bus drove off. *Weird.* Had anyone been paying attention, we'd look like the perfect family with mommy and daddy both standing on the front steps waving. *How deceiving.*

Before leaving home, I checked my phone for missed texts, expecting to see one from Aaron, but there was nothing. *Hmm...strange, no 'good morning' from him.* I removed my sweater from the hanger, and sent him a text telling him to have a great day. Joe startled me as I shut the closet door, he appeared out of nowhere, to standing beside me. I turned off my phone.

"Let me help you with your sweater, sweetie."

My sweater rest over my arm, Joe took it and held it out behind me, so I could slip my arm in. I didn't feel like being touched by Joe, but I let him help me regardless. I turned to head out the front door, Joe pulled me toward him, and placed a kiss on my lips, and said, "Good bye." When Joe was out of sight, I took my sleeve and wiped the wet residue from his lips off of mine. I didn't like the feel of his cold mouth anymore. My body felt no sparks of arousal for him, I had to strain, and push my lips into a pucker when he kissed me because he was repulsive.

At work, I discovered a platter full of cinnamon rolls on the reception desk with a note from Mrs. Lauders wishing me a great day. *She's the best.* Always knowing when I needed a pick me up was her specialty. After a couple hours, my head was overwhelmed from too much thinking, the headache persisted, so I took acetaminophen. By lunch time I was exhausted, Lucy and I couldn't stop for break on account of our high volume of clients. I was in the middle of doing Mrs. Jones' roller set, and Joe walked into my salon. I did a double take towards the door, I couldn't believe my eyes. He hadn't been to visit me in years at work, I couldn't bring myself to smile at him because I really didn't want to. I motioned for him to sit in the waiting area. He quietly took a seat beside Mr. Tyson. I put Mrs. Jones under the drier, and set the timer. Mr. Tyson came and sat in my barber chair, I draped him for a cut. Joe sat quietly and leafed through a magazine. I went over to him to see what he wanted. Joe asked me if I had time to go for lunch. I reminded him that we were overbooked today and it wouldn't be possible. He didn't seem to grasp my responsibilities, and persisted I join him for twenty minutes at The Sandwich Shack. I told him I was sorry, and it was out of the question. Finally, he accepted my answer, and left, but not before placing another peck on my lips. I could feel my face curl up like a hormonal teenaged girl disgusted with life. I glanced at Lucy across the room, who was applying color to Meghan's hair. Lucy's eyes met mine in her mirror, she raised her eyebrows, as if she wondered what my sour expression was for. I pressed my lips together, and turned my head from side to side indicating that it wasn't important.

Sadly, Mr. Tyson wasn't chatty while I cut his hair, which left my mind free to review Joe's behavior. *The whole thing was strange, from the talk last night to the breakfast in bed, and now showing up to take me for lunch. Did Joe have an epiphany due to seeing Aaron and I together? Or was it simply male menopause? Either way, it's irrelevant. I don't like him anymore.*

Later that afternoon, Joe sent me a text, taking me by surprise because he never texts me. The message read, "I'm home, Sweetie, to get the kids off the bus." I wasn't sure how long his mood swing was going to last, so I decided to take advantage. I texted him back saying I'd stay after work to take inventory, and if I wasn't back for supper, there was a salad, and chicken cordon blue in the fridge that only needed to be warmed in the oven.

My last client of the day called to reschedule her appointment because she hadn't been feeling well, so rather than begin my inventory, I helped Lucy with the rest of her clients, hoping to give her a chance to go home early for a change. With the two of us working, we had the clients finished before closing time. Lucy tidied the waiting room, I removed and counted cash from the register. Lucy asked me what was up with Joe today? I told her he and I hadn't been getting along for a while, and I honestly wasn't sure why he was suddenly in a rush to fix things. Lucy thought it was sweet of him and the kids to bring me breakfast in bed, she asked me if I wanted our relationship back to the way it used to be. I couldn't give her a straight answer, so much had changed. After I filled her in on Joe's bad attitude, and the lack of attention he's been giving to the kids and me, she agreed that something seemed off about his recent behavior. She told me to hang in there, and everything would eventually figure itself out. *But would it?* I went into the back room to store the days earnings inside the safe. My stomach began to rumble from being hungry, so I gnawed on another cinnamon roll, and chugged down a bottle of apple juice from our mini fridge. I heard the bell from the front door, Lucy's silvery voice was conversing with a man. I assumed it was someone trying to sneak in last minute for a trim, until I peeked my head around the corner. I saw a man wearing blue jeans with a black and red flannel shirt, and socks on his feet. My body tingled all over in delight. It was Aaron. I tucked my head back around the corner, and kept out of sight. I took a deep breath, my heart pounded. *Lucy hasn't met Aaron. That I know of. And he's never been inside my salon.* I wanted to rush out and throw my arms around him, but I had to get my emotions in order, so Lucy wouldn't suspect anything. I took a few more breaths, and tried to be professional and walk out into the salon. Aaron turned to look at me, as usual his eyes lit up.

"Hello," I said.

"Hey, Missy," said Aaron.

I felt my eyes grow large, and my face froze. I didn't want Lucy to get the impression we were close, I hoped Aaron would pick up on my facial signal of frowning eyebrows to tone himself down a notch. I think it was too late because Lucy's face brightened, "Missy? I take it that you know each other."

I felt heat rush to my cheeks, "Yes, we met at the kids' school."

Aaron had a smirk on his face, I couldn't help but feel amused inside, knowing we had our secret.

"That's cool," said Lucy, "Maggy's never mentioned you."

"I guess I'm not that important," Aaron teased, and snapped his fingers.

Lucy threw her head back and laughed. "Funny guy, eh Mag?"

"Thinks he is," I teased back. "What brings you in today, Aaron?"

"As I told Lucy here, I'd like to get a haircut."

"You know we're closing right?"

"Really? I noticed the cars at the side, so I figured you were open late tonight. Would you like me to come back another day?"

"No, it's fine." I said.

"Mag, do you want me to stay and cut his hair while you do inventory?"

"No, it's okay Lucy. You go ahead home, you're supposed to be off early remember?"

"Thanks, see you in the morning." Lucy extended her hand out to Aaron, "Nice to meet a friend of Maggy's," she shook his hand.

"Same here," said Aaron.

After Lucy left, I locked the front door, and closed the window blinds to prevent customers from thinking that they could pop by for a haircut after hours. Aaron stood by the counter, and watched me in my environment. I walked up to him, "Are you really here for a haircut?"

He removed his hat, his hair looked clean, but unruly the way it fell in every direction.

"What do you think?" he said.

"Come on," I led him by his hand to my station and turned the chair so he could sit, I pumped it up to reach a comfortable height for me to do his cut. I placed the cape over him, and begun to spray his head with water.

"Oooh, that's cold," he said.

"You'll survive," I smiled at him in my mirror.

His hair felt soft in my fingers, as I stretched each section up to cut. Aaron said it felt as if he was getting a head massage. I told him I was a professional, and I could do all sorts of things with my hands. Aaron remained straight-faced, "So, have you ever cut anyone's hair topless before?"

I stopped cutting his hair, and roared with laughter. *I can't believe he said that.*

"I'll never tell."

"Well, if you haven't, there is always a first time for everything." He squinted his eyes, his teeth filled his smile.

I smiled, and waved my scissors in the air. "Careful, Funny Pants, I've got a sharp pair of scissors in my hand."

"I trust you, Missy."

"Are you certain? You never know what I might decide to cut off."

Aaron placed his thighs tightly together, "You wouldn't."

I stood beside him and winked at him in the mirror. "So, did you really just come for a haircut, or was there something else you wanted to talk about?"

I hoped he'd give me some info about his talk with Joe outside the diner, but he didn't mention anything. *If Joe threatened him to stay away from me, he likely wouldn't want to worry me with details. If there is anything for me to know, I'll eventually find out.* I trusted that Aaron was being genuine with me, so I decided to put it out of my mind.

"Actually, I was going to go to Meredith's house tonight for a couple hours, then I saw your van still here on my way by. I wanted to see you, and get my hair cut."

"Stalker."

It was so easy to make Aaron laugh. Every time I said the first thing that popped into my mind, he'd laugh. *I suppose I laugh at a lot of things he says too, I don't want that to ever change.*

"Are you still going to Meredith's tonight?"

"I'll give her a call later, and see if she wants me to."

Cutting Aaron's hair was easier than I figured, when I thought of cutting it before, I assumed I'd be nervous but I wasn't at all. It felt good to run my fingers through his hair because touching him made my body ignite in a sensual way. I joked with Aaron, telling him he was interrupting my inventory time, and I'd get home super-late because of him. He said,

"No point of you going home tonight, you should just come to my place."

I laughed, removed the cape from him, and gave it a shake, watching short strands of his hair fall to the floor. "You know I can't."

"It was worth a try." Aaron stood to his feet, "Thanks."

"No problem," I reached my hand upwards to brush hair off his shoulders, and asked him if he'd like a quick hair wash to get the straggler hairs off of his head.

"Sure."

He leaned back to rest his neck in the sink, I remembered straddling his legs the night of the bonfire, how amazing his hands, and mouth felt on my body. I wet his hair, and scrubbed his head with shampoo. He kept silent, my eyes kept returning to his chest, where the buttons held his shirt together. I remembered the feel of his strength, and when my skin was pressed against his skin. My insides tingled, I began to rinse the bubbles out of his hair when the water pressure from the hose shot out a burst of water, I tried to shut off the tap, it was stuck, the water kept spraying out. Startled, Aaron sprang up in the chair, forcing him out of his relaxed state. He stood, water from his head dripped down and soaked his face, I tried to turn the tap off using both hands, the pressure of the water caused the nozzle to let loose, spraying everywhere, my eyes squinted as beads hit me in the face. I reached for the nozzle but it slipped from my fingertips, drenching my sweater, Aaron then grabbed for the nozzle and in the process water splashed all over his chest. He held the nozzle firmly with his left hand, and with the strength in his right, he was able to twist off the tap. Fixed in the moment, the sound of water droplets falling into a puddle was apparent as I stared at a visibly drenched Aaron.

"Oops," I said.

He looked me straight in the eye, arms stretched out to his sides, "Only you, Missy."

Perhaps if I hadn't have neglected to drape him with a cape beforehand, he would have been protected from the splatter…*or not?*

"I'm sorry."

"Looks like you're going to need a plumber," he said.

"Do you know any?"

I grabbed some towels from the rack, and wrapped one around his head, then handed him another one to soak up the water in his shirt. After drying my face, I looked down to wipe my arms, I could see my lace bra showing through my wet sweater, but it didn't bother me, knowing Aaron could see it too. My feet sopped through the water that rest on the floor, I went to get the mop. When I came back, the sight of Aaron standing there barefooted, shirtless and towel drying himself was enough to make the mess seem insignificant. I set the mop aside, and tossed a few towels on the floor to stop the puddles from spreading any further. I picked up Aaron's wet shirt, and took him by the hand. I dimmed the lights in the salon, and led him into the back room. The foldout couch squeaked as he helped me flip it down. I spread my spare blanket on top, and met him at the foot end, we stood facing each other. My sweater was sticking to me, so I raised both arms above my head. Aaron's hands were at my waist, his fingers slid my sweater up my sides to my underarms, and over my head. I lowered my arms and he tugged at the material that clung to my wrists. He placed my sweater on top of the dryer beside the hamper, along with his wet shirt. I folded my arms and rubbed them to keep warm until Aaron placed a clean towel from the shelf around my shoulders. He stepped in close to me, and pressed his chest against mine. My body absorbed his heat and filled me with warmth, his hands rest on either side of my cheeks, guiding my face towards his. His lips felt smooth as our mouths touched, and found delight in erotic kisses. My hands held his waist, and my breaths were uncontrolled. His breaths rapidly escalated, which intensified my yearning for full-fledged stimulation. The scent of papaya shampoo mixed with Aaron's aqua cologne magnetized my attraction to him, as I rubbed my hands up and down his back, and down to his buttocks. I squeezed each side of his firm ass with both of my hands, and thrust his pelvis into mine, feeling his hard manhood protruding through his jeans. Our tongues had found each other, the taste of minty sweetness covered his tongue. He positioned his hands on my shoulders, the towel dropping to the floor, his hands sensually moved down my arms, and his lips to my neck, sucking and caressing in a gentle motion, my eyes closed, head tilted to the side, indulging in the pleasure. My hands moved again to rub the soft skin on his back, his experienced fingers toyed with my nipples until his right thumb followed the edge of my bra to unfasten the clasp at the back. My breasts had fallen, and he slid the straps downwards to my elbows, I conveniently let them slide down to my wrists, and gravity took care of the rest. He stood back a moment and examined me, eyes filled with lust. He placed his left hand around my back, and he leaned forward and downward on an angle, so his mouth could taste my right breast. He encircled me with his tongue, and grazed his lips all over my fronts. I whined as I hadn't felt invited pleasure for so long. My fingers explored the button on his pants, and with concentration I was able to unfasten and unzip them, with gentle tugs, I was able to shimmy them down to his knees. While he bent down to step out of them, I unfastened my pants, and quickly slipped them off along with my socks, tossing them aside. I stood in my lacey turquoise panties, him in his red boxers. He faced me and rubbed his hands over my ass, and up and down the back of my thighs. I reached inside his boxers, and stroked his erection. He felt harder than I anticipated, there wasn't a trace of hair. He slipped his fingers inside my panties, and thoroughly massaged my womanhood as I spread my legs. I wrapped my left hand around his back and pulled him close enough to rest my head on his shoulder. He and I indulged in each other, both groaning in unison. He pushed my panties down using both of his hands, and I removed his boxers instantaneously. We stood together, naked and inseparable. His boner pressed against my bare pelvis, validating the inevitable gratification to follow. With both of his arms wrapped around me, he lifted me straight up so my breasts reached his chin, naturally, I lifted my legs and wrapped them around his waist. He held me up under my bottom, and rocked me from side to side. "I want to have you," I whispered into his ear.

He squeezed my body, and said, "I'm yours." He carried me to the side of the bed, and leaned down to lay me horizontally, I stretched my arms back to lighten my weight for him as he sat me down. I lay flat on my back, and watched him climb onto the bed. His entire body was well-toned, I saw square indentations that revealed his abs, and green veins bulged in his forearm. His left biceps flexed as he supported his weight, and cautiously placed his body tightly beside mine. I turned onto my right side to face him, and lifted my head to rest it on my right hand. My body was comfortably warm against his, and I ran my fingers through his hair, still damp from the washing. I studied his face, he had a serious yet sincere look about him, his pupils were dilated, and the blue had deepened in color, his face looked youthful because it was free from wrinkles. His lips were thick and perfectly pink. Our lips were drawn together, and without hesitation, he followed my lead. I pulled him on top of me, my arms around his back, my legs apart. He sat up on his knees, and dampened his thumb and fore finger with his own saliva, then proceeded to fondle my genitals. I closed my eyes and accepted his generosity, my entire body was consumed with bliss as he precisely drove his finger inside of me, over and over. My inner temperature had risen, my breathing became heavier by the second until he removed his finger and massaged my lady part faster and faster. I reached for his cock to stimulate him. He was already hard. I stroked him until I heard his moan. The pleasure he gave me was surreal, my body tightened, and I held my breath until I couldn't bare it any longer. I opened my mouth and expelled a loud cry. My body had intensely released from the touch of his fingers. I filled my lungs with fresh air, and opened my eyes. My heart rate was rapid. I sat up enough to pull him towards me, and I laid back down, my hand again reached down for his cock, and I placed his head on my opening. He slid his fullness inside of me with ease, his length filled my depth. He tipped his head upwards and closed his eyes, as he rigorously moved in and out of me. I arched my back for ultimate satisfaction, and squeezed the back of his thighs with my hands. His groans were fierce, as were mine. The feeling was divine. Our bodies were synchronized in favorable motion. The bed creaked, but not enough to cause distraction, his pounding was hypnotic. I wrapped my legs around his waist, and enjoyed his firmness over and over, until he slowed down to a resting point. He looked me in the eye and spoke tenderly, "You are stunning."

I wasn't sure how to respond, so I placed my hands on his face and pulled his lips toward mine. He tipped his head sideways and entirely opened his mouth and pressed it on mine. I fully opened my mouth and lovingly kissed him, our chemical attraction was nothing like I've ever experienced. Total consummation of emotional bliss with Aaron, was sensational. He continued to kiss me, and move himself in and out of me again. I could feel his erection filling up every inch of my insides, my body tingled as I watched his intoxicating facial expressions as he experienced pleasure inside of me. His face was reddish in color, and his breathing was unrestrained, as I could tell he was trying to hold in his mass.

"Can I do it?" he asked.

"Yes," I whispered.

He withdrew and repositioned himself up onto his knees, together he and I elevated my legs above my head.

"Comfortable?" he asked.

I nodded my head yes, he moved in closer and I felt his width deliciously filling me. We both roared in delight as he moved in and out of me, faster and faster for minutes on end. His face was tightening and burning red, a vein in his forehead protruded under his skin. I could tell he was losing his ability to hang on, because his breathing had escalated and his eyes looked like they were in a dream world, as he gazed into mine. Finally he grunted loudly, setting his emotions free by releasing himself inside of me. His groans subsided as he relaxed and gently rest his weight on me. His heart pounded, and pressed against the backs of my legs. He closed his eyes until his breath began to slow. I maneuvered myself beneath him because my legs were losing their comfortability, he moved onto his left side, my skin unsticking from his, allowing me to lower my legs. I turned onto my side to face him, he embraced me, and held me, his lips warm as we kissed again, and again. I could feel his aura entwined with mine. My body overflowed with the sensation of satisfaction, allowing me to relax in his arms. Every inch of me, inside and out, had been soothed in a way I'd been yearning for. I rest my head on his shoulder, and enjoyed the tranquility of the moment, my arm responsive as he stroked it.

Aaron felt too comfortable, I didn't want to get up ever, but I knew I'd fall asleep if I didn't. I pulled away from him, he pulled me back. He rolled on top of me, and carefully brushed my hair away from my face. His hands felt like magic, every time he touched me, my body tingled as delicate bubbles of ginger ale fizzing in a glass. He softly rubbed his lips on mine, back and forth, leading me into a passionate kiss, he then caressed my neck, and sucked my skin. I giggled, as the tantalizing pressure he applied was tickling me, he stopped and laughed, and begun sucking again. I pushed his mouth away from my neck because I knew he'd leave a red mark, I couldn't be walking around like that at my age. I kissed him again, his erection grew against my leg. I reached down to stroke him once more. His eyes closed, as he relished in my touch. In an instant, he wield his manhood and thrust it inside of me. I yelped as I was filled with delectation. His drive was spectacular. I indulged in the pleasure. His firmness was fulfilling. Our bodies were one. I tipped my pelvis upwards to feel his every inch. He was amazing and competent. I laid under him, my hands wrapped around his biceps, I reveled in my own elation as he climaxed. He lay on top of me, I rubbed his back, and embellished the moment with soft kisses on his neck. After a few moments, I could feel him shrinking inside of me, until he slipped out.

The clock on the wall read eight-thirty. I abruptly sat up, reality clicking in, it was the twins' bed time, and I wasn't home to tuck them in. I felt a knot turning in my stomach. I had always been there to tuck them in. I knew they'd be wondering where I was.

"Aaron, I have to get up and call the kids."

"Good idea, I'll give Mrs. Finnegan a call too."

I picked the towel up off the floor, covered myself, and pulled my phone out of my pants pocket. There were two voice mail messages, the first from Jonah asking what time I was coming home, the second from Jody telling me she missed me, and she loved me. My heart strings pulled, I began to feel guilty about losing track of time, and not being home for them. I called home, the phone rang several times, no one answered. *Where are they? What if one of them had an accident and was in the hospital, or what if they drowned in the bathtub?* My mind was temporarily carried away, I called again, still no answer, so I left a message on the answering machine saying I was still at work, and I'd be home shortly to say goodnight. I felt uneasy not knowing what was going on at home, until I was distracted by Aaron standing naked beside the dryer, with his wet shirt in hand.

"Here, give that to me," I walked over to him.

I tossed his socks, shirt, and my sweater into the dryer and turned it on high. "Are you just going to stand there all naked, or are you going to put some clothes on?"

"Would you like me to stand here all naked?"

"I would, so I'll use the bathroom first, and you can stay out here, naked," I teased, then picked the rest of our clothes up off the floor, Aaron stretched out his arms, and caught his drawers when I tossed them at him.

By the time I had my body freshened up, the dryer had buzzed. My sweater felt hot as I pulled it over my head. Aaron wasn't in the backroom anymore, but the couch was folded back up, and the blanket was partially folded and placed on the arm. I took his shirt and headed out to the shampoo room. The floor was no longer filled with puddles, and there was a big pile of wet towels in the hamper. Aaron leaned over at the sink, away from me, he was fiddling with the taps, wearing only his jeans. *I could get used to a view like that.*

"Aren't you handy!"

Aaron turned to face me, "Well Missy, I've temporarily tightened your nozzle to your hose, but it's not going to last, and your taps have begun to rust around the rubbers. I can swing by tomorrow afternoon and put in new ones if you like."

"Are you sure you'll have time?"

"I'd always have time for you."

I handed Aaron his shirt.

"Are you trying to get rid of me?" He put his left arm into his shirt sleeve. I helped him put his right arm in, and I stepped inwards to fasten up his buttons.

"Never," I said.

We embraced each other, he rocked me back and forth, our heads tucked in close to each other's necks. My feelings for him ran deep, but I couldn't let the words out, not yet. I couldn't tell him I'd fallen in love with him. I knew his feelings for me were strong, based on the look of completeness all over his face. Our chemistry was dynamite. *Could he truly love me?*

"Well, Sunshine, how much do I owe you?"

"For what?" *Money for sex?*

"The haircut, Silly."

"Right…the haircut." I held out my hand, "Eighteen dollars please."

Aaron pulled out some soggy bills from his front pocket, and handed me a twenty. "Keep the change, Mam."

"Well, thank you, Sir." I tucked it inside my pants pocket.

My scissor clock read ten minutes past nine. *Had the twins received my telephone message?* I had the urge to be home.

"Everything alright?"

"With you…perfect. It's just late, and we both should be home with our children."

"Okay Boss. Have all of your things?" Aaron took my hand and led me to the front door.

"I'd rather, we leave separately."

"Are you ashamed of me?" he smiled.

"Completely." I looked him in the eye and like a child, stuck my tongue out at him. Aaron immediately placed his lips on mine to kiss me, he entwined his tongue around mine, as I followed his lead. He then quickly placed his lips around my tongue and he sucked the end, toying with me, as if he was trying to catch my tongue as revenge for sticking it out at him. I pulled back from him, laughing, as was he.

"You'll never catch it," I said.

"We'll see, Missy."

"Okay Mr. Out." I smiled, and pointed to the door.

"Have a safe drive home," he said.

"See you tomorrow, Captain."

After Aaron left, I locked the front door, and took a look around the salon to make sure everything was good for morning. I tossed the wet towels in the washer, and left the lid open, so they wouldn't mold in there overnight. I couldn't believe what just happened between Aaron and me. My body shivered when I replayed our night over in my mind. His body was opposite of Joe's, his frame was larger and stronger, he was warm and gentle. His body responded exactly how I needed him to, unlike Joe who always delayed my affection. Every time I touched him, he returned my affection with an even larger gesture than I had given to him. I don't think Aaron realized how much our evening had meant to me. The last time I felt desire that strong was in my teenaged years, maybe this time it was my pre-menopausal hormones starting to kick in, or maybe it was that I had been lacking proper affection for so long that my body was starving an agonizing deprivation. It could easily be any of those things, but I preferred to believe Aaron is the man I've been missing my entire life, the man buried inside my head who I thought could never exist, yet here he was in my life, my perfect match. My body felt fantastic, my spirit and flesh revived, except for the guilt of not being home with my children.

Chapter 10

The first thing I did when I got home, was go directly to the twins' rooms. They both were fast asleep, I couldn't help but try to wake them to let them know I was home. I said Jonah's name a few times over, he didn't respond. He had a faint snore, his lips hung open. I laid my head down on his chest and placed my arms along his sides. I rocked back and forth trying to wake him. He jarred a little, I sat up and started to kiss him several times on his cheek, and told him goodnight. Finally, he opened his eyes a sliver, and smiled.

"Mommy?" His voice crackled, his eyes closed again.

"Goodnight, Jonah." I squeezed him, gave him one last kiss, and placed my cheek on his lips, and he kissed me. "I love you."

"I love you, Mommy."

I sat on the side of his bed and watched his eyes fall back into a deep sleep. He looked so innocent, completely unaware of what I had done. Regardless of how I felt about his father, he and Jody would always be the light of my life, I knew our bond would never be broken.

Jody was easier to wake than her brother, all I had to do was tickle her chin and say, "Goodnight. Jody," and her eyes sprung open, she smiled like an angel, and stretched out her arms to wrap them around me. I kissed her on the cheek, and told her I loved her. She said, "Mommy, I missed you."

"I missed you too, sweetheart. See you in the morning." I couldn't bare to remove my arms from her. I wanted her to feel my presence, and know how much I loved her, I stayed close to her until she fell back to sleep. I went to the washroom to wash my hands, and to take a quick look in the mirror. My facial makeup was lighter than usual, but not enough for Joe to take note of if he was still awake. Turning around in the full length mirror, I checked my body over to see if I could notice any visible differences after being with Aaron, but again, no differences reflected back. The only thing different was how I felt on the inside. Amazing.

On my way downstairs, I could hear the television blaring, along with Joe's snores echoing from the living room. I didn't bother to look in at him, I went straight to the kitchen to get a quick bite to eat. In the fridge, the chicken cordon blue remained on the tray, and there was a half-eaten hotdog left, uncovered on a salad plate. I didn't feel like having a full course meal, instead I made myself a fruit salad of kiwi, apples, and cantaloupe. The cantaloupe tasted a little tart, so I added a teaspoon of sugar. Mrs. Lauders used to say, "A little sugar never hurt anyone." I took my bowl of fruit into the breakfast room, and sat where I could be alone to get my thoughts in order. I smelled my arms, and my sweater to see if I could pick up any trace of Aaron's scent, but I couldn't. I wanted a whiff of him just for a moment, but that'd have to wait until tomorrow afternoon. The kiwi was sweet, and my apple was juicy, before I realized, I had every morsel cleaned up. I stared outside from my bar stool at the darkness, only a few lights shone from inside the homes of our neighbors, same as every night. Everything seemed to be the same—quiet, and normal. Occasionally I'd see an image of someone walking past their window, going from one room to the next. *I guess to them, our house seemed normal too. If anyone was keeping track tonight, the only differences they would notice is my van arriving home later than usual, they'd see a dim light shining from the window on the north side of the house, but they'd have no idea why it was on. They would have no reason to suspect that I came home late because I was fooling around with another man, perhaps they'd think I was late because I had shopping to do, or they might think I was finishing paper work in this very room.* When I was growing up, and to this very day, my dad quotes himself saying, "You never really know someone, even the people you are closest to, and even they have secrets to keep hidden." Years ago, I didn't want to believe him, instead I wanted to have faith that the people I was close to presented themselves as they truly were. Being a hairstylist has taught me that my dad was right. When a client feels close enough, they will share some of their inner most thoughts while their hair is being cut, I assume it's because of the physical contact. I know more secrets than I care to admit. Just a few months ago, my neighbor Shelley was in for a cut, she let it slip that her husband wasn't the birth father of her son. I didn't get the chance to ask her who the father was, because that was the day when I cut my knuckle with my scissors as she was telling me. Lucy had to finish cutting her hair because my finger kept bleeding though the bandage. I later suspected it was the true reason he had left her, but, per the rumors in town, it was him that cheated on her, then he abandoned them both. It's crazy how people go around carrying all of their secrets, living their lives as if they were innocent. *I am now one of those people with a secret. And I'll be the one pretending to be innocent. How could something so wrong feel so right?*

As I scrolled through my last text conversation with Aaron, a new one popped up.

"Hey, how are you?"

"Would be better if you were here."

"That can be arranged."

"Lol, I wish."

"Me too."

"You home yet?"

"Yes."

"Has he seen you yet?"

"No, I'm trying to avoid him until I get my thoughts together."

"Good thoughts, I hope."

"I'll never tell."

"I just can't get over what happened tonight."

"What do you mean, nothing happened. Ha ha."

"I mean, what you coerced me into doing."

"Lol, Mr. Funny pants."

"Lol, really though, are you okay with everything that happened tonight?"

"I am okay with it. Are you?"

"Honestly, Missy, I'm never going to forget it."

"You're not feeling guilty?"

"Nope. You?"

"Not yet."

"Good, because you have nothing to feel guilty about, trust me."

"Lol, what do you mean by that?"

"Nothing, Sunshine. I want you to know how much I enjoyed being with you tonight."

"I feel the same."

"Well Missy, morning is coming fast, I should say goodnight xoxo."

"Okay, Goodnight, Captain."...*Should I write xox, or not? I won't be able to take it back once I send it...* "XOX." *I did it.*

"xoxoxoxoxox."

The sound of glasses clanking together, grabbed my attention. I looked up from my phone towards the kitchen. It was Joe at the counter, opening a bottle of wine. I was so occupied with Aaron that I hadn't heard him until now. I sat still, hoping he wouldn't notice me, but I didn't get that lucky, he casually approached me with two glasses, three quarters filled with red wine. *What the hell is he doing?* I knew he said he wanted our relationship to improve, but his behavior was too much of a change for one day, actually it was borderline suspicious. He placed a glass on the table in front of me, then sat at the bar stool across from me. I left my glass untouched. His long fingers cupped his glass as he drew it up, swilled out his mouth, and downed one third of it. After my night with Aaron, I had a reason to celebrate with wine, but not with Joe.

"Don't feel like drinking tonight?" asked Joe.

I didn't want to look him in the eye, but I knew it was necessary if I was going to act natural.

"Thanks, but no. I've had a nasty headache all day, I need sleep." My headache was long gone, but I wanted my memories with Aaron to stay fresh in my mind. Talking with Joe would draw me away from the closeness Aaron and I had shared.

"I was hoping for us to pick up our talk from last night."

I knew he wasn't going to let me get out of that conversation because he never takes no for an answer. *Just get it out of your system, and we can both move on.*

"Okay," I said.

"I was thinking about the things you said to me the other day, and you are right." He paused to clear his throat. "We need to get back on track with each other, and become a family all over again."

Joe sipped down more of his wine. His voice was honeyed when he spoke. "I think we've lost each other, and we have to…"

I cheated on you. I cheated on him. I nodded my head and smiled as Joe rattled on, I saw his lips moving but the words were muffled, the image of Aaron circling my breasts with his tongue was present in my mind. I could almost feel my nipples getting hard thinking about it. I looked down at my breasts to check if hard bumps were pressing through my sweater, thank goodness my bra had enough padding, so Joe wouldn't be able to tell. Then I felt a quiver in my lower abdomen, visualizing my legs up and Aaron placing himself inside me. My breath was still, I acknowledged that only a couple hours had passed since I had been naked with another man. My thoughts were interrupted when the tone of Joe's voice became tight.

"Magnolia, are you listening?"

"Oh, um, I'm sorry, I'm feeling a bit off tonight."

Joe reached for my hand, my first instinct was to pull away, but I refrained from doing so. He drew my hand towards his lips, and he placed a kiss on top. *Gross.* I remembered the first time Joe kissed my hand, it was at the end our first date back in high school, after he walked me to the front door of my dads' farmhouse. Joe and I stood gazing into each other's eyes, and holding hands, he leaned in to kiss me on the lips, when dad unexpectedly opened the door. Joe pulled back from me, "Mr. Woodward," Joe gasped for air, and let go of my hands. His face turned white, as my dad bluntly told him it was time for him to go home. Dad turned his back because the telephone had rang, Joe swiftly took my hand and placed a kiss in the center before dad had the chance to see. His kiss all those years ago, seemed like a grand gesture of being romantic. He made it his mission to give me that kiss before saying goodnight, I remember thinking he was a rebel inside of a gentleman's body, and that's what sparked my interest in him. The spark was no more, his kiss was unnatural, forced, a turn off. I felt a knot in my stomach, something was off about Joe's behavior. *Certainly he didn't think that our relationship would be repaired overnight?*

"Magnolia, I really need for us to work out. You do want that too?"

I sat quietly, not making eye contact with him. I wanted to say no, but that decision required more thought on account of the twins. The only answer I could come up with was, "It would be great if we both could get what we need."

Joe picked up my glass of wine and guzzled down the entire thing. "See you upstairs." He picked up our empties with one hand and went to the kitchen. I heard him place the glasses in the sink and tread off. I'm not sure how well he liked my answer, but it was the most truthful answer that I was capable of giving. I sat a few more minutes staring outside through the window, most of the neighbors had turned off their lights. It appeared that they'd all gone to bed, perhaps snuggled up with the person they cherished most. *Unlike me, who lays alone in the same bed as the person I've grown to loathe.*

In bed, I lay on my back, Joe pressed his tepid body against mine, his scent was spice and it made me nauseous. I tried taking in slow breaths without inhaling deeply, but my nose was sensitive, a sharp pain darted across my forehead. I turned on my side away from Joe, where the air would be less potent. He threw his arm over me, my body tensed and I wanted to escape him, but I was already at the edge. I did not want his body touching mine. I wanted to close my eyes and recap the feelings of Aaron's body fondling mine.

"Magnolia, I'll go to Kylie's wedding with you."

"What do you mean?" *What??*

"She is my sister, and I think we should go as you mentioned."

"Are you sure?"

"I meant it when I said I needed our relationship back, and I think going to the wedding would make you happy."

I heard sincerity in his voice, unlike the blarney tone he used downstairs. *Could he be telling me the truth? Did he really want to make me happy again?*

"Ya, um, okay sure."

Again, I wasn't sure how to answer him. I was confused with his sudden shift in attitude, it was without warning for him to show interest in my feelings. I wanted to know what he said to Aaron the other night outside the diner. *Could that have been the reason for his change of heart?* I couldn't ask him without the fear of him finding out about Aaron and me. A few months back I would have loved to hear him say those words to me, starting over fresh and receiving love from him as he used to give it, would have filled me up for a lifetime, but he waited too long, too much has changed. The natural love that Aaron showed me, has filled the void that was subconsciously missing and buried below my surface. *I am different now because of him. I don't know how Joe will ever compete with that if he truly wishes to win back my heart?*

Joe's nightly snoring routine had begun, which meant he was completely out of it. I removed his arm from my waist, and slid out from under the covers, to open the window with hopes of ventilating the room from his appalling stench.

I felt Joe's dry lips plant a kiss on mine first thing in the morning, and he said goodbye. My senses weren't fully awake, but awake enough to smell the reek of his morning jungle breath. I wiped my mouth as soon as he left the room and rolled over into the middle of the bed, keeping my eyes closed. The room was fresh because of the breeze from the open window. However, it was a tad chilly, I dragged myself up to close it, then snuggled under my blankets once more to warm up. Aaron's face appeared in my mind. *I'd love to wake up surrounded in his arms.* I pulled the sheets tighter around me, imagining them to be Aaron. From that moment, I couldn't turn off my thoughts, I started to feel aroused remembering how long his erection lasted, and how hard it was. If he were here, I'd have him in a split second. I couldn't fall back to sleep, then I remembered the wet towels in the washing machine at the salon, and how Aaron would be fixing my taps in the afternoon. It was no use in trying to sleep, I rose making an early start to the day.

I ran the brush through my hair, and found delight in thinking of Aaron sweeping my shorter strands away from my face to kiss my neck. Looking in the mirror, I ran my fingers delicately over the spot where Aaron would have left a hicky, had I allowed him. I stared into my own eyes and saw a light, a twinkle of happiness, my body was fixed from the aftermath of complete emotional and physical satisfaction. I felt remarkable until Joe's apology popped into mind, I didn't want negative feelings disrupting my morning, so I pushed all thoughts of him away by deciding to text Aaron, since I knew he'd be awake by now.

"Good morning, Handsome."

"Good morning, Beautiful. How was your sleep?"

"Great. You?"

"Never better."

"Still on for this afternoon?"

"Of course, but it may be earlier because my boss gave me the day off, he has an appointment, and the job we are working on requires two people, so I've got some free time."

"Free time? I know just what to do with that."

"What?"

"You can sneak into my back room. I can have my way with you all morning. Then, you can fix my taps."

"Lmao. Now we're talking."

"Lol."

"Actually, you need a new set of taps all together. I'll have to pick up a set for you, if you want them installed today."

"You would do that?"

"Anything for you, Missy."

"If it's not out of your way, I'd really appreciate it."

"It's settled then. I'll meet you in the back room before I install your taps."

"Lol. It's a date."

"See you later, Sunshine."

The twins came running into my room, already dressed for school. They were full of energy with hugs and kisses for me. I asked them why they were up so early.

Jody said, "I heard your hairdryer and it woke me up."

"Daddy made us go to bed early," said Jonah.

"I'm sorry." I gave them each another kiss on the cheek. "Maybe you two would like to go out for a donut this morning before school."

Their faces looked almost as bright as Christmas morning.

"Yeah," said Jody. She clapped her hands in excitement.

Jonah clenched his fist tightly, and pulled back his arm. "Oh yeah," he said.

In town, we drove through the drive thru to order our donuts and juice. The line was crazy long, but it looked more relaxing than going inside, and standing amongst the desperate people who rushed to fulfill their caffeine addictions. Besides, it was bonus quality time for the twins and me to share any of our lingering thoughts or stories with each other. Jody, stuck out her neck, showed her teeth and started to growl, giving me an example of how a kid in her class acts every time he's upset with their teacher or classmates. She sounded like a vicious dog, and she had saliva bubbling out of her mouth. I have to admit that it did make me laugh, but I told her we shouldn't make fun of people. Finally, the little red sun fire ahead of us zoomed up, enough for me to place our order. Jody wanted a maple dip, Jonah wanted strawberry vanilla, and I was having a sour cream glazed donut. *Nothing like a sugar rush to start your day off.* I insisted that we all get an orange juice. At least that would be healthy.

A young girl with brown hair pulled up into a bun, thick black eyelashes, and had the name tag Jen, said, "Good morning," and took our money at the window. The smell of coffee and sweet bread whiffed out her window and into mine. She returned my change and ripped me off ten cents, I stayed quiet, she already had closed her cash register, and I didn't want to hold up the line. She handed us our juice on a tray and our donuts in a white bag. I told her thanks, and have a nice day.

I parked to the side of the parking lot, out of the way for main traffic, and handed the kids their treats. The sweetness hit my tongue as I indulged in the first bite of my donut. It was scrumptious, as I hadn't eaten one for months.

"Is that Daddy?" said Jonah.

"Where?" I looked out my window.

"Standing by that black car." He pointed out his window towards the other side of the lot. A medium-sized man, with dark hair, and a thin black jacket stood with his back to us. He handed a manila envelope to the man inside the car. They exchanged a few words, and the man turned to walk away. He wore sunglasses.

"Yes, it's Daddy. I wonder what he's doing here," I said.

"Maybe he's hungry for donuts too," said Jody.

"Maybe, sweetheart."

I watched Joe walk to his car. He looked like a gangster wannabe with those dark sunglasses on; his collar flipped up, and his left shoulder twitched forward when he walked. He got into his car and drove off. The man in the black car sat still, possibly taking a look at whatever was inside the envelope. I was finished eating, and told the kids it was time to go. I drove the long way around the parking lot, hoping to get a better view of the man in the black car. I let a few cars go ahead of me, hoping I'd get to stop in front of him. As I approached his car, the traffic slowed before turning the corner. I caught a glimpse of him, whitish hair, square-looking face. He looked familiar, then I saw a lady in the passenger seat. Her hair was shoulder length, parted, and swept to the right. My insides clenched, it's the Westin somethings. *What was their last name? Westin what? The couple I saw Joe with the other night at the diner.* I stopped to stare at them until a honk echoed in my ears. In my side mirror, the reflection of a lady in the car behind me waved her arm out her window at me, as if to tell me to hurry up. The kids told me she was being rude for honking at us. I told them it was my fault because I was holding up the traffic. I sped up and got out of there.

On the way to school, I tried remembering that couple's name, but it wouldn't come to me. It was strange that Joe was meeting with them again. *First was the diner, and now the donut shop, who knows how many other places he's met them? Why was he not meeting them in his office?* I told the kids to not mention anything to daddy or anyone at school about us seeing him, also that he might be working on an important case for work, and he might not want anyone to know what he was doing. The twins were fine with that, and promised not to say anything.

I dropped the twins off behind the row of busses. Bunches of school kids were off-loading at the sidewalk. I watched a few kids run over to my kids to greet them, Landon being one of them. He was the spitting image of Aaron, just a mini version. *I slept with his father. No one at school would ever suspect a thing. It's our secret.* Mrs. Allen, the principal, waved to me, as she walked past my van. I've always gotten along with her. *What would she think of me if she found out? What would I say if she or anyone else confronted me about it? Either I'd deny that any of it was the truth, or I'd brave up and admit it. Then there is always the phrase, "Mind your own business".*

I arrived twenty minutes early for work. *Lucy will be surprised to see me here before her.* I went straight to the back room to start washing the towels in the machine. I took a look around the place to see if everything appeared as it normally did. I couldn't spot any differences, I guessed Lucy wouldn't either. Still, I couldn't believe what happened in that very room, less than twelve hours prior. It brought a smile to my face, and my body felt alive, as the warmth of my love for Aaron rushed through me like wild fire.

I took cash from the safe and put it in the register, turned on the radio, opened the blinds, and turned on the lights over my work station. The red light on the message machine was flashing at the desk. I pressed play, the voice of an elderly woman named Edith requested an immediate appointment for a haircut and style. After checking the schedule, I had to call Mrs. Anderson to reschedule her hair coloring, on account of the taps being only a temporary fix. This left me an opening for Edith, I called her to see if she was free that afternoon at two o'clock. Her voice was clear and precise, she said she would be pleased to come in.

I told Lucy I didn't get much of a start on inventory due to the water accident, she laughed when I explained how Aaron and I both got sprayed with water, and how the floor was filled with puddles. She said it was good that it happened to him rather than a client like Mrs. Walker. I agreed with Lucy, she would have been so disgusted, her lips would have curled up, eyebrows in a frown, and her complexion would turn beet red from the heat produced by her increase of heart rate, then she'd never return. I told Lucy that Aaron was a nice guy, has a great sense of humor, and he joked about me needing a plumber. I could feel my face lighting up when I spoke of him, I knew I needed to tone it down, or Lucy might suspect I had feelings. Lucy asked if I got a hold of someone to fix it. I told her Aaron was picking up a new set for me, and was installing them today. Her eyebrows raised, as if she was surprised at my answer. "Doesn't he work in the day time?"

"Yes, but he's off today. He's looking to make some extra cash, so he agreed to help me out."

"Sounds like a handy guy," she said.

If she only knew how handy he really was. I could feel my insides bubbling with excitement to the point that I was dying to tell Lucy all about Aaron, but I had to contain myself because I didn't want to burden her with my secret. It would have been great to share my inner feelings with her, I knew she'd understand, but the timing wasn't right.

At nine-thirty, I put Mrs. Davis under the dryer, and swept up the hair from the floor. My phone rest on my station and buzzed, so I checked it out. Aaron sent me two photos of different taps that I could choose from, along with the prices. Salon spray hose, plastic nozzle for thirty dollars, or chrome nozzle thirty-eight dollars. Professional salon faucet, plastic handle twenty-one dollars, or chrome handle twenty-seven dollars. Only fourteen bucks difference for chrome. I text him back saying, shiny and smooth things felt better, so I'd go for chrome.

He texted back, "I have something smooth and durable that you might like too."

I burst out laughing. Lucy gave me a strange look as she heard me over top of the buzzing of her clippers. I smiled at her, turned away, and text Aaron back.

"You're in luck, I just happen to love smooth and durable things, I also love firm things."

"Lol, I have something firm for you."

"Good, keep it that way until after I'm finished with you."

"Is that an order, Boss?"

"Sure is, Captain."

"See you soon."

Lucy's client reached into the pocket of his worn out jeans. He pulled out a hand full of nails, washers, coins, and pocket lint, he placed it on top of Lucy's station. Using his index finger, he sorted through it all, looking for tip money as he always did after a cut. Toothless Jake is what we called him behind his back, just Jake to his face. He was lacking his front left tooth, and both of his canines, which made a whistling noise when he spoke, and speaking is what he did most. He was as nosy as an old gossip, and had to keep updated on everything, his memory was better than that of a twenty-five year old. Lucy had her hands full, answering all of his questions. He placed two quarters, one dime, and three nickels in her hand, along with a hard candy that looked as if the wrapper was stuck to it.

"There, that'll be enough to buy you a small coffee," he said.

"Thank you, sir," said Lucy.

He then put everything back in his front pocket, except the granules of dirt that he left behind, and followed Lucy to the cash.

"Eighteen dollars, please," said Lucy.

Jake pulled out his torn black leather wallet from his back pocket, opened it, and handled a large stack of bills. He took out a few hundreds and folded them in half, and stuck them behind his license, a stack of twenties and stashed them in a different section. Then the fifties popped out, he handed one to Lucy, and the others, he put back where he first got them. Everyone in town knew he was loaded, but he was too cheap to spend money on new clothes, fixing his teeth, and leaving a decent tip. As far as a haircut, he only came in once every five months, he had said he can remember the days when a haircut only cost a dollar fifty, and today's prices were highway robbery.

"Here's your change, Jake."

"Thank you." He counted every dollar, and tucked it away with the hundreds. "Have you ladies heard any more about that young lady, Shelley, and if her child's father ever came back?"

That was months ago, I wasn't sure why he'd be hanging on to that one.

"No," said Lucy, as she checked the schedule for her next appointment.

"I've asked around town, and no one seems to know any more about it." He looked at me, as if I could give him an answer.

"I heard he left claiming she had an affair, and she sticks to her story that the husband ran out on her and the child," I said.

Even though I knew Shelley had told me the truth one day in my salon chair, that the child wasn't really that of her husband's, I didn't want her to face the scrutiny of this town, if anyone were to find out. If Shelley wanted people to know she had an affair, it was up to her to spread it around, not me.

Jake pulled out his hanker chief and gave his nose a hard blow. "I feel sorry for that boy, he's going to grow up and learn about this scandal, he'll be affected for life because of it."

I thought he was teary-eyed when I saw him wipe his eyes clean, then I remembered he had a slight allergy to my weeping fig plant that stood on the floor beside the main desk.

"Hopefully Shelley will be able to explain it to him when he's old enough, and he'll understand without any trouble," I said.

"I hope you are right," he said. "Have a good day ladies."

"See you next time," said Lucy.

Jake greeted Mr. Sanders in the doorway upon his departure.

"Come right in Mr. Sanders, I'll be right with you," said Lucy.

I nudged Mrs. Davis awake from under the hood dryer, and gave her a moment to focus after I lifted it.

"Did I fall asleep again?" she asked.

"Don't worry, it was only for a moment," I said. Actually, it was about twenty minutes since she'd dozed off, but she didn't need to know.

I removed her rollers at my station, while Lucy cut Mr. Sanders' hair. I listened to her talk about the church bake sale coming up, and how she'd be donating two dozen butter tarts, and a cheery pie. As I teased Mrs. Davis' hair, I heard the bell chime on the front door.

"You again," said Lucy.

I looked over, and saw Aaron at the reception desk. He wore his usual type of blue jeans, ball cap, and a green flannel shirt. His hair wasn't sticking out around his ears now, due to the cut I gave him. *He looks hotter every time I see him, especially now since I know what he looks like underneath all that.*

"Please excuse me a minute, Mrs. Davis."

I went over to greet Aaron. I felt my mouth forming into a smile as I said hello. When he looked at me, I saw a sparkle of love in his eyes. It made me feel pretty, and sexy at the same time. I tried to not let my feelings show for him by using minimal eye contact, and a professional tone when speaking to him instead of a delightful tone.

"You're early," I said.

"Is that okay?" He stared my body up and down as he could see through my glass counter. My body felt flushed, I was turned on, his focus was almost, as if he could have his way with me then and there on the spot, he would. I would have bet anything to be right in saying his manhood was good and firm inside of his jeans.

"Of course, no one is in the back if you want to go ahead."

"Sure. Do you want me to use the back door to bring in my tools?"

"Yes please, give me two minutes and I'll unlock it for you."

"I'll get it, Maggy," called Lucy on her way to get the broom.

"Thanks, Luce."

I ran my styling comb over Mrs. Davis' hair to smooth out any loose hairs. She asked me what repairs I was having done. I told her the taps were only holding up by a temporary fix, and I needed to get new ones installed. She wanted to know who the repair man was.

"Aaron Freeman," I said.

"He's a nice looking fellow, isn't he?" she said.

I was surprised a lady in her seventies would still notice the looks of a man, young enough to be her child or even grandchild, but then again, it was Aaron. *Who wouldn't find him attractive?*

I didn't dare look at her face in the mirror, in case she could spot any delight in my eyes, I was desperately trying to hide.

"Umm…ya…yep…he is," I said.

"I think he has a crush on you," she said.

I reached for the hairspray, and mist the tips to give her hair a finishing touch. I tried to look focused on her, and not emphasize on her last comment.

"He made eyes at you."

I had no choice but to answer her, she wasn't going to drop it.

"Oh, I don't think so, he's just a friendly guy."

"Well, say what you want." She tipped her head sideways and batted her eyelashes, as if to say that she knew better than I.

I turned her chair around to show her the reflection of the back of her hair in my hand held mirror.

"Lovely," she said, "That should hold up for the rest of the week."

Seeing a satisfied look on a client's face was fulfilling, it gave me a sense of purpose, knowing they could leave feeling better than when they came in.

I went in the back to see if Aaron needed anything.

"I've got everything but you Missy," he said.

I laughed, "Keep your voice down, people are out there."

I watched him spread out his tools on the floor, in what seemed to be in an exact organized fashion. He squat down near the sink, and took a quick look my way.

"That dress looks beautiful on you, Sunshine."

"Thank you." I had on my knee-length, flimsy black dress, with short sleeves, and little red flowers all over. It was comfortable to work in, and since Aaron was coming in, I wanted to look girlish to express how I was feeling.

I watched him roll up his sleeves to his elbows, preparing himself for the job. *His fingers were all over my body last night, I'd love him to be all over me right now. If I stand close enough to him, he could slide his fingers up my dress and fondle me without removing my panties.*

"You alright?" he asked, and began to unscrew the bolts from under the sink.

"I'm great, but I have a client waiting. See you in a bit."

136

I loved the sound of Aaron tapping, and fiddling in the back room, while I worked because it meant he was close by. We were both accomplishing things at the same time, every so often I could feel the calmness of his aura reaching me. Every client asked what was going on in the back, I had to explain the same thing to each one. Lucy had left for an extended lunch break with her niece. She put in enough hours each day. I never minded when she asked for time away. My next appointment wasn't until after lunch, he phoned to ask if it would be alright if he came in twenty minutes late. I said sure. His hair was so thin that it'd take minimal time to cut, and it would give Aaron and I some alone time. I went to the shampoo room, Aaron was seated on the floor, searching through the tap box.

"Everything okay?" I asked.

"Buggers left the washers out of the box, I can't go any further until I have some."

"Really?"

"The hardware store should carry some."

"Um…Okay. I don't want you to waste your whole day on my taps. Is there somewhere else you should be?"

Aaron grinned at me. "Yep. I'm supposed to be at your cousin Meredith's place."

"Ohhh, sorry to mess up your plans."

Aaron set the box aside and stood to his feet, he pulled me into a passionate embrace.

"Yes, you are messing up my plans."

He leaned in, tilted his head to the left, opened his mouth and kissed my lips. A warm rush ran through me, I followed his lead. Our connection was stronger than ever, had he let go of me, I would have melted onto the floor in that very spot. His lips tantalized, I wanted more, and pulled him even closer to me, absorbing every sensation. I allowed him to lead me with his hand into the back room. He placed my back against the wall. I put my hands on his shoulders and jumped up to wrap my legs around his waist. His breath increased as he held me in position, his hands groped and squeezed my thighs and ass from underneath my dress. I reached down, unbuttoned his jeans, and let the zipper down. My hand toyed with the waistband of his boxers. He sucked in his gut to allow room for my hand to slide inside. I rubbed his manhood up and down, until I saw his face becoming flushed. My fingers felt their way to the opening in his boxers, and slipped his firmness out of the hole, allowing him to be free. I removed my hand and held the edge of my panties off to the side. I took his firm head and rubbed it all around my opening until I was wet enough for him to slide himself inside. He let out a groan upon penetration. I wanted to scream as he uncontrollably thrust himself in and out of me. Instead, I took deep breaths, allowing myself to slowly exhale in quick, short intervals. I tucked my hands inside of his back pockets, clutching him and pulling him closer as I endured the pleasure. We placed our mouths together and kissed until he pulled back and tucked his neck in close to mine. He was getting ready to climax, and I heard the bell on the front door. I instantly pushed him back, his erection slide out of me, and my feet dropped to the floor. My heart was pounding. Someone had come into the salon. I wasn't going to allow them to find us back here together. Aaron quickly tucked himself back inside his jeans and zipped up. I adjusted my now damp, panties back in place, and straightened my dress. Aaron's face was flushed, I don't think he's ever seen me move that fast.

"I'm sorry, didn't mean to mess up your plans."

I shot him a wink before I dashed off to the washroom to clean my hands, I turned on the taps, and no water came out, then I clicked in that Aaron had shut off the main water line to fix the shampoo sink. I scampered to the mini fridge and grabbed a water bottle, then ran back into the washroom, squirt soap on my hands, and used the bottled water to rinse with. I dried my hands as quickly as possible, and tossed the towel in the sink. I took a swig of water and rinsed out my mouth. Aaron stood in the back room, his expression wavering, likely uncertain if he should stay hidden.

"Magnolia?" I heard my name being called.

I inhaled and exhaled to settle my jitters, as I knew there was only one person who called me by my full name. Aaron was leaning against the dryer. I mouthed the words, "It's Joe."

"Coming," I called.

I almost made it to the door, when Joe came into the back room. My body jumped as I made eye contact with him. He quickly looked away from me and studied Aaron.

"What's going on back here?" asked Joe.

My heart skipped, "I just came from the ladies room."

"Really?" said Joe. "What is he doing?" Joe stood in his grey suit with beige tie, and pointed at Aaron.

"He's installing a new set of taps for me."

"What wrong with them?" he asked.

"My spray nozzle cracked and they needed to be replaced."

"You should only have to replace the nozzle, instead of replacing them entirely."

Joe couldn't fix squat. I knew he was only adding in his two cents worth to try and intimidate Aaron. I also knew Aaron wouldn't be intimidated because he and I both had the upper hand, in knowing that Joe was clueless to the fact that the taps being fixed were in the other room.

"They were rusted out underneath. I had no choice."

I fully knew Joe wasn't able to give an educated response. This was not his field of knowledge. He quickly changed the subject.

"I believe he and I weren't properly introduced last week?" said Joe.

A sour feeling came over me, as I knew the two of them already knew each other, and Joe was trying to cover it up. I pointed to each of them and said, "Joe, this is Aaron. Aaron this is Joe."

Joe extended his hand in a professional manner to shake Aaron's hand. Aaron hesitated, then locked eyes with Joe, his jaw clenched tightly. The two of them grasped hands and exchanged one firm shake. The tension in the room was so thick that you could cut it with a knife. Neither one would speak a word. The two of them stood facing each other. Both tucked their hands into their front pockets and glared at each other. It was obvious neither was going to back down from whatever was going on between them. I spoke up and asked Joe what was the reason for him stopping by?

He turned away from Aaron and said, "Have you any time for lunch today?"

"Right now? Um, no I can't. My client will be in any minute."

I saw Aaron roll his eyes, as if he were thinking, 'What an idiot.'

"I thought you'd say that, so I brought my lovely wife a sandwich."

I could hear bogus charm in his voice, he was trying to put on airs in front of Aaron, perhaps he wanted to give Aaron the illusion that we were a happily married couple, unlike the impression he gave the other day at our house. I had to get these two out of the same room, so I headed out into the salon. The salty smell of French fries took over the place, I saw a Styrofoam container next to the candy jar on my reception desk.

"I thought you brought a sandwich?"

"It's a platter," said Joe.

I opened the container, it was a club. "Thank you."

Joe was too close to me, I felt negative energy surrounding him.

"I've got to get back to work," he said. I could feel him leaning closer to me, I knew he was going to try and kiss me, so instead of turning my head toward him, I reached for a couple fries and shoved them in my mouth. I heard Aaron in the back rattling his tools. *He must have made it back to the shampoo room."*

"They're really good." I muffled, and kept chewing, and shoving more in, so there'd be no chance of lip to lip contact. I saw him look toward the noise that Aaron was making. He then reached for a fry, took a nibble from it, and looked back. Aaron's racket had stopped, I saw his silhouette at the back of the salon.

"See you this evening," said Joe. He slapped me on the ass with the palm of his hand, and left.

I was hoping Aaron hadn't seen that, Joe was only doing it for show, and I didn't want Aaron to think I enjoyed receiving that type of affection from him.

Mr. Jones opened the door, on time for his appointment. I welcomed him in, and asked him to come and sit at my work station. I looked quickly to see if Aaron was around, I didn't see, or hear anything, his presence was missing. *I hope he's not jealous of Joe.* Mr. Jones was silent while I cut his hair, so was I. *That was a close call, almost getting caught.* I thought over everything from Aaron lifting my dress, to the feel of his erection in my hand, and Joe randomly showing up for the second day in a row. *What the hell was that about?* My mind was on overdrive until I heard Mr. Jones say,

"Ouch." I noticed a little trickle of blood seeping from his ear lobe. Immediately I placed my scissors down.

"I'm so sorry, I didn't mean to nip you. I'll get you a tissue."

After getting him cleaned up, and his haircut finished, I told him the cut was free today. He seemed quite pleased, and told me not to spend any time worrying about what happened. I thanked him for being so understanding.

Lucy had returned from lunch with a bubblier than usual attitude, meeting with her niece, always seemed to fill her with extra energy. Aaron had disappeared, and by midafternoon he hadn't returned a reply to the text that I had sent him. At two o'clock sharp, the salon door opened. In, walked an elderly woman, her hair, white shoulder-length, parted, and swept to the right. She wore a white silk blouse, and champagne-colored dress pants with a black belt, designer shoes, and handbag to match which rest on her right shoulder. I felt the color leave my face, as I studied her.

"Hello, I'm Edith."

She approached the reception desk, and I was able to recall her full name. It was the woman whom Joe had been meeting with, Edith Westinmalin.

Chapter 11

Completely caught off guard, I was at a loss for words. She had never been in my salon before.

Why now?

"Edith?"

"Yes, hello."

"You are right on time."

In dismay, I unconsciously lifted my hand, knocked over my water bottle, it poured out everywhere, saturating my desk.

"I'm sorry," I said, droplets splashed all over her blouse. I quickly grabbed handfuls of tissues from the box, to soak up the water before it ran off onto the floor. Ms. Westinmalin crinkled up her mouth in disgust.

"I'll sit in the waiting area, until you are ready?"

"That won't be necessary," I said.

I pointed her in the direction of my styling chair, "I'll be right over," I continued to soak up the water. *What did she want with me? I hoped she hadn't recognized me from the diner the other night.* Her walk was graceful, yet her face remained serious. She examined my chair carefully before cautiously sitting down, she placed her purse on her lap, and examined the surroundings. I tossed the wet tissues into the garbage can, *Get it together, Maggy.*

At my station, I apologized to her once more. Her fragrance drifted upwards, as I covered her with my cape. The scent was cool, possibly jasmine, or a similar floral essence. I asked her if she wanted a trim or a different style. She said she hadn't made up her mind, and wondered if I had any ideas. Her face shape was a perfect oval, suitable for any hairstyle. I suggested giving her layers around the bottom of her hair, or giving her bangs if she didn't mind having them cut often. She turned her head from side to side, gazing at her reflection in the mirror. As I continued to discuss more options, her eyes wandered to her fingers. She used her index finger to trace the outline of each of her pointed fingernails. It was obvious her mind was elsewhere, and she hadn't

142

been paying attention to anything I had said. I wondered what her true objective was for coming into the salon today. I stopped talking to see if she'd notice, after a few seconds she said she'd have to think about it more. She did not acknowledge me when I complimented her natural hair color, every strand a solid white without a trace of grey.

"Is everything alright?" I asked.

Without delay she responded,

"Your last name is Edwards, correct?"

I looked at her in my mirror, "Yes."

"Your husband is Joseph Edwards, correct?"

"He is. Do you know him?"

"I've met him before."

I spoke in a gentle, and friendly tone, playing dumb, hoping she wouldn't detect I already knew the answer to my question.

"You have? Nice." I giggled, falsifying my surprise. "Where did you meet him?"

"We have done business together in the past."

I ran my brush through her hair, and played with different strands to see how her face changed when I added more and less on the sides. "Business? What type of business have you done together?"

"I don't think I'll get my hair cut today, Magnolia."

Magnolia? I tried to keep up my affable front, even though she hadn't answered my question.

"Okay, no rush. Give yourself a few days to think about my suggestions. Get back to me if you like."

I removed the cape from her, and lowered her chair, making it easier for her to get up.

"Would you do me a favor, Magnolia?"

"Um, sure."

"Tell Joseph that Edith Westinmalin said hello."

"I can do that for you, Ms.Westinmalin."

She proceeded to the front door, without asking how much for her consultation instead of a cut, or saying goodbye. *I'm not stupid, I know you won't be back for a cut.* Her only motive that I could see was to talk about Joe, but why?

After Lucy's client had left, she flopped down in her own hair styling chair, as we usually did to rest our feet when the salon was empty. Lucy wanted to know why Edith changed her mind about getting her hair cut.

"I wish I could tell you Luce, but I don't know."

143

Footsteps sounded in the back, I turned to look. It was Aaron, he poked his head into the salon, he said he was able to get the washers, and would have the taps fixed shortly. He gave me a wink before turning back, *Guess he's not upset.*

When I turned to look at Lucy, she fanned her hand in front of her face, and mouthed the words, "He's hot."

I felt my eyes light up, and couldn't contain my smile any longer.

"Oooh, someone has a crush on him," said Lucy. She pointed her finger at me, and said, "Shame, shame."

I felt my face warming up, I wanted to share the truth with her in the worst way, and I almost let it slip out until she said, "If you ask me, there was something off about her."

"About who?"

"You know, Ms. Westin-whatever."

"Edith Westinmalin? I thought so too."

Lucy looked completely comfortable leaning back, legs crossed one over the other, and her foot swaying. "Maybe she was casing the place." Lucy laughed.

I knew that wouldn't have been her motive but I laughed, leave it to Lucy to think of something like that.

"Maggy?"

I heard Aaron calling my name, so I went to the shampoo room, Aaron had completed my taps. "Took you long enough," I teased.

"At least I was able to finish something today." He stressed the word 'something,' so I knew he was referring to his interrupted climax. I looked at him seductively, and lowered my voice, so Lucy wouldn't hear.

"If you're lucky, I will finish you off later."

"Is that a promise?"

"If you want it to be?"

When I arrived home after work, I saw Aaron's truck parked at Meredith's. I sent him a text telling him that I was home alone, naked, and waiting with my back arched on the kitchen table for him.

"Be there in five," said Aaron.

"Too late, bus is here."

Of course I wasn't naked, or waiting, I just wanted to tease Aaron, and let him know I was home.

"Funny, Missy."

"How long will you be at Meredith's?"

"Likely until nine or so, they won't be home for a while. I want to get as much finished as I can."

"Okay, maybe I'll see you later...maybe I won't."

"You're such a tease."

"You like it."

"Maybe."

During supper, Joe mentioned Kylie's upcoming wedding, he said we needed to start thinking of gift ideas. That threw me for a loop, Joe trying to make plans with me was too strange, almost uncomfortable. My mind wasn't anywhere close to contemplating presents. A part of me still didn't believe he'd go, *there must be an ulterior motive.* I was sure he wouldn't give in to his sister on account of me. I suggested we check her gift registry and choose an item from there. He said he wanted to find her something tasteful, and unique that wasn't on her list. He even suggested I buy a new dress. Listening to him going on and on about the wedding was peculiar, and all of his conversation was suspicious, a person doesn't change overnight, and that is exactly what he wanted to let on. I couldn't stop my nagging gut instinct that something was wrong, and I couldn't stop thinking about the visit from Ms. Westinmalin at the salon. I wanted to ask him who Ms. Westinmalin was, and why he was involved with her, the thought put me on edge. After the twins left the supper table, Joe complimented the flavor of my sesame-ginger beef stir-fry, and he asked for an extra helping. He smiled as I refilled his plate. All his smiling, and chatting, and playing Mr. Nice guy was freaking me out, so I just blurt it out,

"Ms. Westinmalin said to tell you hello."

His face turned pitch white, and he began to choke on his sip of wine.

"Are you okay?" I asked.

He nodded his head up and down, and breathed in through his mouth, then he coughed some more until he was able to say,

"I'm fine, it just went down the wrong way."

He took another sip of his wine, and another, and he cleared his throat a few times, then formed his mouth into a forced smile, "Where did you see her?"

"She came into the salon today."

I could see fury boiling up behind his fake smile. He had the steak knife in his right hand, and begun to cut his steak aggressively.

"Has she been in before?"

"No, this was a first."

I knew I'd be treading on thin water, so I gathered some dishes from the table, and placed them on the kitchen counter, giving myself distance from him.

"How do you know her?"

He hesitated a moment, "Nothing for you to worry about, did she say anything else?"

Instead of him looking in my direction, I watched him stab a piece of meat with his fork, and stir it around and around in the blob of stir-fry sauce, as he awaited my reply.

"Just the usual hair salon talk."

He placed the steak in his mouth, "Okay good."

"Good? What do you mean?"

He picked up his plate and brought it over to the counter, placed it beside me, and moved in close to me. "Nothing," he said. "I need to take care of something." He pecked my lips. *Yuck.*

I waited until he was out of sight to wipe my mouth clean from the taste of second hand sauce. His inquisitions told me he was hiding something, I needed to figure out what. As I tidied the kitchen, I ran different possibilities through my mind, it appeared they were working together on a case, or maybe documents. *If they were partners why would Joe be uncomfortable with her coming into my salon? Then again, why would she come into my salon, and decide to not have her hair done? That made no sense. What did Joe need to take care of?* I almost had myself convinced to go and spy on Joe outside of his office door when I heard the doorbell ring.

A tall baby-faced black man stood on my doorstep, holding a large arrangement of flowers.

"Delivery for Edwards," he said.

His hand brushed mine as he handed me the vase.

"Thank you, who are they from?"

"I believe there is a card attached Madame."

"Thanks again, have a nice day."

The bouquet was a stunning mixture of light and dark blue wild flowers. I placed them in the middle of the kitchen table, removed the cellophane covering, and searched for the card. It was tucked deep down near the rim. I read aloud, "Congratulations on your new addition to the family". I didn't recognize the handwriting. I read the card again, there was nothing indicating who the flowers were from, except the name of the florist, Beautiful Bouquets. *What knew addition? There must be a mistake.*

I phoned Beautiful Bouquets to let them know there may have been a mistake, and the arrangement must have belonged to someone else. The man on the phone asked if I lived at the Edwards household on Belle Street, Laudersville. I told him yes, he assured me there was no mistake. I asked him who they were from, he said it was confidential. The only person I could think of to send flowers was Mrs. Lauders, but packaged food was more of her forte. *Aaron could have sent them, he wouldn't be bold enough to send them to my house.* The message alone was a mystery, 'Congratulations on your new addition to the family'. *The last time I checked we weren't getting any pets, and I'm certainly not pregnant. Aaron told me a while back he had a vasectomy, and the last time I did it with Joe was at the end of my cycle.*

Joe came into the kitchen, eyes fixed on the bouquet. "Where did those come from?"

"I'm not sure, maybe Mrs. Lauders?"

I handed him the card, his face turned from pink to red, as if his emotions were bubbling under his skin, as he read the note.

"Do you have any idea who would send them?"

"Not really," His jaw tightened.

"What do you think the note means?"

He placed the card on the table, and said nothing. I believed Joe knew a lot more than he let on, unless my mind had played tricks on me. *What if the bouquet was from Aaron, and he sent the bizarre note as a cover up?* Joe took the pile of mail from the counter and strode off down the hall. I sent Aaron a text asking him if he had sent flowers, he didn't respond. *He must be working at Meredith's, and hasn't had a chance to check his phone.* It was almost eight. I took a quick peek out the window and saw Aaron's truck still there, but no sign of Meredith's car. I figured he hadn't eaten any supper, so I planned to walk over later to give him some left over stir-fry.

The twins read in their rooms before bed, I quickly brushed my teeth, took a quick shower, and changed into a pair of workout pants and top. If any of the neighbors saw me out their windows, it would look as if I was innocently out for a walk.

By the time I had tucked the twins in bed, I'd still heard nothing from Aaron, which made me curious. Joe's office light was on, I had the urge to eardrop at his door, but I wanted to see Aaron more. I didn't want Joe getting all nosy about where I was going, so instead of telling him I was leaving, I scribbled a note saying that I had gone out for a bit.

I put on my runners and a light sweater, then tried to squeeze a container of stir-fry inside my fanny pack, the zipper wouldn't close, so I pulled my sweater over top to hide it.

Outside, I saw my neighbor Shelley pull into her driveway, I ducked down beside my globe cedar, to keep hidden. *I don't need her spying on me tonight.* I saw her carry her son inside, after her front door was closed, I continued on my way. The neighborhood was quiet, except for the hockey game, which echoed from an open window at the Thomson place. I could smell fresh roses in front of Mrs. Morris' place, and the lawn ornaments clattered in the breeze, past the Bailey's house. I kept my eyes open to see if I could spot anyone peeking out their windows, anyone who might see me go into Meredith's driveway. I decided to walk along her hedge so the motion light wouldn't turn on, and go around to her back deck. I heard some crackling in the back yard similar to twigs being stepped on. *Was someone there?* I stopped at the side of the house to peek around the corner, I couldn't see well enough, I inched closer and squat near the lattice work around the bottom of her deck, I couldn't see anything unusual, but the crackling was still there. I focused, then saw a dark shadow of something, or someone. I tucked my head back, hoping I hadn't been spotted by whatever it was. I waited and listened, everything went quiet. I tried to think of every possibility of what could make that noise, and since Meredith and Peter weren't home, I highly doubted if one of the neighbor's would be strolling through their back yard. I decided that it had to be a raccoon, or skunk. I waited a few more minutes in silence because I didn't want to get sprayed, or attacked for my stir-fry. Slowly I stood and looked around the corner once more, everything seemed safe, I stepped out, something rustled in the grass, the shadow was back, and it was moving quickly towards me. Not sure if I should run or hide, it was too late, I fell to the ground, flat on my back from the impact of being pounced on. I let out a yelp, large paws danced around my shoulders, the smell of dog breath filled my nostrils as I turned my head from side to side, trying to escape a tongue bath.

"Rory stop," I said. I tried to get up, Rory barked now standing in one spot, wagging his tail, as I brushed loose grass from my clothes. I reached down to scratch him on his side and laughed at him, he sniffed my bottom half, thank goodness that the lid hadn't come off of my stir fry.

"Come on, fellow."

I lead him up the stairs to the deck, and knocked on the glass door. Rory stuck his nose all over it trying to get in, Aaron wasn't coming, so I slid open the door and stepped inside. I heard the skill saw running, the smell of pine was in the air. Aaron must not have heard me, over top of the noise. I set the stir-fry container on top of the counter, and drew the blinds, so the neighbors couldn't see in. Rory flopped down on his bed, and chewed on his favorite bone. I gave him one last scratch on his head before I followed the zinging noise of the saw. Getting closer, I plugged my ears as the noise was too overbearing. Aaron had his back to me, saw in hand, as he leaned over to cut a piece of plywood supported by two saw tables. His ass looked fantastic in blue jeans, *especially bent over like that.* I decided to stay put, and see how long it would take him to notice me behind him. He set the piece aside, reached for another, and began measuring. The renovation seemed to be coming along well, he had removed the wall, and shelves to the walk in cupboard, and he'd begun building a new wall dividing the room into two separate ones. The old carpet had been ripped out, and it looked like he had put down new plywood on the floor. Aaron was completely focused on his job, I stepped in closer to him without saying a word, still he didn't notice, so I gave him a good hard slap on his ass.

"Oh," he sounded surprised as his body jolted forward. He turned back to face me, "You, Missy." He removed his safety glasses and ear protectors, and came at me with arms wide open, he turned me away from him, bent me over, and began tickling my sides. I laughed and laughed.

"That'll get you back," he teased.

"Stop, stop," I pleaded with him.

He turned me back to face him, and planted a kiss on my lips.

"Took you long enough to get here."

"I wanted to surprise you."

"You did a good job, I'm surprised."

"What time are Meredith and Peter due back?"

"They're away overnight on business. They said I could stay and work as late as I wanted."

"Cool. Did you eat supper?"

"Not yet."

"Hungry?"

"A little."

"I brought something for you."

Aaron brushed the saw dust off his clothes,

"That was sweet of you."

"Of course it was," I smirked at him, "Now go and get washed up, and I'll meet you in the kitchen."

I warmed up the stir-fry, and used one of Meredith's plates to serve it on, along with a slice of fresh bread from the cupboard. I filled his glass with fruit punch, just in time to see Aaron enter the kitchen shirtless, his hair was wet, and he smelled of vanilla.

"Did you just take a shower?"

"Meredith said I could make myself at home, so I did," he winked.

I set his plate on the table, he went over to the patio door and placed his dirty clothes inside his bag, then pulled out a red t-shirt and put it on.

"I didn't mind your shirt off," I teased.

"I didn't think you'd be able to concentrate if I left it off."

His eyes lit up as he looked at his supper plate, I poured myself a glass of juice, and sat across the table from him. He cut a morsel of steak in half, and placed it inside his mouth.

"This is delicious," he said.

"Thank you, I wasn't sure what type of food you liked, except for hotdogs."

"I'll eat anything with meat, but this is really incredible. Do you always cook this good?"

"Maybe I'll cook for you another time, and you can let me know."

"Is that a promise?"

"Maybe."

That was the first time Aaron had sampled any of my cooking, I was pleased to watch him savor every bite, unlike Joe who kept a sour expression no matter what I served. I was uneasy to ask Aaron if he'd sent the flowers, or not. If he hadn't, he might feel as if I expected him to, but I needed to know for sure.

"I can't stay here too long, no one knows I'm gone."

Aaron chuckled, "So you sneaked out of the house?"

It sounded bad, almost elementary, but it was true.

"Yep, you should feel special. I don't sneak out of my home to see just anyone you know."

Aaron took his piece of bread and soaked up the remaining sauce from his plate.

"You'll never guess what I received this evening?"

"Umm, you've got in the mood to put on a sexy pair of panties, and you are wearing them right now," he teased.

I laughed and shook my head, he raised his eyebrows up and down.

"Well, maybe I do, but that's not what I was referring to."

"I'm sorry, Missy, what did you get?"

I hesitated to choose the proper wording,

"A big bouquet of flowers were delivered to my door tonight."

"Nice. Who from?"

"That's the thing, I'm not sure."

"There wasn't a card?"

"Yes, but there was no name on it, just a strange note that said, 'Congratulations on your new addition to the family'."

"Weird, maybe it was delivered to the wrong door."

"I thought that too, so I phoned the florist, he said it was delivered to the correct address, and he wouldn't tell me who sent them."

"You're right Missy, it is strange. Maybe just wait it out, and someone will eventually come forward. Are they nice?"

"Beautiful."

"You might as well enjoy them, after all you do deserve beautiful things."

"Have I mentioned, you are the sweetest ever?"

"You may have said that before…speaking of which…have you given any thought into moving in with me?"

"Of course I have, but things aren't as simple as that."

"They can be if you want them to be."

"Aaron, we need to think of the kids, and the fact that I'm older than you. Would you still want to be with me when I'm fifty-four, and you are forty-six? That is a big difference at that age."

"Missy, it's not about the age difference, it's about how well our personalities click, and how much love we feel for each other. It's about having similar goals, and interests to keep things alive, we have all of those things."

"You make it sound so simple and perfect."

Aaron came over to my side of the table, and pulled up a chair beside mine. He placed my hand inside of his.

"Missy, you are perfect for me, and I want to spend my life with you."

I could feel my eyes starting to tear up, as he hit my most sensitive nerve. Hearing him speak the exact words I've been feeling, was overwhelming. He was right, we were a perfect match.

"Aaron, everything you said is the truth, but I need more time to figure myself out."

"Are you still in love with Joe, is this why you are hesitant?"

"The only thing I feel for Joe is obligation. I've already broken my vows to him, which I would never have done if I was truly in love with him. Honestly Aaron, I just need time to make the right decision for myself and my children."

"Missy, I will wait forever for you, if that's how long you need."

"Forever is a long time."

"You are worth it."

"How do you know that?"

"I just know."

He pulled me to my feet, and hugged me. Once again, his aura had me full to the brim. I placed my hands on his cheeks and brought my mouth to his, the smooth flow of our lips moving together had engulfed me. I was sucked into the moment, and every nerve inside my body was raging with passion. I slid my hands down his shoulders, and then to his arms to meet his hands, placing mine overtop of his. I lead him down the hall to Meredith's spare bedroom, clicked on the dim table lamp, and closed the door behind us.

"Now Missy, are you sure we should be in here?"

"She never uses this room, and I'll wash the sheets before they get back, besides I told you earlier I'd take care of you later."

"Yes, you did."

I knew I was getting short on time, so I ordered Aaron to get undressed, I did the same.

"Bossy much?" he said.

"It's to your advantage, trust me."

I whipped open the bed sheets, and had him sit on the edge of the mattress. I leaned down to kiss him, feeling his passion is what I needed to be focused in the moment, rather than being worried about the time. He pulled me inwards, began caressing my stomach, both sides of my ribs, and up to my breasts. I stroked the top of his head, down to his neck, and around his ears. His touch was gentle, he smoothed his hands around to my back, and turned his head sideways to rest his cheek on my stomach. He embraced my body and remained still, as if his body was absorbing my sexual energy. I slide his hands down to my thighs, and kneeled to the floor in between his legs. His manhood was fully erect, I stroked him with my right hand, as my tongue tickled the inside of my mouth to produce extra saliva. I leaned in toward him and dampened him before I placed him inside my mouth, he was delightfully firm as I moved back and forth on him, he reached the back of my throat, but his base was still exposed, I removed him from my mouth and ran my lips and tongue all over him, ensuring to cover every inch. His breaths were consistently taken in, and let out from his mouth instead of his nose, and were gradually increasing in volume. I placed him back inside my mouth, and my hand was at his base moving in unison with my mouth. I could feel pressure on the back of my head as his hand followed my every movement, he began to guide me indicating that he wanted more. I took him in faster, and faster until he gently pushed me back. I stood to my feet. He pulled me onto the bed to face him. We laid side by side. His hands rubbed me up, down, and around my body. He kissed me again on the mouth; his tongue gliding back and forth with mine. I rolled onto my back, and he slipped his fingers between my legs, caressing my womanhood. My eyes were closed, and my breaths were heavy and rapid, as his fingers applied a lascivious massage until I couldn't handle it anymore, every sensation in my body was centered on this innervation, driving me to a prodigious release. I opened my eyes and relaxed momentarily to catch my breath, the feeling of total euphoria filled me. Aaron moved his hand to rub my outer thigh, his eyes locked with mine, I reached down to stroke him, and when he became firm again, I sat up and told him to slide back, so his legs wouldn't be dangling off the bed. I moved on top of him to straddle him, and maneuvered my pelvis to comfortably slide down on his firmness to get a feel for how deeply I could fit him inside of me. Aaron's eyes were filled with ecstasy as he examined my body, I began to move up and down on him, gratifying both of our needs. He stretched out his hands and placed them on my hips, pulling me into a harder thrust. The feeling of his width was breathtaking, I threw my head back in rapture, and began to move faster and faster. He leaned upwards and watched our bodies consolidate, I rest my hands on his chest, and raised my pelvis, allowing my knees to support my weight, and giving me more freedom to take advantage of his length. He took my hands in his and pulled me closer so my breasts rest on his chest, he lifted his head, so his mouth would reach mine, he kissed me once more, I could feel his love consuming my soul, and in one swift movement, he swapped places with me. I laid on my back, he inched his way down to my sweet spot and twirled his tongue all over, up and down, around in circles, gentle and quick, over and over until my body tensed absorbing every sensation, until I was lead into absolute deliverance. He then placed himself inside me, my every nerve was deliciously oversensitive, which pulled me into an exhilarating state of indulgence. I placed my hands on his tight ass, as he rammed in and out, in his eyes I could see the pleasure of our bodies escalating inside of him, the vein in his forehead was visible, his face flushed, jaws tightened until he roared and gave into his inner relief. His body relaxed on top of mine, I wrapped my arms around his back, tucked my legs around his, and squeezed. I felt his heart pounding into my chest, for a few moments we laid in silence, our bodies winding down from our shared felicity. I felt as though our bond was stronger than ever, I wanted to tell him I was in love with him, but I was reluctant to do so in fear of losing him. A part of me wanted to hear those words come out of his mouth before mine, then I'd be sure he really meant it and not just saying it because I said it first. The tenderness in his voice, his general concern for me, and his affectionate manor told me he felt the same way, yet he had not let those three words slip out of his mouth. *Why he was holding back, perhaps for the same reason as I?*

I knew it'd be hard to break away from him that night, but time was getting on, I was pushing my luck being there with him at all. Aaron was taking a while cleaning himself up in the washroom, so I threw my clothes on and decided to clean myself up when I went home. I removed the sheets from the bed and tossed them in Meredith's washing machine with extra soap and bleach. I gave my hands a good scrub and drank down some water at her laundry room sink.

In the kitchen, Rory lay on his mat, eyes closed, he must have tired himself out from his last romp around the yard. I washed the few dishes from supper. Aaron's plate wasn't messy, he had cleaned up every bite, just as he did the night at the diner. I remembered him teasing Jody about taking her hotdog and eating it, and how it felt like we were a real family out for the evening. We were enjoying each other's company until I spotted the Westinmalins with Joe, and later the confrontation between Joe and Aaron. *What had been said between them?*

Aaron came up behind me and placed his arms around my waist, and snuggled me.

"Missy, I'll finish taking care of the bed, and tidying up if you are wanting to leave."

"Trying to get rid of me?"

He spun me around to face him.

"Never," he said.

"Don't you have to get home for Landon?"

"I spoke to Mrs. Finnegan on the phone, she said Landon had fallen asleep at her place, and she'd keep him for the night. I don't have to rush home."

"I hate to leave you, but I need to get back before Joe notices how long I've been away."

I tucked my container inside my fanny pack, and put on my shoes, the image of Aaron with Joe outside the diner stuck in my mind.

"Aaron, I need to tell you something, and I don't want you to get upset."

"You can tell me anything."

"The night at the diner, I saw you and Joe talking outside."

Aaron looked surprised, he let go of me, and took a step back.

"What were you two talking about?"

Aaron hesitated, "I didn't want you to get involved, and that's why I haven't said anything."

"Aaron, please tell me."

"He wanted to know if I was the one that the Westinmalins had hired. I told him it was none of his business."

"Westinmalins? Did they want you for a renovation?"

"No, something else. Do you know them?"

"Not really, except that she came into my salon this afternoon."

"For what?"

"A haircut, until she changed her mind."

"Why did she change her mind?"

"I'm not entirely sure. She seemed more interested in having me say hello to Joe for her."

"That makes no sense."

"She said they did some business together. Why did she want to hire you?"

"We need to sit."

We both sat at the kitchen table, me curious about what he'd reveal.

"Missy, what I'm about to say, I need you to understand, and I need you to trust in our feelings for each other."

155

My stomach began to twist, suddenly I was nervous, and began to get the chills because of the serious expression on his face. I remained quiet, and waited for his reveal.

His speech was rickety as he begun." As you know...I have been working a lot of hours. I've been trying to earn extra cash to help pay for Mrs. Finnegan's husbands' anti-rejection medication."

"Did her husband have an organ transplant?"

"Yes, his liver. He means everything to her, and she is a special person to Landon and me. They are like family to us. I want to help them out, as they help me out with Landon."

"That is a wonderful thing to do for them, but what does that have to do with the Westinmalins?"

Aaron looked uncomfortable, he fiddled with his wrist watch, as if it were to pain him to get the words out.

"The Finnegan's are great people, and only a few others knew that I was working to help them out."

"Okay."

"A couple months ago, I received a package at my house. I opened it to find a letter. The letter explained that I could earn thirty grand if I did this one job. At first I thought it was a home renovation, and I knew I had to take it, because it would help the Finnegan's. As I read on, I found out that the job wasn't a renovation, it was taking care of a personal matter."

"What type of personal matter?"

"The kind that is unethical." Aaron rubbed his forehead, as he continued. "I was asked to break up a marriage for thirty thousand dollars."

"What do you mean?"

"The letter said that I would be paid to seduce the wife away from her husband."

"This doesn't make any sense. Why would someone pay to break apart someone else's marriage?"

"That is the question I needed answers for, so I phoned the number that was left. I was told that I would be doing the wife a favor because the husband had been misleading and dishonest with his wife."

"They could have been lying to you."

"True, but I was only thinking about earning fast money for the Finnegan's.

"What did you decide?"

"I thought it over for a couple weeks, and after, I found out that Mr. Finnegan was decreasing his dosage of meds because he couldn't afford the full dosage, I knew I had no choice but to accept the offer."

"Who's marriage were you to break up?"

"The marriage of the most beautiful woman I've ever seen."

The knot in my stomach grew tighter. I could see remorse on his face, as he looked into my eyes.

"The woman on the phone told me to set up an account to receive my deposit, and she gave me the address, and description of the couple, but I was not given their names. I did as she asked, and drove to the address to keep my eye out for the woman I was supposed to seduce. It was a Wednesday, just after 4pm, I parked across the street from a large stone house, with stained glass windows, and a four-tier bird house out front. The house was lifeless until the school bus arrived and two children, a boy, and a girl, got off. After the bus went by, I saw a gorgeous woman with blonde hair, standing outside greeting her children. She wore a knee-length, flimsy black dress with little red flowers, and short sleeves."

His eyes squinted, and he quieted. *He is talking about my house, my children, and my dress. I cannot believe my ears.* I felt the color leave my face.

"I watched you take the children inside, I thought there must have been a mistake. I swear, I didn't know it was your house."

Utter sadness filled my body, I felt tears forming in the corners of my eyes, and my throat began to close up. "You have been using me?"

"No, I haven't. After I found out it was you, I called the woman and told her I wouldn't do it. They said it was too late because they'd already made the deposit into my account, and it I didn't do it, they'd take away what I love most in this world."

"Landon."

"Yes, my son. I was afraid, so I had to figure out a way to get closer to you, and since our kids were already friends, I knew it would make things easier."

"Easier to make a fool of me?"

"No, just easier to get close. At Landon's birthday party, I saw how wonderful you were, and I knew I couldn't do anything to hurt you. After the party I called the woman again, and told her I wouldn't do it. She told me that it would be impossible for the Finnegan's to keep an eye on my son every minute of the day."

"Why didn't you go to the police?"

"I have a buddy, Jacob, who is an officer. I had him run the phone number through the system, and he traced it back to Edith Westinmalin."

"Ms. Westinmalin?"

"Yes. Jacob found out she didn't have a criminal record, and her husband Milton was not known to be involved in anything illegal, that's when I knew she was bluffing about hurting Landon."

"Why didn't you mention anything to me sooner? Like the night we went to the diner, or the day after, or...I don't know...maybe before we had sex?"

"Missy, I'm so sorry, but I didn't see a need to."

"Didn't see a need to? What about the night at the diner, the Westinmalins were sitting at the same table as Joe. Did that not rattle your conscience? Did you think that was alright?"

"It would have, had I known he was sitting with them."

"You had as clear of a view as I did."

"Yes, but I've never met them in person. I didn't know it was them."

"And, when Joe approached you outside on the street?"

"Maggy, I could feel how close you and I were becoming, I didn't want anything to interfere with that."

Maggy...that sounds odd. "Close? You've been lying to me the whole time. And now that you've managed to get me in the sack, do the Westinmalins throw in an extra five grand or something?"

"Look, I know it sounds bad, but my feelings for you have nothing to do with the Westinmalins."

"So, everything we feel for each other is a bonus on top of the thirty grand. I get it."

"Missy, I haven't touched the money, it's still in my account."

"Of course it is, because they saw us together at the diner, and they assume you are doing what they asked."

"I don't care what they think. I only care about you, please don't let this ruin what we have."

"How could you look me in the eye all of those times, and keep this information to yourself?"

"It was stupid, but I didn't think that you'd continue seeing me if you knew the truth."

"You are right, I wouldn't have. I'd be too busy trying to find out why the Westinmalins want to break Joe and me up."

"Maggy, we can find out together."

"How?"

"They said the husband was being dishonest, and misleading. We just need to find out what Joe is hiding."

"Aaron, you have been misleading." Tears flooded my eyes, and ran down my face, "I don't trust you right now. I want to go."

He reached out to touch my arms, I pulled away from him.

"Maggy, I love you. Please, don't go."

Love me? That was the first time I'd heard those words come out of his mouth, and it was also our first fight. I wasn't expecting our magical moment to be like that. I'm not sure how I was expecting it to happen, perhaps in the middle of a love making session, or gazing across the table from one another at a fancy restaurant, or holding hands while walking through the trail at his home. I couldn't say it back to him, I was too upset, and needed time to think things over and process what was going on. *The man I love has been keeping this secret from me, how can someone say they love you and keep secrets from you?*

Chapter 12

At home I peeked in on the kids. Thankfully, they were snuggled up in their beds, same as when I left. I wanted to climb in beside them, squeeze each of them, and spend the night laying as close as possible. I knew their love would forever be unconditional, unlike the ever-changing love of a partner. I needed to feel the physical security and comfort in that, but I didn't want to disturb their rest, or risk waking them to see my bloodshot eyes, instead I settled for placing a kiss on each of their cheeks.

After I got out of the shower, I noticed a text from Aaron saying he was sorry, he wondered if we could meet up the next day to talk in person. His message tugged at my heart strings, I wanted to hurl, but instead I tossed my phone aside without responding.

I heard Joe coming upstairs. *Gross, he's not seeing me naked.* I threw on my nighty to cover up. After everything I found out, I didn't want to face Joe until my mind had settled, so I stayed put in my washroom, hoping he'd fall asleep. I heard him click off his light. After a few minutes, I opened the door a crack to see what he was doing. I saw the outline of his body in the darkness. He was tossing back and forth, and fluffing his pillow by slamming his hand into it. It was hard to assume what type of mood he was in. I wasn't ready to go out yet, so I put in time by clipping my toenails. I heard Joe's cell phone ring, and the gruffness in his voice, he said, "What?"

Who'd be phoning him at 11pm? I stood close to the door and tried to hear what he was saying, but everything was a mumble. He was too far away. His voice deepened, making him sound provoked. Through the opening in the door, I saw him walk out into the hall, and pull our door part way shut. I had to know what he was saying. I switched off the bathroom light, and quietly slipped out into our room. I inched closer to the hall door, being careful not to squeak the floor boards. His voice became more clear.

"Three hundred grand is absurd," he said.

I heard him pacing back and forth along the hall.

"How would I come up with that?"

Joe listened attentively as I saw him leaning against the railing.

"I need more time."

Someone wanted him to give them three hundred thousand dollars. Aaron and the Westinmalins were right. He is hiding something. But what did it have to do with Joe and me breaking up? His footsteps were coming too quickly for me to make it into bed, *he can't find out I was listening*, I grabbed my grandma's blanket off my rocking chair, and draped it over my arm. Joe flung our door open with force. It startled me enough to drop the blanket on the floor. Joe flashed his phone light my way, as I stood in the middle of the room.

"Magnolia? What are you doing?" he snapped.

"Oh, hi. Nothing…I mean, I was feeling a chill, and I wanted an extra blanket on the bed."

"Are you sick? It's boiling in here."

"My shower was too cold. I need to warm up."

Actually, our room was warm, so was my shower, but I needed a quick cover up. After his heated phone conversation, no doubt he was boiling. I turned on my table lamp to see him throwing the bed covers down, then sit on his side of the bed, staring off into no man's land.

"Something wrong?" I asked, and spread the blanket out.

"No." His response was quick and sharp. "I don't want that blanket on my side," he said.

I wanted to find out what his conversation was about, so I tried to guilt him into telling me. I climbed into bed, forced myself to place my hand on his shoulder, and in my sweetest tone said, "Joe, I know how much you wanted for things to get better between us and it looks like something is bothering you. I'd like to help."

He tossed his phone on his night table, ignoring my touch, and laid down. Mr. Nice guy from the past few days had disappeared. I was with Joe—the ass, who I know well. I kept up my sugary front despite his tone. "Let me know if you change your mind." He did not respond, "Goodnight."

I needed to find out who he was talking to, and the only way was to get my hands on his cell. I laid awake waiting for him to fall asleep, so I could sneak over and look at his phone. He kept rustling around in the bed, turning from side to side. I felt like smacking him, but refrained because in an irritating kind of way, it helped to keep me from falling asleep.

I thought back to the evening with Aaron, how amazing his body felt in my touch, and how amazing my body felt to receive his touch. We were a perfect fit, a once in a lifetime type of love. He presented himself as everything I've ever wanted in a man. My feelings for him overpowered my moral integrity, *I should feel ashamed, but I don't.* Aaron had brought out my internal intimate desires which I've kept buried for so long. Without him, I would not have realized that I was still capable of experiencing our level of connectivity. I freely allowed myself to be involved with him, I couldn't blame him for that, but his lie was completely his own doing.

An hour had passed, Joe was still restless. *What he had been dishonest about?* The image of the flowers came to mind with the note congratulating us on our new edition to the family. *Aaron sounded legit when he said they weren't from him, but then again everything he said sounded legit. On the other hand, Joe was acting too peculiar for it not to have meant something to him. Was it a secret code for something? Or was it a message intended to upset Joe?* My eyes were getting heavier, every minute that passed, I found it harder to keep them open. My phone light had been flashing for the past thirty minutes, I was trying to avoid it, assuming it'd be another message from Aaron, by then I was desperate for a distraction to keep awake, so I gave in and opened it.

"Please talk to me, Maggy."

For sure, it was from Aaron. *Had he put the sheets back on the bed in the spare room?* I hoped everything looked presentable for Meredith and Peter when they arrived home. *Why did he have to lie to me? If I hadn't mentioned anything about his conversation with Joe at the diner, how long would he have kept it a secret? Would he have told me that he loved me if I hadn't have gotten upset with him? I know the connection we shared was real, you can't fake a bond as powerful as ours. I thought I knew Aaron better, but his lie proves that I don't know him.* Once again, this goes back to what my father always said, "You never really know someone." Dad was right, and Aaron was a perfect example of that.

Joe had been still for ten minutes, I gradually turned to look his way to see if he was sleeping. His mouth hanged open, as he breathed, a sure sign that he was in a state of oblivion. I sat up in bed to test out my theory, still he didn't budge. Discreetly, I slid my feet out of the covers, to touch the floor, and vigilantly followed his breathing pattern for changes. I stood and lifted grandma's blanket off the bed in case he woke and saw me, I'd say I was putting it back. I took a few steps to the end of the bed, he began to snore, a telltale sign that he was out cold. I made my way to his side of the bed, keeping my ears focused for any motion indicating that he might wake. I couldn't see where his phone was, I leaned down to the night table and felt around for it until something flat and smooth was in my grasp, *it's the phone.* I held my breath, he stopped snoring, and rolled over to face me. I was glued to the spot, hoping his eyes would not open. I waited a few moments until he started snoring, and meticulously crept out of our room, with thanks to the night light in the hall, I was able to make it all the way downstairs. Into the bathroom and locked the door.

His phone was password protected, I typed in his mother's maiden name, Bailey, because that is what he used to use for everything. It was not working, so I tried the twins' birthday, his birthday, our anniversary, and a bunch of random other guesses, but nothing would unlock it, then I clicked the message icon and voila his last three text messages appeared. The first one was from Judy, his secretary, asking him to review the affidavit in case # 93 3009647. The second was from the bank, with a list of two possible dates and times to meet for an appointment. The third was a random number that I didn't recognize, (437) 279-3470. It said, "Seal our deal, or you will lose a lot more. Enjoy the flowers?"

Every text was incoming only. I wasn't able to see what he had texted back, or any of the previous conversations.

"Crap."

What was Joe involved in? 'Enjoy the flowers'? I was right about the look on Joe's face when he read the card. He knew who they were from, but lied about it. 'Seal our deal, or you will lose a lot more?' What kind of deal? I tried a couple more random occasion dates to unlock his cell, but it was no use, I wasn't able to get in. *What was the appointment at the bank for? Joe didn't mention anything to me about it.* I sat on the toilet, and pondered over various ideas, but there weren't enough facts to put things together. I needed to find out who that phone number belonged to, so I memorized it.

I sneaked the phone back upstairs to our room. I caught my foot and tripped on a lump in the middle of our floor. I lunged forward, but was able to stop myself before my entire face hit the floor. The phone however slide out of my hands and landed somewhere. I couldn't see where it went. It made a solid plunk sound, as if it landed on the foot rug beside the bed. I saw Joe's bathroom light on, and I heard him clearing his throat. I felt around the floor in the direction I heard it drop, but I couldn't find it. I had to get back in bed before he came out. *What if he noticed his phone missing?* I scurried to pick up Grandma's blanket to avoid tripping again, and tossed it on the bed. I heard Joe clunking around at the wall cabinet, then he gargled. I got under the covers as fast as possible. My chin ached from the impact of it nicking the floor. The bathroom door squeaked open, and the light went off. I closed my eyes, Joe's tired footsteps staggered across our floor. He got into bed. I couldn't stand the putrid smell of his fruity mouthwash. The sheets came in handy to pull over my nose, to prevent myself from vomiting. He repositioned himself several times before settling down. He didn't say a word. *Maybe he was tired enough to not think of his phone.* I wasn't going to risk getting out of bed again to find his cell. He'd have to find it in the morning. The light on my phone flashed again, but after all of the drama that evening, I left it. My brain was overwhelmed. I needed sleep.

At work, I felt like a chicken rushing around with its head cut off, especially after sleeping through my alarm, and having to drop the twins off late for school. I put on my fake smile, and managed to rough it through the morning with the help from Mr. Caffeine, and Mr. Acetaminophen. I hadn't checked my cell phone all morning. I couldn't bear to hear anything more from Aaron. The pain in my gut was brutal, every time I thought of him lying to me. It was a good sign I hadn't heard from Joe, the last few days of him pretending to care about me was nauseating, I didn't need any more mind games from him. *I don't love him, and I don't need him tricking me into feeling guilty. At least when he acts like a prick, I know where our relationship stands. Why was he pretending to win back my affection?* He must have found his cell phone because it was gone from our bedroom floor that morning, I even checked under the bed, it wasn't there either.

At lunch, I made a trip to the bank to find out when Joe's appointment was. The tellers passed me off to the manager, who refused to give me any information about Joe's appointment. I explained to him that I am Joe's wife and I have every right to attend the appointment. He brushed me off saying he'd have to speak with Joe about it first. I told him to forget it, then I threatened him that I was going to withdraw all of my investments, and every cent from his bank. The offended look on his face told me he wasn't going to change his mind about telling me, and that he had me pegged for a crazy woman. The truth was I didn't feel quite like myself, the accumulation of circulating thoughts, and the pressure of not knowing what was really going on with Joe, was beginning to drive me crazy.

The five cups of coffee had kicked in, and my brain was on overdrive. I told myself I needed to get it together before going back to work, I stopped in at the Sandwich Shop to chill off. There was one teenaged girl ahead of me in line, I didn't have a long wait. The counter person, Jade, said I had come in at the perfect time, the lunch rush had just finished. I ordered a toasted meatball sub, and a water. My stomach was gurgling, I was starved. The first bite into my sub was delicious, the melted mozzarella cheese combined with the aroma of oregano was divine. I took a few minutes to try and clear my inner havoc by focusing on chewing slowly, and appreciating the salty flavor. I sat alone at the table for two near the window, overlooking the street, I watched the cars drive past, and the odd person walk by. The Small Clothing Company was directly across the street, they had a display of autumn-colored clothing on mannequins, and plastic pumpkin cutouts hanging in the windows, and fake leaves on their front door. The first week of October had just begun which reminded me that Kylie's wedding was only a few days away, I needed to buy that new dress. I heard my phone buzz in my purse, I ignored it, and swallowed the last bite of my sub. Jade wished me a good afternoon as I headed for the door. I walked a short way up the street, north of the bank, where I had parked the van, I saw Shelley, my nosy neighbor with her son. I forgot his name, but he was a cutie. I watched his light brown curls bounce up and down, as he walked beside his mother with his right hand in hers, his left held a sippy cup to his mouth. His little legs were moving as fast as possible to keep up with her pace. To be neighborly, I put my fake smile back on, lifted my hand, and waved at her as they strode my way.

"Hello," I said.

"Hi," said Shelley.

"Wow, he has grown," I pointed to her son.

"Thank you, he just turned three."

The little fellow babbled on and on saying, "Mama, goba new tup." He waved his cup around in the air, as if he was so proud of it.

"Oh, my mother got him a new sippy cup with his birthday stuff."

"You are a lucky boy," I said.

He babbled on some more, and started to drink from it again. There was something familiar about the boy, he had a cheerfulness about him, and his bright eyes were filled with wonder.

"He is so sweet, I can't believe he's that old already. It doesn't seem that long since he was a baby."

"Did you have a nice walk last night?"

Changing the subject, she stressed the word 'walk', as if she wanted to make sure I knew that she saw me. A gust of warmth shot up to my face, *did she know I'd been at Meredith's place with Aaron? Had she been spying on me?*

"It was alright."

"Kind of late to be out for a walk?"

I'm an adult, how dare she question me?

"I needed some fresh air. You must have been burning the midnight oil as well."

"Actually, Kaden has been having nightmares recently, he hasn't seen his father in a while, so it could be his body's way of coping." Shelley checked her watch. "I have to go, I don't want to be late for an appointment."

"Okay, well, if you need anything, let me know." I smiled at her. I've gotten really good over the years at pretending to be happy to see people, when really I'm not. I've always figured, if you never tell someone your true feelings, then you've got the upper hand, and as long as you are always polite, you'll never give them a reason to say anything to damage your reputation.

Shelley's attitude was slightly off today, *was she trying to tell me that she was keeping an eye on me last night? Or was I just paranoid?* Shelley wasn't the kind of neighbor to ask for my help, however she always seemed to be keeping watch.

Shelley tugged Kaden's hand, "Let's go," she said.

He went with her, no complaining, or whining. *Kaden must be a happy kid.* I noticed Shelley had put on weight since the last time I saw her up close. Her belly looked rounded out, almost pregnant, I didn't dare ask her, in fear of hurting her in case she wasn't. I hadn't heard of her dating anyone, my guess, she was around four or five months along. It wasn't cold enough to dress in layers, so I knew it wouldn't be an extra sweater bunched up underneath her thin jacket. *Perhaps she'd put on a few pounds since her husband left, or her weight wasn't important to her.* The bright face on

166

Kaden did bring joyous thoughts to mind, I remembered the twins being that age, everyone commented on how well-behaved they were. I knew different though, at home they had fits, threw tantrums, and scrapped over toys, out in public they were angels. *I'm certain Kaden's at home actions would be like those of my twins', and any other three-year-old. Not perfect, yet so perfect.*

Later that night, I took a time out to sit on the front deck. Aaron's truck was back at Meredith's. I had an intense urge to go over and see him. My body ached for him. I pushed his lie out of my mind, long enough to remember the intoxicating sensation of his shaft inside of me. His strong hands on my hips, pulling me toward him, his soft lips on my bare breasts, his unrestrained tongue entwined with mine, and the weight of his body resting on top. The vanilla scent from Meredith's soap, mixed with his own aqua fresh smell made him more desirable. I closed my eyes, leaned my head back, and rest it on the back of my rocking chair. My memory of the seductive look in his eyes made my insides clench, and my stomach muscles tighten. I missed talking to him that day, the unhappiness from not communicating with him, left my entire mid-section feeling hollow. *It's only been twenty-four hours since we'd spoken,* that was no consolation. My emotions had begun to get the best of me, my eyes started to tear up, and I felt a hard lump in the middle of my throat. I heard a pitter patter of tiny footsteps, Mrs. Morris' cat, Mel had come up on the deck. Her meow was delicate, I opened my eyes to see her big yellow eyes staring up at me. I extended my hand down to her, and she knocked her head into my hand. I wiggled my fingers to pet her under her neck. She purred, and ran her whole body back and forth along my hand, she continued to knock her head into my hand for affection. Her fur was shiny and black, velvety to the touch. She jumped up on my lap, and dug her paws carefully into my leg, her claws did not protrude into my skin. I picked her up, and snuggled her in my arms, her face rubbed on my jaw. The vibration of her purr sang against my chest, she comforted, and entertained me long enough to refocus my feelings. I heard Mrs. Morris calling, "Mel?" In a mad dash, she knew it was her cue to go home. The evening had begun to pass, the sun had disappeared into the west. I could see Aaron's truck hadn't left Meredith's, he must have been trying to take advantage of another day off from his day job. It was time to go inside, to finish my last few chores before bed. I placed a few dishes in the dishwasher, and swept up the kitchen floor. The bouquet of flowers looked gorgeous on the table, I figured the only reason Joe didn't throw them out was because he wanted to keep from looking suspicious. The note alone likely drove him crazy. At supper he had gone back into his mute mode, and after, he went to his office, and remained unseen the rest of the evening. I peeked out the back window to spy on Joe. His office light was not on. I assumed he'd gone to bed. I needed to find a way to figure out the connection between Joe and the Westinmalins, and that three hundred thousand dollars. I planned to keep my eyes open, and pay extra attention to Joe without him noticing.

Upstairs, Joe wasn't in bed, I saw the bathroom light on from his ensuite, I heard the shower door close, *Joe must be taking a shower.* I knew Joe spent on average nine minutes in the shower, making him unaware of my whereabouts during that time. That'd give me nine minutes to search his office desk for information. I darted downstairs on tiptoes, and clicked on the light by the kitchen sink, and in the little bathroom. I scooted down the hall to Joe's office, and clicked on my phone flashlight. I shone it on top of his desk surface. All of his loose files had been cleaned up. Every pen and pencil was in place. Only his daily agenda was left out, I took a seat in his desk chair, and flipped through it, to see if I could spot anything unusual. I knew I had only a couple minutes before he'd be out of the shower, everything appeared to be legit. Appointments with clients, dates and times, no special notes along the margins. I put the book back in the exact place that he had it. I set my phone on his desk to let the light brighten up the room, I wanted to take a quick glance around out of desperation for clues. I opened his file cabinet, but it was too dark to see names on the files without removing each one individually. My phone buzzed, startling me. I closed the cabinet drawer and grabbed my phone, it didn't appear to have any new messages. The last few messages were from Aaron's number, which I hadn't opened yet. As much as I missed him, I needed to hold off to get my thoughts organized. I knew Joe'd be finished in the shower, *likely drying off.* I had to get out of there. I clicked the flashlight off and headed to the door. I heard the buzz again. It wasn't coming from my phone that time. I turned back to listen for the sound. It was near Joe's desk. I went over to the desk and heard it again. Nothing was flashing, the buzz was coming from inside the drawer. I slid it open. There was a flashing light in the back of the drawer. I reached in and pulled out a little flip phone. It wasn't Joe's regular phone. *I've never seen this one before.* I flipped it open, "Two new messages" beside a little picture of an envelope. I clicked "Open," and it revealed the message. No pass code required. My nerves rattled, not sure of what I'd find, I was afraid Joe would catch me in his office, I put the phone in my pants pocket, and went into the downstairs bathroom. I locked the door, stood still and listened for Joe, in case he had come downstairs without me realizing. The only thing I could hear was a fly buzzing around in the light fixture. I flipped open his phone to check out the first message.

"Time is up."

Three simple words with so much force behind them. The next message read,

"Meet tomorrow at noon. Bring the three hundred grand."

What kind of mess was Joe into? Perhaps he'd rubbed a person the wrong way and this was his payback, or he had been caught in the middle of something and now he was being threatened. Was this the reason Joe had been acting so miserable over the past while? I had no way of knowing what was going on, and it wasn't as if Joe would voluntarily give me information. I sat and pondered over the possibilities of what it could be about. I thought back to the phone conversation Joe had in the hallway, he mentioned three hundred grand was absurd, and he couldn't come up with that amount. I knew Joe was lying to whoever was on the phone, because when Joe's parents passed away four years ago, they willed him a half million dollars, which we used some of for our house renovation, and between the two of us with our GIC's, and RRSP's combined, we had over three hundred thousand in savings. Joe always insisted on putting away every last cent, and avoided wasting money on 'foolish' items. I didn't know why he would fool around with people threatening him, *why not let the police handle it?* With everything else going on revolving around the Westinmalins, I had to wonder if it didn't have something to do with them. *Was this the reason Joe was making an appointment at the bank? Did he need to withdraw three hundred thousand? Something was seriously off about this situation, Joe wouldn't just hand over three hundred thousand dollars to someone, unless there was something major at stake.* That stupid fly was beginning to drive me crazy with its buzzing and zipping past my head, when it came to a stop near the lights over the mirror I stood, reached for the hand towel and folded it in half, the fly was twisting itself around in a circle on the wall, and buzzing, I swung the towel and whacked it before it had the chance to escape. It fell dead to the floor, I picked up the fly with a piece of toilet paper and put it in the garbage can. "Got you bugger."

The silence in the room was a relief, I wished I would have smacked it sooner, which got me thinking that it is always better to take care of an unsavory situation immediately, rather than let it linger on and on. *If I sit around and wait to find out what Joe is up to, I might go crazy.* I decided to try and take matters into my own hands, same as the fly.

Given the information that the Westinmalins were trying to break up Joe and I, it only made sense that the messages on the flip phone were from them. As much as I despised Joe, that three hundred thousand was rightfully half mine, and no one was going to be taking it.

I studied the telephone number, but didn't recognize it. *Maybe it was the same number Aaron used to contact the Westinmalins? I'm not contacting him to find out.*

After I pondered and evaluated my options to find out more, I irrationally decided to text the number back and pretend to be Joe.

"Where do you want to meet?"

I stared at the phone and waited for a reply, after a couple minutes there was nothing, so for entertainment I searched other information on the phone. I looked in photos, phone calls, contacts, recents, and redial, but everything was blank except for the last two texts. Joe must have cleared everything after each conversation, and that would be his reason for no pass code. *What to do with this phone? I can't sit here all night and wait.* I knew not to put the phone back in Joe's desk, but I couldn't take it upstairs either. *He can't find out I have it.* I had to pick a place and hide it where Joe would never find it...*the game trunk in the TV room. Joe hates playing games with the kids, he'd never find it there.* Barely breathing, I tiptoed into the TV room, slid open the bottom drawer on the wooden trunk, I emptied a box of poker cards, and placed the phone inside the empty box. I closed the drawer, then proceeded to the kitchen for a glass of water. If Joe questioned me about being downstairs too long, I'd say I was thirsty, and went for a drink.

I set my water down on my night table, beside my phone which was still flashing. I got in bed, Joe was already asleep. *Would I get a response by morning on the cell? If I did get a chance to meet up with this person, what would I say to them? Would they tell me what was going on, or would they expect me to have the money?* I wasn't sure what I was about to get myself into, but to continue on with my life, I had to find answers.

I closed my eyes, but every event flooded my mind, and kept me awake. I tried to think of pleasant thoughts, like that afternoon how the twins rushed to me after they got off the school bus to tell me about playing Dr. Dodgeball in gym class, but my thoughts always went back to what I was going to do if I happened to meet the man or woman on the other end of that phone. Then there was Aaron, and how he said he was trying to earn money for Mr. Finnegan's anti-rejection meds. When I thought about that part alone, it seemed like generous and heart felt action. I knew how important the Finnegan's were to him, and I tried to put myself in his position of someone offering me money to help someone I cared for. I knew I'd likely have made the same choices, but I wasn't sure if I'd be able to hold the secret inside, as Aaron did. I wanted to speak with him, it was almost midnight, but if I texted him, I wouldn't be able to untext him. I imagined him laying on top of me, as he did the night before, the devoted look in his eye after he kissed me. An emotional rush seized my body, I wanted to feel him so badly, a sadness came over me, I felt wetness forming underneath my closed eyelids. I wished everything could be the same as it was before he told me the truth. It seemed our feelings had been tainted with darkness, I wasn't sure what to do. Several drops ran down my cheek and onto my pillow, I took in a deep breath through my mouth, my hand wiped the dampness from my face. I lacked the feeling of inner fullness, which I'd become accustomed to after chatting with Aaron. I decided to read my phone messages from him, it was the only way I could get a sense of his presence. He had sent four messages. The first said, "Missy, please forgive me."

The second said, "I've made a huge error in judgement, I'm really sorry."

The third said, "Please talk to me, we can work through this."

The forth said, "I love you, beautiful. I want you in my life."

His messages hit a soft spot, I could feel his plea for forgiveness, I knew he was sincere and meant every word. I wanted to text him in the worst way and tell him I loved him too, but I couldn't, not yet. I wrapped my body tightly inside my blankets searching for comfort. I imagined Aaron's arms around my body until my eyes became too heavy.

I woke up early to join Joe for breakfast, I wanted to keep him distracted with hopes that he wouldn't think of his flip phone, and discover it missing from his desk. He sat at the table and munched away at his cinnamon raisin toast, and read the morning paper. I sipped on a small glass of grapefruit juice. I wasn't sure how he was able to sit there, and pretend everything was normal. I suppose after months or even years of practice, he was used to putting on an authentic front around everyone. I told him I may try to pick up a wedding gift, and new dress that afternoon for Kylie's wedding. He reminded me to select a memorable gift, one that would stand out from the rest. I knew he only wanted to make himself look important. Again, I wasn't sure why he was set on impressing his sister whom he hasn't spoken with in years. His facial expression remained emotionless as I assured him I'd choose something special. He neatly folded the paper, and set it off to the side. I got up and took his dirty dishes to the sink, to portray the image of a caring wife. I asked him if he'd be needing a new suit, or if he planned on wearing his regular one. He approached me near the counter, and said he was having one tailor made as we speak. That was news to me, he hadn't mentioned anything about it. I saw him check the clock, he then leaned in and placed a peck on my lips. I couldn't have him sense how much I despised him, so I forced a smile upon my face, and told him to have a nice day. Unexpectedly, I felt his hand rub over my ass through my nighty, I halted my actions wishing he'd remove it, with a quick gesture he slapped my right cheek, and walked away. My ass tingled, not in a good way. I hoped he wasn't trying to tell me he was beginning to get in the mood for wanting, because I certainly wasn't in the mood for giving, and if I was, it wouldn't have been with him. He headed down the hall towards his office, I strained my ears and listened attentively to pick up any signals that he may have discovered his flip phone missing, but there was nothing until his footsteps on the hardwood were returning. I placed the dishes in the dishwasher, he passed by the kitchen carrying his briefcase, he must have retrieved it from his office. I yelled out to him, "Goodbye." I heard back a faint, "Bye".

It was still early, the twins weren't out of bed, I waited until I saw Joe's car leaving the driveway before I rushed into the living room to get ahold of that phone. I pulled it out of the card box, the light was flashing. I flipped it open as fast as possible to read the new message, sent at two minutes after six 6 am.

"Same place as last time."

I had no idea where that would have been, I had to come up with a reason to meet them someplace else. *If I can at least meet this person, maybe I can get some answers to solve my questions.* I wanted to find out for sure if the Westinmalins were involved, or not. I had to be careful how I responded to them, I needed them to believe I was Joe. Joe was bossy, the message had to commensurate with that part of his personality. I texted back,

"Pick a different location, or the deal is off."

I sat on the carpet, and waited restlessly staring at the phone to see if they'd bite. Every minute that passed seemed like an eternity, until finally the phone had flashed, they'd taken the bait.

"Be at 44452 Autumn Rd. Manotick, no later than twelve noon today. Bring all of the cash, and come alone."

I didn't respond back to whoever was on the other end. I had to remember to act like Joe, and it would be just like him not to reply in a situation like that.

That was easy. If someone was bringing three hundred grand to me, I'd meet them almost anywhere too, but I'm not a professional, a professional would have a criteria to follow, this person was cooperative...they are not professionals. Unless they are, and they want me to think they're not. Hmm...Autumn Road? I hadn't heard of it, I'd driven through Manotick several years prior, I remembered it as the town where all of the rich people live. The houses looked like they were worth two or three million dollars each, all having their own tennis courts, inground pools, and overlooking the Rideau River. I searched up directions, and discovered Autumn Road was approximately forty-five minutes away from Laudersville, I needed to leave early because I wanted a chance to scope the place out before going inside.

The salon wasn't overly booked, which gave me a legitimate excuse to leave around ten o'clock. I asked Lucy to hold down the fort so I could go out and search for a wedding gift, and dress, which was what I intended on doing if I made it out alive after the confrontation set for noon. Lucy made me promise to stop back after and model the dress for her. I told her I would if I had spare time before the twins were due home from school.

On the drive to Manotick, I questioned myself if I was doing the right thing? *Was I getting in over my head?* I chose the fastest route on the GPS, and followed directions for forty-three minutes to Manotick. The drive was filled with leaves, beginning to change into gorgeous orange, red, and yellow hues of fall colors. There wasn't much traffic for a Thursday. Driving on the outskirts of town, I noticed the houses were every bit as wealthy as I remembered. I had to wonder, what type of careers those people had to afford such a lifestyle. Joe and I had a fancy house, but compared to those ours would be considered a downgrade. The GPS told me to turn right in one hundred meters on Autumn Road. The moment was becoming a reality for me, as I neared my destination, *I should have taken kava root to calm my nerves.* I tried to reassure myself that everything would turn out fine. After turning onto Autumn Road, I traveled along a bush area, both sides of the road were filled with tall pines that blocked the brightness from the sunlight. I looked on up ahead and saw a clearing of a wet marsh area with fallen trees, and tall pussy willows. The GPS said I'd be at my destination in three minutes, as of then, I hadn't seen one house on Autumn road, my mind had begun to play tricks on me in thinking that the person would capture me, burry me alive in the woods to rot, and I'd never see my children again. My stomach had begun to twist and turn, as if I was about to throw up, I distracted myself by putting the van window down to breath in some fresh air. I tried to concentrate on the wet and woodsy smells, it only reminded me that I wasn't prepared to die a premature death. I kept driving, only one minute to go, I spotted an abandoned two-story home on the left, *glad that's not it.* A gorgeous log house to the right, number 44443. *Almost there.* I drove past a few more houses, and I began to feel slightly better knowing I wasn't all alone in a strange area. I passed a field with piles of brush lined up in rows, and a large white billboard with the name Pineview Estates, it was an area being cleared for the development of a subdivision. GPS said destination thirty yards on the left, the mailbox read 44452, *this is it.* I slowed down to ten kilometers per hour, and crept past a Victorian farm house. The diminishing red barn to the side of the house looked as if the farm had been out of commission for years, the house looked tidy and well kept. The clock said eleven twenty, I had forty minutes to decide if I was going to go inside or not, I drove up the road a ways, turned right at the stop sign to park on the shoulder. *Whoever this person is will be expecting to see Joe. Will they recognize me, or even know who I am? What will happen when they realize I don't have the three hundred grand? If I go to the door and ask for directions, I'll be able to see who this person is, but that will only work if they don't know who I am, Ms. Westinmalin knows me. What would I say when or if she opened the door? I might be in trouble if I come out and ask them why they are trying to steal my three hundred grand. Aaron said we could find out what Joe is hiding together, I refused. If I had accepted his offer, he'd be here with me right now, and I wouldn't be in this situation alone, instead I was stubborn, for a good reason.* Time approached noon, I turned the van around, and decided to proceed without a plan. I neared the driveway, a blue car cut across the road and turned in by the farm house. The car did not look familiar, I slowed and inched the van along the side of the road to get a better view. Many trees outlined the property, I stayed tucked behind them as best I could. I saw two people getting out of the car. They walked up onto the porch, facing away from the road. I drove ahead to spy. It looked like a man and a woman, both wearing hats. The two of them went inside the house. I studied the place. *Who the hell are these people?* Five minutes to go before noon, I had convinced myself to just go for it. I hoped they weren't the crazy type to tie me up in their barn, and hold me captive for ransom, but if they were, I'd spray hairspray in their eyes and make a run for it before they had the chance. *I came this far, I'm not backing out now.* I parked behind them in the driveway, crept my way to the front door, and rang the bell. I was hot, and my throat was feeling dry, there was gum in my coat pocket, I shoved a piece into my mouth, and chewed it quickly, releasing the minty cool flavor that moistened my throat as I swallowed. I heard a light tapping of footsteps from inside the house, my heart pounded inside my chest. The door squeaked open, and a short middle-aged woman answered the door.

"Can I help you," she asked.

For a moment I was speechless, a part of me was expecting to see Ms.Westinmalin, but I was wrong. Her light brown hair was up in a loose bun, her nose was pointy, and she wore large eye glasses. An apron was fastened around her waist, I had her pegged for the maid.

"I'm here for a meeting at noon," I said.

"Come right in," she raised her right hand and motioned for me to enter.

It was definitely too late for me to back out. I stepped inside the door, she led me into a sitting room, and told me to take a seat on the sofa against the back wall. Looking around the room, I noticed the waxy finish to the old-fashioned pine floor. It sparkled as if it had just been cleaned. I saw the backs of two brown suede chairs sitting side by side in front of a wall mounted fireplace. Over top was a brick mantle with family photos in frames. To my right, there was a little round table centered in front of a large picture window. The table had a beautiful bouquet of light and dark blue wild flowers in a glass vase, they looked a lot like the bouquet that was delivered to my home. I was curious, and got up to get a closer look, the flowers were the exact same. *Was it a strange coincidence or not?* I remained still and listened for the presence of other people in the house, the only thing I heard was an echo from a vacuum coming from possibly upstairs. I quietly made my way to the mantel over the fireplace to check out the pictures, I wanted to get an idea of what type of people I was dealing with. One photo was of an old couple standing together lip locked underneath a mistletoe, another was a group shot of about eight people sitting on a long bench. A few pictures were of children, and babies, *perhaps the grandkids of the people living here.* In one photo a baby boy, about nine months old, was dressed up in a bright yellow furry duck costume. He was sitting on the floor surrounded by rubber duck bathtub toys. The words 'Grandson' stood out on the bottom of the frame. It was cute. I remembered when the twins were almost two years old. I dressed them up like the tortoise and the hare.

I heard voices, a man, and a woman. I couldn't hear what was being said. It sounded like a little scrap. His voice was raised. Hers was irritable. It didn't sound as if anyone was winning the argument. Then it came to a halt, complete silence. I started to get a feeling like it was a bad idea, I decided I should sneak to the front door and skip out unnoticed. I moved closer to the entrance of the sitting room, when a lady poked her head around the corner.

"Whoa," I said.

My heart raced, she was in my face, startled I took a step back, as I recognized her from my salon, it was indeed Ms.Westinmalin. She lifted her head, held it high, and walked past me, if I hadn't have stepped out of her way, she might have walked over top of me.

"This way, Magnolia."

Her stance robust, she proceeded into the living room without looking back. I hesitated a moment, then followed her to the sofa. She neatly tucked her long skirt under her rear, and sat down. She flipped up her palm, and motioned for me to sit.

"Please," she said.

The sofa was firm, and made of leather, I carefully sat at the end, opposite her.

"What brings you here?" she asked.

I felt my courage build, I was somewhat relieved to know I was not dealing with the type of crazy person who would stick me in their basement for months on end. I was feeling strong enough to ask questions, and get the answers I came for.

"I'm the one who set up this meeting with you, not Joe. What business do you have with him?"

Her face remained serious. "Any business conducted between Joseph and I are none of your concern."

"You are asking Joe for three hundred thousand dollars, fifty percent of that belongs to me, it is my business."

"You have no idea who you are married to."

What an insult. After eighteen years of marriage, I well know who Joe is, the only thing I didn't understand is why he had turned into an ass.

"Enlighten me with details, please."

"Magnolia, you need to go home, do not mention any word of this encounter with anyone."

"Why do you want three hundred grand? Are you bribing him for it? Does he owe it to you?" My anger was building, she had answers, and wouldn't give them. "Tell me now."

Ms.Westinmalin appeared calm. Her face hadn't changed its expression since the moment she sat. Her right leg crossed over her left. Her hands folded neatly on her lap.

"Stay out of this, and your life doesn't have to change."

"Is that a threat? I know it was you who had the flowers delivered. And, the message on the card, 'Congratulations on your new edition' what does that mean?"

Her words were stern, "I'd like you to leave now." She stood to her feet, and walked toward the door.

"You are not having my money. Do you understand?"

Her thin eyebrows arched, "Come this way, please."

There was no way she was going to spill the beans, so I followed her to the front door.

"I could contact the police."

She opened the front door. "You wouldn't dare, because if you did, your beautiful fantasy life would be ruined. Get out, please."

"Eventually I will have the truth." I stepped out onto the deck, she closed the door behind me.

Out of fury, and frustration, I sped out of their driveway. *That lady is impossible, she knows everything, and refused to share. Mr. Westinmalin must be involved, likely it was him who had been bickering with her. Did he hear our conversation? Would he have been easier to break down and let me in on the details? It didn't matter now because I'm sure I'll never get a chance to ask him.*

The situation must be bad if Joe was considering handing over three hundred thousand. I had to find answers somehow. I wasn't sure how to get Joe to talk to me, but I had to figure something out fast.

On my way back, I drove into the town of Manotick to find that outstanding wedding gift for Kylie and Benjamin, and see if I could get myself a dress. Manotick had all kinds of fancy boutiques, and designer clothing shops. It's the type of town for those with deep pockets, and extra change to spare. I went into a few shops, the sales people seemed friendly, of course they'd have to be if they wanted a person to spend two thousand dollars on a dress, or four hundred on a crystal fruit bowl. I felt ridiculous looking for a gift for the sister of a man who I didn't want anymore. It would have been easier for me to forget about the whole goose chase and leave Joe, but I had to find out whatever possible danger Joe has brought to our children, and protect them. All of the shops had gorgeous items of glass this, and glass that, but I knew after the thrill of unwrapping had passed, the bride or groom would shove it into the back of a cupboard, or shelf to collect dust forever. I wasn't having any luck in finding an over the top gift, so I texted Mrs. Lauders to see if she had any gift ideas, then I ventured to the dress shop. Beautiful gowns of every color, and style imaginable from wall to wall, displayed on mannequins, and racks. Some had rhinestone sequence, others had lace, they carried long-sleeved, short-sleeved, and strapless. My goal was to find one that fit well, and looked good without upstaging the bridal party. After about thirty minutes of checking everything over, I had my selection narrowed down to three for trying on. The tight-fitting navy blue one with silver sequence around the waist was pretty, but I thought the color might be too dark for a wedding. The green one made me look like a giant emerald, so it was a no go. The last one that I tried on was an ankle length burgundy gown with short sleeves, it had an empire waist with a row of subtle looking diamond rhinestones that sparkled all the way around to the back. The square neckline was see through, beginning one inch below my clavicle down to the top of my breasts. It was a perfect fit. It didn't say tramp or showoff. It simply said elegance. Fifteen hundred dollars later, I walked out with a new dress. I hadn't had lunch yet, so I zipped through the drive through, and bought a chicken wrap to fill me up. As I sat in the van and ate, Mrs. Lauders texted me saying, "Vacation, vacation, vacation."

"Bingo," I texted her back.

I spotted a travel agency in a strip mall across the street. There was billboard outside that read, 'Weekend Getaways – Half Off'.

After a thirty minute chat with the travel agent, I decided to spend two thousand dollars and give Kylie and Benjamin an all-inclusive weekend trip to Las Vegas. Penthouse room at the hotel, dinner, drinks, and gambling, what better way for newlyweds to make memories that last a lifetime, as well, it would be the attention-grabbing type of gift that Joe was after for the benefit of making himself look important.

I spent the drive home, trying to piece together all of the facts I had, and what the connection would be between Joe and the Westinmalins. *What did the Westinmalins have over Joe, and what was the purpose of the congratulations message on those flowers? What new edition to the family were they referring to?* I couldn't figure out why they demanded three hundred thousand dollars, it was obvious that Ms. Westinmalin didn't want me to find out. Nothing made sense. I tried to fit Aaron into the mix. *Why did they choose him to get involved to break up Joe and me? He said they found out he needed to earn some quick cash? If everything Aaron told me was true, it would seem he was the innocent bi-standard that was caught up in their turmoil, and when he tried to get out, the Westinmalins threatened him. Could it be possible that they used Aaron as a pawn to threaten Joe into paying them the money? Perhaps they told Joe to pay the money or they'd make sure his family was broken apart. That scenario would only work if Joe wanted to keep me, frankly I'm not sure why Joe would want to stay with me, how could he possibly be happy living as we are, no communication, no having fun together, no affection? One thing I know that the Westinmalins likely don't, is how much Joe loves his money, and I'm sure he'd choose it over me in a heartbeat. Matter of fact, if I left Joe, I'd be entitled to fifty percent of everything we own, he would be furious if that happened, as well, he'd have to pay me child support for the next nine years, and spousal support forever because he earns more than I. It would be smarter on Joe's part to stay with me, compared to paying out the Westinmalins because if I left he'd lose a lot more than the three hundred grand. Maybe that was why he said he needed to fix things between us, he was afraid I'd run off with Aaron, and he'd lose half of everything. That would make sense for the confrontation Joe had with Aaron, outside the diner that night. If I left Joe penniless, he'd be devastated, so he told Aaron to back down from the job that the Westinmalins had hired him to do. I could always contact Aaron and ask him for more details about that night, he did say that we could figure it out together, but I can't. But I want to. But I won't. I miss him.* My stomach felt like it had a massive empty hole, big enough to stick my whole hand inside and wiggle it around and around. *I don't know how I will ever get past my yearning for him?* I always felt respected by him, and his feelings felt genuine. When he said he loved me, my heart sank because I was overthrown by anger that he had been lying to me. Had I found out sooner, Aaron and I might not have had the chance to fall in love, I would have continued to exist without having experienced the jolt of magnetism every time we touched. With Joe, there was always that one little thing missing, and for years I couldn't put my finger on it, now I know it wasn't a fabrication of my mind, it was real, and I felt it with Aaron.

Earlier when I had lunch, my phone rang. It was Aaron's number. I didn't answer. Then, he sent me a few texts. I didn't open them. I needed to stay strong, and keep focused on my task, which was getting to the bottom of the situation. For a moment, my mind unwillingly drifted back to the bonfire, and us making out. I wanted to have him so bad that night, *I want him now*, my body ached for him all of the time, and it was killing me to hold off in responding to him.

If my theories were true, and Joe hadn't any intention of parting with his money to keep our "fantasy life" safe, why did he need a bank appointment? The bank manager wasn't all hushy hush for nothing. What am I missing?

The whole 'Congratulations on your new edition' thing sounded like someone was getting a pet, or adding something to their life. It was a weird message, I'm certain that Joe understood it completely.

Chapter 13

The next day and a half felt like agony, I kept Joe's phone hidden in the card box, to keep an eye on it for new messages from the Westinmalins, perhaps I had scared them into thinking their money was in danger because they hadn't sent even one. I kept my eye on Joe, to see if I could pick up any clues to what he was hiding, but his usual routine hadn't changed, I wondered if he was going to give in and hand over the money, or simply wait them out. His attitude remained mundane, but calm despite his situation. Aaron's truck was parked at Meredith's, every night that week, he must have been getting close to being finished her renovation, I would have loved to have went over and seen the changes, but I needed to keep my distance. Each night before bed, I read over my text messages from Aaron, it helped to fill my longing, if I pretended things were normal between us my mind could relive my past feelings. By doing that, I felt refueled with an overpowering energy that couldn't be fulfilled any other way. It had also brought on an internal sadness, knowing I couldn't be with him.

Kylie's wedding day had finally arrived, that morning I had Lucy put my hair up in a French twist with a silver hair clip in the back. My earrings were 80-carat diamond studs, and I chose to wear the silver bracelet that Jody gave me for my birthday, and my mother's pearl necklace. It wasn't a perfect match, but I didn't care. My shoes were black sling backs, three-inch heels with an open toe, and to match, I carried a black clutch purse in my hand. Joe wore his new tailored suit, with grey dress shoes, I had to admit he did look handsome when he was all dolled up, but it did nothing to ignite my fire. He reminded me of our wedding day how his hair was trimmed and short, he was clean shaven, wore a black jacket with grey trim around the lapel, white dress shirt, black pants, and shiny shoes. His boutonniere was a single white rose. He held his head high with confidence, yet he had a devilish twinkle in his eye. He smiled at me a lot that day, I thought I'd be the center of his world forever, but after year eleven, I began to feel him judging me and every decision that I've ever made. I've stopped telling him about the minor details in my life because he usually had a negative response, or he wasn't interested in what I had to say. He was not my best friend, after all this time, I've come to realize that he never really was.

What was the true reason for his change of heart in deciding to go to Kylie's wedding? Was it because Aaron had offered to take me if he wasn't available? Was it part of his cover up to try and appear he was keeping me happy, or did he truly want to repair his relationship with his sister?

The wedding was only thirty minutes from home. I assumed it was the bride's decision to be married in her childhood church. It may have been her way of uniting her past with her present. It would be well understood if that was the reason she wanted Joe to attend her wedding, she wanted closure from her past disagreement with Joe, and to start over fresh in becoming as close as they used to be.

I was going to hire a babysitter for the evening, but my dad insisted on keeping the twins at the farm with him, for an overnight. He told me on the phone last week how much he missed them, he wanted to take them fishing at the old dock. Dad used to take me there as a child, where I have many fond memories. We used to put a worm and a couple kernels of corn on a hook, and cast for hours until one of us would finally get a bite, Dad would let me reel in the fish, while he got the net to scoop up the old Charlie—that's the name we made up and used to give to every fish that was fooled into that thinking our hook was food. There was no better way for my children to bond with their grandfather, I could picture them all standing on the dock, wearing their bucket hats, and casting their line into the water, excitement would flourish from the smell of seaweed, and fish. A ray of sunlight would stretch down below the surface, causing them to stare into the rippling water anticipating a catch, while the big Charlie swims inches from their bait, deciding if he was hungry or not. The twins loved their grandfather, he always made them laugh, and he always had stories to tell them, most of them made up. He was really good at being a grandfather, I was happy he was healthy and able to live his life to the fullest. I knew they'd be well taken care of for the night.

On the drive to the church, Joe was relatively quiet, which was fine with me because I didn't have much to say to him anyway. The only thing I was interested in talking to him about was the

Westinmalins, and why they were demanding three hundred grand, but I didn't know how to bring up the question. I wasn't sure what his reaction would be if he found out I knew as much as I did. I assumed he'd either deny the whole thing, or he'd say my information was incorrect, or he'd be furious. I wanted to stay on reasonable terms with him for the wedding because I did want to see Kylie, as Joe's younger sister whom I remembered as being responsible, and mature, with a great sense of humor. I wanted to reunite with someone I used to call my friend.

I turned on the radio to fill the silence between Joe and me. I scanned to find the top one hundred hits on the local pop station because Joe had the radio of his impala programed to only instrumental music. I flipped down the visor to check my makeup in the mirror. I had put on my own face as usual, just a little foundation with powder on top, blush, grey eyeshadow, with black mascara, and burgundy-colored lipstick to match my gown. I was lucky I didn't have even one blemish on my face after all of the stress I'd felt over the past couple weeks, however I had been drinking plenty of water.

The weather was splendid for an early autumn day, the sun was out, the wind was calm, and there wasn't a trace of a cloud anywhere. I could tell the chill of autumn was just around the corner because the trees had now come to a full flourish with leaves of bright colors standing out in their glory, as we neared the church.

The parking lot was full, so we parked across the street in the 'weekend only' parking lane. I covered my shoulders with my hundred dollar see through shawl simply for looks, I knew I'd be overheated before the end of the service.

The church was beautiful, grey brick with two tall steeples, and stained glass windows. There was a handmade wooden sign, standing on an aisle outside the church that read 'Kylie + Benjamin' The walkway and stairs were bordered with four large pots of Asiatic lilies, green cedar foliage, and baby's breath. The Reverend wore a long black robe with a white stole around his neck, he greeted all of the guests with a friendly 'hello' upon entering the church. The usher asked Joe and me if we were on the groom's side, or the bride's. I told him, we were with the bride. He was a short, chubby, blonde-haired man, about twenty-five years old, dressed in a navy blue suit with a black bow tie, and blue boutonniere. He locked his forearm around mine and ushered me half way to the front of the church, Joe followed behind. When we were seated, I thanked him, he nodded, and proceeded to the back of the church. Joe sat closely beside me, I slid over a touch, not wanting his leg to rub against mine. All of the pews were beautifully decorated with slender white ribbons, wrapped around orange lilies, and green foliage, similar to the flower pots outside. The front of the church had an archway made from wood, with a delicate white ribbon wrapped around, with more of the orange, and blue lilies, green foliage, and baby's breath. On either side of the archway, was a lovely bouquet of orange, and white daisies. Looking around the church, I tried to see if I could recognize anyone, I wasn't having luck as most of the elders in Joe's family had already passed on, or had moved away from the area. Kylie's side was filled, must have been her friends, or colleagues. Traditional music played softly, as all pews filled to the back. Everyone was dressed in glamorous gowns, and suits, most were conversing amongst themselves in a civilized manner. I was happy that I'd spent the fifteen hundred dollars on my gown, anything less would have looked cheap. The three groomsmen, and the best man had begun to take their places at the front of the church with the Reverend. The handsome groom clenched his hands tightly together, his face pale, he appeared nervous, as any groom-to-be should. He was about thirty-five years old, short blonde hair, and square jaw. He wore an ivory tuxedo with navy blue trim, bow tie, and white boutonniere. The bridesmaids' processional had begun, everyone looked back as the first bridesmaid entered the church. It was hard to get a good look at her because a lot of heads were blocking my view, as she made it to our row, I saw only that her dress was aqua blue. *Aqua blue...aqua cologne, Aaron. Lord, I miss him.* The second bridesmaid began to walk up, but I was caught off guard by one of the guests sitting a few rows behind us. Her necklace reflected the light causing a glare in my eye. Her hair was brown, shoulder-length, and in curls, her dress appeared to have spaghetti straps, black in color. The second bridesmaid passed our row, she appeared to be wearing a duplicate dress of the first bridesmaid. I looked back to the third bridesmaid, and that lady's necklace again caught my eye. I looked at her face, it was Shelley, my neighbor. *Strange,* I wasn't aware she knew Kylie. As the wedding party proceeded, and the next three bridesmaids made their way to the front of the church, I was distracted, *how does Kylie know Shelley? If they had been that close, they would have visited one another, and I don't ever remember seeing her visiting Shelley, unless she had been there and gone before I had the chance to get home from work. Joe never mentioned Kylie stopping by for a visit, or seeing her at Shelley's place. It would have made sense for her to stop by our house since we lived so close together. I knew they wouldn't have been work colleagues because Shelley was a stay-at-home mom. Kylie doesn't have kids, so they wouldn't know each other from a playgroup.*

The music had stopped, drawing my attention to the front of the church, the maid of honor was standing in a navy-blue gown, her hair pulled to her left in a side ponytail with curls, and her flower bouquet was white, and orange lilies. The bridesmaids cheerfully held their bouquets of white, and blue lilies. The flower girl, dressed in a white frilly knee-length dress, and carried a basket with white and blue ribbons, she happily bounced around in front of the bridal party. The groom stood tall, and the bridal chorus had begun. Everyone looked to the back of the church. The doors opened wide, the bride stood arm in arm with Uncle Sam, Joe's last surviving uncle. The congregation stood to face the bride, as the two of them walked over white rose petals that covered the aisle. She turned her head back and forth to greet her guests. As she approached her groom, Kylie wore an enormous smile that shone through her lace vail. I didn't get a good look at her wedding gown until she reached the front of the church. After everyone had sat back down, she hugged Uncle Sam. He kissed her on her cheek through her veil. He then stretched his arms out, and held her hands in his, he fixed his stare on her, as if to say he was proud of her. Her ivory gown was off-the-shoulder with a V-shape neckline, see through lace from shoulders to cleavage, the sleeves were long with see through lace, the rest was satin, and it gathered at her waist with a delicate belt made of pearls, the bottom flared outwards, and had the see through lace about six inches up from the bottom, and continued down the end of her train. Her flower bouquet was white lilies, and a mixture of the blue, and orange lilies. She handed her bouquet to her maid of honor, her groom took her by the hand, and they stood facing the Reverend.

As I listened to the two of them exchange their vows, and proclaim their love for one another with the promise to love, cherish, and honor, I wondered if they realized what they were getting themselves into? *It's easy to promise to love someone forever, but how can you possibly love someone after they've changed into an unrecognizable being, completely opposite of the day you were first married? Either you stay with them and live the rest of your life in agony, hoping that they'll change back into the person you fell in love with, or you can make a nice clean break and be finished with them.* The day Joe and I were married, I had full confidence he'd be my one and only until death do us part, *now I feel as if I'll be dead if we don't part. How can one know at the beginning of their marriage if it will work out? It's hard to keep faith when both parties aren't giving it their all.*

Shortly after the I do's and the kiss, the church cleared out, it was time to make our way to the banquet hall for the dinner and reception, while the newlyweds, and wedding party went to get photos taken. There was an open bar, a table with cheese and crackers, mixed veggies with humus, cinnamon buns, and muffins. They also had a candy bar, the table had glass bowls filled with every kind of candy and chocolate you could imagine. I'd never seen that at a wedding reception before, it was delightful. Joe placed our gift on the table with the rest of the beautifully wrapped boxes. Ours was the only box that had a flashing red light that read Vegas on it, apparently Joe had ordered it online, *how embarrassing.* We sat in our designated places at a round table that seated eight, our name cards set on the table to the left of our wine glasses. The table was covered with a pale blue lace table cloth, the centerpiece was an orange Lili floating in a crystal water bowl with tea lights. I didn't know most guests at our table, except for Joe's dateless Uncle Sam who sat beside him. As Joe and he talked, I sat quietly and watched the guests slowly pile in to the hall. Everyone had the same routine to follow as they entered; first, stand under the trellis and have your picture taken with a polaroid camera, second, sign the guest book, third, wait until your photo was developed, fourth, stick your photo inside the scrap book, sign your names and leave a message of advice for the bride and groom. Following that, the guests were expected to grab a beverage at the bar, check the seating chart, and find their places in the dining room. The DJ was playing a variety of smooth jazz ballads, and love songs, I sat with my knees together, ankles crossed, my elbows rest on the table, and my chin rest on my entwined fingers. I glanced at Uncle Sam. He winked at me. I smiled back. He was almost bald, but his chin had plenty of hair, a white goatee about an inch long, his suit jacket rested on the back of his chair, and his tie was unfastened and hung down his chest. He slouched back in his chair and chugged back another glass of wine. Joe turned his full attention to Uncle Sam who rambled on and on about the stock market, which was of no interest to me. I sipped my red wine, and tried to make eye contact with the others at our table, hoping to start a conversation, but they all seemed too involved in conversing with themselves, and playing with their phones. I noticed my neighbor Shelley was seated across the room near the candy bar, I was beginning to get hungry, so I thought I'd make a trip to the cheese and cracker table, then swing over to get a handful of candy to spike my energy level. I made my way through the crowd with a smile on my face, I could smell raspberry scented perfume as I passed a group of finely dressed ladies, perhaps in their early thirties, they were standing in a circle, laughing, and hugging one another, as if they hadn't seen each other in a while.

At the cheese table, I filled up my plate with Havarti cheese, and vegetable crackers, before making my way to the candy bar. I spotted Shelley, she was seated at her table and chatted with a man and woman whom I assumed to be married. The chair to her right was free, so I decided to go over.

"Hi, Shelley."

She turned and looked at me, her smile fell into a serious expression. I pulled out the chair and sat beside her.

"Maggy, Hi."

"I wasn't expecting to see you here."

She nodded her head, "Ya," she said.

She turned back and began to chat with the couple at her table, completely ignoring me. I took a few bites of my cheese, she talked about the politics of the new housing development project in Manotick. *What does she know about that?* As far as I knew, she had never been involved in any type of work. The shimmer of her necklace caught my eye once more. It looked familiar. She turned my way to reach for the sparkling water. The necklace was clear in my view. It was a delicate silver chain, with a charm made in the shape of a circular ring about the size of a quarter with diamonds making up the outside edge, one larger diamond about the size of a small pea dangled down into the center of the ring. It was one of a kind. It was mine. I won it for Christmas years ago from the Charm Diamond Center in Brockville. The jeweler said it was the first piece designed by the famous Bridget Sampson, before she became famous. It was worth five hundred dollars. *How did she get my necklace?* It went missing a few years back, I thought it was gone forever.

I interrupted her conversation with her lady acquaintance, "I love your necklace."

She placed her fingers around the charm, and rubbed it around in a circular motion, turned her head my way.

"Thanks."

"I don't think I've seen anything like that in the jeweler stores, it must be antique."

She looked downwards, not making eye contact with me.

"Maybe. I'm not sure."

"I used to have one just like it."

She tossed her head back, and laughed without smiling. "Isn't that something," she lifted her glass, and swallowed every bit.

I felt a vibe off her that she knew what I was getting at. *How did you get my necklace?* The music stopped and caught my attention.

"Would everyone please welcome, Mr. and Mrs. Walker?"

I turned my head towards the entrance, as did everyone in the room, the newlyweds were standing under the trellis, holding hands, grinning and looking outwards at all their family and friends. Everyone began clapping their hands, as they took a bow. I knew the wedding meal would be served shortly because I could smell rosemary spice and chicken. Kylie and her new hubby made their way to the head table, which was adorned with candle votives, blue flowers, with a backdrop of sheer white lace and curtain lights. It was time for me to go back to my own table, and leave my necklace with Shelley, I couldn't prove it was mine, or make her give it back. I stood to my feet, and pushed in my chair.

"It was nice to see you Shelley," I forced a smile.

On the floor, under the chair was a little white card, I squat to pick it up, it was a name tag for someone's place setting. I reached to set it on the table, when I read the name Shelley Westinmalin. My blood boiled, quickly I looked away, pretending I hadn't read it, I picked up my little plate of cheese and crackers and took it back to my own spot beside Joe. Our table was filled with guests, a woman in a black dress nodded at me, as if to say hello, I put on my fake smile and gave her a little wave. Joe bragged to Uncle Sam all about the weekend in Vegas trip that 'he' purchased for Kylie and Benjamin. Feeling overheated, I removed my shall and draped it over the back of my chair, then filled my glass with white wine and drank it down, my throat stung a little as the wine was bitter tasting, it left a lingering sweetness on my tongue. I refilled my glass. *Shelley Westinmalin, Shelley Westinmalin,* I could not stop repeating those two words in my head. *Could she be the daughter, or niece of Edith Westinmalin? She must have gone back to her maiden name after her husband left her. Shelley Westinmalin has my necklace, but how? Was she sent to this wedding to collect the three hundred grand from Joe? I wish I knew what was going on.* Ten servers, dressed in white and black, in groups of two's began to bring out individual salads on large trays, and set them down in front of each person, beginning with the head table, and making their way around the room of approximately four hundred people.

"Excuse me, Garden or Caesar?"

I looked up to see a young thin woman, early twenties, long brown hair pulled back into a French braid, her lips pink, plump, and curved upwards.

"Garden please."

She carefully set my plate in front of me, while the other server set three distinct types of dressing on the table, they continued to Joe, and of course he picked the Caesar salad, opposite of mine. The plate of salad looked fresh and crisp, with spinach, mini tomatoes, cucumber, red onion, and peppers. I selected French dressing because it was my favorite, and Joe did also, I wasn't sure why he didn't go with the Caesar dressing? Joe reached for the wine bottle to fill his glass, and he refilled mine as well. I assume he wanted to put on airs in front of Uncle Sam. It seemed everyone at our table was chatting in pairs of two, except for me, I felt totally left out, but it was probably for the best because I wouldn't have made the best conversationalist due to my new obsession over Shelley, and my necklace. She didn't seem to possess criminal qualities, I couldn't picture her breaking into my home and stealing it, and I knew I didn't lose it outside somewhere because I remembered the last time I took it off was Thanksgiving night, after we brought the twins back from having supper at my father's place. That night Dad teased me saying he was surprised I hadn't lost it like I did everything else as a child. I placed it inside my jewelry box, and it disappeared shortly after. That was six years ago. The only way she could have gotten it, was if someone went into my box and got it for her, but the twins were too short at that time to reach it, and the only other person who would be in my room is Joe. *Why would he take it, and give it to Shelley? Unless, she was blackmailing him, after all she is a Westinmalin.*

"Chicken or Steak, Ma'am?"

The server had come back to the table to take my salad plate, and offer me supper.

"Chicken, thank you."

She smiled and set it on the table, Joe picked the steak, again the opposite of myself. I was beginning to feel more confident than I had earlier, it must have been from my four glasses of wine. My grilled chicken breast was served with seasoned potatoes, and caramelized carrots and yellow beans, a basket of fresh buns had been set on the table. The music had picked up in pace, and the guests had become louder, every so often the guests would clank their glasses with their spoons, indicating for the bride and groom to stand and kiss. I kept my eye on Shelley because she was a Westinmalin, and I wanted to take notice of any suspicious behavior. Uncle Sam had his mouth full of steak, I thought I'd take the opportunity to talk to Joe.

"Are you enjoying your steak?"

Joe nodded his head up and down, as he had just placed a large chunk in his mouth.

"My chicken is scrumptious. Did you know Shelley Westinmalin is here?"

Joe swallowed his meat, and guzzled down a half glass of wine, it was as if he wanted to pretend I hadn't asked him anything, he didn't even look at me. I held my eyes fixed on his grave expression.

"You know, Shelley, our neighbor?" I pressed.

"Um…yes. I know her."

"I think she's wearing one of my old necklaces. It's the one from the jewelry store that I won. Do you remember it?"

"I don't remember."

"Yes you do. It's the one that went missing after Thanksgiving, six years ago. She has my necklace."

Joe wiped his mouth with the cloth napkin, and placed it on his lap, still refusing to look my way. "That's far-fetched, don't you think? How would she get it?"

I could feel the wine starting to loosen my inhibitions, I wanted to keep quiet, but it felt so natural just to blurt out what I was thinking. "Well Joe, I thought it over, and the only person I could think of who could have given it to her was you."

"Magnolia, that's enough with the detective work tonight." His voice was calm, but he sounded as if he was scolding a child.

"It's mine Joe, it's a one of a kind, and I want to know how she got it."

Joe set his fork and knife down on the table, and finally looked at me. His cheeks were pinkish, as if he was embarrassed. His voice became stern. "We'll talk about this later."

"Why would your sister invite her?"

"It's her wedding, you are overreacting."

"What do you mean by that?"

"Nothing, just enjoy the evening, after all you're the one who wanted to attend."

"Is everything okay over there," said Uncle Sam, as he picked food out of his teeth with a toothpick.

"All good here," said Joe, turning to Uncle Sam, "Magnolia doesn't handle her alcohol well, I'm going to have to cut her off shortly."

I winked at Uncle Sam, "Never mind what Joe says, I'm fine, he's just teasing. Nothing to worry about." I filled my glass again with wine, and took a drink.

"If you say so dear," said Uncle Sam.

Uncle Sam was the sweetest man, I didn't know why he never married, perhaps it was because he used to smell like body odor, he always appeared clean, I think he was negligent to the use of under arm deodorant, likely scaring off every woman because they weren't brave enough to tell him, or they feared hurting his feelings.

I munched down as much of the meal as I could, until I forced myself to stop on account of saving room for desert. A lady dressed in a pink gown sat with her husband at the table next to ours, *I bet her necklace isn't stolen, like Shelley's,* the two of them looked to be so in love, how close they sat together, his arm wrapped around her shoulder as he leaned inwards to whisper into her ear, she smiled and quietly spoke back to him, I couldn't make out what they were saying, but I imagined it to be something like Aaron would have said to me if he were here. I was missing him, I studied the couples in the room, some laughed together, others walked hand in hand to get some fresh air on the balcony, maybe some hoping to steel away a quiet moment together. *What did other people think when they looked at Joe and me? I think we looked like decent people, dressed appropriately, manor's intact, except for my minor outburst with Joe, but no one from afar would have known about that. Perhaps they'd think we look like the perfect couple, sitting together enjoying an evening out.* The expression I have found to be most truthful is 'Looks can be deceiving'. *With all of the perfect looking couples in the room, which ones were being deceived by the other?*

Dessert was your choice of chocolate raspberry swirl mousse, or vanilla strawberry swirl mousse. Everyone at our table chose chocolate except for oddball Joe, who chose vanilla. The supper had made me exceptionally thirsty, I poured another glass of wine, to go with my desert because it was the only beverage on our table, I didn't feel like getting up to go to the bar to ask for water. Uncle Sam asked me to fill his glass as well, I think he'd had at least as many glasses as I, maybe more. Joe said he needed to stretch his legs and left the table. I wondered if that was the moment he was going to hand over the three hundred grand to the Westinmalins, or, Shelley, but she was still at her table. I was about to follow Joe when Uncle Sam started to talk to me, I didn't want to be rude.

"How are those children of yours?" he said.

"Very well, thank you. They're ten now, and still full of energy," I said.

"Glad to hear that. And the other one?"

"Other one what?"

"The other child?"

I thought the wine must have been getting to me, or him, but I wasn't sure who?

"Oh no, we just have the twins."

"Well, I could have sworn that Kylie said Joseph has three children, and another one on the way.

I couldn't contain my laughter, two more children would have meant that Joe and I would have had to have sex more than once every few months, meaning actual penetration, and him not pulling out at the last second, if a conception was going to happen. I'm sure Uncle Sam didn't understand why I was laughing, but he laughed along side of me, I was sure the wine was due credit for that.

"I think the story has gotten mixed up somehow, Uncle Sam."

"Kylie said, two boys, and a girl, with another coming in March."

"Last time I checked, Joe and I weren't having another."

Speaking of Joe, where was he? The waitresses had cleared the tables, and the speeches were about to begin. I was about to get up and start to look for him, when I saw him approaching our table.

"What took you so long?"

"I had a call on my cell," he pulled up his chair.

"Really? From who?"

"Just business."

"What kind of business?"

"Magnolia," his tone was sweet and calm, "Just business."

192

"As in business with the Westinmalins?"

Joe whispered, "Magnolia, don't cause a scene."

After Allan, the best man, did his speech in front of everyone, it was Lauren, the maid of honor's turn. They both basically said the same things which covered topics such as, funny childhood stories, how proud they were to be friends, and blessings to the bride and groom for a lifetime of happiness with their new spouse. Then it was Kylie and Benjamin's turn to get up and thank everyone for coming, and sharing in their special day. I watched Kylie closely as she professed her exuberance to everyone. She had a tissue in her hand, where she occasionally wiped tears of joy from her eyes, she was graceful, and seemed to truly appreciate everyone's presence on her special day. She deserved to be happy after having waited until age thirty-five to tie the knot with her chosen one, even though I hadn't been close with her for some time, I wished her marriage would turn out to be one that would last a lifetime, unlike so many other of my friends who have been married and divorced before the age of thirty.

I heard my phone vibrate inside my purse. I read the words, "I miss you," across the top of my phone. My stomach leaped as I saw it was a message from Aaron. I wanted to open his message, and text him back, Joe was occupied chatting with Uncle Sam, and sipping wine, so I knew he wouldn't notice if I did, but I couldn't bring myself to open it completely to read the rest, or any of his messages from the past few days, it was secretly killing me. I had to stay strong, and refrain at least until I could figure out if I could truly forgive him or not.

The lights were dimmed, and the DJ cranked up the tunes, guests had begun to take to the dance floor. Kylie and Benjamin were making their way around the room to say hello to the seated guests at their individual tables. I needed to use the ladies room after drinking non-stop all evening, I told Joe I'd be back, he didn't respond, I got up and left anyway. The washroom was spacious and tidy, there was a wicker basket on the middle of the counter, filled with supplies such as hairspray, brushes, deodorant, mini toothbrushes, and toothpaste, perfume, and facial powder. A nice touch for anyone who was in need to freshen up. I was all alone to do my business until I heard a few ladies enter the restroom. I didn't know how they could even understand each other all chatting and laughing at the same time, they must have had too much to drink and were in the giddy phase. I heard one of them go into the stall, while the other two made use of the product basket. One was spraying hairspray, and grumbling about how her hair was losing its volume, and she needed to fluff it up. My pantyhose had a run near the top, so I took some clear nail polish out of my purse and painted it to stop the run, I had a few minutes to kill until the polish would dry, which forced me to stay in the stall. The lady fixing her hair mentioned how gorgeous Kylie looked, and what a well-organized wedding it was. The other lady had a raspy voice, she asked if Kylie had a wedding coordinator? The woman in the stall yelled out, "She had Shelley Westinmalin help her."

At the mention of her name, I tried not to breathe, in fear that I'd be found out for listening in on something that wasn't intended for my ears.

"Isn't that the pregnant one?" said the lady with the rasp.

I heard the stall open and the tip tap of the lady's shoes on the floor, "Ya, Kylie said she's almost five months along." The water from the taps began to run, I assumed she must have been washing her hands.

I was right to suspect her being pregnant when I saw her last. Her husband had been gone for almost a year now, I hadn't ever seen her with another man, she hadn't brought anyone to the wedding, perhaps she's had a one night stand, and now she's facing the consequence. I was lucky not to have been in the same situation as her, however I might have been had Aaron not of had his vasectomy. Aaron was more than a one night stand, he went from attraction, to lust, to desire, to having an emotional grasp on me, I just couldn't seem to get him out of my head, or my heart.

"I heard she was divorced. Who would the father be, like...does she have a boyfriend?" said hairspray lady.

"I'm not sure, I heard she's the one who had that affair a while back, and that's why her husband left her. Apparently she was going around telling everyone that her husband was the one who cheated on her," said the tip tap shoes lady.

I remembered Shelley hinting the same story to me that time when she came in the hair salon, but she had told me she's the one who cheated. *Why would she tell me the truth, and lie to everyone else?*

"Kylie is nothing like that, how did she get hooked up with someone like Shelley?" said raspy lady.

"I heard she used to be the cleaning lady or something at Kylie's parents' house a long time ago," said tip tap shoes lady.

"So, basically maid turned friend turned wedding coordinator?" said hairspray lady.

"More or less," said tip tap.

"Hey ladies, do you hear that?" Excitement exploded from the hairspray lady. All three of them started to hoot and holler.

"It's our favorite song," they screamed.

"Let's go dance," said tip tap shoe lady.

The three of them scattered out of the bathroom, as I could hear the bass guitar stringing out their jam. The polish was dry now. My pantyhose were sticking to my leg. I gently pulled it off my skin, and adjusted them comfortably.

I washed my hands at the sink, and checked out my face in the mirror. My pupils were dilated from the wine, my cheeks rosy. I powdered my face, and tried to put together the whole Westinmalin thing, and the connection between them, Kylie, and Joe. The only thing that made any sense was they had some information that Joe didn't want getting out, so they were trying to bribe him for the money, *what information could be that important? Then there's the whole Shelley being the maid thing, I'd never heard any mention of her before, did Kylie just become friends with her parent's helper? The necklace thing was a mystery in its own, if Joe had given it to Shelley, could it have been for a bribe too? But...it's been missing for six years. Would they have been holding something over his head for that long? Had it been because of lawyer/client privacy privilege, I'd understand, but last time I checked bribing wasn't a part of that.* I was trying to enjoy the wedding, but I was beginning to get a headache from all of the mystery. I was overthinking. I needed to give my mind a rest for the night, and just try to have a good time, maybe mingle a little, and get reacquainted with some of the others.

Back in the banquet hall, most people were out of their seats, and dancing on the dance floor. I wasn't comfortable enough to dance alone, so I went back to our table. Joe was gone, but Uncle Sam was there, reclined back in his chair, he had a wide grin across his face. I think his mind was in the blurring phase of getting wasted because his hand was unsteady when he tried to pour himself another glass of wine, he over flowed his cup, and tried to lick it up off the table. I didn't see Shelley at her table either, perhaps she was up dancing, or perhaps she was collecting the three hundred grand from Joe? *Where are they?* I was supposed to be enjoying my evening and resting my mind, but I couldn't, not until I knew the whereabouts of those two. I poured myself another glass of wine to carry around with me, my purse was tucked between my left elbow and my side. I took a stroll around the dance floor in search of Joe. I saw Kylie dancing with her bridesmaids. I must have missed her visit to our table while in the ladies room. I made a plan to catch up with her later. I looked through the crowd, which was stupid because I knew Joe wasn't a dancer, he wouldn't want to risk embarrassing himself in front of everyone. That was always his reason for never dancing with me, he said he refused to look foolish, so he refrained from ever being involved in the act of physical expression. Everyone looked to be having a good time letting loose, without a care in the world, I couldn't remember the last time I went out and let loose, except with Aaron, but that wasn't exactly going out. It was sneaking out, and however satisfying it was, it wasn't the same as being chilled and carefree. I wandered over to the bar, and asked the tender to pour me a shot of whiskey, I thought it might help to sooth my ever-growing headache. I slugged it down, burned my esophagus all the way to my stomach. "Another one, please," I said.

"Sure thing," said the guy with the friendly smile.

I slugged that one down too, burning every bit as much as the first.

"Thank you."

There was an empty table near the back hallway, I sat on the table to rest my legs for a moment, and to settle a stomach that wasn't used to straight alcohol. A slow song begun to play, a handful of singles walked off the floor, others stayed and pulled their partner in closer and swayed together as the music played. I watched how some couples nestled up together and considered each other's eyes. Some had their heads resting on their partner's shoulders. Others were engulfed in passionate kisses. It made me think of Aaron, and how his lips sent tingles throughout my body, how I could feel his aura inside of mine before we even touched. It was magical, and beautiful, it was true love. I pulled out my phone to read his last text, "I miss you, please talk to me". The one before that read, "I'm so sorry, we can work this out." The several messages before that basically said the same things over and over. The one that stood out the most read, "Sunshine, I love you. I promise to never hurt you again."

That one cut like a knife, my insides tightened, and my heart stung. I chugged down the last bit of wine in my glass, then refilled again after opening a fresh bottle that sat on the table, *why not?* I chugged it down too. After a moment, the slow song ended only for another one to begin. My head was feeling better, the whiskey and wine must have finally kicked in, I was beginning to feel giddy. A lady I saw earlier wearing the bright yellow gown, now resembled a large duck with her butt stuck out as she clung to her partner, the black drake. I felt like giggling, and I did, no one looked my way, and I frankly didn't care if they did, or not. I was having a party for one with my bottle of wine. I was in the mood to dance, I didn't feel like asking a stranger because none of them were hot enough, if I was going to get close to someone, they'd have to be buff like Aaron. I flipped out my phone and typed, "Hey, wanna dance with me?" A moment later, Aaron texted back, "Sure."

I burst out laughing, and texted, "Get down here, Funny Pants."

"Anything for you, Missy."

"Too late...song over, ahaaa."

"I can't really dance, anyway."

"U R silly, no one will notice anyway."

"Can you teach me?"

"I would if you were here, but you're not, so I can't."

"Tell me where you are, and I'll meet you."

"Nope. Goodbye."

I giggled some more, knowing I teased him, it was fun. I drank back some more wine. The pace had begun to pick back up again, the duck lady was really shaking her tail now. It was just like watching one of those reality dance shows on television, where everyone tries to dance, some can and others resemble cats, trying to balance themselves on their back legs while their front legs swing in every direction. I was entertained, but began to get bored. My phone buzzed again, I put it back in my purse. *It's likely Aaron.* I remembered that I needed to find that ass Joe, and that thief Shelley, so I didn't text him back. I was a little unsteady on my feet when I got up from the table, so I stood a moment to catch my balance. I saw Kylie chatting it up with a little midget man who appeared harmless, I decided to go over to congratulate her.

"Hey, Lady," I called and swooped over to her, as shorty took off with his much taller lady friend. She looked surprised to see me, but held out her arms and greeted me with a tight embrace.

"I'm so glad you could be here," she said, her eyes flashing with excitement.

"Congratulations to you and your new man. I'm so happy for you." I held on to her forearm, and she rest her hand on mine, and squeezed.

"Thank you. How are you doing?"

"Right now, feeling good. I've been taking advantage of the booze."

She let out a hoot, throwing her head back, "That's what it's here for." She paused a moment, and all seriousness washed across her face, "I'm sorry that I haven't kept in touch with you."

"Don't worry about it, I'm just happy to share this with you now."

She pulled me into another embrace, and then leaned back to face me. "I stayed away from you because of the rift between Joe and I, enough time has passed now. You'll learn the truth soon."

"The truth about what?"

"It has never been my place to tell you, but I was hoping you'd see things clearly by coming to my wedding."

"I know Joe is involved with something. Please tell me what it is."

"Magnolia, look closer and you'll figure it out."

Her statement was confusing, "Figure out what?"

The MC announced it was time for the cutting of the cake. She squeezed my hand, "I've got to go. Take care."

"Nice to see you," I said, as she was escorted away by her maid of honor.

My head had a million and one baffled thoughts rolling around inside. Kylie was trying to give me a message, she knew what Joe was into, possibly about the Westinmalins, but she wouldn't tell me. I've always known how strong her loyalty was for her brother, based on the many times she came to his rescue as a teenager, even if he was in the wrong, she protected him.

The music went on, and people continued to dance after the cake was served, I didn't have any because my stomach swished from too much liquid. I had an inclination that Joe had abandoned me, but before overreacting, I decided to look outside. The entrance to the patio was surrounded with white and blue flowers, delicate white lights twinkled along the railing, and were strung overhead along wooden beams with flowers intertwined. There were enormous bouquets of flowers mounted on barrels spread around. The fragrance was sweet musk mixed with cigarette, from a few guests leaning on the railing, taking a drag or two while conversing. The music was quieter outside, the air was still, yet fresh, it was peaceful, refreshing for a change. Joe was not on the patio, neither was the thief, for all one knew, she'd gone home due to her pregnancy. Overlooking the grounds from the railing, perfectly trimmed flowering shrubs were adorned with the white lights, and grew on either side of a cobble stone path leading to somewhere. I noticed a couple strolling along, holding hands, then disappeared around a bend. I was curious to find out what was at the end, perchance I'd find Joe sealing his deal, or possibly it would lead me to a breathtaking botanical garden, either way I couldn't lose. I started down the path, it was tranquil, except for the echo from the dance, and the odd bug flying into the solar lights. The night sky was filled with patches of brightness, I wished I'd put my shawl back on, minute goosebumps were forming on my arms. I heard laughter of a woman's voice up ahead, then a man's voice rumbling. Sounded like they were either drunk or intensely enjoying each other's company. That's the kind of relationship I have always wanted, *how is it fair that everyone else is entitled to be happy with their partner except me?* Around the first bend, I gasped as a little white rabbit hopped out from behind a bush and crossed the path in front of me, then disappeared into the night. The sound of crickets chirping was pleasing to my ears, as long as none of them decided to jump out at me, everything would be good. I continued on until I reached a spot light to my right, shining upwards on a large stone statue, a pair of love birds sitting on a twig. I stopped a moment to admire the piece, I was saddened in thinking I was there experiencing the beauty of the path all alone, when it was obviously meant for lovers. An emptiness washed over me, I desired to rest my head against Aaron's chest, and feel the warmth from his body. Really, we hadn't spent much time together, but our relationship had left a profound impact on me, one that I'd never forget. I continued down the path and saw another statue on my left, a man and a woman sitting to face each other on a tree stump, naked, her left leg crossed over her right, his right hand rest upon her left thigh, her left arm around his neck, her head tipped upwards to meet his lips with hers. My insides sank, I was hollow and lonely, wishing I had brought a glass of wine with me, as my buzz was wearing off, reality was sinking back in. *Would I ever have my deepest desire? Would I ever find out what Joe was up to?* I turned and walked under a wooden trellis, meeting another couple, his arm around her back, he nodded at me, she said,

"Hello."

I nodded back, "Beautiful evening."

They both smiled, and squeezed past. I proceeded forward until the path came to an end, with an arrow pointing to the left.

Some lights flickered through the trees, I took a few steps forward, and saw a path made from stepping stones with wildflowers on either side, I was lead to a gazebo covered in tiny white lights, with blue flowers, and an ivy garland wrapped around the railing. I climbed the steps, and stood a moment to admire the beauty, over the railing, I saw a shallow man made pond, about one hundred square feet, in the center, a fountain sprinkled water about ten feet high. It was surrounded by a rock garden. I followed some stepping stones which led me to a bench, I sat and watched the water change colors as the spot light produced pink, then purple, then blue, green, and finally yellow. I was mesmerized, I wanted to stay there forever. I folded my arms and rubbed them, as my goosebumps were growing. Across the pond I heard voices, I couldn't get a clear view because of the sprinkling water, and the sky was dim. She laughed. He laughed. *Was it the same couple I heard when I first set out, or not, who knows? Loving couples are everywhere at this wedding. Is that the truth Kylie wanted me to see, everyone had someone special, except me? If so, she had to be aware that Joe and I were at odds.* I realized I had been feeling sorry for myself, I needed to stop wasting time, and get back on my mission to find Joe. I doubted he'd be having a secret meeting, all the way out here with the Westinmalins. If anything he'd be in one of the back rooms inside the banquet hall, making his deal. I took one last look around the pond, I wanted to take a picture, but I forgot my purse with my phone on the table before I came out. Tip tap, tip, tap, tap, I heard footsteps from the couple across the pond, figments of their body shapes moved across the stepping stones, they must have been heading back to the reception. I held off a minute before leaving, so it wouldn't be awkward for all three of us to walk back the path together, especially when I wasn't sure who they were, and being a third wheel wasn't my thing. They stood under the gazebo, the vines and flowers disabled me from seeing their faces, but I could see them standing together in a tight embrace. Their bodies looked as if they were dancing without music. I was uncomfortable in watching them, but I needed to see when they left, so I could leave too. I stayed seated at the bench out of their sight, listening to them babble on and on about how they wished they could be together every day, and how much they missed each other after spending several days apart from one another. I was getting impatient, I could either wait a while longer, or head straight for them and interrupt their intimate moment. I had a bright idea that if I made some noise they'd hear me and move on, so I picked up a couple of loose pebbles and tossed them at the gazebo, but it didn't affect them at all. I grabbed a few dime-sized stones from the garden, took few steps closer and flung them, hoping there'd be a greater impact, clueing them in to the fact that someone wants to pass by, but no, they were in their own little la la land, oblivious to everything around them. *Who was this couple?* As a peeping stocker, I sneaked closer and looked through the ivy-covered spindles, to see the woman sitting on top of the table with her dress hiked up, and legs apart. The man was standing in between her legs, pants intact. They began kissing, and holding each other tightly. My stomach flipped, I turned my head away. I needed to get out of there, the only other way was to climb over the picket fence but it was too close to the gazebo that I wouldn't be able to get by without them noticing. I stayed hidden and held my breath, hoping they'd leave. I heard clanking of a belt being unfastened, then a zipper being let down, I thought he was getting ready to take a leak, until I heard the satin rustling from her gown. My instincts told me not to look, but I had to be certain that I wasn't imagining things. His pelvis thrust forward, and both of them expelled a hard grunt. I couldn't believe it, they were doing it, *how disgusting, me, stuck here, listening to them carry on like porn stars.* I squat down behind the nishiki willow, and covered my ears to prevent their sexual escapade from infecting my memories for life. I could still sense the vibration from the table being lifted from him sticking it to her, a few minutes seemed like an eternity, until it finally stopped. I uncovered my ears and heard her say,

"I love you."

"I love you too," he said.

I heard moist lips kissing, then one of their phones buzzed. He said,

"I should check that."

There was a faint light gleaming inside the gazebo, I took a quick look, the brightness from his phone shone onto his face. *Joe.*

Chapter 14

Joe? What the hell? My nerves scrambled, my heart pumped against my chest. *Joe and who?* I started to breathe harder, and my body began to shake.

"It's just a message from my secretary."

"Is it really work, or is it another side girl?"

Joe laughed. "Here take a look."

He shone the phone on her face, allowing her to read the message. I saw the outline of her pointy nose, and the mass of curls cascading down to her shoulder. She reached for his phone and the light shone down on her chest, a sparkle caught my eye, the same kind of sparkle that caught my attention earlier at the dinner. It was the sparkle from my necklace, the one that Shelley stole. It was Shelley with Joe. *Shelley Westinmalin.* Every muscle in my body tensed, I wanted to scream, but with discipline, I held myself together without budging.

"Okay, I believe you," she said.

"Come on, we need to get back before someone notices us missing," said Joe.

"Magnolia is going to ask you where you've been, what are you going to say?"

"Same thing I've always told her. I was on a business call."

"Has she not picked up on that one yet?"

"I've always gotten away with it, so no she hasn't."

They seemed so comfortable talking about me, and equally comfortable with each other. Their voices were without shame, as if their conversation was the norm.

"Why don't you leave her? You've been unhappy for too long."

"I've worked too hard for that Shell, you know she'd get everything, and I'd have nothing left for myself...and you, and the kids."

202

The kids? Is he referring to my kids, or her kid, or her unborn kid? My mind ran wild, *oh my goodness, Uncle Sam said Kylie told him that Joe had two boys, a girl, and another on the way. Kaden is Joe's child, and Kylie knows about it. Joe's been having an affair.*

"My parents will have nothing to bribe you with if you tell her about us."

"I can handle your parents. They are not getting one red cent of my money."

"How are you going to stop them from telling her without paying them?"

"I'll find a way to smooth them over. I need more time, that's all."

"Maybe I can try talking them out of it again."

"That worked with the first child, I don't think it will work with the second."

Her parents, the Westinmalins were bribing him, if he doesn't give them three hundred thousand dollars, they will tell me the truth, and he doesn't want that because he's afraid I'll leave and take him to the cleaners. What a selfish jackass. Is she ever stupid to accept his behavior, maybe that's why her parents are bribing him, they want better for their daughter, and this is their way of telling him to either buck up or pay up.

"You and I could spend our lives together with our kids, you'd be much happier."

"We've been over this, I can't give up everything that I've spent my life working to have."

I could not believe what I was hearing. *How could I have been so stupid,* my stomach was twisting, acid moved up my esophagus and burned the back of my throat, I swallowed to prevent myself from vomiting.

"It's my wishful thinking, but as long as we love each other, we have everything."

"We'll always have each other, no matter what," he said.

I was beginning to think that they'd never leave, and I'd be stuck there forever, listening to my husband with his mistress.

"Come on, we have to get back."

I heard them kiss again, *gross,* then their footsteps across the wooden plank floor of the gazebo. I was trapped in my squat position, unable to move, in shock, my nerves sizzled like bacon in a pan. I managed to stand to my feet, unsure of everything. It was late, I didn't have time to process what I had learned, I needed to get back and pretend I didn't know anything until I could figure out what to do. One thing I knew for sure is that I wasn't walking through that damn gazebo where they had screwed, *heels or no heels, over the fence it is.*

I gave them a few minutes to get a head start, before proceeding. Their moans, and grunts haunted me to the point of nausea. The trail was quiet on the way back until I reached the statue of the man and woman, the thump from the bass was faintly heard, and giggles from Shelley and Joe told me that they were up ahead around the next bend. She sounded as if she were being tickled, his chuckle sincere, he was enjoying himself, something I hadn't heard for years. *She's the reason that he's been treating me like dirt, what a slut, sneaking around in a public place where no one would pay attention to who was with whom due to the loud music, and vast consumption of alcohol.*

"We're almost there, we need to go our own way," said Joe.

"I'll see you in a couple days then?"

"Or sooner."

They were making plans of when to meet next, *how pathetic.* I inched up a ways to get another look, to clarify if it was Joe and Shelley. He had his arms around her from behind, his chin resting on her shoulder, his hands rest on her abdomen, *her baby, their baby.* She snuggled against him, her hands rest on his. They appeared cozy. *How sickening.* I tucked back behind the shrubs until I heard them trod off.

I knew I'd have to act normal when I saw Joe, and Shelley *who screwed my husband while wearing my necklace.* I was having a hard time calming my nerves, and my stomach refused to settle, my body temperature raised, as it does when you have the flu, I knew I was about to hurl, off the path, and a mad dash into the bushes, I bent over, the wine and half-digested chicken spewed out of my mouth like a funnel into the grass. I kneeled to the ground, and wiped my mouth with my hand, then my hand on the grass. I hunched over, hugged my stomach, and breathed. The queasiness stopped, I needed to get a grip, and get back to the reception.

Inside, the banquet hall the party was still going on, now a slow song was playing, and couples filled the dance floor, a few singles stood around chatting, I snuck over to the table that I was

204

at earlier, to retrieve my purse. I needed to get to the washroom, and freshen up from vomiting. At our table, I saw Joe talking to some guy, my insides clenched, and my teeth clamped down, I wanted to scream as soon as I saw him. I hoped I could slip past him unnoticed, but I could see the two of them pointing at me, he motioned for me to go over. I forced a smile and went over.

"Well Joseph, she's just as pretty as I remember."

How pretty and pale I must look after heaving up all of my supper.

"Hello," I said, greeting him with my fake smile.

"Magnolia, you remember my old neighbor Clyde, don't you?"

"Clyde, I didn't know you'd be here?"

Joe grew up living beside Clyde, the only African-American man on the street, I remember when Joe and I were dating, he used to say if we didn't stop in to visit him once a week, he was going to make up a story and tell Joe's parents that he caught us making out in his tool shed, and we'd be in trouble. He was a riot, I remember Kylie being fond of him as well, must be the reason she invited him.

"I'm getting old, so you two had better come for a visit, and bring those children for me to meet."

Children, which children of Joe's was he referring to? I bet he didn't know how many Joe really had.

"They'd love that," said Joe, putting on airs again.

Clyde looked as handsome as ever, with his short corn rows pulled back into a ponytail. "Joseph, aren't you going to ask your lovely wife to dance? That's how you keep the romance going."

Joe smiled at Clyde, and looked up at me, "Care to dance?"

No way I was getting anywhere near him after his performance outside, I felt like regurgitating all over again, but I was on empty. Joe was trying to impress Clyde by asking me, *Had he even washed her off his hands after he'd come in?* It took everything I had to refrain from grabbing the empty wine bottle on the table and smashing it over his head.

"Thank you, Joe, but I need to make a trip to the ladies room. Clyde, it's nice to see you, take care." I kept my composure and left them both at the table.

In the restroom, I rinsed my mouth with water, touched up my face, and smoothed my hair. A few ladies came in, did their business and left. Mrs. Lauders texted me to see how the night was going, I wasn't sure how to respond, so I sent her an emoji ghost with "ttyl".

Kaden is the half-brother to my twins, and now they'll have another sibling in March. How will I ever explain this ambiguous affair to them? We had a close to perfect family, before things changed. *Everything makes sense now, Joe got involved with Shelley seven plus years ago, and he's been lying to me ever since. How could he deceive me like that? Had he stayed faithful, would our marriage have grown into an unbreakable love that lasts a lifetime? Would I have been happy enough to keep focused on him, not allowing Aaron to turn my head? I suppose I'll never know.* My head began to pound from the shock. *Time to go home.*

It was hard to sleep beside Joe that night knowing he'd had his pecker inside of another woman only hours before. I made sure my body stayed within its own proximity, never to have contact with him.

The kids were staying with my dad until late afternoon, leaving me a free day to recover with a double dosage of acetaminophen. Around ten o'clock, Joe said he had to prepare for a case that he was working on, so he was spending the day at the office and wouldn't be home until after supper. I assumed he was lying to spend Sunday with Shelley and Kaden. *What a dick, he looked me straight in the eyes and lied, the same lie he's been telling me for years.* He was convincing, as was I when I told him to have a nice day. *I suppose if a person tells the same lie repeatedly it becomes a truth in their own mind, and it's as natural as breathing.*

About thirty minutes after Joe's car left the driveway, I saw Shelley's car leave her house as well. I thought about following her to find out the location of their hideout, instead I wanted to go through Joe's office again, to see if I could uncover any more secrets he had to hide. I didn't care if he caught me or not, I had the upper hand. I went through his desk drawers, file cabinet, bankers boxes, and storage closet, I found nothing except legit client files, and supplies. Nothing concerning the Westinmalins or Shelley, or evidence of their affair. I sat in Joe's desk chair, and noticed that Joe had a clear view of Shelley's backyard from his window opposite our deck. She had a child's play structure with sandbox set up in the back corner, an iron fence surrounded her property. *All those years Joe sat here and watched Kaden grow up and kept his eye on Shelley. How the hell could he live a life like this? Our twins running around inside, while his illegitimate child was running around outside, how twisted for him to be okay with that. He'd have to be comfortable lying to me every day, for the purpose of keeping this house and the money. He seemed happy with Shelley yesterday, how could money be more important than love? I've been miserable every day for too long, wondering how my marriage could have went wrong, and why Joe was distant? Eighteen years is a long time to stay with someone whom you're not completely in love with, I suppose it was around the twelve year mark that did us in. I wish I would have found out sooner, the last six years have been wasted on hopes for a change. I'm sure he could have felt my discontentment, but he'd rather put me through this than leave me. At least Shelley knew what she was getting into, me on the other hand, complete darkness. How long was he willing to do this to me? How many times did he sit in this very chair and wish he was there with them? What did he see in her that I didn't give him? Sure, she's a few years younger than me, but I honestly don't know what she could possibly give him that I hadn't already? Maybe it was the slut factor he was into, some might say I was a slut for doing it with Aaron at my salon, but the key words are, 'my salon', and it was behind closed doors, those two were literally out in the open, and her being pregnant makes it much worse.*

I lifted the double photo frame standing on Joe's desk, it held pictures of the twins from their toddler years. Staring at it, their smiles were so innocent and perfect, I had no idea what I'd tell them when the time was right. I remember feeling blessed when I gave these photos to Joe, he hugged me, and said, "They are beautiful, they must take after their mother." He was sincere, and I felt loved. That was forever ago, *but exactly how long ago?* I flipped over the frame, and lifted the backing off, the date said 2011. *That's not right, 2011 would make Jonah age four, and this picture was when he was one or two.* I took the picture out of the frame, and a few others fell out with it. Baby boy photos, that were not of my baby boy. One looked like a first birthday photo, baby in highchair, cake in front with one lit candle. Other was a baby boy dressed up in a bright yellow furry duck costume. He was sitting on the floor surrounded by rubber duck bathtub toys, date on the back October, 2011. *Oh my goodness, it was a duplicate photo of the one I'd seen at the Westinmalins house. It's Kaden as a baby, and Joe's had them stashed here all along. How could I be so naïve? I am married to a liar. If he would have stayed faithful, our* marriage might have been a rare one that defied the odds of divorce. He could have stayed focused on our family, and through hard work and dedication, we could have had an amazing thing. He acted concerned the day I couldn't find my necklace, he even moved out my dresser, so I could check to see if it had fallen behind, then he went out to check the car. *What a deceptive ass. How dare he give her my necklace! I want it back. It's been on her neck for years. I saw them screw while she wore my necklace, gross. No, I don't want it back.*

I put the photos back in the frame, and made sure everything in the office was up to the standards of Joe, he wouldn't even know I'd been in there. *What will the Westinmalins do when they find out I know the truth? Will they be happy that their little girl can run off and be with the man of her dreams, or will they be disappointed that they won't be getting the three hundred grand...unless Joe goes through with it and pays them before I break it off with him. It would be fun to see him suffer a while longer, having them on his back, torturing him. Joe and the Westinmalins deserve each other with all of their lying, cheating, and bribing. I want no part of it. Sadly, my children are connected to them because of their half siblings, I hate that. If I stayed with Joe, the twins will grow up being unaware of his other kids, because he'll continue to keep it a secret. I can't live the next eight years like that, waiting on the twins to grow up. I'd be keeping a secret from my kids, and I'd be no different than the Westinmalins, or Joe.*

I knew the next few weeks would be challenging, I texted Lucy and told her I'd be taking some time off, so she could go ahead and hire her niece, Everlea to take my place, if she hadn't found work elsewhere.

I sat in the breakfast room and tried to drink down my blueberry smoothie. Looking out through the stained-glass window, I took a moment to admire our tallest maple tree, bright orange with yellowish-green leaves spiraled to the ground, in groups of five or ten, then stopped. *Would this be my last autumn in this house, next year it could be Shelley sitting in this spot, looking out my window while holding her baby.* Strangely, I was bothered more by the fact that Joe'd been living a double life, rather than the idea of moving on and divorcing him. *Was I crazy to be relieved that Joe was fooling around? Now I have a legitimate excuse for leaving our miserable life.* I should have been feeling guilty for cheating on him, but I wasn't, a sure sign that I was finished with him. If I had felt truly loved by him, I never would have strayed. He didn't love me, and I was certain he wouldn't be pining under a rock for me after I was gone. He'd be able to move on no trouble, with the exception of losing my half of everything. *If he loves Shelley, he should be with her, then the two of them can spend their lives admiring my necklace.*

Aaron had texted me a few times that morning. The first one at 8am said, "Good morning, beautiful," with a happy face emoji. Funny how a single text from Aaron brings light to my world. I returned his text with a wink. I figured he deserved that much after I drunk texted him last night. At 10am, he texted me, and said, "I'm ready for that dance, Missy."

I wanted to tell him to get on over here, I would have loved to see his smile, and feel his warmth. I wanted to tell him about the Westinmalins, but it was too soon.

"Maybe someday, if you are lucky." I texted back.

"I'm patient, I'll wait," he said.

I drove to Dad's to pick up the twins late afternoon as he requested, per the twins they had spent most of the weekend fishing, and caught enough to eat for supper, for the next two weeks, which was a given by the smell of fried pike when I walked in the door. I hugged them both, they kissed my cheeks. I didn't realize how much I'd missed them until my body absorbed the bounty of love they expelled. They tugged my arms and pulled me to the couch, both eager to tell me all about their eventful weekend, their voices overlapped as I tried to fit each story together. Dad sat in his recliner, and listened to the kids. His eyes were full of life, he always said his grandkids were more entertaining than the television.

"Mommy, wait here, we have something to show you," said Jody.

The two of them dashed off outside.

"The kids look good, Dad, thanks for watching them."

Dad stretched back in his chair, unrolled the sleeves of his flannel shirt. "It's my pleasure, darling. How was your weekend?"

Goodness, I wasn't sure how to tell him what happened, "Um…well, the wedding was beautiful, the rest wasn't what I expected."

"What do you mean?" Dad leaned forward.

I put the couch cushion behind my back to get comfortable. I was aching to talk to someone, but once I let the words out. I wouldn't be able to take them back. I struggled to get the proper wording, "I found…I learned…um…I found out Joe's been having an affair."

Dad's face twisted in disgust, "We don't do those things in this family. What is wrong with him?"

"He doesn't know I've found out, but I'm going to be leaving him."

"Are you sure that's what you want?"

"He's been lying to me for at least seven years, and he has child with another woman, and the woman is pregnant again."

Dad looked shocked, "Darling, I'm sorry. Are you alright?"

"Honestly, Dad, I've been unhappy with him for a long time, and getting divorced will be the best thing for everyone."

"That's not the kind of life I wanted for you, sweetheart. Who would think after all of these years he'd do something that stupid?"

I heard the back door squeak, two sets of footsteps dashed across the kitchen. Dad cocked his head to the side, both of us went quiet. It was the twins, each carrying a blanket in their arms rolled up into a ball, both had smiles from ear to ear, Jody was giggling.

"Look, Mom," Jody tipped her blanket down, and a furry orange head stuck out.

"Ohh, so sweet," I reached to pet it.

Jonah opened his blanket, I heard a tiny meow, and a striped grey kitten peered out.

"Can I hold him?"

Jonah placed the blanket on my lap, and handed me the little fellow. I rubbed his soft head, as he remained still and his blue eyes stared at Jonah whose chin was resting on my lap, staring back at the kitten. "Can we keep him?"

"Ya Mommy, there are two, one for each of us," said Jody.

"I do love kittens, but they don't look big enough to take away from their mother, and besides your father is allergic to cats." I caught my tongue, it was a habit to think of what Joe's needs were, but his needs wouldn't matter much longer, nor if he was allergic. We'd have our own house soon enough, free of Joe, and free to have kittens if we wanted. Dad raised his eyebrows at me, I knew what he was thinking, 'Poor kids.'

"Please, Mom," they begged.

"I'll think it over, but if we did take them, it wouldn't be until they are drinking on their own, and only if grandpa doesn't want them."

"Grandpa, do you want them?" said Jonah.

"How long will that be?" asked Jody.

I looked at Dad, "Are they five weeks yet?"

"About four."

"Can we have them grandpa?" said the twins.

Dad winked at me, "It's okay with me."

"Yay," Jody screeched.

"Thank you, Grandpa," said Jonah. "Ya."

"You two can start saying goodbye to the kittens, we have to leave soon."

I handed Jonah the kitten, he carefully wrapped it back up.

"Come on, let's take them back to the barn," said Jody.

Dad scratched his forehead, and looked toward the floor, as he did when trying to make sense of something. After the kids were out of earshot, Dad said, "I didn't want to get involved in your business, but I've noticed before that Joseph seemed different than he used to, more stressed, I chalked it up to his workload."

"He's been distant, I used to try to make things better, but now, too much has happened. We can't go back."

"Darling, you deserve a man who respects you, and shows you every day how lucky he is to have you. You deserve to have the kind of relationship that your mother and I had."

I blinked back my tears, I remembered very little about my mother, except one day my dad came in from doing chores, my mom was cooking in the kitchen, dad stared at her from across the room, and said, "There's the beautiful lady." Her face looked like a teenaged girl crushing on a cute boy, as she faced him. He asked her to bring him a cold glass of water, when she took it to him their hands touched. He said, 'Thanks, sweetie' and he kissed her on the lips. I was so grossed out, I had to cover my eyes.

"Your mother took care of me, and I took care of her, and that's how a relationship should work. It's not one taking advantage of the other, and that's what Joseph has done to you."

"You're right, Dad. He has. I just want what's right for the kids."

"It might be hard at the start, but those kids have Woodward blood in them, they'll be just fine."

"I hope you are right, Dad."

"I'll help you anyway I can, they are good kids."

"Thanks, Dad."

"Why don't you move back home for a while, until you get things figured out."

"With you?"

"Yes, I'd love to have you all here."

"That's generous, but I'm not sure. Can I think it over?"

"Of course."

My dad is officially the sweetest father a girl could ask for, so supportive, and loving. He has been there every time I've needed him. I hope Jonah grows to have his traits, and not those of Joe.

The scent of fresh fish filled the van on the way home. Dad had cleaned a bunch and insisted on sending it home with us. The kids tried to come up with perfect names for their kittens, while I tried to come up with the perfect way to tell my kids we'd be moving. After hugging Dad, he handed me credentials of his friend Michael Adams, the lawyer, who had thirty-five years of experience, more than Joe who had only fifteen. Dad wanted me to get the best legal counsel possible, someone who knows the ins and outs of the law, incase Joe tried to pull one over on me.

I planned on calling Michael Adams first thing tomorrow morning, to set up an appointment. I had to start making plans for my new life with the twins. I needed to find a house for us, Dad was kind to offer letting us stay with him, but I didn't want the twins to get settled into Dad's, then move them again after finding our own place. Laudersville was my everything, and I wanted to stay close to my family. I wasn't sure what Joe's reaction would be upon finding out that I was leaving him. I knew he wouldn't threaten to take the twins from me because he hasn't an interest in spending time with them, let alone giving up his own time for their day-to-day care, he had no idea what they were doing on a regular basis, and I knew he wouldn't want to start now. The kids would choose me over him because ten out of ten times they come to me, and not him. He'd be mostly concerned about losing his precious house, and cash in the bank over the kids, if he was given the choice.

Joe arrived home around seven-thirty, I thought I'd have some fun with him and see what kind of a lie he'd tell me that time.

He sat in his chair, clicked on the television, and started to flip through the channels. I pulled up my rocker beside him,

"How was your day, dear?"

His eyebrows frowned, he looked out of the corner of his eye at me. "Good," he said.

"Did you get much work finished?"

"Yep."

"Good. What case are you working on?"

"That's confidential."

"I won't tell anyone. Besides I'm your wife, you can tell me anything."

"Magnolia, I'm tired. It's been a long day."

"You said you wanted to work on our marriage, so I thought if we spent more time telling each other things, we'd be closer."

He placed his hand on top of my left hand that rested on the arm of my chair. His voice soft and sweet, "I do want that for us. Really, I'm just tired out."

I wanted to pull my hand away, I was repulsed to think of where his hands had been today. Knowing that he wouldn't take me up on the offer, I said, "Sounds like you need a stress reliever, how about after the kids are in bed, I give you a warm massage, and then we can get all up in each other, if you know what I mean." I reached over and gently squeezed his upper thigh, as I used to.

"Sounds nice, but I really need some down time."

"Okay, maybe next time."

"Maybe."

What a snake, we haven't had sex for over two weeks, any man who wasn't getting it elsewhere would snatch up that offer in a flat second. How could he be fine leaving his own wife wanting? Of course, I'd never give it to him again, I wanted to hear what lame excuse he'd give me for not having it. Partially convincing he was, by the charming way he stroked my hand. It's amazing how he could look into my face and lie over and over.

"Well, I'll leave you to relax then."

Around nine, I could hear his stupid documentary blaring all the way upstairs, that was one thing I wouldn't miss after I was gone. I wanted to take a shower and freshen up, we had Dad's deep fried fish for supper, and it left the smell of grease on my skin, clothes, and hair. I stood under the hot water, and closed my eyes. It felt good trickling down my body, I turned from back to front, and back again, then lathered up with lavender scent body wash. It was the same wash I used the last time Aaron and I made love. Flashes of us in Meredith's spare room invaded my mind, the scent of my lavender mixed with Aaron's vanilla-aqua scent was delicious, I remembered the look of ecstasy all over his face as he touched me, the natural awakening of my senses as he fondled me, the firmness of his erection giving me pleasure. *Lord, I want to feel him.* Looking downwards, my nipples had hardened, the mere thought of him turned me on. I didn't want to be without him. Our connection was unbreakable, at least that's what I was beginning to believe, he hadn't given up on me, and I still desired him. *Had he not given me his information about the Westinmalins, would I still be in the dark about Shelley and Joe? Would I have been out searching for him at Kylie's wedding, or would I have remained inside chatting it up with Uncle Sam?* The Westinmalins had screwed with my life, but they didn't force Joe to cheat on me, they wanted to force Joe and I apart, and they were about to get what they wanted. Aaron and I had a connection before they stirred things up, but I had it under control. Had Joe not been involved with Shelley, none of it would have happened. Joe was the root of the problem, he made his own decisions, and I'll be glad to rid myself from him. I dried off, wrapped up in my towel, and pulled my pink cotton nighty out of my vanity drawer, when I unfolded it something fell from it onto the floor. I picked it up, and realized it was the sweater I had stuffed in there, the night of the bonfire. My body went limp as I held it up to my nose, delighted in the faint aroma of Aaron's cologne and smoke. I held my sweater up against my chest, snuggling it, I closed my eyes and imagined it was Aaron. I smelled it again, wanting to let out a roar in yearning for him. Tears ran down my cheeks, I sat on the edge of the bathtub and wrapped my shoulders with the sweater. I took deep breaths, trying to control my cry, my throat ached from holding it in, tears flooded my eyes, I covered my face with my hands, trying to get myself together, but more tears flowed. All I could focus on was Aaron telling me that he loved me, I wished I had declared my love for him the first moment I'd felt it, but I was afraid.

I dried my face with the hand towel, managed to get a grip, and got dressed. After drying my hair, I climbed into bed and covered my chest with my sweater. Aaron's hands had been all over that sweater, my skin quivered wanting to feel his captivating touch. An uncontrollable tear slipped down the side of my face, dampening my pillow, and then another. Joe hadn't come to bed yet, frankly I wished he'd stay downstairs all night.

Chapter 15

I woke to the buzz of my alarm, and no Joe in sight. My wish had come true, his side of the bed was untouched, leaving me alone with my now crumpled Aaron scented sweater. *Had he snuck over to Shelley's in the night? I don't care.* I was relieved I wouldn't have to feel guilty about leaving him, or for my affair with Aaron. That was the deal breaker for me, knowing I could cheat and not feel bad about it, was the truest sign that leaving Joe was the right decision, yet it was surreal. Other people did things like that, not me, but there I was glad to have had tasted what I've been craving my whole life. Had it been someone else other than Aaron, I'm not sure what I'd have felt. I placed my sweater over my face and inhaled an imaginary strong scent of Aaron, my insides ached to feel him inside me, and run my hands down his back, and kiss his sweet lips, I indulged a few moments longer. My phone buzzed forcing me to get up.

"Good morning, Beautiful."

This man...what to do with him? I sent him an emoji of the sun, without words, hoping he'd know I hadn't forgotten about him.

"Have a great day, xoxo."

"Thanks, you too."

He continued to send xoxo after everything, maybe he was hoping I'd send it back sometime.

After the kids got on the bus, I contacted Dad's lawyer friend, Michael. His secretary said my dad had already contacted him, and cashed in a favor to have me squeezed in today for eleven o'clock. That gave me enough time to jot down what I wanted for a divorce settlement, I knew exactly what to ask for due to the numerous times that I've fantasized about divorcing Joe.

Around nine-thirty, I popped by the salon, to see if everything had been working out for Lucy and her niece. When I walked in the door, the two of them were gabbing up a storm with their clients; Lucy doing a cut, Everlea finishing a roller set comb-out, which looked fantastically symmetrical, at that point I knew the salon would be in good hands for a while. After Lucy's client left, I had her slip into the back room with me for a minute, to give her the short version of what's been going on, excluding the part about Aaron and I. She hugged me, and said she'd be here for me anyway she could.

My phone buzzed in my back pocket, it was Meredith.

"Hey, stop by and check out the renovations when you have time."

"I promise, I will soon."

"I'm home all day today."

"Possibility for this afternoon."

"Okay great."

I was eager to see the renovations, but I needed to let Meredith know what was going on with Joe and me before it was out in the open.

Michael's secretary told me to go ahead in and have a seat. His twentieth-floor office smelled of fresh paint, and stationary, reminding me of Laudersville's print store. Behind his wooden bureau was a wall to wall window, illuminating the skyline. From my chair, I could see the blue sky with white fluffy clouds, a flock of geese shaped in a 'V' flew overhead. *If my salon looked like this, I'd never get any work done.* Everything was placed in an exact order on his desk, computer to the left, telephone to his right, a single pen rest beside a black note book, all free from dust.

"Mrs. Edwards?" A modulated voice addressed me from behind. I turned to see a medium build man with dark glasses, dressed in a brown suit, and grey hair swept to the side covering his bald spot in the center of his head. His face earnest, he approached me with his hand extended for a shake.

"Please don't get up," he said.

"Just Magnolia, please." I stretched my hand to meet his firm grip. He continued around to sit in his suede rolly chair.

A little uneasy, *how would I explain to him that I needed a divorce and keep my smile on?*

"If you don't mind me saying, you are the spitting image of your mother."

"My mother?" My eyes grew large, "…thank you. You knew my mother?"

"Of course, I met her years back when your father took us out in his boat. A beautiful woman," he moved his head from left to right. "We caught five largemouth bass that day, your mother caught an eight pounder. She skunked us both out of our two dollar bet on biggest fish."

216

He made me smile. "Yes, Dad had mentioned Mom being an avid fisherwoman, alongside her other talents."

"She was a great lady, with a wonderful sense of humor, and she was a fantastic cook. That night she fried our catch, it was the best I've ever tasted."

I was calmed, knowing he liked my mother, and she must have liked him enough to go fishing with him and Dad, it made everything better. "I have her recipe."

"If your cooking is as half as good as hers, you should be proud."

"I do my best."

He picked up his pen and flipped open his notebook. "We need to get started."

I handed him my notes about what I thought'd be a fair settlement. He put on his glasses and read diligently, then came back with the response that I should be asking for more, based on our net worth. I explained to him that my mother had a life insurance policy on herself that she willed to me when I was five. My dad invested the entire thing, said he could get by without it, over the years the investment grew, and as of next year—my forty-first birthday, it will be worth four hundred thousand dollars. He explained that Joe and I had been together for eighteen years and fifty percent of everything belonged to me. I was aware of that but it didn't seem right to take away the only home my kids had ever known, in order for me to get my half. I wanted them to have a familiar place to visit their father on selected weekends. Michael explained to me that if I didn't take my half, my control would be lost, and what Joe did with the remaining assets would be his business, and no guarantee it'd go to our kids. He presented me with different options, I settled on taking thirty-three percent of our net worth, and leaving my remaining seventeen percent with Joe to secure the house, and in trust for the twins. If he decided on selling the house, my seventeen percent would automatically go to the twins. Joe would also be responsible for paying fifty percent of the children's' extra-extraordinary expenses, and a monthly child support according to the federal child support guidelines of Ontario. I signed off on spouse support, I was not greedy, I could earn my own cash, I didn't need to rely on him to support me, and I wasn't after revenge. What I was after was a clean and easy break, with as little attachments as possible. Michael said he respected my choice to not run Joe into the ground and take every cent I could get.

Michael stood to his feet reaching to shake my hand, "I'll have the papers drawn up now."

"Now? I don't have to wait a week or so?"

"Your father has always been a great friend to me, and he's never asked for anything in return, until now. Go and have lunch somewhere, and the papers will be ready within the hour."

"Thank you so much." Once more, I extended my hand to meet his.

Troy's Restaurant smelled of pizza and grease, before I had the doors open. A sign out front said All-You-Can-Eat-Buffet, I figured that'd be the quickest service, and I was craving pizza. I filled my plate with Caesar salad, bread sticks with tomato sauce, meatballs, and fresh vegetarian pizza, and sat in a booth. The pizza had mixed Italian spices, the oregano, and basil were the strongest scents, one of my favorite combinations. I picked up a slice of pizza, and noticed my diamond engagement ring, I'd been wearing it so long that there was a permanent indent on my wedding finger. It sparkled under the ambient lights above my table, I could see my reflection in its smooth face, and if I angled it, I could see other objects in the room as clear as day. In only a short while, I'd be taking it off for good, and that'd be what I'd miss. Around the restaurant, sat people of all ages, some were couples, others were singles...single men. In a few months, I'd be free to date, I didn't have the urge to meet anyone else, but the idea of being allowed to was nice. Not one of the men in the restaurant looked remotely appealing, they looked either unshaven with bushy hair, or had stains running down their shirts, one man was picking his teeth with the fork. *Gross.* The staff looked tidy, and the restaurant appeared clean, except for those yuckies. One man sat alone in the corner, his back to me, with neatly trimmed hair at his neckline. He wore a blue flannel shirt, reminded me of Aaron, and my insides clenched, wanting it to be him. I pictured myself walking over to him, and single handedly clearing the table with a quick swipe of my hand. He'd lift me and set my bottom at the end of the table, we'd kiss frantically and breathy, he'd rip my blouse open to expose my naked breasts, and begin fondling them with his tongue and lips. I'd unfasten his jeans, and let them fall to his knees, penis erect, I'd moisten my hand with my saliva and stroke him, he'd throw his head back absorbing the pleasure, he'd lift my skirt up around my waist, my bare bottom resting on his hands, I'd arch my back and loosely wrap my legs around his waist, with my right hand, I'd stretch his firmness to massage my opening, and he'd

218

buck himself inside me, both of us letting out a wail of heedless blithe. The table would rattle and teeter on the floor, as it wouldn't be sturdy enough to support the action. We'd both release at the same time, as the revelry between the two of us would be too much to handle.

"Can I get you another water, Madame?" said the waitress.

Startling me out of my daydream, a blonde lady stood with a jug of water in her hand.

"Yes, please."

She smiled and filled my glass to the top, then went to the next booth. I checked my watch, still had twenty-five minutes to kill, which was fine, I got up for another slice of pizza, cheese. I wanted to text Aaron and let him know what I was up to, but I knew it'd be best if I didn't mention anything to him yet. My little fantasy really had me missing him, finally I gave in and texted him.

"Hey." I waited only a minute for a response, long enough to take a few more bites of my pizza.

"Hello, Beautiful. How is your day so far?"

Hello beautiful, that never gets old. "Good. I was thinking of you."

"Everything sweet I'm sure."

"I'll never tell."

"Sunshine, I need to see you."

"Of course you do," I teased.

"Will you meet with me soon?"

"I'll think about it, and get back to you, okay?"

"Don't think too long, just meet me."

"Okay."

Lord, I want to meet him right now, I knew I wouldn't be able to keep my hands off him if I did, but there was no time today, I had to stay focused on getting my plans together.

Back home, I read over our settlement papers, everything was in order, including my sole child custody agreement. Thank goodness for my dad asking his friend to help out. I wasn't sure how I'd present the papers to Joe, so I hid them in my bathroom drawer under my box of tampons. Meredith texted me again around two o'clock. "I see your car in the driveway. Are you coming over?"

"Sure. I'll be there in five."

I felt like texting the Westinmalins and telling them they could call off their bribe because I knew the truth about their daughter and Joe, but they'd want to go straight to Joe, blowing my cover, so I held off. I pulled out Joe's phone that I hid in the games chest, to see if the Westinmalins had sent anymore texts, the battery was dead. I stuffed it inside my purse, to deal with later.

I wrapped on the front door and let myself in, Rory came running toward me the moment he heard me. I reached down to scratch his side. Meredith, dressed in flannel pajamas, popped out of the kitchen.

"Hey, Mag," she said, rushing over to greet me with a hug. *The last time I was hugged in this spot was from Aaron,* looking at Meredith, I brushed him out of my mind.

"You're not sick, are you?" I asked.

"No, just taking a break today. I'm so happy to see you."

"Same," I said.

"Same taking a break, or same happy to see me?"

"Both."

"Come in and sit, I'll put on the kettle."

Rory followed us to the kitchen and sat at my feet, staring up, as if to say, "Please pet me."

We had a few minutes to spare before the kettle was ready, Meredith took me into the TV room, it had been turned into a cozier sanctuary since it'd been squared off and separated from the other half. The new sun room had bay windows, and a skylight above, it practically looked like we were standing outside, with the amount light it allowed in. The floor was solid maple, and the walls had been painted a lovely white grape. Meredith had placed an extra-large couch under the skylight, it'd be perfect for star gazing in the comfort of home.

"It's amazing."

"Big difference, right?"

"Yes, I love it, and the new paint too."

"Your friend Aaron is so talented, I'm so happy you recommended him."

Aaron had many talents, but I wasn't going to tell her which one I preferred.

"Well, I knew he was looking for work."

The kettle whistled, "Coffee or tea?"

"Tea, if you have it?"

"Coming right up."

I stood admiring the results of Aaron's handiwork. *The same hands that transformed this room are the same hands that brought me so much pleasure.*

"Everything alright?" asked Meredith.

"Yes, great." I went into the kitchen, and sat at the table across from Meredith stirring her coffee.

I removed the tea bag from my cup and placed it on my saucer. Meredith chattered on and on about how nice of a guy Aaron was, and she was going to pass his name around to give him more business. *Had she known what he and I had done together in her house, she might think differently.*

"Are you sure everything is okay, you seem off today."

"Actually, I do have something to tell you."

I started in on the whole story with my relationship with Joe, Shelley, the Westinmalins, Aaron, and now the divorce. I was expecting Meredith to show some sadness, or give me a motherly piece of advice, even though she was younger, but no, she didn't. Her eyes lit up, almost as if she'd just won a lottery.

"When are you handing him the divorce papers?"

"As soon I have a few more things arranged."

"You are sure this is what you want?"

"Absolutely."

"Maggy, I just have to get this out," almost bursting up and out of her chair, "I'm so happy for you," she screamed.

Totally shocked me, "You are?"

"Yes, I could never stand Joe, he has no personality, I don't know why you stayed with him so long? Good riddance, Shelley can have him. Now tell me more about Aaron."

I filled her in on more details, and that he said he loved me after our fight, and he hasn't given up.

"I understand why he'd want to help the Finnegan's, they are the sweetest couple in history."

"You know them?"

"Of course, they are my boss's Aunt and Uncle. I've met them several times. Mr. Finnegan used to volunteer at the company after he retired, never missed a day until he was diagnosed with cancer in his liver, which lead to him having a transplant. I heard they were having a tough time coming up with fifteen thousand per year, to pay for the anti-rejection drugs. Rumor has it, between the cost of his meds and daily living expenses, their old age pension isn't cutting it."

"I had no idea."

"I can understand why taking thirty thousand from the Westinmalins would be tempting."

"It would cover two years of meds for Mr. Finnegan."

"Hun, I believe Aaron truly is in love with you."

" He had a chance to take that money and run, but he chose to turn them down."

Had I given Aaron the chance to fully explain the situation, I might have understood instead of running out on him, we could have spent the last couple weeks working together to find out Joe's secret. It could have been fun playing detectives by day, lovers by night.

"I want to see you happy, Maggy. Talking about Aaron has brought life to your face, and I haven't seen you look like that, ever, when mentioning Joe. I can tell he completes you, why don't you go to him?"

"There's nothing I'd love more, but the timing is wrong. I have to think of the kids, and what is best for them. I'm not sure how bad the divorce will impact them, and they can't see me with Aaron yet."

"At least let him know what you're feeling, and if it's meant to be, it will be."

It felt like forever since Aaron had told me the truth, I hadn't been compliant, and still he remained persistent, that meant a lot. He could have said, 'forget about her', or started chasing someone his own age but he continued to pursuing me. I had to admit, finding out the truth about Joe, had made Aaron's truth seem minor. And, I had to give him points since he hadn't touched the thirty grand that the Westinmalins had placed in his account, especially when he needed it. *What am I to do with Aaron?*

Chapter 16

That night, I saw Joe's suitcase open on our bed. He came out of his walk-in closet with some dress pants draped over his arm, and a few shirts on their hangers.

"Where are you going?" I asked.

"I'm leaving for Toronto in the morning."

"That's news. How long will you be away?"

"Two or three days."

I raised my eyebrows at him, wanting to accuse him of sneaking away with his tramp, but I held myself together.

"It's last minute. Our trial was bumped to tomorrow afternoon. I have to be there."

"It's a four-hour drive. Won't you be too tired?"

"Thirty minutes by plane, should be there by nine."

"Sounds important, is anyone going with you?"

"All of my cases are important, Magnolia."

He completely avoided my question. *No doubt, Shelley'd be on that flight with him. What an ass lying to me for seven years. Other than money and this house, I still don't know why he hasn't asked me for a divorce if he wishes to run around? He's not happy here, he must know that I'm not.*

5am came early, pretending to be asleep, I heard him gather his things, I didn't budge in case he made a lame attempt to kiss me goodbye. After twenty minutes had past, I heard the door to the car garage close, then his car speeding off. I got up and looked out my bedroom window towards Shelley's house. There was a dim light inside, and a black car was parked in her driveway. It was her parent's car, the one they drove to the donut shop that morning to meet Joe. I kept my eyes peeled and sure enough, I spotted Mr. Westinmalin packing a red suitcase inside the trunk, then Shelley came outside and got in the driver's seat. He leaned down to talk with her at the driver's window, then he gave her a wave. She backed out and onto the road, and vanished up the street. *Her parents must be staying with Kaden while she runs off to Toronto with Joe, how could they be so supportive of the two of them one minute, and blackmailing Joe the next? Those two deserve each other, I can't believe how naïve I've been to not notice before.*

I tried to get a few extra hours of shut-eye but my mind was working overtime, so I jotted down a list of preparations to do before giving Joe the divorce papers. I looked online in Laudersville Real Estate for a home suitable for the twins and myself. We didn't need anything as fancy as what we were living in, I'd have been content with an updated farmhouse that'd only require some fresh paint, and a touch up here and there, things I could do myself. With Joe gone, I'd have the chance to go and check out my favorites. I sent emails, inquiring about three houses. The next three days would give me enough time to find house, tell the kids, pack up, hand Joe the papers, and get out, then my children and I would be free from our dysfunctional family. Mrs. Lauders' hair appointment was on Wednesday, no matter what was going on, I wasn't going to forget about her. Aaron wanted to meet with me, but I wanted to hold off a while longer, if I told him my plans, he'd want me to move in with him, that would be rushing things, and extremely confusing for all of our kids. What I really needed was time to get to know Aaron better without jumping in too quickly, time to figure out who I was without Joe, as much as I loved Aaron, there was no way I'd be ready to move in with him.

Tuesday flew by quickly, I grabbed about fifty empty boxes from the grocery store in town, and packed as many things as possible, and stacked them in the garage. When the kids arrived home, I explained that Daddy and I hadn't been getting along for a while, and we needed to move. After about one hundred questions from them, Jody said, "Mommy, I know you don't get along because Daddy never talks to you, and he's always in a bad mood."

Jonah said, "He never talks to us either, or does anything with us. I don't think he likes us."

I assured them their father loved them, but he wasn't good at showing it. *However, he had no trouble showing it to Shelley.* That night the twins packed a bunch of their things, I told them they could take the next day off school, we'd go and look at the houses I inquired about.

Laying alone in bed felt amazing, no Joe stench, no snoring, I could keep my table lamp on if I wanted, how free I was, except that my mind kept going back to everything that needed to be done, at the same time, I was excited to be starting over fresh. *The twins and I, to be liberated from Joe and his poorly fermented attitude.* Being able to do as we please, without having his negativity weighing us down, was exhilarating to fantasize about. I tossed Joe's pillows onto the floor, buried my face into mine, in the center of the bed, I spread my limbs as far as they'd reach. I was on vacation in a valley surrounded with a warm covering of down and fluff, so comfortable, my mind was settled, about to drift off into the world of sugar and spice until my phone buzzed. *Grrr,* I didn't want to budge, but somehow I felt it was Aaron.

"Missy, I really need to see you."

"Hey, Captain. Yes, we have a lot to talk about."

"There's a name I haven't heard in a long time."

"I'm sorry that it's taken me so long."

"Remember Sunshine, I told you I'd wait for you."

"Yes you did."

"I miss you, when can we meet?"

"I'm sure you don't miss me as much as I miss you."

"Impossible."

"I've got a busy day tomorrow, are you free tomorrow evening after eight?"

"What about Joe?"

"He's away, and won't be back."

"So, you'll be alone and waiting naked for me?"

"You'll have to wait and see."

"You're such a tease."

"You like it."

"Yes, I do."

"Good night, Handsome."

"Good night, Beautiful. I love you. XOXO."

I wanted to write that I loved him too, but I wanted the first time I said it to be in person, so I left him with, "xoxoxoxx."

Mrs. Lauders grabbed an arm each belonging to a different twin, she tugged them into her grasp and squeezed, "How are you, darlings?" She placed a firm kiss on either of their cheeks.

The twins cackled and squeezed her back, "Good," they both replied.

"I'm glad," she said.

Her eyes were almost even with Jonah's, she stood four-feet, eleven inches. The shortest, and richest woman I've ever known, her height never seemed to get in the way of her confidence, even before she became rich, always held her head up, no matter how many strange looks she'd get. I remember growing up by age twelve, I was two inches taller than her, she took me to a garage sale and a couple kids told her she looked like midget. She quickly responded in saying, "That's right, short and sweet, unlike the whipping I'm going to give you in front of your parents, who are standing over there." She pointed, and laughed like a crazy woman, the two kids scattered as fast as the speed of light. From that moment, I learned the valuable lesson, to never judge someone from their looks.

"Can we go through the maze?" asked Jonah.

"You sure can," she said.

Mrs. Lauders' backyard was ten acres, complete with inground pool, botanical gardens, pond with water fountain, and the sixty-by-sixty-foot cedar maze. The kids loved when I took them to see her, they usually spent most of their time adventuring out back with her little pooches, Sadie, and Max.

"Be careful out there you two," I said as the two of them headed for the nearest exit. Mrs. Lauders and I went into her laundry room, where she had one corner devoted to a mini salon with sink, hairdressing chair, and mirror. She designed it like that as soon as I began hairdressing school, she said no matter how busy I became, she expected me to visit her once a week and style her hair, and I always had, excluding the odd time she'd go to my salon. She had a talent for reading me like a book, even at my age, she loved to give advice whether it was asked for or not, her wisdom was something I learned to value. Her voice had become raspy with age, but her sweet smile always made me feel at home. After a washing, I had her sit in the cutting chair where I draped her for a style. I could feel her prolonged gaze fixed on me, in the mirror.

"Everything alright, Magnolia?" she tipped her head up and looked down her nose at me. I couldn't lie to her and tell her everything was fine, instead I worked away and gave her the short version of everything. She listened attentively, her lips sealed. After I finished drying her hair, she spoke,

"You poor darling. I don't blame you one bit. Tell me more about the Finnegan man."

I explained that he needed the expensive medication or his body could reject his new liver, and he'd die. She appeared to be pondering over that until I finished curling her hair.

"That's an unspeakable act for those Westinmalins to try on the young man, knowing he was kind of heart in trying to help the man, and trying to bribe Joseph was untactful, do you think he'll give in to them?"

"I assume Shelley has them settled down for now, because they are babysitting Kaden, Joe's and her child, while the two of them run off to their secret destination."

"The young man must be their back up plan."

"Aaron?"

"Yes, they used the three hundred thousand dollar bribe to put pressure on Joe to tell you the truth, and if he didn't comply, they'd have Aaron work on the side to spilt you apart. As I view it, they want Joseph together with their daughter, and they want you out of his life."

"I had that part figured, but why wouldn't they just come to me and say, 'Your husband is having an affair with our daughter?'"

"Perhaps, they were afraid you would stay with Joe and take the little boy, and raise him alongside your own children."

"I hadn't thought of that. You are saying they needed me to fall in love with another man, so I'd leave Joe on my own, and Kaden would be safe with Shelley."

"Makes sense, they could be their own happy family."

"Shelley can have him, I'm finished. I'm not sure Joe will feel the same about her, knowing he has lost fifty percent of his assets. You see, Joe wants the best of both worlds, he wants power and money with me, and sex and fun times with her."

"Magnolia, you are an exceptional woman, you deserve a man who values and appreciates you. One who will give you his whole heart, and is devoted only to you."

"Those types are hard to find these days."

"I believe you have already found one."

I back-combed her curls, and felt my cheeks getting red.

"Aaron is his name, correct?"

My pulse began to increase at the mention of his name, my mouth formed into a school girl's smile, as my lips formed the word, "Yes." In the mirror, I could see my teeth, and a light in my own eyes, I stood behind her, my face above hers.

"You're in love with him, aren't you?"

Yes, completely, head-over-heals. "It's complicated, he's younger than me, and he's the father of one of the twins' friends."

"I know it's none of my business, but..." *Time to listen. She always says that before her words of wisdom spew out.* "...it's a rare man who turns his back on thirty thousand dollars for a woman, it speaks volumes about how he feels for you. He could have taken the money and given it to Mr. Finnegan, but he chose not to because he is an honest man. That's the type you want in your life, and never mind him being younger, age is only a number."

"Funny, that's what he always says."

"It's true. Are you aware that Mr. Lauders was nine years younger than me?"

Wow, surprise, I remembered him having more wrinkles than her. "Um, no. You always looked younger than him."

"You see, Magnolia, if you stay out of the sun, drink plenty of water, and use a good facial cream, you can keep yourself looking young. Men don't fuss too much over their looks, that's why they appear older than they are." A smug grin came over her. "Plus, a younger man is capable of keeping up with the needs, *she emphasized on 'needs'*, of an older woman. Trust me, Magnolia, a younger man is a gift from above, if you are lucky enough to capture the attention of one, don't let him get away."

I threw my head back and laughed, as did she, I couldn't believe she was giving me sex advice. "He did withhold the truth from me, you know."

"Oh pity patty, such a waste of time thinking like that," she smoothed her fingers over the top of her hair. "I'd like you to comb it to the side for a change."

"Did I tell you, that the Westinmalins threatened to hurt Aaron's son Landon if he didn't do what they asked?"

"Did they follow through?"

"No. They were bluffing."

"The way I see it, he did accomplish the goal that they set out for him."

"I suppose Aaron may have sped up the process, my relationship with Joe has been stale for years, it was just a matter of time before I walked out."

"Aaron deserves to have the thirty thousand dollars that the Westinmalins promised him, for a job well done, wouldn't you agree?" She winked at me, before I turned her chair around. I knew what she was getting at, and it was time for us to throw together a plan to get Aaron that money. We sat in the parlor, where she had her personal assistant, Brigit, bring us some tea, and take cookies to the twins outside, who I could now keep my eye on through the French doors, overlooking the back acres. They were playing fetch with the dogs in the clearing behind the garden. Before our second cup of tea was finished, our Six-Step plan had been developed.

Step One – I have to remain living with Joe for two more weeks without serving him the divorce papers.

"I have a bunch of things packed already, things Joe won't notice missing. I could rent storage space."

"Nonsense," she said. "I'll have one of my guys pick up your things. You can store it here."

"We'd better not. The Westinmalins might see your trucks, and the plan will fail."

"I'll send a delivery truck, they'll think you have ordered something. The small truck will fit inside your garage, and they won't see anything."

"That'd work, it'll have to be this evening because I'm supposed to be looking at houses this afternoon."

"Why don't you and the twins move in with me, after the fundraiser?" *Step Two – Mrs. Lauders, start making plans to host a charity fundraiser in support of donor recipients of anti-rejection medication.*

"I don't want to burden you, and besides I've already turned down Dad's offer to move in with him."

"Your father's house is too far away. I'd love to have your company, and those twins are growing fast. It'd be nice to spend time with them before I'm dead." I stared into her face, and she stared into mine. We both let out a hoot, as that was the same guilt trick she's been playing for the past twenty years.

"We might be too loud, and drive you insane."

"This house has forty rooms, if I need a break, I'll go and hide." She chuckled, and reached up to place her satiny hand on mine. "You have always been my pride and joy. I would do anything for you."

I let out a breath, and squeezed her hand. "I'm so blessed to have you."

That afternoon, the twins and I went and checked out the houses for sale, but nothing would fit our needs, I didn't want to rush into purchasing a house where we wouldn't be content. I was feeling thankful that Mrs. Lauders was so generous in offering us her roof. The twins were really excited about staying with her, Jody said her house looked like a castle, and it did, with the circular tower out front. I explained to the kids that we needed to keep quiet about moving for now because it was our secret.

By that evening, I hadn't heard anything from Joe, and I was glad. The moving truck showed up around four-thirty, it had blue lettering on both sides that read, 'The Furnishing Trunk.' Mrs.

Lauders had vast connections, when she called for something, it was done in the blink of an eye. I was surprised that Edith Westinmalin was brave enough to come outside and gape towards my house without concealing herself. If she thought I had purchased furniture it'd mean I was staying with Joe, and that idea would fit into our plan. After the movers loaded up my things and left, I needed to complete the next step. *Step Three – Get a hold of Aaron.*

"Hey."

"Hey, Sunshine."

"You still meeting me tonight?"

"For sure."

"I need you to do one thing first."

"Anything for you, sweetheart."

"I need you to get ahold of The Westinmalins and tell them you've decided to take their deal. Tell them you are going to break Joe and me apart."

"WHY???"

"I can explain when you meet me, just tell her you are desperate for the thirty grand, and you're willing to do anything."

"Missy, I'm not sure about that."

"Do you trust me?"

"I do."

"BTW, tell them you can start working on it tonight because you heard that the husband was out of town."

"Anything in this for me, Sunshine?"

"Me."

"I'll get on it, Boss."

"Thank you, and try to stop by before dark."

"Sounds mysterious."

"Lol."

The twins were asleep by 7:45, between talking about moving, packing, and running around with the dogs, they were tired out. Aaron's truck pulled in my driveway shortly after. I couldn't wait to see him, smell him, touch him. He rang the bell, I opened the door, as if I was surprised to see him incase Edith was watching. "Aaron, what a nice surprise," I shouted.

He turned his head sideways, and smiled. "Why so loud?"

I placed my hand over my mouth, as to scratch it and whispered, "Play along, and pretend like we're acquaintances." I looked out of the corner of my eye because I thought I caught movement behind Shelley's curtains.

"What brings you by?"

"I was on my way home, and I realized your son's sweater was in my truck, and I wanted to return it." He looked around as if he wondered what I was looking at.

I smiled, "Good...where is it?"

"In the truck."

"Okay, we'll get it later," I whispered. "Did you want to come in for coffee?" I shouted.

He whispered, "Am I supposed to say yes?"

Ignoring his question, I motioned for him to come inside.

"What's going on?" he asked.

I closed the door the moment he stepped inside. His aqua scent consumed my senses. I was instantly aroused. My heart pounded long, hard thumps. His aura bounced against mine. Our eyes locked together into a burning stare, his arms surrounded my waist, and he lifted me, and squeezed me, and rocked me back and forth, his head embedded in my shoulder. My arms stretched around his back, I wanted to use all of my strength to keep him there and never let go. I leaned down and our mouths were like magnets, attraction pulling us together by an unstoppable force. His lips were tender, and aggressive, same as mine, when they touched. He put me down, our lips remained together, my knees were about to give out, I wanted to sink deep into him, and he stopped kissing me, his eyes were locked once more with mine. His voice was calm, "I'm so in love with you."

My emotions controlled me, and tears trickled down my face, "I love you too."

His complexion turned flush, as if my words had shot him in the heart. He held me, without kissing or rubbing, we both were held in a moment of completion, and vulnerability until he broke the silence, "Took you long enough."

I burst out laughing, and wiped the dampness from my face, "Just be happy, I said it at all." He lifted me again and squeezed me, and turned me around in a circle. We enjoyed a few more moments of divine bliss before heading into the kitchen. I started from the beginning, and explained everything to Aaron over coffee. After he understood Mrs. Lauders' and my plan, he told me that the Westinmalins had withdrawn the funds from his account again, and they weren't the kind of people to just hand over thirty grand.

"I know that, and that's why we have to get them to the fundraiser. Any ideas how?"

"At the beginning, she said she needed to see proof that you and I were a couple. She wanted to be sure you'd be out of Joe's life forever."

Step Four – Get the Westinmalins to the fundraiser.

"Tell them that's the night your plan will be complete and they need to be there to witness the breakup of Joe and I. Then they can hand the thirty grand to you for tearing Joe and I apart."

He placed his right hand on top of my left, "Or…we could forget all about them. You serve Joe the divorce papers, and be free. We could live happily ever after."

I placed my right hand on top his right, still on top of my left, "Or we could teach them a lesson for trying to threaten you. Don't you think it'd be fun to have a little fun with them?"

"Missy, you are not one to mess with, are you?"

"I think they need to be taught a life lesson."

"Mrs. Lauders' fundraiser will be two weeks from now, so we have that long to make the Westinmalins think you've won me over."

"Think?" he looked puzzled. "I thought I already had."

"Maybe, maybe not," I teased.

"Maybe not?" He got up from his chair and began tickling my sides. "Maybe not?"

I laughed, and laughed, then quieted, being careful to not wake the twins. "Okay, okay, I'm yours, but we have to keep it quiet for now, except that Meredith and Mrs. Lauders already know."

"Meredith, your cousin…and the rich woman?"

"Maybe, I might have said something."

"You've been talking about me, hmmm, that's a good sign." He leaned in and kissed my neck, and began sucking. I was lost in ecstasy for a moment, not caring if he left a red mark.

"I remember you saying, not under his roof, what happened to that?"

"It's a different ball game now, you are leaving him, and given what he's done to you, all respect is lost."

"I like that theory." I led him into the breakfast room, and kindly ordered him to remove his clothes, while I closed the curtains, and slid the door to the kitchen closed, locking it in case the twins came downstairs. He stood firm and strong, penis erect. Approaching him, my womanhood became aroused. His body looked like a masterpiece, waiting to be glorified. I rubbed my hands all over his upper and lower body, he drank in my touch as I felt his allurement. His erection was the most beautiful I'd ever seen, thick, tall, a bulging vein running up the side to meet his oversized perfectly rounded head. I kneeled in front of him, and took him in my mouth, he let out a discreet moan, my lips were soothed from the ease of his size sliding in and out, my hands massaged his thighs up to his buttocks, where I held him firmly to prevent my mouth from losing him. He smelled of fresh laundry and shower gel, his hands rest on my shoulders and reached down to my underarms, bringing me up to my feet. He placed his hands on either side of my face, and passionately kissed me, every sensation of pleasure ran through my veins, our lips in perfect favor. He lifted my sweater up and tossed it on the floor, I removed my bottoms. We stood bare, bodies pressed together, his excretion of body heat warmed me, I led him to the bar stool, and I sat up on it, pulling him in between my legs, he pulled back, in a swift movement he scooped up my bottom, hands supporting my back, he lifted me up, so my legs would rest on either side of his shoulders, and his tongue could fondle my sweet spot. His strength elated my desire, his tongue steady and stimulating, it was a turn on, looking down to watch his invigorating motion, his expression indulgent, his moans, as if he was enjoying a forbidden delicacy. My skin was sensitive from lack of sexual contact, orgasm was long overdue, my mind was lost in staggering ecstasy, I held onto his biceps and clenched my teeth together to contain my urge to squeal, I threw my head back and my accumulated emotions were emancipated. He set me back down to the chair, I stroked his firmness, his face entranced, he took himself from my hand and found his way inside of me. We both let out a roar of delight, it was instant pleasure in its highest form. I leaned back and tipped my pelvis upwards for maximum impact of depth. Amazing sensation as he thrust in, and paused, and thrust again, he pulled out, leaving only his tip inside, he slid his tip in and out teasing me over and over, leaving my insides begging for more. I pushed him back, and stood to my feet, I aggressively stole kisses from him, and looked him in the eye smiling deviously, I stood and turned away from him to bend forward on the stool, I checked him out over my left shoulder, he was even hotter than the first time I'd laid eyes on him, he bent his knees and drove his width inside me, my body trembled, his expression, focused, he placed his hands on my hips, bracing himself and continued his in and out motion. We were in paradise for two, as he filled me with his length, my breaths were intense, I could have easily collapsed onto the floor, but I held on, his breathing escalated in speed, finally he gave in and let loose. He leaned forward and rest his upper body on my back, his hands slide up to my breasts and he massaged them, his breathing slowed, as did mine.

"You are so beautiful," he said.

I pushed my body upwards to a stand, turning to face him, I said, "So are you."

He exhaled, and stared at my face. I smiled. We embraced each other, our aura's together in perfect harmony. I felt a little trickle running down my inner thigh, I tightened my muscles, and quickly crossed my legs in a standing position. "Oh no."

"What's wrong?" he said.

I smiled, "I'm dripping, got to go." I kept my muscles tight, gathered my clothes, and rushed to the washroom as fast as I could.

After Aaron cleaned up, he joined me in the kitchen. "Thanks for the coffee," he said.

"Best one you ever had." I smirked.

He pulled me into a snuggly embrace and rocked me, "Yes it was," he whispered.

Tingles ran throughout my body, same as always when he touched me, or when I thought of him. "You'd better get going because the Westinmalins are likely counting the minutes of your stay."

I showed him to the front door, outside I shouted, "Thanks for stopping by."

He tried to conceal his laughter, knowing I was trying to get the attention of Edith. "No problem."

I would have loved to have walked him to his truck and plant a goodbye kiss on him, but if Edith was watching, it'd be too soon to showcase affection.

Chapter 17

A lot had been accomplished over the following two weeks. I had to let on as if I knew nothing about Shelley, in front of Joe, which was hard since every time I saw her and Kaden walk by our house, or play in their backyard, I wanted to slap him. I wanted to study the boy's face to check for a resemblance between him and my twins, but I didn't want to risk getting caught. Aaron had to make up random stories to keep Edith Westinmalin believing that he and I were growing closer by keeping her updated with the fake progress. By the end of the first week, Aaron had the Westinmalins convinced to attend the fundraiser, where they were to witness the two of us as a couple and hand Aaron the thirty grand. Mrs. Lauders hired an event planner to help organize the charity. By the sound of it, she had everything covered from music and decorations, food and wine, she had invitations printed and sent to everyone on town, sent email invites to her contacts out of town, and she made a formal announcement in the local paper. She was able to get thirty local vendors to donate items for an auction, one-hundred-percent of the funds going to charity. It was to be an exquisite event, one the Westinmalins would never forget.

I was nervous getting ready, unsure of the outcome of our plan, or what kind of impact it would have. One thing I knew was that after the evening was all said and done, my life would be changed forever. I put on my new gown, sleeveless, black, below the knee, and well-fitted, curving in all the right places. Neckline plunging to center cleavage, my mother's pearl necklace resting above, earrings also pearls, 7mm in size. Silver sling back shoes with three-inch heels, and elbow-length fingertips gloves to match. I was going to wear the dress from Kylie's wedding, but I decided to splurge on another new one, because…well…why not? My eyes were smoky, and lips ruby red, complexion light. I set my hair on one and a half inch rollers earlier, to achieve soft flowing waves. I pinned back the left side just above my ear.

Joe was planning on showing up around eight, he said he had some urgent paper work at the office that couldn't wait. *Sure he did.* Normally, he'd refuse to attend with me, but anything to do with Mrs. Lauders, had him intrigued. Since the death of Mr. Lauders, four years ago, he was infatuated with her wealth and power, but it wasn't until after she hired him to take care of her own last will and testament documents, he learned that every cent of Mr. Lauders' dynasty was willed to her, leaving her the richest old gal he'd ever known. Mr. Lauders had written a note saying Mrs. Evelyn Lauders was the love of his life, and the only one he knew to be trustworthy and deserving of it. Joe kept track of every newspaper article, announcements, and businesses she was affiliated with, even though she'd never hired him for anything else afterwards. He made it his mission to learn as much as possible about her, it was clear he didn't respect her because he used to make frequent remarks to me such as, "What has an old hag like her ever done to deserve all that doe?" It angered me, but I stayed quiet to avoid conflict. One thing I knew about Mrs. Lauders, is if she doesn't hire you back the second time, it's because she doesn't think highly of you, she's never mentioned anything about Joe to me, but I could tell she was never one of his fans to begin with.

Either way, I didn't care if Joe showed up late, I wouldn't need him until later, as he was the guinea pig in our plan. *Step Five – Secretly remove my belongings from home.* I had a list of my things prepared for the movers to retrieve while the fundraiser was going on. They were to transport and hold everything at Mrs. Lauders' warehouse until I instructed them otherwise. They were to wait until Joe left our house that evening, then proceed with caution. The twins and Landon were safe at Meredith's place, thankfully she was willing to help. *I can't wait to see the appalling looks on the Westinmalins' faces when they find out what I have in store for them.*

On top of the hill, sat Mrs. Lauders' estate, lit up as well as Times Square on New Year's Eve. Tiny white lights adorned the tallest of trees, almost baron due to the cooling temperature. Rows of cars parked to the west, a valet waited under the car port at the main doors. Tall porcelain vases with pampas grass stood on either side of the entrance. The doorbell chimed like choir bells, when I rang. The maid opened the doors, and whispered, "Best of luck tonight," she took my overcoat.

I smiled at her, "Thank you."

Montel the server approached me with a silver tray in the palm of his hand. "Champagne, Madame?"

"Yes, please," I reached for one, it was a melody of sweet and sour on my tongue. Beautifully dressed guests in gowns, and suits mingled around the place, waiters walked amongst serving hors d'oeuvres. The main room was twenty-four-feet high, oval in shape, and ten-thousand-square-feet, the walls were white limestone, the floor solid marble, making it the largest room in the house. A stage had been brought in, with the auction items placed on tables to the left, in front of a row of windows. Chairs were placed in rows in front of the stage, taking up one-third of the room. A few cushioned benches were set up along the right side of the room with glass coffee tables, flower bouquets were placed on top of decorative lamp posts. Jazz, Mrs. Lauders' favorite, played over top of the babbled voices that filled the room. A few of my clients from the salon came to greet me, but I couldn't give them my full attention, I needed to find the whereabouts of the Westinmalins, *had they arrived yet?* Mrs. Lauders was sitting in the corner of the room in her royal throne look-a-like. Guests would go and greet her, always humble, she looked confident dressed as a queen, wearing a white pantsuit with butterfly sleeves, and a diamond broach over her heart. Watching her, she was a lady of grace and wisdom. I loved her from the first day she came into my life. My dad introduced me to her as Miss. Brooks, Brooks being her maiden name, one week after my mother passed away.

I made my way through the crowd, walking around in her mini castle was surreal, as if I was attending a gala for the rich and famous. As of that moment, this was to be my temporary home because of her generosity, at least until I found my own place. She acknowledged me from across the room with a discrete wave, I nodded giving her a half smile. I texted Aaron a short time before, he said he couldn't find his bow tie, and was making himself late searching for it. *Crazy guy.* I approached Mrs. Lauders, she was chatting with an older couple, I heard her say, "Mr., Mrs. Finnegan, it's been a pleasure."

To me, they were the guests of honor, without them the fundraiser wouldn't have happened. Aaron wouldn't have been tempted by the Westinmalins to earn the extra cash, he may not have asked me to be a driver for Landon's birthday party, in attempt to get close to me. Aaron and I wouldn't have had an affair, and I would have been clueless at Kylie's wedding when she advised me to look closer, which lead me to discover Joe's secret. I'd still be in the dark about Joe, Shelley, and their kids for who knows how long. It's strange how one incident can turn into a chain reaction, causing everything else to swing out of balance, but in my case, it was into the right balance. The Westinmalins would have tried a different method to rid me from Joe's life, if it hadn't been for Mr. Finnegan.

Mrs. Lauders took the stage and gracefully thanked everyone for attending, before the auction kicked off, she asked everyone to make their way to the dining room for a buffet dinner.

Close to three hundred people gathered in four separate rows. Tables filled with food selections of Canadian, Italian, Indian, and my personal favorite, Chinese. About mid-line, the succulent aroma made me wish I was at the front because, my stomach was growling. I scanned the lines for the Westinmalins but I had no luck in spotting them, if they didn't show our plan would dissipate, letting them off the hook. A familiar tingle washed through my body, it was enlightening, and breathtaking. A force was pulling at my left side, I felt sparkles wield my eyes, over my shoulder I saw a man in a black tuxedo, white shirt, and silver pocket puff, his hair was short and dark, his hands rest inside his pant pockets as he casually walked in my direction. The rest of my body followed my head, to make a complete turn to face him, he was stunning, my heart almost plummeted out of my chest. I wanted to go to him, but my legs were locked in place. Now six-feet away, I noticed his bow tie was missing, and his top button was open, revealing the hollow at the bottom of his throat. His eyes glistened from the reflection of the chandelier, his smile looked as sweet as sugar. *Lord, I love this man.* Now twelve inches from me, "Hello, Sunshine."

My head tilted left side to right, "Hello, Captain."

He ran his hand around my back and rest it on my right hip, my chest filled with the same warmth it did the night of the bonfire. If the room had been empty, I would have taken him on the spot and indulged in his every inch. I don't think anyone noticed the two of us, but it didn't matter anymore, by the end of the night, everything would change. We filled our plates and took a seat together at the private dining table that Mrs. Lauders had reserved for us and a few others whom we've never met before. Moments later, the Westinmalins made their not-so-grand entrance, her dressed in a designer bobby pleated skirt and mid-length suit jacket, him in a single breasted dinner suit and stripped tie. Everyone consumed by their own conversations, barely noticed them. Heads held firm and mighty, they went directly to the buffet tables, the lines had cleared out to the last few couples. Aaron and I studied them, as they filled their plates, their eyes scoured the room as they looked for a seat. I wanted to wave at them and yell, "Hey, witch. We're together now, so give us the thirty grand," but I remained composed to keep from being unlady-like. Aaron and I sat cool-headed, enjoying each other's company, and eating our dinner. An uneasiness came over me, as if I was being watched, I looked around and spot the Westinmalins seated two tables from our right. That was our chance to make an inconspicuous scene for them to take note of. Aaron was finished eating, so I leaned in closer to him, batted my eyes at him, and pretended to whisper in his ear. I threw my head back and laughed, as if what I had to tell him was an exchange of words only for lovers. I put my hand on his forearm that rest on the table, hoping they'd notice. Of course as far as they knew, Aaron had no idea what they looked like, and they'd have no idea that I knew about them hiring Aaron. I tried not to look their way, so Aaron did it for me. He said they were drinking wine and gaping our way. I got up and went to the dessert table and chose the chocolate lava cake, and a butterscotch cheesecake, I wasn't sure which was Aaron's favorite, as close as I was to him, there was still much I had to learn. On my way back, goosebumps filled my arms as I brushed past the Westinmalins' table, I proceeded as if I didn't see them. I placed both deserts in front of me at our table. "Where's mine?" said Aaron.

"Be patient," I said picking up my fork. "Are they watching?"

Aaron discreetly glanced at the Westinmalins, "Of course."

I gently stabbed my fork into the butterscotch cheesecake, and fed it to Aaron, then I repeated the same with the chocolate. "Which is your favorite?" I asked.

"Chocolate, silly."

His favorite is chocolate, awesome. "Great." I fed him the rest of the lava cake, with me taking alternate bites off the same fork. Putting on a show for the Westinmalins was fun. Aaron and I spoke intimately, our elbows rest on the table and our fingers locked together, we nestled as close as our chairs would allow, I placed my arm around his back, and he pretended to speak sweetly to me. The Westinmalins weren't taking their eyes off us.

Mrs. Lauders announced that there'd be thirty minutes of dancing on the dance floor before the auction kicked off. After an arrangement of fast songs, I saw Joe enter the house. I pretended not to see him and stayed with Aaron. *Step Six – Break up with Joe in front of the Westinmalins.* A slow song began, about half the crowd remained on the floor, the lighting dimmed and a kaleidoscope of colors flooded the walls and ceiling. Aaron and I locked bodies and danced to the slow rhythm, my heart beat increased, unaware if Joe was watching us from wherever he was. I keep an eye on the Westinmalins seated at their dining table. As we pressed against each other, carnal desires filled me. I was secure, *no matter what else happens tonight, I'll have the love of this man.* The second slow song began, I wanted to kiss Aaron, I knew that'd be too much of a juvenile act, and I wasn't sure what Joe would do. As we turned in circles, Aaron came to a stop and pulled back. I turned my head and saw a sour-faced Joe tapping him on the shoulder. He was wanting to cut in on our dance, Aaron looked back at me. "No." I said.

Joe's expression turned angry, I didn't comply.

"Magnolia, don't cause a scene."

"You heard the lady," said Aaron, "now run along."

Joe looked furious, "Hey, you stay out of it." I feared a fist fight coming, it had to be stopped, Joe's face a blazing red, Aaron's chest puffed out. I had to remind myself that our actions needed to remain subtle enough to get the point across to the Westinmalins only, not the entire room, after all, it was a charity event for organ recipients, not a high school brawl. I needed to prevent the two of them from getting into it.

"I'm sure Shelley will dance with you," I said. "Did you bring her Joe, or is she tired out from morning sickness?"

Joe's face turned white as snow, it glowed in the now dimmed lighting, his head tipped downwards, as if he were ashamed. He stood motionless, speechless, perhaps shocked, he was caught off guard. Aaron kept firm in his stance. I saw the Westinmalins watching Joe, as he turned and trod off into the crowd. I wondered what his next move would be, knowing that I knew the truth? The couples dancing near us were staring, Aaron put his arms around me to draw the attention away, he led me into a dance. "You okay?" he asked.

"Now I am." I closed my eyes for a moment. The song came to an end, music stopped, and lights came on. Mrs. Lauders' chipper voice echoed from the microphone, announcing, in ten minutes the auction would be starting, she recommended that everyone take a final look at the items up for grabs on the tables. I figured now'd be the time for Aaron to confront the Westinmalins about giving him the thirty grand, since they'd witnessed us together as a couple. The crowd was moving around as Mrs. Lauders had suggested, the Westinmalins had disappeared. Aaron and I decided to split up and search for them. Finally, I spotted them near the coat room, and Joe was with them. *Crap, the last thing we need is him screwing with our plan.* I text Aaron and let him know, I took a glass of champagne from the server's tray to blend in as he passed by. Amongst the crowd, were ladies handing out bidding paddles with a number registered to each individual. Joe walked out the door just in time for Aaron to meet the Westinmalins. I saw him talking to them, Edith was pointing her finger at Aaron and her lips appeared to be moving a mile a minute, he buffed up and said a few words back. I didn't see a money exchange, or envelope passed. The Westinmalins began making their way to the door, they couldn't leave, not before handing over the money. Tonight was our only chance to get them back. I moved in closer to Mrs. Lauders, and waved my hand for her to notice the Westinmalins trying to escape.

"Attention everyone, take a seat, buckle up, and open your wallets, no one is leaving here tonight, lock the doors boys." Mrs. Lauders let out a bray laugh, the guests began to chortle, not realizing how serious she was. I saw the two security guards step in front of the Westinmalins and lock the front entrance. Edith and her husband looked bewildered, the guard looked down at them and motioned his hand for them to join the crowd. The guards walked behind them, forcing them to move away from the doors. Aaron texted me,

"They refused to give me the money because Joe told them that he broke things off with you."

"Once a liar, always a liar."

"They said that you and I had set them up to get our hands on their thirty grand." Our six-step plan had failed. Well, the last part anyway.

"Time for plan 'B'," I texted, "Keep your eyes on the Westinmalins."

Mrs. Lauders announced that the bidding paddles were all handed out and it was time to begin. Aaron texted me, "I'm ninth row from the front, right side."

I texted him, "Westinmalins are thirteenth row from front, left side." I ducked in behind them without them noticing.

The bidding begun, the auctioneer pointed to the first item. "Listen up folks, you could be the proud owner of this antique end table. Let's start the bid at one hundred dollars. One hundred, one hundred, good one hundred from number 18, anyone for one fifty dollars? Who can give me one fifty? Good, number 67, thank you, anyone two hundred dollars." He carried on and on, and made it all the way to two thousand dollars for a sell. After thirty minutes, the auctioneer had made it half way through the items everything from a glass vase to diamond earrings, which sold for twenty thousand dollars. The Westinmalins hadn't raised their paddle once the entire time. Next item up was an oil painting. *Beautiful.* Two lovers intoxicated with passion, an intense exchange of romantic chemistry, and love. *So perfect. So befitting.* The auctioneer began the bid at five hundred dollars. Who's got deep pockets here? Five hundred, five hundred, who's got five hundred?"

I texted Aaron, "This item."

"Come on folks, 'Passion' is a stunning original, palette knife oil painting by World-Renowned Artist, Leonid Afremov."

Aaron texted me, "Let's do it."

"Okay, we've got five hundred from number 22. Can I have seven hundred?" I lifted my paddle. "I've got seven hundred, now nine hundred. Nine hundred from number 186." The bidding had reached up to sixteen thousand dollars, people being generous with their wallets for the name of the cause. "Come on people, who can give me seventeen? Seventeen? Oh number 22 has offered seventeen thousand. How about eighteen?" I raised my paddle number. "Number 71 has eighteen. Can I get nineteen? Number 22, thank you. Now twenty?" I raised my paddle again. "There seems to be a bidding war here between 22 and 71. Does anyone else want to jump in?" No one else made an offer. The room was filled with muffled voices. "Okay, 22, can I get twenty-one thousand dollars?" Number 22 raised his paddle. "I've got twenty-one, can I get twenty-two?" I flipped my paddle again. Number 22 and I kept going back and forth raised by one thousand dollars each time, finally reaching thirty thousand dollars. "Can I get thirty? Come on number 71, how deep are your pockets? Can you donate thirty thousand dollars to a worthy cause, and keep this exquisite piece of art?" I flipped my paddle. "Yes, number 71, that is phenomenal. Now, 22, how about thirty-one?" The paddle didn't raise. "Folks number 22 is throwing in the towel, the oil painting is sold to number 71, that is quite the contribution. We should give a warm thank you to…" he turned his head to the side, and placed his hand to the side of his mouth, but the microphone picked up his words, "Mrs. Lauders, who does paddle 71 belong to?" She sat in her bergère chair to the left of the stage, and flipped through the list of recorded paddle numbers along with each person that the number was assigned to, then approached center stage and took the microphone.

"Indeed, that is a generous gift, and the donors are Edith and Milton Westinmalin."

The crowd scanned the room searching to find out who the couple was. The two of them sat looking petrified in their seats. "Ladies and gentlemen, I believe this couple deserves a round of applause, we just need to find them."

I stood up behind them and shouted, "Here they are." Everyone in the room turned to face them. They lifted their heads, shell shocked.

"Come on up you two, and claim your gorgeous painting." Their faces were beet red, the guests gave them a standing ovation. I would have loved to have known what was going on inside their minds. Perhaps it was full out embarrassment, or the realization that their threats had finally caught up with them. I tapped Edith on her shoulder,

"You'd better go up, I believe you can leave your check with Mrs. Lauders." She did not quibble against my words.

The guests clapped for them, two of them must have caved under the pressure and made their way to the stage. Everyone in the room had witnessed them writing out their check and handing it over. *Plan B Complete – forcing the Westinmalins to hand over the thirty grand.* The auctioneer held up the next item for grabs, and started taking bids. I made my way over to Aaron, and put my hand inside his.

"Great job, 71," he said.

"Same to you, 22."

By the end of the auction, five-hundred thousand dollars in donations had been collected, one-hundred thousand alone came from Mrs. Lauders who bid on an antique lamp. After everyone cleared out, Mrs. Lauders, Aaron, and I sat in the dining room and drank some tea. We all agreed that it was a relief to be over with the night, and rejoiced that the Westinmalins got what they deserved. Before Mrs. Lauders retired for the evening in her bedroom, I gave her a hug, and thanked her for being supportive of me. She told me I was the daughter she never had, and she only wanted the best for me.

It was late but I wasn't ready for Aaron to leave, I asked him join me at the window seats overlooking the pond. The sky was dark, but the yard lights made everything translucent. This was the beginning to a new start for me, finally free from a loveless marriage, out of the darkness and reprieved of Joe's lies. *He must have found the divorce papers by now.* I laid them out on his desk at home before leaving that evening, along with his flip phone, and the two photos of Kaden that I removed from the picture frame. He was likely fuming at home while examining every word of the settlement agreement, and child custody arrangements. He'd likely be furious that his entire life was about to change and there wasn't a thing he could do to stop it. I removed my heals and tucked my feet under the cushion, as I lay with my head on Aaron's shoulder, his arm around me.

"Where to from here, Missy?" Aaron leaned down to kiss the top of my head.

"One day at a time, Captain."

After a restful sleep in my temporary bedroom, I awoke to my phone buzzing. I squinted my eyes, the sunlight was bright and shining in through the window, that filled the wall over the head of my queen-sized bed. A warm smile melted across my face, the text read, "Good morning, Sunshine xoxoxo."

Will Aaron ever tire from sending me those texts? If we were living together he could just say those words to me every morning as I snuggle in his arms. I had a lot to do before that fantasy would even become a possibility, finding my own place, getting the twins settled, the divorce finalized, and learning to be a strong single Mom. If it was going to work between Aaron and I, we'd have to spend quality time together getting to know one another, our attraction was a given, but there is much more to a relationship, not to mention the future challenges that may arise because of our age difference.

"Good Morning, Handsome xoxox."

"Plans today?"

"Picking up the kids, Silly."

"Want to go together?"

"I sure do. Meet you after lunch?"

"Looking forward to it."

I wanted to prepare a special breakfast for Mrs. Lauders to show her my appreciation. I spent an hour slicing fruit, making homemade waffles, home fries, and sausages, all her favorites. My appetite was stimulated from the delicious assortment that I had spread across the counter. Mrs. Lauders was taking her sweet time in joining me, so I went to check on her in her room. I knocked gently on her door, she didn't answer. I waited a moment then called her name. Still, no answer. I turned the door handle opening it a crack, and called her again. Nothing. I stepped inside, her room was three times the size of mine, floral walls, and white carpeting. Her bed was king-size with fat wooden bedposts, and had a ruffled bed skirt. Her blankets looked to be hanging off the opposite side of the bed.

"Mrs. Lauders?" I called, no answer. I thought she might have gone into her ensuite bathroom, I wanted to get closer to tap on the door, as I walked past the end of her bed, I saw a dark lump on the floor. I looked down, *No,* my body shuddered, nerves in disarray, it was Mrs. Lauders. "Oh no." I rushed to her side, she lay stiff as a board. "Mrs. Lauders," I said, she lay on her left side, eyes closed, chin tilted up, right arm and leg extended away from her bed. She did not budge, I rolled her onto her back and touched the side of her neck, her skin as ice, without a pulse. "No," my emotions poured out in somber tears of woe and anguish…Mrs. Lauders was dead.

A week after her funeral, a lawyer arrived on the doorstep with documents, stating that Mrs. Lauders had willed her house, her assets, companies, and properties all to me. Everything was mine, a net worth of five billion dollars, it was a moment of joy, but a moment of pain.

It wasn't long after news spread around town that I was the new queen of the castle, Joe thought he deserved a piece of the pie because he was the one she hired to take care of her estate, and we weren't legally divorced yet. He brought a copy of the will that he had drawn up for her, which stated that her entire estate was to go to Joe and me. What he didn't know was that Mrs. Lauders had Joe's copy of her will made void and she replaced it with a new will and testament, two weeks before her death, removing his name indefinitely.

Joe stood on my front doorstep and bellowed that I had been a wench to live with, and he had stayed with me for the sole purpose of gaining Mrs. Lauders' estate after she kicked the bucket, and for the investment from my mothers' life insurance policy. I told Joe maybe he could gain some extra cash by selling my necklace, the one he stole from me and gave to Shelley. The deplorable look on his face was priceless. He then accused me of brainwashing Mrs. Lauders into removing his name from her will. When I was tired of listening to his rant, I had security haul him off my property, kicking and shouting.

It was going to be a huge responsibility getting familiar with Mrs. Lauders' undertakings. She had her trustworthy assistant appointed in her will to show me the ropes, and the tricks of the trade. My training would be a gradual process as the twins were still young and my first priority would continue to be them for a few more years. I had a talk with Lucy about her taking over the salon permanently, and since everything was working out great with her niece filling in for me, she gracefully accepted my offer.

Dad stopped by the house to see how I was getting along, he couldn't believe how big the house was, he jokingly suggested for me to put fish in the pond out back, so he could fish there. Jody and Jonah were so excited when they saw Dad with the kittens. They each had made little cat beds out of blankets, on their beds for the kittens to sleep in. I knew having pets would help bring happiness and comfort, however Mrs. Lauders' dogs would have to get used to them pouncing at their legs while they slept.

The twins seemed well adjusted after our separation, one thing Joe agreed on was it'd be in the best interest of the twins to keep quiet for now about their half siblings, otherwise they'd find out he'd been lying and cheating, and I didn't need that weighing on their innocent minds.

The twins, and Landon didn't realize how serious Aaron and I had become, all they knew is we were dating, and they were loving spending extra time together on the weekends with us. Since the fundraiser, Aaron didn't have to spend as many hours working to help the Finnegan's, so he used his extra time for "the more important things in life" as he called it. Either we'd invite Aaron, and Landon, to our place, or vice versa. While the kids played together, Aaron and I would have a coffee together and talk in the kitchen, or sit outside beside Mrs. Lauders' favorite autumn garden. One afternoon, he took me for that walk he promised through the trail in his back yard, it was beautiful, not as romantic as I had pictured, with the three kids running around trying to tag us, but Aaron being the kid he is, played along with them, as did I. I could see his pleasure in making the kids laugh, and when they weren't looking, he'd pull me behind a cedar and plant passionate kisses on my mouth, and neck. We enjoyed taking the kids out to a restaurant, or movie, and when the snow finally came, we took them sledding down the largest hill in town. We were having a blast getting to know each other, at the same time, it was hard keeping our hands off each other around the kids, it was like we were forming our own little family.

Chapter 18

The Friday before Christmas break, the kids were invited to go on a weekend field trip with their school, to Winter Village, which would be the first uninterrupted weekend that Aaron and I could spend as a couple.

After profound hugs and kisses, and a bitter sweet goodbye, the twins, Landon, and their classmates left for their weekend adventure. Aaron, myself and the other parents waved to our children as the bus vanished up the street. One of the mom's woefully rattled on and on about how this was her daughters first time away from home, and she'd be counting the minutes until her child came home again. The other parents, including Aaron, managed to escape this gloomy woman, but I felt it'd be rude to leave her there alone willowing in sadness. *Why didn't you volunteer on the trip if you're going to miss her that bad?* Anyhow, I didn't think I'd ever get away, until Aaron phoned me, giving me an 'out' of the conversation, I smiled and waved to the woman as I escaped to my van.

"Thank you," I said, holding the phone in one hand, putting on my seatbelt with the other.

"Your place or mine?" *He didn't waste any time getting that out.*

"Yours. But first, I need to pick up a few things at home."

"Want some help picking up the things at your house?" he teased.

"If you go to my house, we'll never make it to yours."

"True. Just hurry."

"See you soon, Captain."

"Bye, Sunshine."

With the exception of the kids visiting Joe on the weekends at his place, and Landon spending time with the Finnegan's, Aaron and I hadn't much alone time, except for the few quickies we squeezed in while the kids were at school. Aaron and I had grown closer emotionally and physically. He was everything I've never been able to see in anyone else. His sense of humor was uplifting, and his body was captivating. I couldn't wait to get to his house and unleash my deepest sexual desires.

At home, I removed any unwanted body hair, did a self-mani/pedi, took a shower, applied make-up, dried my hair, and gave it a thorough brushing. I wanted to look perfect for Aaron, even though he'd seen my body several times by now, I wanted the weekend to be special.

"Come on already," Aaron texted me.

"I'm leaving in five, Mr."

"Ok but I'm coming to get you if you're not here soon."

"Impatient, are we?"

"I just want to spend every minute with you, Beautiful."

"I want that too, be there ASAP."

I threw together a weekend bag, mostly consisting of lingerie, and clothing that was easy to slip out of. It was a great feeling to know that we could spend the weekend together because we were allowed to, not because we were sneaking around with hopes of not being found out. I had let the important people in my life know how serious Aaron and I had become, as for the others, they could wonder from afar based on the rumors that were spread around town. As for Joe and Shelley, they still weren't living together, perhaps their relationship wasn't as exciting since they didn't have a reason to sneak off behind my back.

The smell of wood ablaze, lofted in the crisp air. Gentle flakes of snow landed on my head, and danced on my nose, like a school girl, my stomach in butterflies from excitement, and friskiness. I rang the bell at Aaron's front door and waited with my bag in hand. I heard his willing footsteps approaching, then the spring in the door handle turning, and the creak of the door opening. My sexual desire kicked in the moment I laid eyes on him, he stood before me shirtless, and barefoot, wearing only a pair of blue jeans. *I get to have all of that.* The heat from the house warmed my face as I stepped inside, it must have been over eighty degrees. In the far room, I could see blazing orange flames glowing through the glass door of his fireplace.

"Hello, Sunshine," his voice was low and seductive.

"Hi." I bat my eyelashes at him. "Do you always answer the door half naked?"

His eyes lit up, "I'm just getting a head start," he beamed.

"I didn't realize that we were having another race."

"I'll race you alright." Like a gentleman, he reached for my bag, and set it aside as I removed my coat and boots, then flicked the tiny pieces of snow from my hair.

"I like the sounds of that." I took him by his hand and led him upstairs to his bedroom, I'd been waiting far too long to have him in his own bed. I unfastened his jeans and nudged them downwards until they fell to the floor, leaving him standing in black boxers. He leaned down and softy kissed my neck, my libido was raging, I wanted to be naked with him now. I pulled back from him and removed my sweater, and slid off my pants, leaving myself in my bra and panties. He put his arms around me and unfastened my bra, letting it fall to the floor, his hands moved down to my waist and slid them under my buttocks to lift me, my legs encircled his waist, and he carried me to his bed. Standing there a moment, he sucked my breasts, and ran his tongue over my nipples. I grasped his shoulders, and biceps, his skin was delicious to the touch. His embrace was tight, as he spun me around then sat on the bed, my legs still clinging to his waist, now in a seated position. I rubbed his back and leaned down to kiss his open mouth. I was fiercely engulphed in a lustful fury, I wanted more of him. I pushed him down onto the bed, kissing him, sucking him, his hands exploring my sides and back, I rubbed my hands all over his chest, he reached up to my breasts and gently tugged my skin. I moved to his right side, shimmied down his boxers. I dampened his erection with my tongue, my legs bent, and parallel to his shoulders, he pulled me over on top of him, my legs straddled his face. His tongue trickled along my femininity, causing me to bawl in gratification. I raised his erection with my hand, to hold him steady as I took him in and out of my mouth, squeezing my lips around him. His sobs turned me on, and his head was turning reddish in colour, I didn't want him to get off early, so I dismounted him and pulled him off the bed and onto his feet. I leaned over on the side of the bed, my arms stretched out, elbows bent to support my weight, I felt his hands move down my sides, his left index and forefingers made their way to my front and buffed my snatch. His pelvis pressed against my buttocks, his right hand glided from my hip down to hold his token, I spread apart my legs, and he searched for my gap with his head until he slipped inside of me. I clenched his bed comforter with my hands, both of us panted, and thrusted against each other simultaneously for maximum gusto, my insides were pleasantly manipulated, he moved faster and faster, freeing himself to satisfaction. Leaning forward, his heart throbbed onto my back, he continued to work me as I unwound to his soothing touch. He caressed my left shoulder with the tip of his nose, "I love you," he whispered.

His very words sent shivers through my body, I jolted upwards, both of us planted our feet on the floor to face each other. I looked up at his pinkish face, and pulled him close,

"I love you too."

How comfortable it was to rest my head on Aaron's chest, under the softness of the blankets on his bed. His right arm wrapped around me, his left stroked my forearm, the smell of his blue aqua cologne ravished my senses with delight. My stomach was at ease, my body tranquil, life seemed perfect, and in that moment it was.

"Missy, I'm still waiting for the answer to my question."

"You didn't ask anything."

"Sure I did. I asked you, if you'd move in with me?"

"Maybe one day, Captain. Are you sure I'm not too old?"

He rolled over on top of me, "Are you sure I'm not too young, Boss?"

"Never."

We kissed provocatively, made fiery everlasting love, and held each other, the rest of the night.

When morning arrived, I opened my eyes to find Aaron sitting beside me on the edge of his bed, looking hotter than ever, his bare chest aroused me, his bright smile brought joy to my soul, and his seductive eyes said 'I want you'. He leaned down and placed a kiss upon my lips. I sat up to meet him, and he handed me a single pink rose, "Good morning, Beautiful."

"Good morning, Handsome. I held the rose up to my nose, it was a refreshing fragrance of sweetness and beauty.

THE END